BREAKING THE RULES

A SINNER AND SAINT NOVEL

LUCY SCORE

Bloom books

ISBN: 978-1-945631-04-7 (ebook)
ISBN: 978-1-7282-8276-3 (paperback)

Published by Bloom Books, an imprint of Sourcebooks
P.O. Box 4410, Naperville, Illinois 60567-4410
(630) 961-3900
sourcebooks.com

lucyscore.com

090122

To Polly, raiser of good men.

1

The whine of the jet's engines did nothing to block out the nagging pain in Waverly Sinner's side or the calamitous thoughts that swirled in her head. She shifted in her seat and grimaced as Lake Tahoe fell away beneath her.

"You're still bleeding, but it's slowing down," her friend and personal assistant Kate York said, probing the gauze.

Waverly set her teeth as Kate prodded a little too hard.

"Did you call in?" she asked.

Kate nodded and let Waverly pull her bloodstained sweater back down.

"Yeah, when the doc was stitching you up."

"And?"

Kate shook her head. "No bodies."

"What about Dante?"

"No bodies," Kate said again. "No Dante."

Thank God. It meant there was a possibility that he was still alive after the ambush. Waverly would cling to that hope that the man who had given her a chance to change her life could still be among the living. "Okay, so what's the plan?"

"Belize. They're flying in a very nice, very discreet plastic surgeon to patch you up so you don't look like you just got shot. Your orders are to lay low, very low."

Waverly's phone signaled in her lap. It was her mother. "What's the story?" Waverly asked before answering.

"You're going to hate it," Kate warned.

Xavier Saint's attention was fixed on one of the three TV screens in his office. The one with a publicity shot of Waverly Sinner floated about the ticker that threw out the news casually as if it hadn't moved the earth under his feet. *DUI accident. Injuries. Rehab.*

The vulture announcers with their peroxide grins gleefully speculated on the scandal and what it would mean for the actress's career. There was speculation, of course, that Waverly had been on a downward spiral since her last breakup with leading man Dante Wrede. Their on-again, off-again volatile relationship had been fodder to the gossip sites and tabloids for two years.

Xavier wanted a drink. A cigarette. A coma. Something, anything, to get the need for Waverly out of his system. It had been five years. Five years since they talked, five years since he felt her body under his, five years since she'd nearly died in front of him. And yet it felt like yesterday. He could still remember her scent, that layer of exotic spice and a sweetness that never faded.

He muted the TV and made himself another cup of coffee.

Nothing he'd done in those five years had been able to erase her from his mind. Invictus Security had grown, first from the blood and sweat that he and his partner Micah Ross had put into the start-up and then from the notoriety of the Ganim case. Now they had offices in L.A., New York, D.C., and a brand-new chapter starting in London. He'd long-since retired from fieldwork and instead focused on training, consulting, and the day-to-day of running the top private security firm in the country.

Everything he'd worked for since his time in the Army and Defense Clandestine Service was now his. *Except her.*

He'd followed Waverly from the safe distance that entertainment news provided. Every movie, every award, hell, even her college graduation. She'd finished a degree in psychology and international relations from Stanford in three years while still managing to release a movie a year. That still lit the spark of pride in him. She'd been smarter than anyone around her gave her credit for. And now the world was taking notice.

The last two years had been one hit after another. The following that she'd earned from being the near victim of serial killer Les Ganim five years ago had grown into a huge, legitimate fan base.

Waverly Sinner was officially a star in her own right now. She pulled in bigger paydays than most of her male co-stars. And comparisons between her and her mother, screen goddess Sylvia Sinner, were now entirely complimentary.

He barely recognized her public persona these days. Gone was the frightened girl who built walls to protect herself. In her place was a ballsy, vivacious woman who didn't take shit from anyone.

When her publicist announced that Waverly was dating her co-star Dante Wrede, Xavier polished off a bottle of whiskey alone in his apartment, and when he surfaced from his hangover, he vowed that Waverly Sinner was out of his system. He tried to get over her. He'd dated, casually. And even attempted not-so-casually dating. He'd met a nice enough woman who had a busy career of her own. They'd talked marriage a few times—well, she had—but he'd never made a move in that direction. And when she'd ended things, he felt as much relief as he did guilt.

Xavier stared at Waverly's picture on the muted screen and felt it. The buzz that something wasn't quite right. He *knew* her, and despite the last five years of distance, he was sure there was something rotten with this story.

He'd watched her for the last two years as Waverly had put herself in every situation that she'd despised within the Hollywood experience. She'd club-hopped and shopped and gotten into shoving matches with aggressive photographers. Her new best friend, Petra, was the daughter of a Russian billionaire, and the two downed vodka tonics by the gallon as they partied their way around L.A.

Her hair was a little shorter now, a darker honey blonde instead of the silvery Rapunzel tresses he'd had his hands in years ago. But the eyes, those sea witch eyes, were the same.

This wasn't some rebellion. Not the timeless Hollywood trap that she'd made herself immune to. This was something else.

Xavier punched a number into the phone on his desk.

"I need a favor. I need a police report."

WAVERLY HID her wince as she climbed aboard the private water taxi on the dock in San Pedro. The in-your-face island beauty had never failed to strike her since the first time she visited Ambergris Caye shooting a movie. And this visit, though wounded and exhausted, was no different. The blinding turquoise of the water butted up against sugary sand beaches. On one end of the island was the bustling golf cart hub of San Pedro. On the opposite, endless peace and quiet. She'd bought a home here a year ago, finding the easy commute between L.A. and Belize City irresistible, and made sure to escape here as often as she could. The airy, canary yellow two-story was tucked in between resorts and protected by a thick grove of palms.

There wasn't a housekeeper or a paparazzo to be seen. Here, she traded Hepplewhite for hammocks and bulletproof SUVs for a golf cart. And hopefully she would heal here.

The water taxi captain must have been under orders to go slow because they clipped along at a far more relaxed pace than the usual break neck speed. The town blurred by in a hodge-podge of colors. The docks became farther apart, the resorts more spectacular. And finally, there was her own little dock, jutting out into the Caribbean waters, a palapa offering shade and a place to swing in a hammock at the end.

They bumped alongside the dock, and Kate helped Waverly out of the boat. Their only luggage, two go bags, was easily hefted over the side. Kate tipped the captain, and with a wave, the taxi zoomed away leaving the two women alone.

They turned their back on the boundless blue of the ocean and slowly made their way down the dock. Palm trees shivered a welcome in the balmy breeze.

Waverly made it up onto the wraparound porch of the first floor before lowering herself onto the rust orange cushion of an outdoor sofa.

"Don't get blood all over that," Kate warned her as she jiggled the key in the lock. The side door, a thick wedge of tropical hardwood, opened inward.

Waverly gingerly held herself upright while Kate bustled inside. A moment later, the storm shutters that ran the length of the first floor began their intrepid journey upward. Shutters stowed, Kate shoved open the accordion glass doors until the porch and interior living space became one.

Kate joined her on the porch and flopped down in one of

the wicker chairs. "Okay, there is literally no food here, and since we left in such a hurry, I didn't have time to call the grocery service. I can leave you here and go into town, or I can call them now."

For once, food didn't sound remotely good to Waverly, but some time alone to think did. "If you don't mind going into town, that would be great. Just start with some basics until we know how long we're going to be on lockdown."

Kate nodded and rose. "Cool. I'll stop at that tiki bar place on the way back and bring home dinner."

"Kate?" Waverly stopped her. "Thanks for being awesome. You don't know what it means for me to be able to count on you like this."

"I love your face, too." Kate threw her a grin and a mock salute before heading back into the house.

Waverly dragged herself to her feet and plodded inside.

The main living space was a towering two-stories with glass from floor to ceiling, taking advantage of the ocean views. There were two wings each with a bedroom downstairs and a master upstairs.

Waverly slowly made her way up the concrete staircase to her room. With her last ounce of energy, she opened the storm shutters and pushed open the terrace doors. She grabbed towels from the bathroom, tossed them on the bed, and let herself collapse.

It was just a flesh wound. But there were other, worse implications that would come out of the events of today. Rehab? She snorted into a pillow. The studio didn't care what a ding her reputation would take or how the lie would hurt her still healing parents. After all, a splashy comeback from rehab would only up her pull at the box office and make her other role as Hollywood's party princess more sellable.

If she were to think about how she got herself into this

mess, she could pinpoint the exact second she'd set off down this path. When Xavier Saint had walked out on her.

It had been a different wound then, five long years ago. A knife instead of a bullet. She'd been utterly helpless at the deranged hands of a serial killer and again when the only man she'd ever loved had told her she was damaged, toxic. She'd made a vow to herself that she would never again be helpless, never again be vulnerable.

She would never let herself be dependent on someone else for safety or love.

And that's what it had been, she thought, fingering the medallion she wore around her neck. A gift from a lover. Even though she loathed the man who gave it to her, she couldn't bear to part with it. A lucky charm, a superstition. And as long as no one knew what hung on that long chain dangling between her breasts, what harm could it do?

She would never understand why Xavier left. Not after watching the footage of her brutal attack. It had taken her months before she felt strong enough to face the visual evidence of the night that had cost Waverly her heart and very nearly her life. The screams, the headlights, the knife.

And then Xavier, tenderly curling over her, blocking out the rest of the world so he could whisper his love for her over and over into her ear. He had killed for her, and then he had held her as if she were fragile glass. Tears and pleas slipping from him, gently, reverently. She remembered everything from that night.

He had loved her, and he had left her. That was all there would be to their story. She would never forgive him for conning her into opening up to him, to giving him her heart, only to destroy that fragile trust, that delicate confidence.

Her mother had been right about so many things, even in the depths of her alcoholism. Chasing happiness and love only lead to heartache. The real satisfaction in life came from pride in her successes. No one could take that away from her. She was in control of her effort and her outcomes. There would be no going back to helpless and vulnerable.

No matter how many times she dreamed that she was still in Xavier's arms only to wake alone. Nearly every night, but she shouldn't be thinking of Xavier now. She needed to be thinking of Dante.

How ironic, she thought. That neither of the men who had changed the course of her life was hers.

2

*M*arisol Cote was very displeased with the groceries Kate had stocked in the kitchen.

"You girls will not always be able to burn ten thousand calories," she said, sternly shaking a box of doughnuts at Kate. Her dark hair was more silver now, but she was still a tiny and formidable woman. Now the house manager for Waverly's parents, she had originally been brought on as the nanny. She had single-handedly raised Waverly during Robert and Sylvia's volatile years.

The Sinners had settled down now, each with a healthier purpose, and Waverly was still adjusting to the new normal. And Mari, who knew Waverly's secret had hopped on a plane immediately after Kate contacted her.

"Well, Mari, no one asked you to show up here and rummage through the cupboards," Kate told her.

"No one needs to ask me to come check up on my girls. My reckless, irresponsible girls."

Waverly plucked one of the doughnuts out of the box and took a bite before Marisol could slap it out of her hand. "Where did you tell Mom and Dad you were going? They don't know I'm here do they?" She eased herself onto one of the barstools under the long kitchen counter. Almost a week into healing, and she was feeling stronger every day and more determined to figure out exactly how everything had gone so sideways.

Marisol gave her a long dark-eyed stare. "I told them I was visiting my aunt in the Dominican. They are hopeful that your 'rehab' will lead you down a healthy path." She snorted.

"The cover was not my idea," Waverly said defensively.

"This job should not have been your idea," Mari said with equal fervor. "It is dangerous. You already have a job: you make movies. Why this too?"

It was an argument they'd had at least a dozen times in the last two years. "Mari," Waverly sighed. "You know I wanted to prove that I could be more than just an actress."

"So you proved it. You got shot. Now you can quit."

Waverly shifted on the barstool and refused to wince at the twinge in her side. She'd been shot in movies, and her characters recovered much faster. Reality was turning out to be a bit of a disappointment.

The plastic surgeon the studio had sent in under the cover of night had had a steady hand and asked no questions. She'd sewn Waverly up on the couch in her bedroom with exquisite stitches and offered pain meds, which Waverly had declined. She needed her mind to be sharp and stay sharp so that when she was recalled to L.A., she could find Dante. Or find out what happened to him.

Until then she was to rest, heal, and stay invisible to the outside world, which thought Waverly Sinner was whiling away the hours in an undisclosed rehab facility for a DUI accident that never happened.

~

To gain a modicum of peace, or at least quiet, Waverly sent Marisol and Kate into town. Her go bag, while not typical of the average fast escape stash, wasn't exactly stocked for a tropical vacation. She arrived in Belize with a cocktail dress, a pair of Zanotti Swarovski sling backs, a pair of distressed designer jeans, workout capris, a black tank, and a gray cardigan.

The clothes she'd arrived in had too many bloodstains to salvage. Kate and Marisol were on a mission to appropriately outfit Waverly's closet here.

Waverly pulled on the black tank, a pair of bikini bottoms she'd left in a drawer on her last trip, and the silk robe from her bathroom.

She'd lay out by the pool and watch the ocean. And go through every single moment of last Saturday again until she could pinpoint where everything had gone wrong.

She chose a striped lounger in the sun and eased down onto the cushion to contemplate life.

Waverly had a good life. A solid life. One she'd chosen. She had a beautiful home, her pick of projects, and the occasional excitement that her side job offered. She and her parents had made great strides in repairing a relationship she'd once thought was a lost cause.

So her sex life was non-existent. She was very busy, and the few times she'd ventured down that road, sticking a toe into the relationship waters, it had been at worst a miserable failure and at best moderately disappointing.

No one had lived up to *him*. Waverly cursed the memory of Xavier Saint, his memory a shroud that clung to her.

It had been five years, yet not a day passed that he didn't cross her mind... repeatedly. She'd finally put an end to her hobby of cyber-stalking him, reading interviews with him covering Invictus, scouring the gossip sites for his rare pictures. Since their time together, entertainment bloggers and even the mainstream media had been endlessly fond of him. But when he and the painfully beautiful Calla were linked together, when marriage speculations were made, Waverly had finally stopped looking and stopped hoping that she'd find that one piece of information that she needed to move on. *The why.*

Their time together had sparked hot and bright and then burned out, extinguished by anguish.

She wished she could forget him, wished she could move on. But something always held her back. So she focused on the other areas of her life. She made movies, started producing, and decorated a house that finally felt like home. She held her small circle of friends close and she waited for the something that was missing.

Five days earlier...

BEHIND THE WHEEL of the rented Aston Martin, Dante Wrede was whistling the theme song to his last movie. For all of five seconds, he'd not-so-secretly dated the pop star who had recorded it.

"Don't tell me you're missing Penelope?" Waverly teased from the passenger seat.

"Haven't you heard, Waverly darling? I only have eyes for you now," he said, grinning over his Prada sunglasses.

"Oh, is *that* where we stand? I can never remember whether we're dating or broken up or secretly engaged—"

"Or having torrid love affairs with other people," he filled in. "I just read the tabloids in the grocery store, and they tell me what our current status is."

Waverly laughed. "You in a grocery store? Please, the day Dante Wrede shows his domestic side is the day snow cones go on sale in hell." A very large population of women had succumbed to his British-accented charm.

Dante scoffed. "I fully intend to fall madly in love someday and spend the rest of my days spoiling the life out of the beautiful, lucky lady. What's your excuse?"

"Why, Dante!" Waverly fluttered her lashes. "How could I possibly fall in love with someone else when I'm so enamored with you? At least for today."

He stuck his tongue out at her.

"Very James Bond of you," she snickered.

"Since you brought up work, Money Penny, let's talk mission."

Waverly studied Slide Mountain as it loomed in front of them, leaving Reno behind them. "You mean the oddly vague yet suddenly imperative mission to continue our blossoming friendship with Petra Stepanov?"

"That would be the one," Dante said, accelerating down the highway looking every bit the careless playboy.

"You know something, don't you?" Waverly accused him. "You think this job stinks, too."

"I think there's a possibility that there's something rotten in Lake Tahoe," he agreed.

"Aha! I knew it." Waverly kicked back in her seat. Her gut had been telling her there was something wrong with this assignment from the start. Usually their jobs were straightforward. Get into this diplomat's home office during the cocktail party and bug the phone, drag some information out of an under-the-influence, chatty son at the club regarding his father's shady weapon dealings, put a tracker on so and so's yacht while partying on it.

But the studio had remained tight lipped about the why of

this particular assignment. Waverly had been tasked with establishing a relationship with the Russian billionaire's daughter who had recently settled in Los Angeles in a cozy $20 million estate. Just Petra and her herd of tea cup Chihuahuas in a nine bedroom home with two tennis courts, a full-size movie theater, and one of the best views in Hollywood Hills.

She'd coordinated an introduction at a club a few weeks ago, and the two had hit it off, partying together, enjoying flashy shopping sprees that attracted every paparazzo in a ten-mile radius, showing up on red carpets as each other's dates. Once the relationship was cemented—when Petra's bodyguards felt comfortable leaving the two women alone—the studio insisted that Waverly and Dante resume their relationship charade to get his foot in the door. When Petra invited them both to Tahoe for a long weekend, the studio gave the trip the thumbs up with no added instructions.

"Which is precisely why you are to keep our little billion-airess occupied while I do some recon around daddy's lake house."

"Don't do anything stupid, Dante," Waverly warned him. "With the bodyguards he's got on her, I can only imagine what security is like in a house that he actually uses."

Dante was technically her mentor. With the ink still hot on her diploma from Stanford, Dante had brought her on board to the dual purposed "studio," making movies on the public side and running contract clandestine operations for government programs that needed the special access that celebrity afforded. She'd lost her green and found her groove quickly, becoming an effective agent. She was still playing a role, as the party girl or the spoiled celeb, but it was a role she chose. A role she controlled.

But sometimes Waverly felt as if she were the senior agent

running herd on a bullheaded new recruit. Dante was impulsive and, on occasion, a little reckless. She worked hard to keep him in line.

She'd done some digging on the Stepanov family. Grigory, the father, was a billionaire several times over. His vast holdings included everything from real estate in seven countries, a football club, the majority stake of a very successful oil company, and, to further round out his investments, the patents on forty prescription drugs.

Petra's mother was Mrs. Stepanov Number Two, and Grigory was now on Number Four. Nothing popped for any of the wives. In fact, besides being outrageously wealthy, nothing was ringing a bell for Waverly. No hints at tax evasion or drug running or weapons smuggling. Nothing their usual clients would be interested in.

The weekend needed to yield answers. Waverly wasn't a fan of working blind.

But the weekend had only yielded more questions.

Perched on a bluff, the five acre-estate boasted a timber frame home that was filled with every kind of Americana luxury that reflected the Old West. A butler dressed in jeans and a pressed plaid shirt led them upstairs to a room with an unobstructed view of the lake. And for one second, Waverly recalled another room in another lake house. But she did what she always did when faced with an unbidden memory of Xavier. She ruthlessly shoved it aside.

This room wasn't in a cozy family home in Idle Lake, Colorado. No, this timber behemoth included eight thousand square feet of living space including a basement bowling alley and nightclub and third floor cigar lounge. This particular bedroom could have shamed any five-star luxury resort in the country. The highlight, besides the wall of windows that peered over the rusts and oranges of fall foliage to the glistening lake below, was the bed. Hand-turned posts thick as tree trunks held up the metal scrollwork of the canopy.

There was a stone fireplace, less grand than the one downstairs but still impressive, with window seats tucked into each side.

Waverly wandered into the bathroom and raised eyebrows at the opulence. The entire room was done in floor to ceiling stone. The walk-in shower had enough square footage and jets for a modest party of six. The copper soaking tub was set against a window offering optimal views of forest and lake.

She was examining the heavy timber frame of the mirror that ran the length of the vanity when she heard a groan from Dante.

She found him facedown on the bed buried under half of the dozen pillows mounded at the head.

"Dibs on the bed," he said, his voice muffled by goose down.

"We'll switch off," Waverly corrected him.

Dante rolled onto his side, propped his head on his hand. "You know, this would be much easier if we were actually sleeping together." He looked every bit the British movie star lying there in tastefully distressed jeans, the gray V-neck sweater worn casually over a white button down and topped by a dark corduroy blazer. His short blonde hair curled lightly around his face.

Waverly threw a pillow at him and hit him square in the handsome face. "If by easier, you mean messy and complicated, then I totally agree."

He laughed, flashing her a pearly grin. They joked about their fake relationship turning real, but neither of them was interested. Dante was not the kind to settle down, and Waverly wasn't interested in the complications of a fling or a relationship. She'd dated a little in college, enjoying the normalcy of being removed from Hollywood, but she could still never be one-hundred percent sure that the guys were interested in who she was becoming or who she had been.

"You are here!" Petra Stepanov, decked out in leather leggings and a furry vest, trotted into the room in her five-inch Tom Ford stilettos. She had a tiny dog clutched to her chest.

She wrapped Waverly in a one-armed hug and gave her a smacking kiss on both cheeks. "I am so glad you could join me this weekend," she squealed.

The daughter of an Italian dancer and Russian tycoon, Petra was a unique blend of cultures. She had the heart of her mother, her father's head for investments, and a love of everything American from baseball to the Kardashians. She wasn't the typical spoiled rich girl. From what Waverly had gathered, her father had dragged her to the office just as often as her mother brought her to the theater. She was bubbly and sweet, and Waverly suspected she wouldn't survive a day in the wild on her own.

She made the introduction and rolled her eyes behind Petra's back when Dante amped up the charm, kissing the woman's knuckles.

"Thank you for having us, Petra," Waverly said. "Hi, Pixie." She rubbed a knuckle gently over the dog's round forehead.

"You are so good with names!" Petra gushed. "You must teach me your trick." Waverly wondered what the studio would think of her educating a Russian on tradecraft.

"This room is incredible," she said, gesturing at the bed that Dante was dragging himself off of.

"I'm so glad you like it," Petra gushed. "It took Papa six years to get everything just so."

"He's certainly got an eye for design," Dante complimented.

Petra looked at him from under her lashes. "I helped, too, in some rooms."

Waverly hid a snort.

"I will let you get settled," Petra announced. "Dinner is at eight."

～

THEY DINED ON RUSSIAN CAVIAR, white truffle pizza, and lobster tail at the dining table. Backed in leather, the dining chairs had foot-long tassels that hung from the seat cushions. They currently doubled as a chew toy for Pixie, the teeny Chihuahua. Dante regaled them with tales from movie sets all over the world and plied Petra with innocuous questions about herself and her father.

Dante's value as an agent came primarily from his uncanny ability to draw information out of women. They couldn't seem to help themselves and spilled every detail of their lives to him.

None of Petra's answers were striking warning bells, though. Grigory was in Russia for the next few weeks working on a new real estate deal. He planned to join his daughter in L.A. at the end of the month.

After dinner, Dante excused himself to take care of some vague business, which Waverly knew was cover for checking in with the studio and, knowing Dante, do a little snooping.

Waverly kept Petra occupied by insisting on an evening walk to the lakefront. It was dark, but Grigory had the landscape designers flank the stairs and path with solar lights. Pixie wore a pink turtleneck sweater to protect her from the cold, and two of Petra's bodyguards tagged along to protect them from the shadows.

The first round of gunfire had Waverly shoving Petra behind her back against a tree.

"Fireworks?" Petra asked, trying to peer over her shoulder. The guards took up their positions in front of them, weapons drawn.

"I don't think so," Waverly whispered. "I think someone's trying to get in the house."

"What? What do they want?" Petra's voice trembled.

"I don't know," Waverly said grimly. Her gun was in her room. All she had was the knife strapped to her ankle under her boots. Where the hell was Dante?

"Do you have your phone on you?" Waverly asked Petra.

The girl shook her head, her dark ponytail trembling. "It's charging in my room," she whispered.

Another burst of gunfire ripped through the night. *Shit,* Waverly thought. They needed to move. They were sitting ducks if they stayed here. One of the guards was growling into a radio in Russian.

"Anatoli to house. Do you copy?"

There was no response. Nor was there one on his second attempt.

"Okay, we need to find a better hiding place," Waverly told Petra. "You're going to stay right behind me and be quiet."

Wide-eyed Petra nodded and then flinched at a new volley of gunfire.

Waverly signaled to the guards to follow her. They weighed their options briefly in the language they didn't know she spoke fluently while Petra trembled at her side.

"Oh for fuck's sake, guys," Waverly muttered in Russian. "We need to move." She pointed toward the boathouse at the edge of the lake a hundred yards away. Finally the short, thick-necked one with the radio nodded his assent. Wishing she had a gun or at the very least a dark shirt, she dragged Petra along behind her. The guards brought up the rear. They darted from tree to tree and tried to stay out of the moonlight.

For goons, Petra's guards moved with relative silence, which said training. It was Petra stamping over twigs and leaves that made them sound like a drunken circus bear stumbling through firecrackers.

The last thirty feet to the boathouse were out in the open. Waverly paused for a second and listened. The air was eerily silent as if everything alive was listening desperately at the same time.

She gave Petra a three count, and they began the sprint toward the boathouse. There was more gunfire, and Waverly heard wood splinter next to her head as she shoved Petra inside. There was an active shooter targeting them in the dark, which meant nightscopes, and that meant not your run of the mill break-in. They were here for someone, not something. The bigger of the two guards rushed in the door behind them.

"Anatoli," he said, gasping the name of the other guard and pointing to the door. "He is shot!"

Another round of bullets tore through the wood, and they dropped to the cement.

"Please tell me there's a boat in here," Waverly asked Petra.

"Yes!" she said through chattering teeth. "A m-motorboat."

"Thank God, I thought we were going to have to kayak out of here. Okay, you! What's your name?" she asked the guard in Russian.

"Yurgei."

"Yurgei, you are going to put Petra and Pixie in the boat and motor your asses out of here. Stay on this side of the boathouse to block your escape and then stay down in the boat. Go to the other side of the lake and call this in."

Yurgei grunted an okay.

"What about you, Waverly? Will you come with us?" Petra asked, shaking so hard Pixie whimpered.

"I'm going to find Dante."

She waited until Yurgei had started the boat and raised the garage door before moving back to the side door. She would be a distraction while they made their escape.

The second the engine revved, Waverly was out the door, low and running. She zigged and zagged through the dark, hearing the bullets that hit the ground near her.

She saw the fallen guard. He'd dragged himself to the trunk of one of the pine trees that ringed the rocky beach, but he was still in the line of fire. She hustled to him. It was a leg shot, thankfully not life threatening unless the hilltop shooters decided to wander closer.

"Anatoli, can you walk?" she whispered.

"Not well, but yes," he told her in thickly accented English.

She slipped his arm over her shoulder and helped him stand. She thanked God it had been him and not the heavier set guard who'd taken the hit. Anatoli weighed a good forty pounds less than his healthy counterpart.

"We're going to run for those canoes," she said, pointing at the heavy timber rack that held six polished wood boats. That should give you better cover."

"Okay," he gritted out.

"On my mark." They tottered and stumbled, changing direction twice. Bullets tore into the ground, and Waverly felt a stitch in her side. They made it safely and she shoved him under the lowest canoe. "Gimmie your tie," she instructed. His blunt fingers were shaking too much so she worked it free for him. She tied it around his thigh above the wound. "You got an extra piece on you?"

"Ankle," he told her, this time in Russian.

She found the clutch piece on his left leg. It was a thirty-eight and wouldn't hold up long against whatever semi-automatics her friends up the hill had. But beggars couldn't be choosers.

"You have any ideas who would do this? 'cause they sound serious."

In the dark, she could just barely make out his headshake.

She wasn't buying that but didn't have time to run an inquisition. She'd go in blind. "Stay here and stay alive," she told him.

"Petra?"

"She's safe. Your buddy Yurgei got her on a boat. They're probably across the lake by now."

"Who *are* you?"

Waverly flashed a grin. "I made a couple of spy movies," she said.

She left him under the canoe and darted around the stand into the edge of the woods. She waited for the hail of bullets, but none came. They were probably pulling out. If this had been a kidnapping attempt, they knew they were shit out of luck and it was only a matter of minutes before some serious law enforcement came knocking.

She stayed off the path, away from the lights, and battled her way uphill over rocks and tree trunks. She paused every thirty seconds or so to close her eyes and listen, but the night was quiet.

Waverly pulled herself onto the deck at the far end of the house and belly crawled under the teak table. Lights were on in the house, but they had been when they left. There was no movement.

Holding the gun in both hands, she moved to the patio doors. Seeing no movement inside, she slid the door open. The gun battle had happened here, she gauged from the broken glass and blood. Upstairs all the way to the right, she spotted one doorway open, a spray of bullet holes decorating the wall around it. Grigory's office.

Shit. Dante had been snooping, and that's probably exactly where he went.

She cleared the room, stepping around debris and puddles of blood. There had been wounded, but no bodies.

She ran up the stairs, heart pounding. Would she find Dante? Was he alive?

She sprinted the length of the walkway to Grigory's office door. There was blood here, too, but no body.

There were lights turning into the driveway. Someone was coming. Waverly ran down the hall into her room. She grabbed her phone and bag. There was no time to search all three floors of the house. She hustled back to Grigory's office, did one final sweep, and finding nothing, let herself out the balcony door.

By the time the new arrivals pushed through the front door, Waverly was two-hundred yards into the woods on her phone.

She stumbled once and pressed on. She found a spot against a boulder under the cover of a copse of pines and pulled out her phone. "Kate, I need a way out and a lift." She closed her fingers around the coin she wore on the long chain. The sharp pain in her side drew her attention, and she probed it. When her fingers came away wet, she swore. "I think I was shot."

WAVERLY CLOSED her eyes on the lounger. Where the hell was Dante? It had been five days with no contact. Was he dead? Was he hurt? Was he being held prisoner?

If the studio knew, they weren't spilling it. They had a

cover story for him though. According to the entertainment news, Dante was enjoying an impromptu vacation in the Seychelles cementing speculation that his relationship with Waverly was once again on the fritz. The news about Petra had been just as vague and less than truthful. There were reports that after a home invasion by an unstable suspect in Lake Tahoe, Petra was on lock down in a safe, undisclosed location. It was clear that someone was doing major clean up on what must have been a shit show on all sides. *How many players were there?* she wondered.

Dante had to be alive, Waverly told herself. He wasn't just a pretty face. He had the skills and training that an intel officer would have, but he also knew how to talk himself out of any situation. He was alive, and she would find him... and kick his ass for making her worry. But he was out there. And she was going to drag him out of whatever deep shit he'd gotten himself into. They were partners, friends. He was the first man she'd trusted since Xavier.

Waverly needed answers, and if no one was going to give them to her, she was going to go out and get them herself. She wasn't the helpless kid she'd been. Now, she was just as dangerous as the bad guys.

But right now, all she could do was heal and wait. She let the sun and the warm breeze soothe her mind until it floated away into dreams. Dreams that Xavier invaded. His hands stroking her skin, his voice, rough and raspy. Those brown eyes that held the fire of a thousand hearts.

Something woke Waverly where she dozed on the lounger. Even before she was fully conscious, she knew she was no longer alone. She was slowly reaching for the gun she had tucked under the magazine at her side when he spoke.

"Nice rehab, Angel."

3

*X*avier Saint, all six-feet-three-inches of him, leaned against the trunk of a palm tree looking entirely too relaxed. He'd finally grown out his military haircut. Now his hair, a shade darker than the dirty blond she remembered from years ago, was worn short on the sides and longer on top in a stylish cut. He was missing his trademark dark suit and instead wore golf shorts and a short sleeve white button down. A very nice watch flashed on his wrist, and aviators covered his eyes. He had a day or two's worth of stubble covering that granite jaw.

He looked like a rich playboy on vacation. But she knew better.

Waverly hated the instantaneous physical reaction her body had to him. Her palms were sweaty, and a deluge of adrenaline sent her blood pumping fast and hard through her system. Her nipples—the traitors—tightened with memories of what that stern looking mouth had done to them.

"This is private property," she said evenly. She wanted to march over to him and slap him across the face with a blow so hard it would echo across the entire island. But she didn't want him to see her wince when she got up. Besides, she knew what happened between them when they let anger get physical. Fireworks. Orgasmic fireworks that shook her to the very core.

And she was never going to let that happen again.

"Don't disappoint me, Waverly. Aren't you dying to know how I found you?"

She was, and that pissed her off. "I couldn't care less what you're doing here. So why don't you do me a favor and take a nice long walk off of that dock?"

He pushed away from the tree and ambled toward her. Her pulse thudded louder with every step that brought him closer to her. Every cell in her body was screaming in recognition. She couldn't hear the ocean over the blood pumping in her head.

She realized the gauze from her bandage was sticking out and yanked down the hem of her tank top. If he was surprised that she didn't jump up or try to run, he didn't show it. Xavier just sat down at the end of her lounger, comfortable as could be.

"I missed you," he said.

No other combination of words in the English language could have pissed her off faster. She hung onto the anger with both hands in a white-knuckle grip. "I'm going to give you to the count of five to get off my property before I call security."

It was a bluff, but besides pulling the gun from under the magazine and shooting him, it was all she had at the moment.

He grinned. "Don't you know better than to lie to me, Angel?"

"Stop calling me that," she snapped. It had been his code name for her and had morphed into an endearment. There had been a time in her life that she had longed to hear that word from Xavier's lips. Now it felt like lemon juice in a gunshot wound.

"Or what? You'll call your security?" he smirked. "Go ahead, beautiful. Let's see who comes to your rescue."

Now she really wanted to shoot him.

"I don't need to be rescued anymore. I learned a long time ago that you can't depend on anyone to keep you safe."

It was a dig and a deep one.

Xavier said nothing but reached for her foot, a move he'd made dozens of times before. She yanked it out of his grasp and planted it squarely in his chest instead. "Back off, X."

That gorgeous smile, and the hand he ran up her calf, told her she wasn't pissing him off. No, she was turning him on and that was worse. She didn't want to test her immunity to him when she was already weakened. With her entire body already singing, she knew how it would go if he made a move on her. So she shut it down, unleashing the inner Ice Queen.

"You're wasting your time here. I got over you a long time ago, Saint."

The noise he made was somewhere between a growl and purr. "I never got over you. And I finally gave up trying."

Words that she would have given anything to have heard years ago. But the time for that, for them, was long over.

"Stop talking and get your ass back on the boat." The ice was melting as the rage bubbled to the surface. She hated him, hated her reaction to him. He was coming at her when she was at her weakest, but she wasn't going to fall under that spell again. She would never go back to that.

"I'm not going anywhere, Angel."

"Last chance before I call security," she said. Her fingertips brushed the grip of the gun, and it gave her strength.

"Angel, I am security."

She was shaking her head before the word left her lips. "No."

"Oh, yes. Say hello to your new head of private security."

"I didn't hire you!"

He leaned casually on his elbow, enjoying himself.

"You didn't have to. Your father took care of that."

It brought her to her feet and the anger masked the pain enough that her scowl was all for him. "We are *not* doing this again."

Xavier stood, and she felt the prey drive jumpstart her heart. She was always the prey with Xavier. He closed the distance between them. "Oh, but we are, Angel. And I'm looking forward to it."

"How did you find me?"

"There's my girl. I could bore you with the details like flight manifests and Marisol Cote's spontaneous family vacation to the Dominican Republic only with a ticket to Belize City. Then there are the property records... clever girl buying this place under a corporation name, by the way. But the important thing is I'm here to help you."

"Help me?" she couldn't think. Not with his fingers toying with the edge of her silk robe. Not with anger and lust roiling within her to create one emotional volcano.

"Your parents and everyone else in the world think you're in rehab after an accident that didn't happen."

Her eyes must have betrayed her because he stepped in on her leaving no room for escape, no room to breathe.

"That's right, Waverly. There's no police report of you and a DUI or you and a traffic accident in the United States or Canada. And I highly doubt the media was reporting on a fender bender with a golf cart in Belize."

"I don't know what you're talking about."

"You flew here from Reno, Nevada, on a private jet five

days ago. And judging from your wardrobe," he paused to look her up and down, "it wasn't a scheduled trip. So why don't you tell me, Angel, why exactly you'd be willing to let everyone, including your five years sober mother, think that you were going to rehab after hurting yourself in a wreck?"

"It's none of your fucking business, Saint."

"That's where you're wrong. Everything you do is now my business."

"My father hired you?"

"He did."

"Then I'm firing you. I'm twenty-five now, X. I make my own decisions."

"Try it, Angel, and I'll be on the phone to your father in ten seconds telling him that his little girl isn't getting her life together in rehab. She's sunning herself on the beach in Belize. And I won't stop there. I'll get our pal Gwendolyn Riddington-Macks to draft a statement for the media, and I'll have your lawyer file a suit against every publication that printed the story and the unnamed source at Target Productions who confirmed it."

He was blackmailing her. And ironically enough, he was blackmailing her with the truth. But the truth was what could do the most damage right now.

"What do you want?" Her voice was calm, almost bored, but inside she was seething.

"A whole lot more than you're willing to give me right now. But I'm a patient man." Xavier ran a thumb over her lower lip, and she didn't bother stifling the urge to bite it. Her teeth sank into the flesh. Xavier tossed his sunglasses onto the cushion and backed her up until she found herself pinned between him and the thick trunk of a palm tree. "God, I missed you." His mouth was on hers, and her last coherent thought fled her mind as the ghost of flames long extinguished consumed her.

She refused to open for him, refused to yield. She stayed cold, at least until his tongue teased the seam of her lips. On a sigh, a moan, she opened to him. But she wouldn't yield. She fought to be the aggressor in a tangle of lips and teeth and breath. It was violent, beautiful, cruel. The pain of the last five years reared its head and poured itself into the kiss. She wanted to brand him with the hurt that had scarred her so long ago.

Xavier whispered dark promises against her mouth that had her shivering with desires rekindled. He was hard and throbbing against her. Her breath came in jagged pants.

His hands skimmed down her sides toward the curve of her hips, and she yelped in pain as he cruised over her wound. That quick slice of pain brought her back to earth faster than gravity. She shoved against him, needing space more than she needed oxygen.

"Did I hurt you, Angel?" His hands were suddenly gentle, his voice soft.

Yes. She wanted to shout it through tears. Yes, he'd hurt her. He'd destroyed her, and just looking at that gorgeous face was killing her now.

This couldn't be happening. She'd promised herself, vowed, that she would never again let herself be gutted by Xavier Saint or any man. She was Waverly Sinner. She bowed to no one. Remembering the hurt, clinging to it, she drew herself back.

She looked at him coldly. "You'll never be able to hurt me again, Xavier."

"Waverly." Her name on those lips brought a new pain blooming to the surface.

"What? You're on the payroll again, so you think sex with me is one of your benefits?" She wanted to draw blood, to hurt him the way he'd hurt her.

30

His hands dropped to his side and she felt victorious... and guilty.

"Who said anything about payroll? I volunteered."

"Good, then you'll be even easier to get rid of," she snapped.

"Angel, there's no shaking me loose this time. I'm going to find out what's going on, and I'm going to help you out of this mess, even if I have to drag you out by your hair."

"Hey, Wave, wait'll you see the dress Mari found y—holy fuck." The shopping bags Kate held tumbled to the deck as she took in the scene.

"Are your fingers broken?" Mari snipped at her from inside. "Don't just throw—Aye, *mierda*."

"Ladies," Xavier said, inclining his head to where Kate and Marisol stared open mouthed on the deck.

Waverly took control—and another step away from Xavier. "Kate, Mari, I don't know if you two remember Xavier Saint. He was with us for *such* a short time and left us so suddenly."

Xavier stepped up to her side. "God, I missed your smart mouth," he murmured.

"Fuck you, Saint."

~

"WHAT DO you mean he's working for you again?" Kate said several decibels above conversational level.

Waverly pulled the pillow off of her face and glared at Kate from her position on the bed. "My father hired him to guard me after I get out of rehab."

"So fire his ass and send him packing. What's the studio going to say when they get wind of this?" Kate demanded from where she lay on the floor next to Waverly's bed.

"I'll find a way to get rid of him before that becomes an issue," Waverly said with more conviction than she felt.

"What are you going to do, kill him?"

"Maybe just maim him," Waverly decided. "He wouldn't be able to keep up with me with a leg shot, right?"

"Is it just me, or is he even better looking now than five years ago? I mean, it should be criminal to look that fine," Kate said wistfully.

"Kate!"

"What? I'm sorry, but he's like a freaking god or something. How are you going to control yourself with him under the same roof?"

"Kate!" Waverly yelled it this time.

"Sorry." Kate pulled herself up and put her elbows on the bed. "I'm just... thrown. He is the last person I would have expected to show up here. I would have been less surprised to see some gun-wielding maniac from Tahoe or—"

"For the love of God, Kate, shut your mouth!"

"Sorry. Sorry. I just—Are you okay?"

"No, I'm not okay! Dante's missing, the studio isn't telling me anything, I got shot, and Xavier Saint just waltzed back into my life threatening to blow my cover!"

"Do you want something to eat?"

"No... maybe."

XAVIER SET up his laptop on the eat-at bar in Waverly's kitchen and ran his WiFi password hacker.

It had gone better than he thought. He'd been braced for bloodshed, deserved it even. Walking out on her hadn't been easy, and looking back, he knew it hadn't been right. He deserved worse than what she'd dished out, and that concerned him. Her energy seemed off. Oh, she was mad enough, but it wasn't sparking out of her like it would have five years ago.

She'd eased into pissed off like someone sinking into a tub of hot water as if she didn't quite have the energy to roll into a full-blown tirade. That made him wonder. She moved slowly, carefully, almost like a victim of an accident. But there had been no accident. Maybe she'd been sick or gotten hurt? He'd make her see a doctor just to be safe.

Xavier had been prepared for that visceral, physical reaction to seeing her again. He hadn't planned on kissing her, but then again, he wasn't surprised that he hadn't been able to help himself.

Waverly Sinner was even more spectacular now than she had been at twenty. She was stronger. He felt it in the way she pushed him away and in those tight muscles when they bunched under his hands. What had been all soft curves had transitioned into a lean, athletic body that looked and felt capable. She was tougher, too. Gone was the delicate brittleness she'd once protected. He wondered if her panic attacks were gone, too.

There was nothing that was going to keep him from her this time, not even Dante Wrede. She was it for him, and there'd be no more denying it. Xavier didn't care how dirty the fight got. He was sticking. He'd make her see it, eventually.

"Oh, you're still here." Kate's voice was flat as she made her way into the kitchen.

"Hi, Kate." He flashed her a grin that wasn't returned.

She ignored him and pulled a container out of the refrigerator. He watched her pour soup into a pot and light a gas burner on the range.

"Hungry?" he asked. Again there was no response.

Xavier sighed and pushed his laptop aside. "Kate, I know I fucked up."

She whirled around as if it was the opening she'd waited for. "I'm so mad at you. I can't even imagine how she feels," she said pointing up the stairs. "I can't believe she didn't shoot you on sight."

He pushed his barstool back and rounded the peninsula. "I would have deserved it," he said agreeably.

"You crushed her when she was at her most vulnerable, Saint. I didn't think she was going to snap out of it."

Xavier hung his head. The guilt that had ridden his shoulders for years got heavier. "I'm going to fix it, Kate. I won't hurt her again."

She whirled on him. "What do you think seeing you is doing? She's upstairs, laying on her bed wiped out because you showing up here just rocked the world she's worked so hard to build. You're fucking everything up!"

"Enough!" Marisol's tone left no room for argument. She stood next to the stove as if she'd appeared from nowhere. She crossed her arms over her chest, frowning. "And just how do you think your friend would feel about you painting her as a vulnerable little kitten to Mr. Saint."

Kate blew out a breath. "She would hate it."

"And you? You expect Waverly to welcome you with open arms after the way you left her?"

"No, I didn't expect that. I deserve whatever ill will you all hold against me," Xavier said earnestly. "But I'm going to earn my way back, and I'm not leaving again. She's in trouble. I know it, and you know it, and I'm here to help."

He watched Kate and Marisol exchange a glance.

"Whether you can be trusted remains to be seen," Marisol sniffed in disdain. "But if you can prove that you can keep her safer than that Dante Wrede, you'll have my support."

"Where is Wrede?" Xavier asked, his tone even. He wasn't going to hesitate to fight for Waverly this time around. Even if that meant declaring war against Hollywood's most famous leading man. And if Waverly's accident story was bogus, odds were that meant that Dante's vacation a hemisphere away was also false.

"Maybe you should start there," Marisol said with an imperious glance. She turned back to Kate. "The soup is boiling. I'll take it up to her."

"I'll help you," Kate said, lifting her chin.

They left Xavier alone in the kitchen, but unless he was mistaken, Marisol had deliberately given him a starting point. And he'd take whatever he could get from them.

4

*H*e made them dinner, grilled fish and vegetables, under the stars on the patio. Waverly didn't join them, but Kate grudgingly offered Xavier a cold beer when she took the chair on his left.

"Here," she said, shoving the bottle at him.

"Thank you, Kate."

She grunted a response. Marisol stuck to wine and watched him like a hawk as he doled out foil packets of fish and summer vegetables. Conversation was strained and awkward at first. It wasn't until Xavier handed Kate a second beer and topped off Marisol's wine glass that he got down to business.

"I imagine you both are wondering why I'm here."

"Duh," Kate snorted over her bottle.

"I think if I explain my motivations, it will be easier for you to accept that I'm back and maybe even support my efforts."

They both watched him suspiciously. He passed a loaf of fresh bread around. Kate made a grab for the bread, but Marisol looked at him like she sensed a trap.

"I plan to help Waverly out of whatever trouble she's gotten herself into and then I'm going to marry her."

Kate choked on a gulp of beer, sending a fine spray of it across the table in all directions. As she gasped for breath and reached blindly for her napkin, Marisol didn't take her dark eyes off of him.

"I imagine, Mari, you're wondering how serious I am," Xavier continued on conversationally. He pulled the small box out of his pocket and put it on the table between the two women.

Kate stared at it as if it was a rattlesnake. "You've got to be fucking kidding me."

Xavier shrugged one shoulder. "Open it."

Kate grabbed it and opened it. "Holy mother of bling." She gaped at the ring and made Xavier feel even more confident in his choice. The cushion cut, all four carats of it, winked at them in the candlelight, as did the diamonds lining the thin band.

"I don't care how long it takes or how long I have to wait out her feelings for Dante Wrede. He doesn't deserve her. I don't deserve her, either, but I'm the one who will spend the rest of my life trying to." Xavier speared a piece of fish with his fork and stared both women down. "And I'll do it with or without your help."

Marisol looked at him for a long, silent beat and then nodded. "It is good you've finally come to your senses."

"Good luck," Kate said, chancing another sip of beer. "Even with a ring like that, you've got your work cut out for you."

He didn't doubt it.

Xavier insisted on clearing the table since it was Marisol's last night with them, and when she and Kate wandered off to their respective rooms, he plated up the last piece of chocolate torte and carried it up the stairs.

He rapped lightly at her door and heard a quiet "Come in."

He found her propped up on pillows against the headboard of the gigantic bed. The bed faced the patio and the doors were open wide. The sheer curtains billowed inward on the night breeze. Behind the bed, a wall of stone carried the eye upward to the high, pitched ceiling and its white timber rafters. Waverly's face was as pale as the white duvet she lounged on. When she saw him, she slammed her laptop closed. "You didn't use your Invictus knock," she accused him.

Xavier grinned. "So you do remember, even though our 'time together was so short,'" he said, turning her words back on her. Xavier and all of his staff in every Invictus location knocked the same way. One hard rap followed by two short taps and Waverly had once asked him about it. A long time ago.

"You disguised your knock to get into my room. That's cheap."

He'd been right about her energy. She seemed even more tired now after spending the whole afternoon and evening resting in her room. She hadn't even thrown anything at him yet.

"I didn't want you to miss out on everything from dinner," he said, pulling the plate from behind his back.

"I'm not hung—" She spotted the plate and stopped mid-complaint.

"Chocolate torte from a bakery down the road," he said, waving it in front of her face like a bouquet of flowers.

He saw her hands clench the light blanket that covered her legs. "How about I leave it here?" he offered, placing the plate next to her on the duvet. "Then you can eat it without shame when I leave."

"Oh, you're leaving? Gee, what a pity."

"I'm leaving your bedroom to go downstairs and unpack in mine. Unless, of course, you'd like me to stay here." He tested his luck and sat on the mattress facing her. The bed's arched headboard rose above her, dwarfing her and making her look fragile, as did the dark circles under her eyes that looked like bruises.

He brought his palm to her forehead, and she gave him an annoyed look as he felt for fever.

"I'm not sick, and I'm not stupid. And you're not welcome in my room. Chocolate or no chocolate."

"You look like you're exhausted. You've been lounging around on a beach for five days, and you look like you got hit by a car at the end of a triathlon. If you're not sick, you're hurt, and if you're not hurt, you're worried."

She looked away. Waverly Sinner never backed down from a good argument. Now he was the worried one.

"Why are you here, Xavier?"

He nudged her chin until she looked at him again. "I'm here because of you. I'm here because I was a scared, stupid asshole all those years ago, and I'm going to make up for it. I'm getting you out of whatever you've gotten yourself into, and I'm sticking around after."

"Is that an apology?" she asked, picking up the plate and taking a tiny bite of torte. "Because if it is, it sucks."

"I'm bad at groveling, Angel. And you wouldn't respect a groveler. So how about this? Walking out on you was the biggest mistake I ever made in my life. And I've been sorry for it every day since. I've never gotten over you, even when I tried. I'm done trying to forget you. And I'm not going to stop doing whatever it takes to win you back."

"Oh, really? What about Dante?"

Xavier looked around the room. "I don't see him here."

Her eyes welled with tears. "No, you don't."

He laid a hand over hers. "Waverly, if you need a friend, that's what I'll be. For now."

She withdrew her hand and shook her head. "I don't need a friend, and I don't need you."

"Angel, you need someone, and right now I'm your best shot." He got up and skimmed a hand through her hair before she ducked away.

"Don't get too comfortable, Saint."

"Get some sleep, and we'll fight in the morning, okay? Bring your A game, though. This whole listless thing isn't working for you. You're not any better at wallowing than I am at groveling."

She tried to hide it, but he saw it all the same, that ghost of a smile on her pale lips.

WAVERLY WOKE up the next morning after her first solid night's sleep since the accident and felt ravenous. It must have been the chocolate torte that she'd polished off the second Xavier closed her bedroom door. It certainly wasn't because of Xavier. No, the man had lost any right or ability to mold her moods long ago.

She pulled on a pair of shorts and a colorful tank that Mari and Kate had picked up for her the day before and headed downstairs. It was still early, and the house was silent. She craved these pockets of quiet in her life. She had more control over them now that she had her own home—*homes*, she corrected herself. But they hadn't gotten any less precious with increased frequency.

Nothing had gotten any less precious in the last five years. She'd faced death and faced it so publicly that there was no way to turn away from it, no way to shield herself as she had so many other times. So she'd faced the rest of it, the fears, the failings, the wounds and scars. She lived it, walked it, talked it until every sliver of pain and doubt had been brought into the sun and wiped clean.

If only she'd been able to do the same when it came to Xavier. But that hurt? That went into the marrow of her bones. He'd walked her right into the face of her deepest fear, that she was too damaged to be loved. And then he left her there.

So she'd faced it, accepted it, and finally, finally moved on. So what if she was damaged? She used it in her work. It made her deeper, more empathetic. What had harmed her in her personal life turned out to be a gift in her professional life. She had a deeper understanding of both characters and people and used it.

She'd finally forgiven herself for falling in love with him. She'd been young, wounded, and ready to be swept off her feet. And as long as she never let it happen again, she'd stay forgiven. *Fool me once*, she thought wryly.

And with that magical summoning, Xavier padded out of the bedroom he'd confiscated off of the living room. He wore a pair of cotton pajama pants that rode low on his hips. The drawstring was untied. His hair was tousled and he still hadn't bothered shaving.

The bag of coffee slipped from her hands and hit the tile floor with a soft thump.

He grinned a slow, sleepy-eyed smile and knelt down in front of her to retrieve the coffee. He took his time getting back up and surveyed every inch of her body as he did.

"Morning." His voice was still thick with sleep.

Waverly felt her cheeks flush with a redness that spread to the roots of her hair.

She turned her back on him and willed herself to get it

together. She would not be thrown by a shirtless Adonis. "Oh, you're still here?" she asked coolly.

"In the flesh."

She heard the laugh in his voice but decided it was safer to stare down the coffee maker than the half-naked man. She fumbled with the scoop and dumped half of the grounds on the counter before he gently, but firmly, pushed her aside.

"Go find eggs," he ordered. "I'll take care of the coffee before you ruin it."

"I'm not making you breakfast."

"No, *I'm* making *us* breakfast," he corrected.

"I don't eat breakfast anymore."

He shot her a look. "You've lost weight, and you've exhausted yourself. You can eat some goddamn eggs."

She paused, debated, and then pulled eggs out of the fridge. She added the package of bacon and loaf of bread to the pile.

The coffeemaker burbled to life, and Xavier moved around her to get to the stove. Waverly dug the toaster out from its cupboard.

"Remember the last time we made breakfast together?" he asked, setting a skillet on a warm burner.

"Don't." Waverly put the bread down. "You don't get to reminisce about the good old days because they stopped being good to me."

He pulled the skillet off the burner and set it aside. Xavier cornered her against the counter and rested his hands on her hips. "Waverly, I'm sorry."

"Is sorry supposed to make it all right?"

"No, but it's a start. Or it will be if you stop being so stubborn and just deal with the fact that I'm back."

"Deal with... you show up here five years after walking out

and blackmail me into letting you stay!" She was good and pissed, and damn if it didn't feel good to feel something.

He grinned down at her.

"What? What the hell is so amusing?"

"Nice to see you again, Angel."

"Ugh," she groaned and pushed him away. "Look I'm rusty. I haven't had too many assholes to fight with since you left, and my verbal sparring sucks before coffee. And I can't form a coherent argument with you shirtless."

"I purposely didn't put a shirt on."

"Go back to your eggs," she said with a roll of her eyes.

"I think you mean *our* eggs," he teased. But he obliged by putting the pan over the flame.

"When did you get to be so chipper in the mornings?" she asked, slamming slices of bread into the toaster.

"When your face is the first one I see."

Waverly made a gagging noise over the toaster, and Xavier laughed.

"Are you going to get pissed off if I tell you again how much I missed you?" he wanted to know.

She poured herself a cup of coffee and then grudgingly grabbed another one for him. "Just a head's up here, but I'm going to be pissed off at anything you say unless it's 'see ya.'"

"Smart ass."

They took their plates outside to eat on the deck. Waverly chose the seat farthest away from Xavier, which put her back to the ocean. But it wasn't a hardship, considering Xavier was still shirtless.

"You seem to be moving better today," he commented as she bit into a crispy slice of bacon.

She was, she frowned. Her side hurt less, and her head felt clearer. Waverly glanced down at her plate and realized she'd already cleared half of it.

"Do I?" she asked with feigned disinterest.

"Those are some good cuts and bruises on your legs."

Waverly fought the urge to look down. She knew her legs were a mess. You didn't drag yourself up a mountainside in the dark with a gunshot wound without earning a few souvenirs.

"Mmm," she said, focusing on her toast.

"Okay," he said, wiping his hands on a napkin. "You don't want to answer any questions. How about you ask some?"

Waverly tried not to look interested. "How's business?"

"Good." He nodded. "The London office is opening this month."

"That's what? Your fourth?"

He nodded again.

"You and Micah have come a long way from when you first started Invictus. Why is it that you're still doing fieldwork?"

"I don't anymore. I made a special exception in this case." That grin winked into existence again.

"Lucky me," she said dryly. Waverly pushed her empty plate away and picked up her coffee. "I heard you were engaged."

"Are you asking if I was?"

She shrugged as if she didn't care, but she was hungry for an answer.

"I was not."

"But you were in a serious relationship?" she pushed.

"I was. I'm not now."

"Why?"

"You."

"Please. We haven't spoken in years. What did I have to do with your relationship?"

"She wasn't you."

He was pushing her off center, feeding her words that felt like truth but couldn't be.

45

"What's Micah up to these days?" she asked, abruptly switching the subject.

"Does Dante make you feel the way I did?" Xavier asked, leaning in.

"You mean full of rage? No, he's pretty low key. And I'm the one asking the questions."

The tic in his jaw was the only sign that he wasn't as relaxed as he seemed to be. "My apologies," Xavier said, picking up his coffee.

"Why now?" Waverly asked.

"I thought you were better off without me."

"I am," she challenged. "What changed your mind?"

"I saw the news."

"And you wanted to swoop in and save me again?"

"I saw the news and knew it was bullshit. How much of the last few years have been fake, Waverly? Since when do you stumble out of clubs drunk off your ass or fly off to St. Barths to party with a bunch of kids with diplomat parents? What are you into that's so secretive that you let your parents think you're in rehab?"

"You think you know me so well," she shook her head. "You have no idea who I am."

"I know more than you think. You're still playing a role."

"I'm playing a role that I choose. There's a difference," she snapped and then cursed herself for letting him get that much out of her.

"Let me in, Angel. Do it before you get hurt."

Waverly pushed back from the table. "I already got hurt, X. I'm a lot stronger now." She picked up her plate and mug. "Thanks for breakfast."

HE HADN'T MEANT to push her so early, but historically his control around Waverly sucked. Some things never changed. He wondered if she felt the difference from yesterday to today that was so evident to him. Even the way she moved was stronger, more energetic. She'd tangled with him, verbally at least, and he saw her color coming back.

She'd never admit it, but arguing with him made her feel more alive. And he felt the same thing.

He needed to be more patient, Xavier reminded himself, *needed to give her time to get used to having him around again.* And he needed to find ways to wear her down. One chip at a time until she was his again.

Last night, he'd ordered his research department to make a few unofficial inquiries into Dante Wrede's whereabouts. He'd also done a little looking himself before turning in. Dante had last been publicly seen in L.A. on Friday. Sunday—the same day that Waverly's stint in rehab was announced—an unnamed source had told a handful of gossip sites that he was enjoying a long, impromptu vacation in the Seychelles, but no one had captured him there frolicking on the beach or otherwise.

Xavier also knew there had been no flight plans filed for the Seychelles by the charter company that Wrede favored. So if he'd gone abroad, someone else had taken him.

One thing he was sure about, whatever Waverly was tangled up in, Wrede had put her there.

He took another minute to stare out over the crystal blue of the water and realized he felt lighter than he had in years. Just being near her was enough to lift the weight of the fog he'd operated under for so long. He could almost picture his mother saying, "I told you so." And she would as soon as he told her he was back on Waverly's security detail. She'd root for him just as she'd lambasted him for letting her go all those years ago.

There were voices coming from inside. The rest of the gang was ready to meet the day. Xavier rose and picked up his dishes.

"Is he still here?" he heard Kate hiss as he walked in from the patio.

"He is," Xavier answered for Waverly. "And you slept through breakfast, so you can fend for yourself," he told her.

Marisol was studying Waverly intently with her dark, all-seeing eyes. "You look better today," she told her.

Waverly nodded and avoided looking at Xavier. "I feel better."

"I wonder why?" Marisol sniffed smugly.

Waverly narrowed her eyes at the woman, knowing exactly what she was implying. "I got a good night's sleep. *Alone*, Mari," she said pointedly.

Xavier knew exactly what Marisol was doing. Sending him a message that he wasn't the only one who'd improved with his visit.

"Whatever you say," Marisol said innocently.

Waverly looked as though she was barely resisting the urge to stomp her foot.

"Hey, before Mari has to head to the airport, why don't we do that dress fitting in case we're back in town for the Fundraiser Fashion Gala?" Kate suggested, stepping in to distract.

"You don't know when you're going home?" Xavier asked. "Is someone telling you when you can come back?"

Waverly gave Kate a shove toward the stairs. "Can't talk! Dress fitting," she announced, and the three women trooped upstairs.

Xavier shook his head. Whatever they were hiding, he'd find out.

He took his laptop and a second cup of coffee onto the patio off his room and set up at the table. It was nice to be working out of a closer time zone to Micah and the L.A. headquarters. He already had a few responses to his requests the night before, including one from Micah.

> *Saint,*
>
> *Here I was, happy as a pig in shit when I saw you put in for your first vacation in a hundred years. I was thinking, "Finally, Saint's pulling himself together and running off to a tropical paradise with a beautiful woman." And then I see your request for Research to look into Dante Wrede.*
>
> *You'd better not be pulling Invictus resources to stalk She Who Shall Not Be Named's boyfriend, or I'm going to have to call for an intervention.*
>
> *Go have yourself a legitimate vacation and at least one drink with an umbrella in it. Or else.*
>
> *Micah*

Xavier shook his head. Micah had had his back for as long as they'd known each other and especially in the days after Waverly's kidnapping and attempted murder. When Xavier had broken it off, he'd thrown himself into a spectacular downward spiral that only ended when Micah broke into Xavier's apartment, threw him in the shower, and then shoved him on a plane headed for home.

He'd spent two weeks with his family until he couldn't stand the smothering and had come back to the job emotionally bruised and battered but alive.

It had taken a long time for him to get his feet under him again. The what-ifs of Waverly's abduction had haunted him.

What if he'd insisted she stay home? What if he hadn't picked a fight with her that night? What if he hadn't left her side in the club? What if they had been one second later on Hollywood Boulevard?

He'd never gone back out in the field after that. At first, his confidence had been too shaken. Visions of the knife flashing above Waverly's head still stalked him at night. But as he regrouped, he realized he could still be an asset to Invictus. He'd developed a tiered training program for new recruits and seasoned staff. It had allowed them to field some of the best assets in the private security industry. Today, Invictus was *the* name in security.

He rolled his shoulders and drafted a response to Micah.

Micah,

First of all, pigs are actually very clean animals. So your "pig in shit" metaphor lacks a realistic foundation. Secondly, I'm not running down some personal vendetta against Wrede, even if he does dress like a douche.

I've got a reliable source who claims he's been missing for almost a week. Just doing my due diligence. Humor me.

X

P.S. I am currently enjoying a very tropical beach view and may seek out an umbrella drink at some point.

Voices from Waverly's room carried down on the breeze, and he heard laughter. God, he'd missed her. Yes, their time together had been short. But the connection they'd forged ran fast and deep. He felt it again now and knew Waverly did, too. It was a vibration in the air between them, an awareness, a hunger.

"Next time you get shot, can you do it in a less conspicuous area?" Kate's voice carried down to him.

"Next time, I'll be sure to ask the shooter to aim for the feet. No one would miss a toe or two," Waverly answered with sarcasm.

But the rest of the conversation was lost to him as Xavier slammed into the house and stormed up the stairs.

5

*H*e didn't bother knocking, just threw her bedroom door open. Kate and Marisol were gathered around Waverly who stood on a footstool modeling a black halter dress. Kate was trying to yank fabric over gauze until she saw him, and then she jumped back a good foot. Marisol ignored him and busied herself in her sewing kit on the dresser.

"Out," he said, his voice eerily calm.

"Excuse me, you're not in charge here," Waverly turned to face him, crossing her arms over her chest. But Kate and Marisol were already jumping ship, muttering excuses of packing and imaginary phone calls.

"Cowards!" Waverly called after them from her perch on the footstool in front of the mirror.

Marisol shut the door quietly behind her.

Xavier didn't say anything, couldn't say anything, for a moment. Whatever trouble he'd imagined for Waverly, it didn't involve her getting shot.

"Show me." His voice was ragged with suppressed emotion.

"I don't have anything on under this." She wore a black halter dress with a hint of shimmer that bared an acre of back.

"I've seen it before," he reminded her a little harshly.

"And you think that's a pass to see it again?" she snapped.

Xavier sighed and looked down at the floor. He wanted to rip the dress from her, to look at the wound, to yell and rage at her, but that would get him nowhere. And she had a point. "No, of course not."

"Good answer," she said, simmering. "I don't have to show you anything. I didn't ask you to come here. I don't need you, Xavier."

"Please, Waverly." He didn't know if it was the please or the tremor in his voice that got her. But she stepped off of the footstool and stomped over to the dresser. With her back to him, she pulled a tank top out of the drawer, yanked it on over the dress and then untied the halter.

"Can't believe I'm doing this," he heard her mutter under her breath. She pulled the tank up under her breasts baring another swatch of gauze just inches to the right of her navel.

"It went through?" he asked, trying to look at it clinically, coldly.

"Clean through. Just a flesh wound," she recited.

"Lay down." The order was out of his mouth before he realized he was thinking it. "I mean, can I have you lay down so I can take the gauze off to see?"

Waverly shrugged one shoulder. "Whatever. I need to change them today anyway." She turned away from him, the skirt of her dress swishing hypnotically around her knees. She lay on her back and pretended he wasn't in the room. Xavier circled the bed and eased onto the mattress next to her. His fingers shook when he reached for the bandage.

With care, he peeled it off to reveal a small red hole closed with ruthlessly neat stitches. A relatively small caliber, but still. One inch to the left, and she wouldn't be laying here now. He could have lost her without ever having found his way back to her.

Rage clogged his throat. She was supposed to be safer without him.

"You're angry," she said softly.

He nodded.

"You're angry, and you're not yelling at me," she added.

He raised his gaze to her face. Those gray-green eyes that held the power to stun him watched him warily. He did his best to swallow his anger enough that he didn't let it lash out but he still didn't trust his voice. He wanted to rail and yell and force her to tell him what was going on. He needed to know, needed to understand the threats that she faced. Because her threats were his.

But he needed her to tell him, to trust him.

"Okay, now you're starting to scare me, X," Waverly told him.

He shook his head. "Can I see the other side?"

Obliging, she rolled carefully onto her side away from him. He repeated the process on her back, peeling away the layers of tape and gauze. The wound was a little larger in diameter as exit wounds were prone to be. But again, the stitches were fine and delicate. The flesh around the bullet hole was pink and healthy.

His fingers traced the area around the wound gently, and he saw goose bumps crop up over her skin.

"Both wounds look healthy," he said.

"Xavier, I'm fine," Waverly told him.

"I didn't say you weren't."

"You sound like you're being strangled. I know you're upset."

Xavier cleared his throat. "Where's the gauze?" he asked, ignoring her statement.

"You don't have to—"

"I'm doing it." The words snapped out of him even though his hands remained gentle, not quite completely under control.

"In the bathroom next to the sink."

He left her on the bed and found the supplies on the quartz countertop. He paused a moment to collect himself. The breath he took filled his lungs with her scent, steadying him. There were a thousand questions racing through his mind, and he needed answers. But he didn't know if he'd have the patience to wait for them.

He returned to her side and gently rebandaged her back before easing her over to attend to her front.

She laid a hand on his arm as he reached for her. "Xavier. It's just a flesh wound."

"Stop placating me, Angel." He stared hard into her eyes.

"What do you want me to do? You're upset."

"I want an honest reaction out of you. Rub it in that I walked away from you and that this is what happened because of it. Tell me the truth. Or tell me to mind my own goddamn business. I want you to be up front about hurting me. Don't try to cheer me up while you hide how much you don't trust me. I'm not your parents."

She did wince then at his words. He began to bandage the wound on her abdomen.

"Fine," she told him. "I don't trust you, and I don't see how I ever would again. I'm not going to tell you how or why I got shot. You're wasting your time here."

He ran a finger down the last piece of tape sealing it to her skin. "Thank you for your honesty," he said. "Now it's my turn. I'm not settling for this. I will find out what happened—with or without your answers—and put a stop to it. No one hurts you and gets away with it. And if I find out that Wrede had anything to do with this, I'll show him what a gut shot feels like."

"This wasn't Dante's fault," Waverly argued.

"But he was involved," Xavier surmised.

Waverly's mouth closed with a snap.

"You could have been killed. Again. Waverly, normal people don't go around getting stabbed and shot. You make movies. This shouldn't be happening." He could hear the emotion rising in his own voice.

"I'm safe now," she said stubbornly.

And she was. He was by her side and not leaving it again. If Waverly Sinner weren't in this world, then nothing else would matter.

He lay down next to her and gathered her close so her back was fitted to him.

She stiffened against him but didn't try to pull away.

"Just give me this. Please. Let me have this," he said, lips moving against her hair. He held her as he had so many nights before, locked in the safety of his arms. He breathed her in and let the feel of her warm body cradled against him calm him.

He felt her relax degree by degree. Xavier wanted to say the words in that moment. To remind her how much he loved her, but she would only pull away. He had to be patient, and he had work to do. But first, he could just hold her, even just for a moment, even if she didn't realize she was already his.

THAT AFTERNOON, they bid Marisol good-bye at the end of the dock. Waverly wrapped the tiny woman in a fierce hug.

"Thank you for always being here when I need you, Mari," she whispered in her ear.

Marisol patted her gently. "You're a good girl. Make better decisions so next time a vacation is just a vacation."

Waverly took the criticism with a grin. "I'll do my best."

Marisol moved on to Xavier. "I trust you will keep our girl safe?"

"Mari—" Waverly began, but Xavier cut her off.

"I will," he nodded solemnly.

"Good. I'll hold you to that," she promised.

She bid her good-byes to Kate, and they waved her off as the water taxi made a sweeping arc away from the dock before heading south toward San Pedro.

"Who's up for dinner out tonight?" Kate asked as they trooped back down the dock.

"Me!" Waverly decided. She'd been here six days and had yet to leave the property.

Kate looked over her shoulder at Xavier. "You in, X-Man?"

"I go where she goes," he said, nodding at Waverly.

"Chicken Shack?" Kate asked.

"Chicken Shack," Waverly agreed.

THEY DRESSED CASUALLY in shorts and t-shirts. Waverly wore a ball cap with her hair pulled through the back in a sloppy ponytail.

Xavier insisted on driving, so they took the golf cart south on the only road that served as a definitive line. It wound along between oceanfront properties on their left and ramshackle abodes on their *right, between* sand and swamp.

They bumped along for nearly a mile before Waverly

pointed out the red roofed shack on the right. A hand-painted sign read Chicken.

"Here?" Xavier asked incredulously.

Kate popped her head between them from the back seat. "Trust us. Would we lead you astray?"

"Yes and have on multiple occasions. You're just dragging me here to give me food poisoning and get rid of me," he grumbled.

"Man up, Saint," Waverly taunted him and slid off the seat. They chose a picnic table close to the outdoor fire pit that was covered with a blackened metal cage that held dozens of chicken breasts over open flame.

"How do we order?" Xavier grumbled next to Waverly.

Kate patiently explained the system. People sat, chicken barbecued, and then everyone ate the same thing at the same time.

Waverly enjoyed his discomfort. It put her back on slightly more even ground after letting him talk her into seeing her wounds... and then after. He'd held her, and as hard as she tried to resist relaxing into him, she'd done just that. Her body still recognized his as her mate. Just like his kiss from the day before, everything physical between them was still as devastating and confusing as it had always been. But the difference was she knew better this time around.

There couldn't be a working trust when all they had was a physical attraction, even one as ruthless as what they still shared. She just needed to keep him at a safe distance until she could shake him loose back in L.A. *If* she was ever recalled. Her phone had been painfully silent for days now. Nothing from Dante, nothing from Petra, and nothing from the studio. No answers, only questions. And no one to trust.

She knew Xavier was looking for his own answers. She'd heard his phone calls, seen him firing off messages. He was looking for Dante, and as much as she didn't want Xavier to get involved, she needed those answers. She'd deal with the consequences of his involvement later.

Three paper plates laden with chicken, rice, and coleslaw magically appeared before them as did beers and waters. Waverly made a grab for one of the waters and slid her beer to Xavier.

He leaned in to whisper in her ear. "I knew the party girl image was fake."

She shot him a glare and focused on her plate, and for just this evening, the three of them pretended they were normal. No wounds. No worries. No painful pasts. Just three adults enjoying the best barbecued chicken that Belize had to offer.

SHE WATCHED the palm trees dance in the hot Belizean breeze from the balcony off her room and plotted.

Waverly had been strictly forbidden from contacting any resources typically used by the studio. And the lack of contact was starting to chafe. They claimed it was to help sell her cover, but Waverly was sure they were keeping her on ice for a different reason. It had been nine days since the incident. And as beautiful as Belize was, she needed to get back to work.

Tomorrow was her self-imposed deadline. Ten days without answers, without contact, without instructions meant she would be returning to L.A. on her own and quite possibly stepping onto an unknown battlefield.

She needed answers, and right now, the only one doing any digging was Xavier, and he wasn't sharing. There was one other person she could call, but that would be sticky, very sticky.

For half the morning, she debated the merits versus the

consequences of asking Xavier what he'd found. He couldn't force information out of her—at least not legally. But maybe she could give him just enough to protect her secret life.

Waverly found him working at the peninsula in the kitchen with a direct line of sight to the stairs to her room. *Always working, always watching,* she thought.

She gave herself one more second to reconsider, but she was out of options. "I'm going for a walk on the beach. Want to come?" she asked.

Xavier's brows shot up. "You're willingly inviting me?"

"You'll just follow me and creep me out and generally ruin the peace of a walk on the beach. So you might as well do it next to me instead of ten paces behind."

He shut his laptop and stood. "I'm all yours."

Waverly slid on sunglasses and ignored his veiled entendre.

She called out to Kate who was working on her room's balcony as they left. Kate waved and looked only a little suspicious.

He looked sexy as usual. He wore a pair of navy blue shorts and a short sleeve button down worn open. She figured it was on purpose. Xavier was well aware that she had no willpower when it came to his chest and abs... and other parts. He was barefoot, and the stubble had turned into a full on beard that was impossibly hot. She wondered what it would feel like against the soft skin of her neck.

Get it together, girl, she warned herself. Wandering off into sexy daydreams about Xavier offered up nothing but trouble.

Waverly waited until they were out of sight from the house and plodding north on pearl white sands. "I need to know what you've found on Dante," she said without preamble.

"I need to know how you got shot," Xavier responded.

She'd expected it, the tit for tat, but it still irked her. "You first," she offered.

His grin made her heart flutter just a little in her chest. "Angel, how quickly you forget how well I know you. This may be an ocean instead of a pool this time, but I still see you setting a trap."

"I'm not in any condition to be shoving your deserving ass into the water," she countered.

"That's the cost of doing business with me," he said, his fingers twining with hers.

She gave a quick tug, trying to free her hand, but when he merely tightened his grip, she gave up for the moment. They walked on another hundred yards while she weighed her choices.

"I'll share information for information," she conceded.

They came to a low seawall built of thick black rock. The surf lapped gently at the foot. Xavier stepped down into the water and gently lifted her down to him. The body-to-body contact was enough to have her synapses frying for one glorious second as she felt his body lean and hard against her. She took an instinctive step back and stumbled. He caught her and guided her down to sit on the lip of the wall.

They sat side-by-side, shoulders touching, and stared out into the blue. Against the shore, the ocean was a translucent turquoise. Sea grass danced beneath the surface. Closer to the reef, the waters darkened to cobalt.

"Give me a starting place," Waverly said.

"I have you and Dante Wrede on a flight manifest from LAX to Reno, Nevada, nine days ago. I have you and Kate in a flight log from Reno to Belize City in the early hours the following morning. I also have a few vague media mentions of a home invasion happening at the Lake Tahoe home of your friend Petra Stepanov."

Waverly weighed her options. The truth was always easier to sell than a lie. The trick was determining how much of it to reveal.

"Petra invited Dante and I up to her father's home in Tahoe for the weekend. We flew into Reno and rented a car and drove the rest of the way."

"An Aston Martin," Xavier filled in. "Which was returned in the dead of night to the rental agency two days later. It was parked away from the security cameras so their feed didn't catch the driver."

The studio cleanup team probably, she thought.

"We got to the house around four or five. Staff showed us to our room, and Petra met us there. We had dinner, the three of us, and watched the sunset on the lake. Afterwards, I suggested a walk."

"In the dark?"

Of course he'd catch that. Waverly shrugged. "There was a moon, and the view was so beautiful, I thought it would be fun."

"Mm-hmm."

Great, she was already losing him. "Dante wanted to make some calls, and I didn't want to rush him by hovering, so I told him to take his time and meet us on the beach if he was able to."

"Was it just you and Petra?"

Waverly gave a half-hearted laugh. "No, Petra brought her dog, Pixie, and two bodyguards."

"Nothing like a nice quiet walk in the woods with an entourage."

"The path and stairs that led to the beach were lit, so we had no trouble getting down there. But that's when we heard gunfire. It sounded like it was coming from the house."

"Where Dante was?"

Waverly nodded. She swallowed hard before continuing. "The guards couldn't get any security in the house to answer on the radio, so they hustled us off down the beach. Someone started shooting at us, and I guess that's when I got hit," she added a tremble to her voice for effect.

He slid his arm around her shoulder and pulled her a little closer.

"I got separated from them. It was dark. I didn't know where to go. Then the shooting stopped for good, so I went back to the house."

His grip on her tightened reflexively.

"I can feel your disapproval," she joked.

"Angel, you could have been killed."

She shook her head. "By the time I got back up to the house, everyone was gone."

"Dante?"

"Gone." She didn't need to fake the prick of tears behind her eyes now. "There was blood and glass everywhere."

"No bodies?"

She shook her head. "Nothing. That's when I saw headlights pulling up to the house, and I panicked."

"Why?"

"I was afraid the shooters were coming back."

"Why didn't you call the cops?"

"I was so scared. I didn't want anyone to think that I was involved in some kind of kidnapping plot."

"Is that what you think it was?"

Shit. She needed to keep her opinions to herself. She shrugged again. "I don't know. It could have been a robbery, but it seemed kind of ballsy to do it when people are staying there since the house is probably empty most of the time."

"How did you get out?"

"I went through the woods until I found another estate. No one was home, so I called Kate. She flew up to get me."

"So you created the rehab story?"

"I didn't know what else to do," she said. "Petra's father is very powerful, and if he thought I was involved in what happened, I knew I could be facing serious charges. I thought that I'd be able to talk to Petra and straighten everything out, but she hasn't returned any of my calls. I don't know where she is."

Xavier swiped a hand over his face. "You just sat there in the woods, bleeding for hours?"

"I tried Dante's cellphone about a million times, but there was no answer." A tear escaped and cut its way down her cheek.

"You haven't heard from Wrede since then?"

She shook her head. "I'm scared that the blood was his. I'm scared I'm never going to see him again, that I'm never going to have any answers." And as she swiped away tears over another man, Xavier Saint stroked her back in slow, gentle circles.

GRIMLY, Xavier paced his room. Waverly and Kate had gone to bed hours ago, but his mind wasn't ready to shut down. His talk with her this morning played on an endless loop. She'd confirmed his suspicion that she'd been at the Stepanov estate. But what actually happened there was still veiled in secrecy.

There was no mention in the media of Petra housing guests for the weekend. The rental car had been returned, so no one had to come looking for it. And all of the players were effectively incommunicado. Someone was doing cleanup.

He'd put in a call to his old friend Agent Malachi Travers at the FBI looking for answers. Someone would have investigated a home invasion on that scale. Someone would have theories. He needed to know what they were dealing with and if Waverly was anyone's suspect.

Xavier had shared with Waverly what he'd found so far, which was nothing. With it being an unofficial investigation, he had let his scary serious hacker, Song, off her leash. She'd turned up a whole lot of no activity. As in no credit card transactions, no emails, no social media since the selfie he'd taken with Waverly at LAX. Even Wrede's phone was inactive. There'd been no calls or texts made from his number since the incident, and tracking it was proving to be impossible. It was as if the phone had been destroyed, Song told him.

He understood now why Waverly was wound so tightly. To her, the bullet holes in her back and abdomen were the least of her problems.

Xavier's dilemma would have been comical under different circumstances. There was one thing he could do to win Waverly's undying gratitude. He could find Wrede for her. But what would happen when he delivered her missing boyfriend to her? Who would she choose?

So he paced his room weighing his options and wondering what Waverly hadn't been telling him today.

6

———————

$\mathcal{W}$averly's Day Ten arrived with still no contact from anyone, including the studio. So she took matters into her own hands and called for the jet. She was done healing, done sitting back and waiting. It was time to go home. And send a message.

They arrived at LAX at six o'clock at night. With Xavier on her right, Kate on her left, and a phalanx of airport security, Waverly expertly navigated the crowd.

The questions flew fast and loud from the swarm of photographers who went nearly hysterical when they recognized Xavier.

"Waverly! How was rehab?"

"Are you ever going to drink again?"

"Xavier, are you on the job, or are you dating again?"

She smiled and waved and looked every bit the happy to be home again actress.

Xavier shoved their way through the crowd to the waiting Invictus SUV at the curb. He held the door for Waverly and Kate before sliding in next to them and slamming the door on the hoard.

"Well, that was pleasant," he said dryly.

Waverly smiled grimly. *That entrance should send a message*, she decided, peering out her window.

They pulled away from the curb, and she realized she hadn't given Xavier her new address. "We're not going to my parents' house are we?" she asked.

He shook his head. "Your house."

Invictus' research department, most likely. Waverly wondered if he'd kept tabs on her all these years. While refusing to use his name in conversation, she'd fallen down the rabbit hole of Internet searches occasionally over the years. Every office opening, every high-profile case, and because the tabloids never forget, every date he was captured on. Had he shut her out completely, or had he slipped, too?

They made their way north on the freeway toward Calabasas, and Waverly used the drive to text her parents and Mari to let them know she was home. Four seconds after she sent the text, her phone rang.

"Hi, Mom," Waverly answered.

"Darling! I'm so glad you're home," Sylvia Sinner chirped in her ear.

"Me, too. How are you and Dad?"

"Oh, we're just fine. We just finished up with the trainer trying to regain our youths. I've got a late dinner tonight with a producer to talk about a certain part," she said airily.

"You got it, didn't you?" Waverly asked with a smile. Her mother had been up for a part in a family drama that was creating quite the pre-production buzz.

"Of course I did. We're talking about casting tonight for some of the other parts, and there's a daughter role. It's not a huge part, but it's tortured and beautiful."

"Really?" Waverly said, knowing where this was going.

"No pressure here, darling. But it would only be about two

weeks of shooting in January, and how much fun would it be to do a movie together?"

A few years ago, it would have been an impossibility. And now? Sylvia's sobriety had changed their entire family for the better.

"Can you send me the script?" Waverly asked. It wouldn't be bad to be attached to a project to help dilute the rehab news.

"Already in your inbox," Sylvia said brightly.

"I'll take a look tonight."

"Glad to have you back, sweetheart! Now, we're still going to have to talk about this rehab stuff. Dinner tomorrow?"

Waverly pinched the bridge of her nose. "It really wasn't a big deal, Mom. I told you on the plane it was more for stress than anything else."

"I know, but we're still going to talk about it," Sylvia said firmly.

"Dinner tomorrow is fine. I need to talk to Dad anyway," Waverly said, eyeing Xavier. "He sent me something that I'm not happy about."

Xavier winked at her.

"It will be good to clear the air," Sylvia predicted.

"Yeah. Listen, set an extra place. I have a feeling someone is going to tagalong to dinner."

"Wonderful! We'll see you tomorrow night. Say, seven?"

"Sounds good." Waverly said good-bye and disconnected. "We're going to dinner at my parents' house tomorrow night and getting this mess straightened out," she told Xavier.

"Looking forward to it."

So was Waverly.

The driver paused at the Hidden Vista gate and showed his ID to the guard. The gates opened. Waverly shot Xavier a look. "How is Invictus on my access list?"

"Just expediting the process," he said innocently.

There were a lot of things that were going to get straightened out in the next twenty-four hours.

But Waverly set it aside as they pulled into the driveway of her home. She'd been here two years and still loved every nook and cranny of the rambling two-story traditional. Here, she'd finally found the home and the privacy she'd longed for all her life. The yellow house sat cozily on two acres up a winding concrete drive. The wraparound front porch was crowded with comfortable furniture, inviting guests to sit down and take a load off.

Xavier and the driver unloaded the bags from the back of the SUV and piled them up at the front door before he sent the driver off with instructions to drop off another SUV for their use. Kate yawned and stretched her arms over her head.

"Wave, if you don't mind, I'm going to go home and reacquaint myself with the rotting contents of my refrigerator."

Waverly grinned and grabbed Kate for a hard hug. "Thank you for coming to my rescue and babysitting me for days on end while putting your own life on hold. I promise to return the favor."

Kate gave her an extra hard squeeze. "You got it. Now try not to get shot or stabbed or abandoned in another state for at least a month or two."

"I'll do my best."

She waved Kate off as her friend backed her SUV out of the third garage bay and headed down the driveway.

"I guess it's just you and me," Xavier said, leaning against one of the stark white columns of the porch.

"Don't get used to it," Waverly warned him. She paused at her front door, debating. She was about to allow Xavier Saint to enter her sanctuary. "Don't you want to go home or something?" she asked.

He shook his head. "I sold my condo here. Whenever I'm in town, I use one of the Invictus properties."

"Fine, don't you want to go anywhere but here and leave me alone in peace?"

"Not a chance, Angel. Open the door."

She slid the key into the lock and opened the arched front doors. She keyed in the access code on the pad by the door. Even with Xavier crowding behind her, she still felt the rush of pleasure she always did when she came home. Inside, the traditional disappeared with an open layout, soaring ceilings, and windows everywhere that encouraged view gawking. The view was spectacular. Canyon and mountain with just a sliver of city lights to the southeast.

The travertine foyer opened to the main staircase and a sunken living room. A contemporary chandelier hung twenty feet above them, showcased in a cupola. There was a formal dining room to the right with a big bow window overlooking the front yard.

She headed straight back the wide hallway until it opened up. The entire back of the house was one cavernous room with windows everywhere. Here, the floor was dark slabs of stone warmed by the sunlight that poured through two stories of windows. She'd gone with dark cabinets and light marble countertops in the U-shaped kitchen. A massive island offered an acre of prep space. The walls were a creamy off-white.

Despite its size, the great room felt cozy with oversized couches organized around a large TV. There were three sets of French doors and dozens more windows here. Massive trusses gave the ceiling a cathedral feel. The fireplace, tucked into the corner and flanked by two comfortable chairs, was made out of the same stone as the floors. Above, a loft led to bedrooms.

Xavier went straight to the doors off the kitchen and stared out at her backyard. There was a kidney-shaped pool with a small hot tub and her favorite feature of the entire house, a pavilion perched between pool and cliff. There a farm table was centered under rafters and ceiling fans. A massive outdoor fireplace was built into the far end of the covered patio.

"This place looks like you," he said finally.

Waverly felt a shiver of annoyance dance up her spine. "Don't pretend that you know me, Xavier."

He turned his back on the view to watch her.

"You knew a scared girl who didn't know how to stand up for herself," she snapped. "That's not me now. You have no idea who I am now."

"I know you're lying to me. I know that there's more to this story than being in the wrong place at the wrong time." He grabbed her arm when she tried to walk away.

"What makes you think I'm lying to you?" She tried to yank her arm free.

"Your lips are moving."

"You really piss me off, Saint," she snapped, shoving her free hand against his chest and shoving with all her might.

"Waverly, you're not getting rid of me."

"I don't have to get rid of you, X. I just have to wait for you to get bored and walk out on me again."

He pulled her against him. "I didn't get bored, Angel. I got scared. I almost lost you because of a mistake I made."

"Bullshit." The word snapped out of her mouth. "That's bullshit, and you know it. You saved my life that night, and the only one who made a mistake was me in trusting you to stick around. Maybe you did get scared, but it wasn't because of Les Ganim. It was because you couldn't love me."

He bared his teeth, and instead of fear, she felt desire, fierce and hot, spike inside her. "I never stopped loving you. I fell for you when you tossed me in the pool, and I have never, not even for a single second since, stopped loving you. You are it for me Waverly Sinner, and the sooner you face it, the easier it will be for both of us."

His mouth crushed down on hers, sealing the words that she wanted to shout at him, the accusations that he deserved to hear. She pushed against him, but her traitorous fingers dug into his jacket and held. And when his tongue slipped between her parting lips, she lost her mind and stopped fighting him.

He consumed her, and she let him. Just for a moment she wanted to forget everything that was going on and just feel something, anything. And Xavier made her feel everything, the heat, the longing, the clawing need. There were still feelings there, still the ignition of chemistry, but that had never been their problem. Honesty had been. And nothing had changed there.

He tasted her as he lifted her up to wrap her legs around his waist.

"I can't be around you and not touch you," he murmured against her mouth. He settled her on the kitchen island, and she bit his lower lip, hard. Xavier growled into her. His hands were everywhere, stroking and teasing. She felt his palm slide under her sweater and cup her waist careful to avoid her wound. And when it moved higher to rest on her satin covered breast, she hissed against his mouth.

No one had ever made her feel the way Xavier Saint did. No one silenced her inner demons and broke through her defenses just to drag her to the jagged edge of pleasure, no one but Xavier.

His hand kneaded her breast, and she hitched her legs tighter around his waist, pulling him against her. She could feel his erection through her jeans and moaned at the friction he was causing.

"Angel, I need you. I need to touch you." He flexed his hips against her, and her head fell back. He shoved at her sweater, and she reached down between their bodies to cup him through the pants of his suit. Xavier groaned at the contact. He found the front clasp of her bra with his fingers and released it. And when his palms skimmed up to hold both breasts, Waverly shuddered with pleasure.

"Do you remember?" he gritted out against her neck as she stroked the length of his shaft through his pants. "How it felt when I was inside you? How it felt when I moved in you?"

She gasped and felt tears burn her throat. She remembered, and she knew there was a price to pay for feeling like that. She didn't want this heat, this need. But she was already tugging his zipper down. Waverly wanted to take him in her hand and make him beg for her.

The ringing cut through the haze of lust that threatened to suffocate them both, her phone, that ringtone.

Her fingers fumbled and then stilled.

"Angel?" He whispered the question against her frozen mouth.

"I...the phone. I have to take it," she stammered out.

He swore softly but lifted her off the counter and let her slide to the floor against him, every inch of their bodies touching.

She stared up at him, dazed by the contact, swamped by the need. He broke eye contact with her, his gaze pinned to her chest. But when his fingers reached for something, she realized it wasn't her breasts that held him captivated. Triumphantly, he held up the coin necklace he'd given her on a long ago night.

She waited for him to say something, to call her out on her reluctance to leave the past in the past as she'd told him she had. But he was silent. His eyes said it all. There was fire in those whiskey depths. Hope. Memories.

Embarrassed, Waverly pulled the pendant from his fingers and tucked it back inside her sweater.

"Your phone, Angel," he reminded her.

Waverly extricated herself from the cage of his arms and scrambled for her bag on the thick-planked dining table between kitchen and living spaces. Her body was still on fire from Xavier's touch. She didn't understand how her heart could be so hardened against him yet her body melted for the man. Her heart needed to have a stern talk with her hormones.

She found her phone on the bottom of her bag. It had stopped ringing, but she had a text from the same number.

Tomorrow. 7 a.m. Palo Comado. Alone.

It looked like she'd stirred up the hornet's nest as intended. She felt Xavier's gaze weigh on her and deleted the text. She didn't trust him not to snoop through her phone. It's what she would do in his place.

"Problem?" he asked.

She turned to face him, her cheeks still flushed with a combination of desire and embarrassment. "Yes, and he's standing in my kitchen with a hard-on like a Redwood."

Xavier wasn't embarrassed. He looked ready to pounce.

She held up her hands when he took a step toward her. "Stay where you are. This is not going to happen."

"It would have happened if you hadn't gotten that call," he argued.

"Then I owe that wrong number a huge debt of gratitude," she said pointedly.

"And I'm going to kill them with my bare hands," he smiled.

She rolled her eyes. "I'm going upstairs to take a shower. Alone!" she added when he made a move forward. *A cold shower. With ice cubes.*

"Where would you like me to put my things?"

"You're not staying here, Saint."

"Agree to disagree, Angel," he said amicably.

She glared at him. "There is something very wrong with you, Xavier."

"It's called love."

"Stop saying that!" she shouted as she stomped up the back staircase.

She shoved through the double doors of her bedroom and for the first time didn't feel the sense of peace and calm envelop her when she entered the space. She'd gone for a creamy khaki on the walls to warm up the room. The hardwoods were a caramel tone complemented by the thick wool rug in cream. The wall of arched windows included French doors that opened onto a small balcony overlooking the front yard.

She moved into the bathroom. The walls were light and creamy in here, and the light flooded in from one large window over the tub—the exact replica of another in a room in Mykonos—and two skylights. The same stone from downstairs covered the floor in here, but the architect had added radiant floor heating beneath it. Even her feet were spoiled in here. She opened the glass door to the shower and turned the faucet on full blast.

Waverly undressed as the steam billowed out over the top of the glass and stared at her reflection in the mirror. She hoped she knew what she was doing, walking into two lion's dens at once. The studio was aware of her return and not happy about it. And to further complicate things, she'd willingly almost ripped her clothes off and begged Xavier to take her on the kitchen counter.

She couldn't trust herself alone with him. Everything clouded when he was around until Xavier was the only thing in focus. She had a thought and tried to push it away but it took root.

Was this what he'd felt for her all those years ago? That destructive need that shoved control and instinct and good judgment out of the way? No, she didn't want to understand or empathize. She wanted to blame him, and keep her distance. She would protect herself now, from Xavier.

He claimed he loved her. But did either one of them really know what love was? They'd had their chance, had their passionate affair. And now it was over.

She stepped under the stream of water and let it gently wash away the hours of travel, the days of worry. She was home and tomorrow she was going to get the answers she sought.

7

She padded into her bedroom in a fluffy white towel, skin pink and glowing from a hot shower, and froze when she spotted him sitting on her bed. She still wore the chain around her neck, he noted. God, the spark of hope he'd had when she'd kissed him back had ignited into a slow burning flame when he saw the necklace he'd given her in its rightful place.

It had all meant something to her, too. And he was going to remind her of that.

"Uh-uh, it's not happening, Saint. Get out."

He held up bandages and tape. "Don't be an asshole. You know I'd never force you to do anything you don't want to do."

"You mean like let you stay here? Or let you follow me around and pretend to be my security again?"

Xavier grinned. "Quit whining and let me change your dressings."

"I can do it myself," she snapped.

"Oh, I'd love to see that. Now, lose the towel."

"I'm naked under here!"

His fully hard cock was already well aware of it. "Then go put something on if you're so self-conscious."

"Nice try," she shot back at him as she stomped into the closet. He'd had a peek at it while she was in the shower. There were no men's clothes in it, which was telling, just rods and shelves and drawers of all the facets of his Angel. There may be a section for club wear—which he would never let her out of the house in—and nearly double the number of shoes she'd had five years ago, but the majority of her wardrobe was still lounge clothes and workout wear. Maybe things weren't as different as she wanted them to appear.

She returned wearing a pair of leggings and a tank top in rich garnet under a thick, cozy cardigan.

"Ground rules, Saint," she said as she worked her thick, damp hair into a braid. "No kissing, no extraneous touching, no sexy talk."

"Think you'll still be able to control yourself?" he baited her.

"Shut up."

She lay face down on the bed, and he made quick work of the wet bandage on her back. She was healing quickly. The stitches would probably come out in another day or two. He sealed the tape to her skin and told her to roll over.

He took his time here, rolling the tank up under her breast to bare her abdomen. When he realized she wasn't wearing a bra every drop of blood in his body pooled in his groin. But he forced himself to focus on the wet dressing, not the sleek flat stomach or those perfect rounded breasts just inches from his hands.

"Your security system looks familiar," he said, trying to focus on anything but her nipples that were demanding his attention under thin cotton.

"It should. It's Invictus," she told him. "Also, stop snooping."

He'd done a lot more than just snoop, but Waverly didn't need to know that, yet.

"You had Invictus install your system?"

She smirked up at him and tucked her hands under her head. "Micah did, actually. We never had the parting of the ways that you and I did."

"Son of a bitch," Xavier muttered, placing clean dry gauze over her wound.

"Don't be a baby. After the whole Ganim thing, I asked Micah to come out to my parents' house. I didn't think it was right to drop Invictus right after that whole stabbing thing just because you were an ass."

Xavier tensed. He'd never be able to joke about it, and there were nights when he wondered if there would ever come a time when he'd be able to fall asleep without reliving that moment, that terror, over and over again.

"It would look like I blamed the company for what happened," Waverly continued.

"You should have blamed me."

"I blame you for being a dick and walking out on me, not for Ganim. Anyway," she continued. "I asked Micah to keep you out of any of my dealings with Invictus."

"I guess I can add 'pound on Micah's face until his jaw is wired shut' to my To-Do list tomorrow," he said, gently sealing the tape the whole way around the gauze.

"Don't blame Micah," Waverly said rolling into a seated position. "It was good business."

He spotted the scar then. A thin streak of silver against the tan skin of her neck. He nudged her chin up and trailed a finger over the jagged sliver.

"Did I not say no extraneous touching?" she reminded him dryly.

He ignored her. "What about the scar on your chest?" he asked.

"You're just trying to see my boobs," she joked.

He gave her a cool look, and she muttered a complaint, but when she pulled the strap of her tank top down Xavier considered it a small victory. The scar was there, another serrated mark, this one thicker, more obvious damage.

He ran his fingers over it.

"The plastic surgeon suggested I have scar revision surgery," Waverly said, doing her best not to look at him. "But I wanted it."

"Why?" *Why would she want a reminder of the night he'd almost cost her her life?*

Her smile was wry. "A souvenir of survival, I guess."

Xavier remained silent, remembering in exact detail how she'd earned that scar. The flash of the knife under streetlights as Ganim wielded it over her head. The impact of the SUV's tires flying over the curb. Three shots as the knife flew downward.

"Did you ever talk to anyone about it?" Waverly asked, finally looking at him.

Xavier shook his head. He'd never discussed the incident with anyone, not even Micah.

She sighed. "I figured you'd go the stoic hero route. I, however, am a normal human being and had to talk my way through it. I used to wish that I could have talked to you about it," she said, her fingers plucking at the creamy satin of the duvet. "You're the only other person in the world who knows what it was like."

"It's over now," he said lamely. He'd never been able to talk about it, never been able to put words to the clawing fear in his throat that he was too late, that the blood spilling on the sidewalk wouldn't stop until she was gone.

"Yeah. It is," Waverly agreed. But he knew she wasn't talking about Ganim. She was talking about them. He decided not to press his luck and to let that remark go. He would find a way to make her see that they were never over. They were just getting started.

He looked at her, really looked at her. Those long, lush lashes over sea witch eyes that avoided his face. The delicate hollows beneath her cheekbones and full, kissable lips. Her hair, the silvery blonde tresses that he still dreamed about, were wrapped in a tight braid. Mile-long legs with a California tan.

If she'd been his dream girl before, Waverly had now grown into something even more desirable. There was a determination, a strength, a confidence about her that hadn't been there before. He liked it on her. Gone was the delicate princess, and in her place was a capable queen.

He'd never been able to resist her before, and why would he stop now?

Xavier lowered his lips to the scar of the wound that had almost killed her and pressed them gently against it. He felt her heart beat toggle higher, and then she was pushing him away.

"I said no kissing. Have you had your hearing checked lately?"

He wanted to pull her back to him, to hold her. But she was already rolling off the mattress on the other side of the bed. "I'm going to see about dinner," she told him and left him alone on her bed thinking about how he'd almost lost her.

~

THEY ATE SALADS—WITH chicken that Xavier grilled to perfection—under Waverly's pavilion by the fire as the sun went down over the mountain. She'd missed home, but Waverly was annoyed at how easily Xavier fit into the scenery here. She didn't want him to fit anywhere in her life... except maybe her bed.

Their connection had always been so fiercely physical. And judging from their earlier encounter in the kitchen, the attraction had only sharpened in their long separation.

She wanted him. After all the time and all the pain, she still wanted Xavier, and that pissed her off. She wanted it to be a cleansing, a closure. But things would never be that simple between them. They were complicated people with complicated desires. Mixing them would only lead to devastation. She was stronger now, tougher and edgier. But that didn't mean she couldn't still get hurt. *Would she be able to walk away if she let him into her bed?*

She steered the conversation away from their history and asked him about his family. In the midst of her stalker's reign of terror, Xavier had spirited her away to his family home in Idle Lake, Colorado, for a weekend. She'd spent two blissful days splashing in the lake with his sisters and crowding around the kitchen table with his smart and sunny parents. The Saints had become her benchmark for normal, and they were still her secret hope for the kind of family she could have someday.

Xavier filled her in on the latest from the Saint family.

"My father has become quite the film buff since he met you," Xavier told her.

"You're kidding?" Waverly put down her glass on the table and gaped at him. Emmett Saint hadn't had a clue who his houseguest was until his wife had educated him.

Xavier shook his head. "He's seen every one of your

movies, multiple times. The whole family goes to opening night at the local theater every time you have a new release."

It touched her that they remembered her as fondly as she them. "I should get them tickets to the next premiere," she mused.

"They would love you forever. Especially since it would mean a family vacation to California."

Waverly laughed. "What would you do with your entire family here?"

"I'd ask my beautiful, generous friend Waverly if they could stay in her house since I don't have one."

"Your family is always welcome here."

"When you say that, I get the feeling I'm not included on that guest list."

"Well, I never said you were stupid," she quipped.

Xavier leaned across the table. "Give me time, Angel, and I'll get back on that list."

"Yeah, well, you can start with the dishes and see if that softens me up." She shoved her salad bowl at him.

Xavier carried the dishes inside while she stayed put under the pavilion. Waverly thought about her meeting in the morning. Would she finally know if Dante was still alive? God, he had to be. And if he was, where was he? Was he hurt? Did he need her? *Or was this all part of a larger plot?* she worried.

She had no one to ask and no one to trust, no one except herself.

When the evening chill chased her inside, she and Xavier companionably cleaned up the kitchen before retiring to the great room with their respective work.

Waverly read through the script her mother had sent over. Smart, funny, and poignant, it was the perfect project for her mother and, if the predicted shoot schedule was correct, it would be a great fit for her as well.

She rattled off an email to her mother and one to her agent, Aisha Leigh, a charming Southern belle who navigated the Hollywood waters like a shark. The woman had style, class, and balls, and Waverly hoped to be just like her when she grew up.

She needed to talk to her publicist, Gwendolyn, too. But she'd hold off on contacting Media Barbie until after her meeting in the morning.

She was confident she could sneak out in the morning without Xavier being any the wiser. Her return would be the problem. But she didn't shy away from fights anymore. She didn't need to avoid conflict as she once had. She could handle Xavier.

Next on her agenda, she needed access to some information about Petra and her father. Waverly's gut told her that the father was the key. Someone wanted something from Grigory Stepanov. But without being able to tap the studio's resources, she needed another asset.

And wouldn't Xavier hate that? she thought with a smile.

She fired off a text, still smiling and when her phone shrilled moments later with Katy Perry's "Last Friday Night." Xavier raised a suspicious eyebrow at her. "Gotta take this," she said, taking the phone into the study off the great room and shutting the door.

"Hey," she said by way of greeting.

"I don't even know where to start!" Chelsea Saint's voice announced. "First there's some weird accident—that there's no police record of, by the way. Then you're allegedly in rehab. And then you fly into L.A. *with my brother,* the man whose existence you vowed never to acknowledge again."

Waverly laughed. "I know, it's all kind of hard to explain, and I don't have a lot of time since your brother is still here."

"Here as in 'your house'?" Chelsea hissed.

"Yeah, I don't know how to get rid of him. Any advice?"

"Try crying and talking about your period. That always worked for me and Mad," Chelsea suggested, referencing her younger sister Madelyn.

Waverly snickered. "I'll keep that one in my back pocket for now. Listen, if you have time, I need a favor."

"Name it."

"I need some information on Grigory Stepanov. He's your typical Russian billionaire mogul."

"And your BFF's money bags dad," Chelsea added.

"Are all the Saints keeping tabs on me?" Waverly wondered.

"I plead the fifth. What do you need on Stepanov?"

"I'm looking for anything seedy. Any hint of rumors or investigations, money squirreled away, anything that looks off to you. Anything that would warrant an investigation by a government organization."

"I take it you're back on the job?"

"Let's just say this is an unofficial peek. I'm still benched, so keep all of this quiet."

"You got it. One more question," Chelsea said. "Are you guys getting back together?"

Waverly could hear the hope in Chelsea's voice and hated to crush her. But the hard truth was always better than a soft lie. "No. He's, uh, helping me look for Dante."

"Ohhh." One extended syllable over the phone said a lot.

"Yeah."

She took a few more minutes to catch up with Chelsea about work and life before disconnecting. She wondered how Xavier would take it if he found out his little sister was one of the best vigilante hackers in the business. Probably about as well as finding out that she and Waverly had maintained a close friendship over the years since her visit to the Saint family in Idle Lake all those years ago.

She stowed her phone in the pocket of her cardigan and returned to the great room. Xavier was still on his laptop, but he'd moved to her couch. She could have picked up and moved over, but what was the point? He'd only follow her around in an evening game of musical chairs until he'd chased her up to bed. And her goal was to keep him up late tonight so he'd buy that she was sleeping late the following morning.

She flopped down on the couch and pulled her computer into her lap, ignoring him. But it was an impossible task. She fired off emails to her agent and drafted one for her publicist to send after her meeting tomorrow. Gwendolyn Riddington-Macks could sell bald-faced lies to a polygraph. And hopefully she could help Waverly repair the damage that the rehab story had done to her reputation.

With nothing else to do but keep Xavier up late, she shut down her laptop, turned on the TV, and picked a fight.

8

Six came awfully early to Waverly's way of thinking as she slipped out of bed and tiptoed into her bathroom. Xavier had, of course, chosen the guest room closest to her bedroom, and she wasn't taking any chances of him hearing her.

She'd snuck downstairs in the middle of the night, testing her luck and Xavier's ears to leave a note on the dining table.

Picking up breakfast. Be back soon.

On her way back to her room, she'd paused at Xavier's door and heard him tossing and turning. She'd been possessed with the urge to open the door, knowing exactly what would happen if she entered his room. Her hand had actually grasped the handle before she'd gotten a hold of herself and crept back to her own room.

She lay awake for a good hour after that, thinking about Xavier in his room. Wondering if his head was as full of her as hers was of him.

It had been a long night. But now she needed to be sharp.

She dressed in her leathers and boots and tucked her gun into a holster inside the waistband at the small of her back and a knife in her left boot. She found her tiny can of pepper spray and stowed it in her jacket pocket. If she was walking into a trap, she was doing it armed and ready for a fight.

She grabbed her phone from the nightstand and some cash and her ID and stepped out onto her balcony, closing the doors softly behind her. There was no way she was going to chance tiptoeing past Xavier's room. She was faster than she'd been years ago, but he could probably still take her in a foot race.

Waverly swung her leg over the railing and found her footing on the edge of the decking. She slid her hands down the railing and lowered herself into a full hang, dangling from the overhang of the front porch.

She dropped the last few feet and tucked into a crouch. She closed her eyes and listened for nearly a full minute. Hearing nothing, she rose and jogged across the drive to her garage. The fourth bay door rose with a quiet whir when she keyed in the code. She grinned when she spotted her baby. The Ducati SuperBike made her feel like freaking Batman whenever she put the Pirelli rubber to road.

She wheeled the bike into the driveway and down to the road. To be on the safe side, she pushed it another hundred feet past her property before starting it up. She snapped the visor on her helmet closed and began winding her way through the neighborhood.

It wasn't the friendly community that Xavier had grown up in. There were no interconnecting backyards or community fire pits here in Hidden Vista. She didn't know her neighbors, but the gate bought her the privacy she'd craved.

Paparazzi weren't even permitted to linger outside the gate, not that they'd be waiting for her at 6:15 in the morning. The sun wasn't even up yet. And there was no sign of Xavier Saint on her tail. Waverly went through her strategy again as she cruised north. Palo Comado Canyon was an arid park perfect for quiet hikes and clandestine meetings.

She'd go in hot, play it pissed off and scared. After all, an ambiguous assignment had nearly gotten her killed, and her partner was missing. And what had she gotten from the studio? Certainly not answers; just a directive to lay low, instructions to follow. Instructions that never came. She was pissed, and she'd play it that way. She had given them two years of her life, finished every job she'd ever started, and on two occasions, had come home with information that had saved lives. She was a damn asset, not a gopher.

She let the adrenaline roll through her. She needed to be sharp, ready for anything. She'd arrived early on purpose, coasting into the parking area as the sky turned a mottled pink.

Waverly stashed her helmet and gloves and grabbed a flashlight from her saddlebag. It was already light enough to see with dawn beginning to break, but the stubby Maglite would add one more weapon to her arsenal in case she needed it.

She skipped the direct path that would take her where she needed to go and, instead, looped around on a longer trail to come up behind the meeting place. If anyone was there lurking, she'd find them. But she found the vista and its surrounding area empty. She was alone in the final dredges of dusk.

The weight of her 9mm at her back reminded her of how far she'd come. A few years ago waiting alone in the dark for the unknown could have triggered a panic attack. And now? Now, she pitied the idiot who made the mistake of targeting her. She'd made the most of her training and expanded upon it with a self-defense coach. With or without weapons, Waverly Sinner was no one's victim anymore.

As the sun began to peek above the mountain, she saw headlights cut through the shadows from the parking area above.

She felt a tingle between her shoulder blades. It was show time.

She stood, her back to the canyon and the safety railing, and waited with arms crossed. She could easily reach for the knife or the pepper spray from this stance, and he'd never suspect anything until it was too late.

In her opinion, the studio bought a little too much of her cover as the bubbly party girl. And she wouldn't hesitate to use that ignorance if it helped her case. She'd learned a long time ago that she was safer when people underestimated her.

She heard the scuff of his shoes and the low cadence of his voice as he approached. Bradley Archibald Tomasso, the youngest CEO in Target Productions' history, sauntered down the decline to the bench chatting on his cell phone.

"Yeah. I saw the numbers. They look good. Listen, I gotta go. I have a meeting."

He hung up the phone and flashed Waverly a pearly smile. "There's my girl! How are you healing?"

He didn't look like a firing squad in his navy trousers and glossy caramel colored Stefano Bemers. He was trim and energetic with thick dark hair that held a lot of product. He looked like every studio executive she'd ever met. But he was the first one, to her knowledge, to have the foresight to double the studio's income by farming out talent to intelligence gathering organizations on a contract basis.

"Just fine," she said with a smile as phony as Brad's wife's breasts. "Maybe a little shaken up, to be honest," she ventured.

Brad joined her at the railing overlooking a portion of

deep canyon. "I can certainly understand. That assignment went to hell in a handbag, didn't it?"

"I got shot if that's what you mean by handbag. Who were those guys?" she asked.

Brad gave a careless shrug of his shoulder, but his eyes were sharp and focused. "I have no idea."

Liar, Waverly thought.

"They just came out of nowhere," Waverly said, adding a quiver to her voice.

"Why weren't you in the house?"

The question caught her off guard, but she rolled with it. "Petra wanted to show me the fire ring down by the lake," she said.

"So Dante was alone in the house?"

Waverly chose her words carefully. She didn't want Brad to know that Dante had been suspicious of the assignment and had gone snooping. "He had some calls to make. He was going to meet us down by the lake when he was done. There was some security and staff in the house, I think. Petra's bodyguards came with us."

Brad jingled the keys in his pants pocket. "I see."

"Do you know where Dante is? I'd really like to talk to him. You know, make sure he's okay."

"You haven't heard from him?" Brad asked, pursing his lips.

Waverly shook her head. "I tried calling him immediately after the shooting, but he never answered, so I followed protocol and arranged an extraction."

Brad nodded briskly. "So no texts or calls or emails from Wrede?"

"No. Why? Is he... he's still alive, isn't he?"

"He's fine," Brad said with confidence. "We sent him away,

too, until everything calms down. Except he followed orders and didn't come back early," he said sternly.

Waverly did her best to look chagrined. "I couldn't stay away any longer," she protested. "I needed to know what happened, and you weren't offering any answers."

Brad's friendly façade fell away. "It's not my job to give you answers. It's my job to give you orders and your job to follow them. You could have jeopardized a lot of plans coming back the way you did. With Xavier Saint, might I add."

Waverly felt the pepper spray with her fingers through her jacket.

"That was my father's fault. I didn't ask him to—"

"You need to get rid of him," Brad snapped. "If Mommy and Daddy are worried about their little princess's safety, tell them the studio will be happy to arrange security for you. But get rid of Saint. I don't need him coming around stirring up even more trouble."

"I'll get rid of him," she promised.

"Good, because more than just your job is riding on this. If Stepanov's father finds out that you were in his house on assignment, if he even suspects for a moment that you were there as anything but a friend to his daughter, your days are numbered. He's not a good man, Waverly. Keep that in mind next time I give you an order and you feel like you know better."

"What do you want with Petra? Or is it Grigory you're after?" Waverly questioned.

Brad turned on her. "You listen to me. Your job is to do your assignments, nothing more. I don't pay you to second guess me or try to wrap your brain around the complex worlds of politics and business. You smile pretty and collect the information we need. Don't try to play hero and save heiress's lives or track down assets."

"I do a lot more for you than just smile pretty," she reminded him coolly.

"Don't overinflate your worth. You're replaceable, and so is Wrede."

"Where's Dante?" Waverly snapped.

"I'm surprised that you don't know." Brad's phone signaled in his pocket. "Now, what I need for you to do is lay low until you hear from me again. Stick to the story and keep your mouth shut or don't be surprised if men with guns show up on your doorstep."

He wrestled the phone out of his pocket and answered it on his way back up the path.

"Mother fucker," Waverly muttered.

"My sentiments exactly."

She jumped a mile out of her skin and was pulling the gun from her back when Xavier stepped out of the scrub brush.

Her fingers brushed the metal, and she pulled back at the last second. "What are you doing here?" she asked. They both froze when they heard the engine rev from the parking area.

But it was Brad leaving.

"I got your note," Xavier said, his voice chilly with calm.

"Yeah, I was just about to go pick up breakfast for us," she said uneasily. With a thirty foot drop to her back and Xavier at her front, she wasn't liking her chances for escape. And he may have pissed her off, but she didn't feel that quite warranted shooting her way out.

"Why don't you sit first and we'll have a little chat?"

"I think I'm good. I don't need to talk," she crossed her arms.

"Let me rephrase that." Xavier stepped over the bench and into her personal space. "Sit the hell down and tell me why you're sneaking out for pre-dawn meetings without telling me."

"Do you really want to go over the whole 'I didn't hire you' thing again? Because we can," Waverly said, jumping on the offensive. "I didn't hire you. You don't work for me."

"And I told you before, I go where you go or I spill all your secrets."

"You don't know my secrets!" Her voice echoed around the canyon. Unless he'd been there for the entire conversation.

"I know that you weren't in rehab for ten days. I know that you were in Petra Stepanov's house when you got shot by a bunch of goons with guns. I know that you haven't heard from Dante since that night, and I also know that when I find him, I'm going to kick his ass for pulling you into this." He ticked the items off on his fingers.

"Dante didn't pull me into this!"

"You're in over your head and refusing to let me help you is just fucking stupid," he snapped.

"You know what's fucking stupid? You underestimating me. You don't want to help. You want to swoop in and take over. And I don't need you to. I have everything under control!"

"Then where's Dante? And why was that guy threatening you? I got his plates when I got here, you know I'm going to run them and him."

She bit back a sigh of relief. So he hadn't heard the entire conversation. That was a plus.

"That ray of sunshine was Brad Tomasso, head of Target Productions. I have a movie coming out with them soon, and he's pissed that I could be hurting the rep of the film with my recent antics. I came because I was hoping he had information on Dante."

"Your recent antics involve a fake stay in rehab confirmed by Target Productions." Xavier leaned back against the railing, a deceptively casual stance.

"None of this is your business, X. How the hell did you find me anyway?"

"Tracker on your bike."

At her gasp of indignation, he grinned. "I know you, Waverly. You want to pretend that we're strangers, go right ahead. But I know every move you're going to make before you make it. Even the stupid ones like meeting someone alone in the dark when no one knows where you are."

She gave herself a second to fantasize flipping him over the railing and into the canyon.

"You wouldn't be able to get me off the ground," he said with a smirk.

"I hate you."

"You hate that you want me," he corrected.

"Dream on," she spat out.

He pounced like a jungle cat, one second relaxed and the next second hauling her up against his side. "The way I see it is you have the drive back to your house to decide whether you're going to let me in, or I can go public with what I do know. I'd be defending your honor, of course. I hate to see your reputation smeared with a fake rehab story, especially since it's causing you problems at work. I'll start with your parents, but I'm sure the media and gossip sites would be happy to have a statement from me about you."

She let the anger spiral through her. It was a safe emotion. She went for a low blow. "If you're trying to blackmail me into a relationship with you, it's not going to work."

He pushed her along toward the parking lot, his arm anchored around her shoulders. "Angel, we're already in a relationship. You just don't want to accept it."

She tried to shrug him off. "No, *I'm* already in a relationship," she reminded him. So what if it was fake? Xavier didn't know that.

He paused and let his arm drop from her shoulders to take her wrist. "I don't see him here, do you? And I sure as hell didn't see him when you got shot. So unless Wrede is dead, he deserves an ass-kicking, which I will provide when I find him."

Oh, he was angry. She could feel it flowing through his grip on her wrist, see it in those molten eyes. Waverly glared up at him. She could go toe-to-toe with him, wanted to even, but she knew what happened when they met in the middle with anger. They always ended up in bed.

She saw headlights coming from the parking lot above, heard doors closing and voices. The day was beginning for the rest of the world. And she was just getting started.

THE RIDE HOME was a quiet one. Xavier refused to let her take her bike home and stuffed her into the passenger seat of his SUV, buckling her seatbelt himself. She thought about what fun the pepper spray would have been but realized the quarters were too close.

Instead, she closed her eyes and thought through her conversation with Brad. He didn't know where Dante was either. She was sure of that now. Which meant there was a good chance that he was alive, somewhere. He'd given her the information she'd been looking for, and as soon as she heard back from Chelsea, she'd have a clearer path to what needed to happen next.

But first she had to survive dinner with her parents and Xavier tonight. She wasn't looking forward to dancing that tight rope of assuring her mother that she wasn't turning into a second-generation alcoholic *and* keeping Xavier under control.

She felt Xavier bring the SUV to a stop and opened her eyes. She frowned at him. "What are you doing?"

"You promised me breakfast," he said innocently.

"Every time we're seen in public together people are going to assume things," she reminded him pointedly.

"What a pity," he grinned.

"Ass."

She followed him out of the car to Zia's Café. The people at the miniscule bar tops at the front of the café basked in the autumn sunshine that poured in through the front windows. The floors were a gray washed oak, the walls alternated with splashes of cream and khaki. A handwritten chalkboard menu hung above both registers. The entire place smelled like a dozen different coffees and fresh baked goods. The baristas all followed a similar dress code. Black on black with green aprons and facial jewelry. There were several early birds already in line and a dozen more patrons scattered about the tables and barstools.

It could have been worse, she reminded herself. He could have rolled up in front of a Starbucks on Hollywood Boulevard. It wasn't likely they'd run into any paparazzi here. But she still heard a gasp and felt the weight of a half dozen gazes on her when Xavier held the door for her.

No paparazzi. But fans, on the other hand, were a different story.

The cell phones were up in seconds, and Waverly did her best to ignore them. Xavier leaned in to whisper in her ear. "You'd better smile and look happy and healthy, or else I'll be forced to plant a kiss on you that no one will forget."

Waverly looked up at him with a smart-ass smile on her face. "Try it, and I'll kick you in the balls so hard you'll be shooting blanks for the rest of your life."

He grinned wolfishly.

"Angel, if you're going for my balls, we both know it won't be to kick them."

She didn't like where that statement took her mentally so she turned her back on him to study the menu. The girl in line in front of her held up her cell phone pretending to take a selfie but was clearly lining up to get Waverly and Xavier in it.

Waverly sighed and grabbed Xavier by the shirtfront, pulling him in with her over the girl's shoulder. "Smile pretty, Saint."

It opened the floodgates, of course, and by the time they walked out of the café—coffees and breakfast sandwiches in hand—they'd posed for a dozen pictures with customers and staff.

The first time someone asked for a picture with just Xavier, Waverly couldn't stifle her laughter. She'd insisted on taking the picture herself and thoroughly enjoyed Xavier's discomfort. It was fun to be on the other side of the camera for a change as she'd found with the handful of production projects she'd done.

"You're up to something," Waverly said with suspicion as they got back in the SUV.

Xavier flashed her that smile that always sent her heart stumbling. "The way I see it, someone's after you. So it can't hurt to let them know that you're not going to be easy to get to."

"And there's the added bonus of making it look like we're dating."

"Angel, don't underestimate your appeal. If I were Wrede and saw those pictures, nothing would keep me from you."

"And if our fake relationship doesn't bring him out of hiding?" Waverly said, struggling under the ironic weight of being in two fake relationships at the same time.

"Then we go hunting."

9

"Okay, have I suddenly entered an alternate dimension, or am I staring at you and Xavier mugging for the camera in a coffee shop selfie?" Kate demanded through the phone against Waverly's ear.

Waverly reached for her tablet on the nightstand in her bedroom and opened a browser. "Which site?" she asked.

"Uh, yeah. All of them. Like seriously, Wave, this just blew the rehab story out of the water. You're even on CNN."

"Crap." Neither she nor Xavier had ever publicly acknowledged that they'd been in a relationship. After five years—a lifetime to the media—she'd hoped it wouldn't be such a big story. But she was wrong. The picture was at the very top of Celeb Spotting's website with a caption that hinted that everyone's wildest fairy tale dreams could be coming true since Waverly Sinner and Xavier Saint stepped out together for an early morning breakfast.

"You look happy," Kate commented.

Waverly frowned at the picture and dismissed it. "I'd just threatened to kick him in the balls. I was feeling pretty good."

"What do you think the studio's gonna say about these pics?"

"Judging from my meeting this morning, they probably won't be happy," Waverly predicted.

"Did you get anything out of Dipshit this morning?" Kate asked, referring to Brad with her special pet name for him.

"Nothing concrete," Waverly told her. "But I've got Chels digging."

Kate snickered. "Xavier is going to freak out when he finds out about her."

"Well, let's make sure he's packed up and moved out of my life before he does."

"Good luck with that," Kate snickered.

"I need to make a move, and soon. I just have this gut feeling that something is going down."

"I hope you're wrong. And I hope Dante comes sauntering back into town with his sexy smile, and then we can watch the two of them fight over you."

"You're insane," Waverly laughed.

"Want me to come over? We can start working on your *mea culpa* for Gwendolyn. She's going to kick your ass over this mess."

Waverly had a meeting scheduled with her publicist in two days. Thankfully, the woman was busy squashing another client's sex tape and wasn't free sooner.

"No, take a couple of days and do something fun. Things are a little tense here since X busted me with Brad this morning," she told Kate.

"That guy never ceases to amaze me."

"It's not so amazing when he slaps trackers on all of my vehicles," Waverly complained. The rumble from the driveway caught her attention. "Speaking of, I think my bike's back. He must have had someone from Invictus bring it over. I gotta go."

MICAH ROSS YANKED off the motorcycle helmet and hooted in Waverly's driveway. "Damn, that's a sweet ride you got there, Sinner." He'd long ago abandoned Xavier's code name for her in favor of what he referred to as her "more realistic" last name.

Waverly laughed from the porch as he cut the engine. "You better not have scratched her."

"Where's your ride?" Xavier asked him, stepping up next to Waverly.

Micah jerked a thumb in the direction of the road. "Burke couldn't keep up with me on this baby." He swung a long leg over the seat and jogged up the walk to them. "Don't you two look cozy?" he commented as they made room for him on the porch.

"Funny, Micah. Can I get you something to drink?" Waverly offered.

Micah shot a look at Xavier. "How about a coffee?"

"I suppose you want one as well?" she asked Xavier.

"Please," he said, offering her that devastating grin.

She led the way into the house and continued on into the kitchen while Xavier pulled Micah into the living room off the entrance.

"Nice place," Micah said, eyeing the room.

"Don't even try to skate on that," Xavier warned him. "I know you've been here. I know you installed the security system."

Micah crossed his arms and sat on the chaise end of the couch. "And you're pissed."

"You're lucky I'm not beating the shit out of you right now. You shut me out of Invictus business." Beneath the anger was a hurt that he hadn't expected. He'd counted on Micah to have his back from battlefield to boardroom.

"Saint, you know I love you like a brother—" Micah began.

"But what? You could have told me."

"She asked me not to," Micah said simply.

"Oh, so if a client asks me to go set your fucking house on fire I should go ahead and do that?"

"Look, she was a good kid, and I felt like we owed her. She could have dropped us like we were hot when you got your panties in a bunch and walked out. She could have taken that out on the business, but she didn't. So I owed her because you owed her and were in no shape to repay her."

"I can't believe you've been lying to me this whole time."

"Chill the hell out, lover boy. I installed a security system. Occasionally we provided drivers and guards to Mr. and Mrs. Sinner. End of story. You were so gone over this girl. Man, when I poured you on that plane to your family, part of me didn't expect to see you again. But you pulled yourself together and got back on track, eventually. But don't think for a second that I didn't see you cringe every time there was a news story about her. Especially when she started dating Wrede."

"Yeah, well, Wrede is out of the picture now."

"Don't fuck this up again, Saint. I don't know if either of you can handle another round."

Xavier shoved his hands in his pockets and stared at the floor. "I'm not fucking this up again. I'm fixing what needs to be fixed, and then I'm going to convince her that I'm the one she wants."

Micah nodded once. "She was leveled over you. Hid it a little better than you, of course. But that's the actor in her. So don't do it again to either of you, got it?"

"Got it." Xavier nodded.

"We good?" Micah asked.

"Maybe. I'll let you know. I still want to kick your ass."

"Well, while things are up in the air, let me get on your ass about getting back into the office."

"You told me it was about damn time I took a vacation!"

"Yeah, I meant like a long weekend to Aruba or something. You've been out for a week, and the natives are getting restless."

"Micah's right," Waverly said brightly from the door. She was carrying a tray with coffees and accessories.

Xavier took the tray from her and put it down on the table in front of Micah.

"You should definitely be getting back to the office." Excitement and hope warmed her voice.

"Nice try, both of you, but I'm staying put. Unless Waverly flies to New York with me to take a day and a half of meetings and then on to London."

"Mmm, sorry. Busy. But feel free to go on your own," she offered, helping herself to one of the cups of coffee.

"We really could use you in-house at least while you're here," Micah began again.

"Let me see your phone," Xavier demanded. He knew when he was being played.

Micah looked sheepish. "My phone?" he patted his jacket pockets. "Hmm, must have left it in the office."

"Okay, I'll use yours," Xavier said, snatching Waverly's phone off the tray.

"How do you know my passcode?" she gasped and smacked him when he keyed into her phone.

"To Micah, 'Please get X out of here. He is not employed by me or my parents. He's squatting in my life.'" Xavier recited her texts. "To Waverly, 'Interesting, I'll do my best.'"

She made another grab for the phone.

"You sneaky little—" he began.

"Careful how you finish that sentence," she warned him, eyes flashing.

"Fine. You want to put cards on the table, stand up."

Waverly stood up and jutted her chin up at him. "What are you going to do? Fight me?"

He yanked her t-shirt up over her head in one swift move. She surprised him by going for his balls instead of her t-shirt, but he managed to deflect the blow and lock her into a hold and held her in front of Micah. "This smart ass got herself shot in some kind of home invasion at a friend's house. Wrede was with her and hasn't been seen or heard from since."

"Damn, Sinner," Micah said, examining her wound. When his eyes inevitably traveled up to her red satin bra, Xavier growled. "Eyes up here or down there. Nowhere in between."

"I'm guessing we need to make these inquiries you've been feeding Research official," Micah said, keeping his eyes glued to the ceiling.

"XAVIER!" Sylvia Sinner's surprise was unmistakable. "When Waverly said she was bringing a guest, I just assumed it was Dante."

And score one for Team Sinner, Waverly thought, hugging her mother in gratitude. Sylvia looked good in the soft spun lavender poncho over white cropped pants, better than good. Five years of sobriety had done wonders. She looked younger, healthier, happier. And that change had changed her career trajectory, too. She was enjoying a revival of sorts. The only thing Hollywood loved more than a public downward spiral was a comeback, and since Sylvia had come out publicly to talk about her alcoholism and recovery, she'd once again become one of the most sought-after actresses in the industry. She'd also started a new yoga-inspired fashion line that had opened up a surprisingly strong income stream.

"Haven't you heard?" Xavier said, swooping in to kiss Sylvia on both cheeks. "Waverly upgraded."

Sylvia's laughter turned into a breathy gasp of pleasure when he revealed the massive bouquet of flowers he'd insisted on bringing for her mother. Waverly rolled her eyes and stepped around the love fest.

She found her father in the formal living room lighting a fire in the hearth. "Waverly!" the pleasure in his voice at seeing her automatically scaled down her attack mode. He was dashing as ever. His dark hair was cut a little shorter than usual for a movie role that he'd just finished filming. The crinkles around his eyes when he smiled were a little deeper. And there was a lightness in his gaze that, despite being there for several years, still struck her every time she looked at him.

The Sinners had been through hell and back together.

She walked into his open arms and held on tight for a moment. What had been a nonexistent relationship just a few years ago had evolved into something real and solid. Robert and Sylvia Sinner had taken her near-death experience and made it into a turning point for their family.

"Xavier's here," Waverly told her father.

She saw her father's face light up. *What the hell did that mean?* she wondered.

"I take it you're not pleased," Robert said with a smile.

"Dad, I don't want him in my life, and now he's driving me everywhere, following me around, staying in my house..."

Robert's eyebrows shot up. "He certainly moves fast."

"He does when he knows what he wants," Xavier agreed, stepping in behind Waverly and offering his hand to her father. "Robert."

Robert took Xavier's hand in his and pulled him in for a one-armed hug. Waverly frowned at the friendly greeting. "What is this?" she demanded. "You barely know each other, and he was not nice to your daughter. Now you're hugging buddies?"

"Your father and I maintained a friendship over the years," Xavier explained. "We'd catch a game of golf whenever I'm in town."

"Are you kidding me?" Waverly groaned.

Robert put his arm around her shoulders. "Now, sweetheart. He did save your life."

"I need a drink." She didn't drink of course and had never done so as a matter of principle. And even if she wanted to, there was no alcohol in the Sinner Estate. When Sylvia committed to a lifestyle, it was all the way. The room that had housed an impressive bar had been reconfigured into a yoga studio and meditation room.

"Darling, don't joke about that so soon after rehab," Sylvia chided her as she entered the room. "Recovery is not a laughing matter."

"Mom, I told you it wasn't that kind of rehab," she sighed, avoiding Xavier's gaze.

"Well, let's enjoy some appetizers on the patio by the fire, and you can tell us all about it," Sylvia suggested. She took her husband's arm and led the way through the glass doors onto the patio.

Xavier offered Waverly his arm, which she ignored. But when she brushed past him, he grabbed her and tucked her under his arm in a headlock. She yelped and swung, catching him in the thigh with a hammer fist. He released her with a laugh, and Waverly straightened her crepe mini dress.

"What's gotten into you?"

"I like being around you." He brought her hand to his mouth, kissed her knuckles.

"You need to stop with the full court press, Saint. It's not happening," she said even as she let him tug her closer.

"Angel," he was suddenly so serious. The tenderness in his eyes took her breath away as she looked up into the face angels had carved. "I really like your boots."

He laid his lips against hers in a surprise kiss.

"Ugh!" Waverly shoved away from him and stalked out to the patio, his laughter carrying behind her. She wanted to hate him, wanted to remember all the pain he'd caused her. But she'd never seen Xavier so playful. A smile played upon her lips. *And her boots were spectacular,* she admitted. Over-the-knee grey suede, they helped ward off the autumn chill. Mile-high heels took them from stylish to sexy. Even now, she could feel the heat of his gaze on her as he followed her outside.

Would she ever not be aware of him? Would she ever get used to his magnetism?

"We thought you two got lost," her father said with a smile. He and Sylvia were cuddled up on one of the outdoor settees by the fireplace.

Louie, her parents' chef that she borrowed from time to time to stock her fridge with meals when she was too busy to cook, swept through another door, a platter of canapé in his hands. He was a trim man with a manicured moustache and inky black hair. He could turn the most basic kitchen ingredients into a silver platter worthy four-course dinner.

"Louie!" Waverly waited until he'd set the tray down on the low wicker table in front of her parents before wrapping him in a tight hug.

"You're too thin," he announced briskly. "I'll come tomorrow and cook for you."

He gave Xavier a frosty look. "Mr. Saint," he nodded coolly.

"Good to see you again, Louie," Xavier said offering his hand.

Louie made a humming noise before reluctantly shaking Xavier's hand and then abruptly turning back to Waverly. "I'll see you tomorrow. I approve of your boots."

And with that, he stormed back into the house.

"Louie is obviously a big fan of yours," Waverly said with a snarky grin in Xavier's direction. She took a seat on the settee across from her parents and didn't bother silencing her sigh when Xavier sat next to her. He took up too much room with his broad shoulders and the spread of his knees. He'd worn navy trousers tonight and a soft blue-gray sweater over a checked button down with the same tones. Why did he always have to be so gorgeous? He still hadn't shaved, and the roughness over his jaw made his dangerous look even edgier, lethal even.

"Waverly." Xavier pinched her in the ass.

"Huh? Sorry. What?"

He grinned at her as if he knew exactly what she'd been thinking. "Your mother wants to know about your recent trip."

He was baiting her, daring her to put it all out there to her parents. Or let him win. She shifted her foot so that the heel of her boot rested on top of his Armani oxford.

When she leaned forward to pick up a canapé, she applied pressure. "I mentioned when I called you, Mom, that it wasn't *rehab* rehab," she began. It was funny how quickly things could change. She'd spent most of her life lying to her parents, but in the past few years as they'd pulled their lives together and refocused as a family, honesty had become a priority.

There was just one thing that she couldn't tell them the truth about. As protective as they'd become since nearly losing her, her parents would never have supported her intel work for the studio. So she'd kept them in the dark, danced around their questions when necessary, and now, lied outright to their faces.

She perched on the edge of the cushion.

"Well, what would you like us to know about it?" her father asked amicably.

It was one way her parents' therapist had taught them to ease into sticky conversations.

Waverly took a deep breath and launched into her script. "I've been feeling like my life's been moving so fast lately. There's always a movie, a project, an event. And then all the social stuff."

"You have been going out a lot lately," her mother agreed.

Waverly nodded. "I started to feel out of control, and it all just kind of came to a head. I wanted to get away for the weekend to think. I was supposed to meet a friend in Tahoe." She felt the pressure of Xavier's hand on her low back. "But I just wanted to be alone. So I went north, and then there's this bear running out in front of me."

Her parents were watching her in rapt fascination. Xavier was watching her with amusement. The smug bastard had won. He was staying, at least until she could find Dante and clean up this mess.

"Anyway, the bear was fine and so was the tree, but the rental car got pretty banged up. And I just remember sitting there thinking that if I'd been going slower it wouldn't have happened. And maybe slowing down was what I needed to do everywhere else, too."

"Oh, Waverly! Were you hurt?" Sylvia asked.

Waverly shook her head. "Just a couple of scrapes and bruises." *And a gunshot wound,* she added silently. "I made a couple of calls and left immediately for a really nice place in Hawaii. They focus on relieving stress and reestablishing priorities. It was almost like a vacation."

"How do you feel now?" Robert asked Waverly, rubbing his wife's shoulder with his hand.

"Focused and ready to kick some ass." That, at least, was the truth.

"That's wonderful, darling," Sylvia glowed at her. "I'm so proud of you for tackling your issues head on. You've always been so brave."

"Thanks, Mom," Waverly squirmed in her seat, and Xavier stroked his hand down her back.

"So forgive me for being so blunt, but where's Dante? And why is Xavier here?" Sylvia asked. "Not that I'm not very happy to see you, of course," she said to Xavier.

Waverly opened her mouth then closed it. "How about you take that one, Saint?" Why should she be the only liar tonight?

Xavier moved his hand to her shoulder. He was staking a claim in front of her parents, and she was mortified. "I saw the news and knew that that wasn't the Waverly Sinner I knew. So I called Robert—"

"*You* called *him*?" When Waverly tried to stand up, Xavier tugged her back down next to him.

"Be quiet," he told her. "We were both understandably concerned, so I flew out to her to assess the situation. It's clear someone was feeding the media false information, and I have concerns that it could be someone with a vendetta against Waverly. So I'm happy to resume my role until we can figure out who's behind the character assassination. As for Dante, we don't know where he is. It's been reported that he's on vacation, and he may not know about Waverly's... accident."

"Oh, dear. Are you two off again?" Sylvia asked.

"No!" Waverly said, looking at Xavier instead of Sylvia. "No. We're just... things are complicated, and I'll straighten them all out when I see him again," she finished lamely.

"I must confess that I'm happy to have you back, Xavier," Robert said.

"There is one other thing I think you both should know in the spirit of full disclosure," Xavier told them.

Waverly turned to stare holes in him. *What was he doing?*

"I plan to marry your daughter as soon as I can convince her to give me a second chance."

Sylvia's crostini tumbled to the patio. Robert blinked rapidly.

"Xavier!" Waverly hissed at him.

"Angel, I just don't want them to be surprised if I cart you off to Barbados, and we come back married."

"I am going to cart your body to Barbados and dump it in the ocean," she threatened. "He's insane," she said, turning to her parents. "He's clearly suffered a head trauma in the last few years and has lost his damn mind."

Sylvia covered her laugh with her napkin. Robert was not so subtle with his amusement. He laughed loud and long. "Remind you of someone, don't they?" he asked, nudging his wife.

"It's like staring in the mirror almost thirty years ago."

"We are *not* together. We are *not* getting back together. We are... solving a problem and then going our separate ways," she said in a near shout. Waverly tried to stand up again, but Xavier kept her hand and pulled her back against him.

"Mmm, good luck, darling. He looks serious," Sylvia said, eyeing Xavier.

"Very determined," Robert agreed.

"Is there really no alcohol in this house?" Waverly muttered.

10

"*I* forgot what a good liar you are," Xavier said, starting the SUV. With the dirty business of lying and covering their tracks finished, dinner had been a relatively peaceful affair. Though Waverly was still reeling from the fact that Xavier and her father had maintained a friendship after all these years. And she didn't even know what to say about his announcement that he intended to marry her. He couldn't possibly be serious.

"Me? What about you? All that character assassination stuff and then marriage? You can't mess with my parents about things like that, Xavier. They'll take you seriously."

"Angel, I am deadly serious. I intend to make you my wife."

"I don't even know how to tell you how insane you are." She thumped back in her seat so hard, she bounced her head off the headrest. "You make me so mad."

"It's because you have strong feelings for me," he said, pulling down her parents' drive and heading home.

She shot him a dirty look. "My strong feelings involve fantasies of maiming you."

The corner of his mouth turned up in a smile, and they rode the rest of the way home in silence.

He unlocked the front door because, of course, somehow he'd made himself a key and then keyed in the alarm code that she'd never given him.

"Make yourself at home, why don't you?" Waverly grumbled.

She stashed her bag on the table in the foyer and stormed back into the kitchen, her dress swishing around her thighs and her boots clicking against the hard floor.

He locked the door behind him and re-armed the alarm before following her back.

"Do you love Dante?" he demanded, leaning against the refrigerator.

She met his gaze and glared. "Of course I do." She did. He was the closest thing she'd ever had to a big brother. They were friends, partners, practically family. But that wasn't what Xavier was asking.

"Did you love me?"

She wanted to lie, wanted to take those words from so long ago back. But she couldn't. "Yes, I did."

"Do you feel for Dante what you felt for me?"

Not even close. She took a breath. "This is stupid. I'm with someone else, Xavier."

"You have no men's clothes in your closet or anything in your bathroom. You've broken up a hundred times, and on every break, he immediately hooks up with someone else. He hasn't once reached out to you since I came back into the picture." Xavier took his time, ticking through the reasons.

"Leave it alone, X." She showed him her teeth and made a move for the beverage cooler. Her throat was tight, and she needed something to loosen it.

But he stopped her and grabbed her arm. "Answer me."

"I don't owe you any answers!" She yanked free, but he followed her into the great room.

"Waverly, if I would have disappeared back when we were together, you would have been devastated. You would have stopped at nothing to find me, even if it was just to kick me in the ass. Dante goes missing, and you lay low. Sure, you're scared, you're worried. But I don't see despair. And that tells me something."

"It should tell you this is none of your goddamn business!"

"I told you before, Waverly. You are my business. I love you."

"Don't say that!" The cry echoed through the room.

"Tell me," he pushed. "Do you feel about Dante the way you felt about me?"

"No!"

His voice was low, but he was breathing heavily. "Then why are you fighting this, Waverly?"

"You said that I was damaged!" There. The words that had haunted her for years were finally free. But they didn't stop Xavier in his tracks. They only egged him on.

"Baby, you show me one person in this world who isn't. Go ahead, point a finger and show me someone who escaped life completely unscathed. Life is damaging, and all we can do is use those scars to make us stronger, better, smarter."

"That isn't what you told me before. You said I was damaged and toxic. That I wasn't good for you."

He reached for her again, gently this time. His hands were warm on her upper arms. "Angel."

She could hear the pain, the regret, in that one word.

"I was wrong. I was scared, and I was so wrong. I had never felt what I felt for you, and I'd almost lost you. My world was upside down."

"Why didn't you talk to me?"

He leaned in, and she could see the earnestness in his eyes. "I'm sorry for that. And I'm sorry for hurting you. But understand this, I'm going to spend the rest of my life fixing this. You give me a second chance, and I'll make sure you never regret it."

"I can't do that! I can't love you again!" The words came out a sob.

He took a deep breath, and she felt him purposely loosen his grip on her arms. "Waverly, I need you to cut me some slack."

"Slack? You want me to cut you slack? You brought me home from the hospital and made me beg you to stay, and then you just walked out on me."

"I'm sorry!" he snapped, his fingers tightening on her again. "I'll say it a thousand times if it takes the hurt away. I'm sorry, Angel."

"You made me think my worst fear had come true. That I was too damaged to be loved." Tears filled her eyes, but there was anger there, too.

He stilled and brought his hands up to gently cup her face. "Oh, Angel. I'm so sorry."

He was. She knew he was, knew he understood now, maybe for the first time, the blow he'd dealt her. He'd known her deepest secrets about her family, about how her childhood had affected her. And by walking out on her, saying the words she'd feared for so long, he'd leveled her.

"Waverly." He said her name with a tenderness that sliced into her.

She squeezed her eyes closed. "No, don't be nice now. I don't want to cry," she sniffled.

"If you cry, it will gut me," he warned her.

"Well, at least there's an upside."

He gathered her to him and picked her up. He carried her

to the couch where he sat with her in his lap. She didn't try to bolt, but she didn't relax either. She just took slow deep breaths and tried to force back the tide of emotion.

Xavier tucked her head against his chest and rested his chin on top. "Angel, don't ever question if you're good enough to be loved. And don't ever, ever let a man dictate whether you can be loved."

She hiccupped softly against him, and he stroked her arm.

"That's what I'm going to teach our daughters. I figure we'll have three. At least to start."

"Xavier." And suddenly she was tired, bone weary.

"Shh, Angel. Just think about it."

"I can't think when you're so close to me," she confessed.

"Maybe don't think. Just feel. This connection is real. Nothing you tell yourself is going to make it go away, believe me. I've tried."

"I'm sure there was a long line of women helping you try," she muttered.

"There have been two since you. Two in five years, Waverly. Same as you."

"What do you mean, same as me?"

He ignored her question. "I think part of me always knew I was meant for you."

She pushed away from his chest but didn't leave his lap. "How exactly were you keeping track, Xavier?"

"I didn't want you to be with anyone who would hurt you," he said by way of explanation.

"Are you kidding me? You ran them? You ran background checks on anyone you thought I was interested in, didn't you?"

"You never stopped being important to me."

"I suddenly know how your sisters feel," she said, with a heavy sigh. "You can't do that kind of stuff, X. You have to trust people to make their own decisions."

"It's what I do," he protested. And her heart cracked open just a sliver for the man who would do anything to protect the ones he loved from hurt, however misguided and controlling his actions were.

A thought hit her. "Are you the reason Trent transferred in the middle of a semester, never to be heard from again?" She'd casually dated Trent her junior year at Stanford. He was cute and charming in a preppy fraternity brother kind of way. They'd never gone beyond kissing, though. She'd never trusted him enough, and there'd been good reason why.

"He was still seeing his ex on the side," Xavier protested.

"Oh my God, Xavier! You didn't have him killed, did you?"

"Jesus, Angel. No! I just had someone scare the shit out of him, and he left Stanford on his own accord."

"I'd found out he was still seeing his ex because *I'm not an idiot*! And when I did, I handled the situation."

"He was still calling you," Xavier pointed out.

"I don't even want to know how you knew that."

"I had a couple of guys have a talk with him. It wasn't a big deal."

"X," Waverly took a deep breath. She felt a war of emotions within. She'd spent so much of her life surrounded by people who used her. Just knowing that Xavier had tried to keep her safe even after they were through undid her. Yet his methods were insane. "You can't run people's lives like that, especially not from a distance."

"What was I supposed to do?"

"How about let everyone make their own decisions and deal with their own consequences?"

"I let you make your own decisions, and you got yourself shot," he pointed out.

"I need to process all of this," she told him. "I'm going to go to bed."

"Did you mean what you said about Dante?" She heard it in his voice, the hope and fear, the need to hear it again.

"I've never felt what I had for you with anyone else," she whispered, closing her eyes for just a moment and burrowing into the warmth of his chest.

"Kiss me goodnight," he ordered, his voice gruff.

"Xavier—"

"Just a kiss. I promise."

She knew she'd regret this, just as she knew if she didn't kiss him, she'd spend the entire night tossing and turning and thinking about what an idiot she'd been to turn down that masterful mouth.

He was leading her into a trap, but did it really count as a trap if her eyes were wide open?

"Just a kiss?" she repeated.

"I promise." His lips moved feather light over her hair. "I won't even offer to help you get out of those boots. His fast fingers traced the tops of her boots around her thighs.

Her lips curved. That earnestness, that playfulness from him was enough to have her ignoring the warning bells and finally give in to the craving.

The pulse in his neck thrummed faster beneath her fingers as she closed the distance between their mouths. Slowly, slowly, she moved with a patience never before tapped. She paused a whisper away feeling his breath hot on her face. Her blood felt thicker, and there was a buzzing in her ears. His lids, thickly lashed were heavy and half closed.

She couldn't shake the feeling that she was sealing her fate with one kiss.

He waited for her. She knew he wanted this to be her choice, wanted to give her that power. And she took it. Lightly, sweetly, softly, she laid her lips to his. They were hard beneath hers, everything about him was, thick biceps, broad chest and shoulders, the granite of his thighs. He'd already been hard when he sat her in his lap, but he'd done nothing to push her.

She wanted to take them both to the edge, to make sure she could come back from it. She spun in his lap and straddled him. He brought his hands that had been fisted at his sides to her hips where they gripped. "Just a kiss, Angel," he whispered. Gentle words at war with the frenetic need she felt from him.

The skirt of her dress rode up indecently high as she spread her thighs over his lap. She brought her hands to his face, stroked his jaw, his neck, and dove her fingers into his hair.

He sighed into her mouth, and she used that access to deepen the kiss. Her tongue stroked into his mouth, claiming new territory.

She could feel his heartbeat thumping against her breast. Still he let her take. She changed the angle of the kiss, went deeper, and when he couldn't take being submissive any longer, she sucked the tip of his tongue as he thrust it into her mouth.

He pulled her hips down so his erection was cradled tight between her spread legs. She whimpered once and felt a glow, warm and bright, spread through her. She'd been kissed before, but this seduction? This lazy sampling of pleasure? It was something only Xavier could give her.

"My Angel."

Her breath caught in her throat. She couldn't breathe, not with the weight of so much desire on her. Not with the current of love that was flowing through her. His love for her, he poured it into her through the sweetness of a kiss. She had no doubt now that he loved her. But that didn't mean she could just blindly follow him.

As if he felt her thoughts, Xavier snaked a hand behind

her head. Holding her against his mouth when she would have pulled back. He deepened the kiss on a long, sinful stroke, and she felt his penis throb beneath her. She wanted him. Wanted to move against him. Wanted to reach into those urbane navy trousers and release him so he could finally be inside her again.

She wanted his hands on her body, stroking and teasing. She remembered everything about every time they'd ever made love. He was sparking an inferno in both of them that would never be extinguished. With just a kiss. Just a kiss.

Finally, he pulled back on a shaky breath, tucking her head against his neck.

She could feel the flush of her cheeks and the swelling of her lips. He'd ravaged her body and mind with a kiss. A kiss that was a promise of so much more.

"Goodnight, Angel."

She trembled on his lap. "Goodnight, Xavier." When she made a move to slide off of him, he stopped her by holding on to her hips.

"Hang on. I'd hate to embarrass myself so early on in our reconciliation." He picked her up off his lap and deposited her on the cushion next to him. He leaned forward, hands on his knees, and took a few deep breaths.

"That hard, huh?" she asked, suddenly feeling smug.

"If you don't get your perfect ass and those sexy boots up those stairs by the time I count to three, I'll show you just how hard."

Waverly jumped away from the couch but took her time sauntering up the stairs. She felt him watching her the entire way.

IT WAS a little too early to deal with Gwendolyn Riddington-Macks, but Waverly made an exception that morning. "Hello, Waverly," the cool, blonde publicist grimly swept in through Waverly's front door wearing a cashmere coat and Jimmy Choos. Behind her, Waverly's agent, Aisha Leigh breezed in, dropping a kiss on Waverly's cheek.

"Hey, gorgeous," Aisha said, her tone miles friendlier than Gwendolyn's. "How ya feeling?"

Al, as she preferred to be called, was a Mississippi-bred champion of contract negotiations for actors and writers. She wasn't afraid to get dirty in a fight. And her fierce loyalty was what had convinced Waverly to hire her after she and her mother's agent, Phil, had amicably parted ways while she was still in college. She'd never regretted her decision to hire Al. The woman had Waverly's back in every negotiation and showed her support at every event. Her flawless dark skin was complimented by a curve hugging peacock blue turtleneck and crisp charcoal slacks. Suede booties clicked on the floor.

Next to them both, Waverly felt like she was wearing pajamas. But she was in her own home and felt no need to put on airs. Her capris and cozy hooded sweatshirt would keep her comfortable during what was sure to become an uncomfortable morning meeting.

Waverly led the way back to the kitchen where she had coffee, water, and a few Hollywood-approved snacks arranged on a tray on the dining table.

Gwendolyn, still frowning, accepted a mug of coffee and ignored the rest. "So why don't you tell me why you decided to jaunt off to rehab without giving your publicist a head's up?" she said, her tone clipped.

Waverly didn't bother taking offense to Gwendolyn's comment. With her list of high-profile clients, the woman had literally already seen everything and nothing fazed her. Al, on the other hand, picked up a cherry Danish and sat back, ready to absorb whatever it was that Waverly was going to share with them.

"It was supposed to be more of a vacation. Like a yoga retreat," Waverly began. "It had nothing to do with drugs or alcohol. I just needed a break to reprioritize."

"Mmm," Gwendolyn frowned, sliding on a pair of gold-framed reading glasses to take notes on her tablet. "So no drugs or alcohol involved in the accident. I'll see if we can get law enforcement to confirm. What facility did you go to?"

"There won't be any confirmation from any law enforcement, and I'm not willing to talk specifics on where I was."

Gwendolyn set her tablet down on the table with a snap. Al's perfectly sculpted eyebrows lifted, appreciating the entertainment of the brief show of temper.

"So what exactly am I doing wasting my time here?" she asked.

"I'm telling you that there are certain aspects of the story that were leaked to the media without my permission that aren't entirely accurate. So rather than going to war with Target Productions, I'd like to find a way out of this without pointing fingers and maybe earning a couple of bonus points with fans."

"You want me to spin a vague stay in a potentially non-existent rehab facility so you come out on top?" Gwendolyn clarified.

"Yep."

"Well, then let's start with some misdirection. Where is Xavier?"

Of course Gwendolyn had seen the photos of them flying in to L.A. and yesterday's cozy coffee shop stop. Waverly's attention was caught by movement outside on the patio. An arm rose out of the steaming water of the pool and then another, followed by Xavier's head and torso. The son of a bitch was wearing the scandalous swim trunks her mother bought for him in Greece all those years ago. The red and blue Grigioperla suit left absolutely nothing to the imagination.

"Holy hotness," Al breathed next to her, the Danish fell unheeded from her fingers to the tabletop. Even Gwendolyn's armor showed some cracks as she slowly removed her reading glasses to stare.

Xavier reached for a towel and slowly dried the water that beaded across his vast expanse of chest. Steam rose off of his muscled shoulders in the morning chill. "Is he moving in slow motion, or am I drunk?" Al wondered.

He padded barefoot to the door, the saunter of a man with an audience and no cares in the world, and let himself in.

"Ladies," he greeted them.

No one said a word. Waverly couldn't stop staring at the indecently short trunks that barely concealed what looked like a weapon. But that wasn't a gun in his shorts.

Xavier swooped over her and snagged Waverly's coffee. He drank and winced at the sugar.

"I can make you your own cup," Waverly muttered. She was embarrassed that she couldn't seem to stop looking at him and annoyed that Gwendolyn and Al seemed to have the same issue.

"Yours is fine," he told her and playfully tugged the hood of her sweatshirt. "I'm going to go shower."

They all watched in reverent silence as he loped up the stairs and crossed the loft above them to his room. He shut the door, and all three women let out the collective breath they'd been holding.

"Oh, boy," Gwendolyn breathed. "I can work with that."

"Please tell me he wants to get into acting," Al sighed and picked up her Danish. Waverly had seen the men who accompanied Al to events. The woman knew fine male stock when she saw it.

Waverly snapped her fingers at them. "Focus, ladies." She rose and returned to the coffee maker for a new mug to replace her stolen one. "We need a message that deflects from the whole rehab thing without coming right out and saying it was bullshit."

"I'll handle the message," Gwendolyn said, returning to her reading glasses and tablet. "As long as you're comfortable with playing up a little romance with Mr. Hard Body Saint up there."

"Do I have a choice?"

"I checked in with Kate last night," Al told her. "Traffic to your social media accounts exploded in the last forty-eight hours. You and Xavier are the world's living, breathing love story."

"The world is a twisted place," Waverly complained.

"Honey, if you're not taking advantage of having Xavier Saint living under your roof, you're the twisted one," Al warned her.

"So we've got a message, or we will have one by noon," Gwendolyn said, checking the glittering Cartier on her wrist. "Where do we want to shout from the rooftops?"

"I've got the perfect forum," Al grinned. "You're going to love it," she told Gwendolyn.

"Good. The sooner we clean this up, the sooner we can start pushing the new release."

"Agreed," Al nodded.

The next film in Waverly's release line up had been written by one of Al's other clients, a hot screenwriter named Jackson Pierce who had strutted onto the scene a few years ago with talent and guts, taking Hollywood by storm. She was particularly fond of this film as she'd made it with Dante.

"There's one more thing. I need to be prepared to handle questions about Dante." She could tell by their expressions that all it had taken was Xavier Saint in indecent swimwear to wipe any memory of Dante Wrede's existence from their minds.

11

Waverly skimmed through the interview notes again from Gwendolyn. Happy, healthy, and coy about her love life. She was to flirt and laugh and speak earnestly about the importance of priorities. She knew Gwendolyn was painting a picture of a breakup with Dante and a reconciliation with Xavier but without actually saying anything.

She fidgeted with the hem of her dress in the backseat of the Invictus SUV. She'd gone with classic and virginal white to show off the healthy tan she'd gotten in Belize. The dress was fitted from the chest to the hips before flaring out into a subtle tulip skirt. It could have been demure with the three-quarter length sleeves, but the plunging V neckline and red patent pumps kept it from being boring. She'd worked her hair into a messy, curly ponytail, keeping her makeup bright and fresh.

She was the picture of glowing health. The picture of glowing health that was about to go on national television to lie.

"Nervous?" Xavier asked.

He knew how she'd felt about crowds. But that was a

previous life. Long gone were the panic attacks and debilitating fears. She still didn't love crowds, but she certainly found more enjoyment in them than she had. After her attack, something had changed. She'd found power in vulnerability and confidence in being herself. Once Waverly had become authentically herself in public, the boundaries she set stuck and appearances were something to enjoy rather than dread.

She shook her head. "I'm good. I've been on Max's show before."

"The last time you were, you wore black, if I recall."

Burke, her favorite of all of Invictus' drivers, pretended to be deaf to their conversation.

Waverly raised her eyebrows. "So you saw that episode, did you?"

"I saw that you found a short version of that dress I begged you not to wear to the awards show and wore it on national television," he told her. "Tell me the truth. That was a message to me, wasn't it?"

A few years ago, when she'd first been invited on Max Heim's late night show, she'd taken that dress that Xavier had once so vehemently vetoed and had it altered from an evening gown to a mini dress. She'd strutted out on stage knowing he'd be watching from wherever he was. Knowing there was no way he'd miss her. Knowing that he'd get the metaphorical middle finger loud and clear.

"I don't know what you're talking about," she said innocently. "I can't possibly remember all the outfits I've worn in public."

He leaned into her until his arm was pressing against her body. "Angel, you remember the dress, and I've never forgotten it either. I didn't want to walk around a cocktail party with a hard-on all afternoon," he whispered darkly.

"You seem to handle the blood flow just fine these days," she said, looking pointedly at his lap.

He adjusted himself. "I just hope to God you still have that dress because I have this fantasy of ripping it off of you."

Her breath caught in her throat. The image he brought forth seared into her brain.

"I'd start you standing up," he continued, lips moving against her ear. "I'd spread your legs until the skirt rode up high enough for me to see what sexy little lace thing you had on, and then I'd slowly pull them down to your knees. Then I'd take these fingers—"

The SUV pulled to a stop in front of the production building, and Waverly clapped a hand over his mouth. Her thighs trembled when she pressed them together while her nipples stood at attention. "Jesus, Saint," she gasped.

Burke got out of the car, and Xavier used the opportunity to bite her earlobe. "Someday you're going to let me show you all the things I've fantasized about," he promised.

"You're..." Words failed her.

"Ready whenever you are, Angel." He buttoned his suit jacket over the vest he was wearing and adjusted his hard-on again, pinning it under his belt.

Burke opened the door for her and she stepped out onto the sidewalk with a healthy flush on her cheeks.

By the time she marched out on stage in front of two-hundred strangers an hour later, she'd finally gotten herself back under control. A reluctant Xavier was locked away in the green room giving Waverly her first easy breath in days. Max Heim, the middle-aged host, looked dapper in his pinstripe suit and kissed her enthusiastically on the cheek.

The crowd applauded at a slightly above appropriate level, and Waverly took her time waving and smiling before taking a seat on the buttery soft sofa next to Max's desk. She blew a kiss to the bandleader, who patted a hand over his heart.

Max, his grin permafrosted in place, neatly stacked note cards in front of him. They were blank, just a prop. Something familiar for the older generation who still watched the show every night despite the fact that Max was the sixth host of the institution.

"Welcome back, Waverly. It's always good to see your beautiful face."

She rested her head on her hand and stared adoringly at him. "I was just thinking the same about yours, Max." He mugged for the camera while the audience hooted.

The warm-up was easy and friendly, and the audience broke into laughter a few more times before Max got down to business. "Alright then. We've got a lot to catch up on, so I think we're going to go rapid fire."

The music cued a dangerous riff, and Waverly and Max both turned to Camera One in mock looks of terror.

"Are you ready?" Max asked.

Waverly rolled her shoulders and feigned some stretches. "Okay. Let's do this."

"You just got back from rehab, true or false?"

"Kind of sort of true," she nodded.

"Drugs, alcohol, shopping, gambling?"

"None of the above."

"Sex?" Max pressed hopefully.

Waverly laughed. "Stress. It was more a boot camp for people who are making crappy life choices such as these..." She waved behind her to the screen.

The video cued up and the crowd laughed through a montage of Waverly wearing questionable outfits, stumbling out of clubs, and enjoying every carb known to man.

"So to clarify, when an unnamed source said I went to

rehab, I was actually sitting on the beach and absorbing some life coaching," she filled in. "And then I came back and everyone was like 'Are you sober?' and I'm like 'I just learned to meditate.' It's not nearly as sexy a story as if I were all coked up and laying in a gutter."

"That would be incredibly sexy," he agreed, eyebrows high.

Waverly laughed.

Satisfied with her answer, Max changed the subject. "Moving on. What is your spirit animal?"

They ran through the pre-approved list of questions rapid-fire. And Waverly felt like she'd done her best to sell the "time out for health" angle.

"Now, I know you don't answer questions about your love life," Max said, sending a pouty face to the audience. "So we'll skip that part. Instead, we'll move on to the rapid, rapid fire round. You just say the first thing that comes to mind."

Waverly agreed and prepared herself to escape the trap that was being laid.

"Favorite holiday?"

"Fourth of July," Waverly answered decisively.

"Favorite farm animal?"

"Chickens?"

"Who was the last person you texted?"

"My friend Kate."

"What is in your refrigerator right now?"

"Leftover pizza."

"If you could be a pro in any sport, what would it be?"

"Pro wrestling."

"First thing that comes to mind when I say Dante Wrede?"

Waverly smiled big. "Charming."

"How about when I say Xavier Saint?"

She smiled bigger. "Lifesaver."

The crowd cheered with enthusiasm.

"I understand that Xavier is here with you tonight," Max said, and an "oooh" went through the crowd.

Waverly nodded. "He's in the green room." She was going to kill Gwendolyn.

"I feel like we should bring him out, don't you?"

Oh, yeah. Gwendolyn was a dead woman. "Uhh—" Waverly was weighing her options while the crowd made their opinion deafeningly clear. When the screen behind her cut to a moving shot from the green room, she knew the decision had already been made.

Xavier was standing up and buttoning his jacket over his vest. Every woman in the studio whooped. A production assistant led him through the short maze of hallways to the studio while the camera followed. And when he stepped onto the stage, the noise was deafening. Max stood to greet Xavier with an enthusiastic handshake. Waverly stood, too, and accepted the peck on her cheek that Xavier delivered as he stepped to her side.

The crowd continued to cheer, and Xavier waved politely before taking a seat next to her.

"You're pretty popular, X," Waverly commented under her breath while the din could cover it.

"I'm going to stuff Gwendolyn in a trunk and bury her in the desert after this." His words were in direct contrast to the wry smile plastered on his face. The producer finally had to gesture for people to sit back down again.

Max could barely suppress his glee at having landed the first interview with Xavier Saint and Waverly Sinner together. *This was going horribly wrong*, Waverly thought. The studio was going to see this interview as her going rogue. And everyone in the country would be drawing conclusions that she and Xavier were together.

"Thanks for being such a good sport, Xavier," Max beamed at him.

"Thanks for not giving me a choice, Max." Xavier said with a sharp smile.

Waverly saw Max swallow nervously before pressing on. "Right then. So now you two have never given an interview together, I'm told."

Both had spoken to the media separately over the years. But Xavier had always refused to answer questions about the night Les Ganim had abducted Waverly. And Waverly had stuck to her guns about never answering personal questions about Xavier.

"We have not," Waverly agreed. "He's too argumentative."

"She's too stubborn," Xavier argued.

"No, I'm not!"

"You are," he nodded.

"I can see that neither one of you has a point," Max quipped. "Let's talk how you two met."

Waverly and Xavier exchanged a glance. It was a relatively safe topic, but they both knew he was just warming them up with softballs.

"Waverly's parents hired me five years ago to help with some security concerns," Xavier said.

"They hired him to keep me in line," Waverly corrected.

"And she wasn't very happy with the idea," Xavier grinned at the memory.

"I threw him in the pool," she admitted. The audience roared.

"I wasn't happy," Xavier said, raising an eyebrow at her.

Waverly laughed at the memory of the sopping wet Xavier. "I felt really good about that."

"But I assume you eventually became very happy to have him in your life," Max said, switching gears into serious.

Waverly heard the murmur in the crowd and knew that the screens behind them were playing some of the footage from that night. She reached over and grabbed Xavier's wrist. Her nails dug in. She didn't need strength, she needed him to not flip out and commit murder on national television.

They kept their backs to the footage, a unified front with the past solidly behind them. It was the longest thirty seconds of Waverly's life. She could feel Xavier vibrating under her hand. She didn't blame him. They'd been ambushed into opening up about something so private and painful. Something they'd both rather leave in the past.

It was her price to pay. She had to willingly give up the privacy that others had in order to be successful in this industry. But Xavier had never made that bargain. And it wasn't fair to make him pay for her choices.

"That night was an emotional one for all of us who are such big fans of yours, Waverly," Max began. The audience didn't even need the cue to cheer.

"Thank you," she said once they'd settled down. "It wasn't a walk in the park for us either."

"Can you tell us what you remember about that night?" Max asked in his mellow baritone.

Waverly released Xavier's hand, but as she gave her white-washed version of the events of that night, she felt his arm on the back of her chair reminding her that he was never far away.

"What a horrifying ordeal," Max said sympathetically. "How about you Xavier. What do you remember?"

"Doing my job."

Max let the silence stretch on for a few moments before moving on. "And you clearly did it well. Now, is it true that you had a parting of the ways after that night?" Max prompted them.

She felt Xavier's hand on her back and Waverly nodded. "It was a traumatic incident, and I think we both needed to get away from the reminders of how difficult that night was."

The audience was riveted.

"And now?" Max leaned forward.

"Now we're getting to know each other again," she said.

"So your relationship is strictly professional?" Max pressed.

"Let me put it this way, Max." Xavier said the man's name as if it left a bad taste in his mouth. "Waverly and I have been through a lot together to the point where 'strictly professional' isn't possible. I care for her very much, so whether it's in a personal or professional capacity, if anyone wants to hurt her, they're going to have to go through me first."

The audience thought that was awesome and got to their feet.

"I'm here with Waverly Sinner and Xavier Saint," Max said turning to Camera One. "Don't go anywhere because, when we come back, we'll be playing puppy poker with our favorite Sinner and Saint."

A KATY PERRY tune filled Max Heim's green room and had Waverly snatching up her phone, hoping Xavier stayed out in the hallway for a few more minutes.

"Chels?"

"Hey, I don't have much for you, but hopefully it's a starting place," Chelsea began.

"Okay, go."

"Stepanov looks clean. Squeaky clean. That doesn't mean he's not into something dirty. It just means if he is, it's buried deep. He juggles about a gajillion business deals a year, real estate, manufacturing, etc. I did come across something that lines up with your timing though. About two months ago, this biotech firm—Axion Pharmaceuticals—says they want to buy some of his pharmaceutical manufacturing licenses, a hypertension drug and an antimalarial."

"Did they make an offer?"

"Several, but the deal never went through. It's not like Stepanov makes a ton on the formularies. Pills of each are sold for between seventy-five cents and a buck apiece."

"So what happened to the deal?"

"The biotech company lobbied pretty hard, but Stepanov turned them down flat in August."

Right around the time the studio had assigned Waverly to befriend Petra. The timing lined up, Waverly mused, but what would prescription drugs have to do with Petra? And where did Dante fit in?

"Thanks for digging. You are, as always, a lifesaver, Chels."

"Always happy to help. I'll keep snooping and see if there's anything that rings funny for Stepanov. In the meantime, I'm sending you my report so your eyes can glaze over and go crossed while you read through it."

"You're the best!"

"How are things with my brother?"

"Tune in to Max Heim's show tonight and find out. Make sure your parents are watching, too. Two words: Puppy poker."

"Oh, this is going to be good."

They disconnected, and Waverly was ready to stuff her phone in her bag when a text from Kate came through.

Petra's at Club Volt! Celeb Spotting just reported it!

Waverly jumped to her feet. *Finally, she could get to Petra and get some answers.* She looked down at her dress. But first she needed to change. She poked her head out into the hallway and spotted Xavier speaking with a production assistant. She flagged him down.

"I'm going to change. I feel like going out." She held up her phone with the picture featuring Petra's arrival with her two bodyguards at Volt on the screen.

"I'll tell Burke."

"You're not trying to talk me out of it?"

"Fastest way to get answers," he shrugged.

"I promise it will be better than the last time we went to a club together."

He glared at her. "Not even close to being funny."

She winked. "Thanks for being a good sport with all this."

"It goes with the territory, and I want the territory." He rubbed a finger under her chin. "Go change."

She felt the zing when she closed the door. She'd been out of action long enough that she'd almost forgotten the adrenaline an assignment brought on. She felt sharp, ready. Or was that the Xavier effect? She pushed the thought aside and dug through the weekender bag that accompanied her everywhere.

Her go bag had been replenished since Belize to better cover both sides of her professional life. Tucked between evening clothes and workout wear, she found an outfit that could pass for club wear. And in the bottom of the bag, inside a soft-sided case, Waverly found a small handgun and a fixed blade knife in a skinny sheath.

She pulled on the pleated black miniskirt and tucked the .38 into the built in waistband holster. Next came the top. It was a long line bustier that stopped a few inches above the waistband of the skirt. It's molded cups with their butterfly print not only made her boobs look incredible, but they also provided secret access to a tiny pocket that was designed to hold her knife.

She dragged on a cropped leather jacket and examined her reflection. No one would ever guess she was carrying with this outfit. She took a minute to freshen up her make-up and was repacking her bag when Xavier knocked. He stuck his head in the door, "Ready to go?"

Waverly zipped the bag closed. "Oh, yeah."

12

It feels good to be doing something, she thought as Burke sped through downtown as fast as traffic would allow. She'd spent enough time waiting. It was time for action.

"So I take it you have a plan?" Xavier asked, tucking his phone into his jacket and shooting yet another judgmental look at her outfit. He hadn't demanded that she take it off, which she considered progress for him.

"I'm going to talk to Petra and find out what she knows. And I'm probably going to need your help distracting her bodyguards." She shot him a look. "They're pretty big guys. Are you up for a little two on one?"

"Exactly how rough is this going to get?" he asked dryly.

"I just need to get next to her. She'll call them off," Waverly said with confidence. At least, that's what she hoped would happen. She had no idea what had happened after Petra and Yurgei had driven off in the boat. She assumed the girl had been on lockdown since. It's what she would have done if she were Petra's father. But there was a chance that Petra could have connected her to the mess in Tahoe.

There was only one way to find out.

When Burke eased up to the curb in front of Volt, Xavier held her arm in his warm, strong grasp. "I'm not leaving your side this time," he promised her.

"She might not talk in front of you," Waverly warned him. "I need whatever information she's got, X. And if that means you have to take a couple of steps back, I need you to do it."

"I'll give you six feet."

It was better than nothing.

She made another move for the door, and again he stopped her. "I need you to be careful."

"Xavier," Waverly said, squeezing his knee. She realized that tonight had stirred up a lot of memories for them both, and he was probably thinking about the last time he'd taken her to a club, the night she'd been abducted. "I swear to you this time is going to end differently."

Reluctantly, he let her go when Burke opened the door for her. But he was sliding out directly behind her, and his hand settled on her back before she made it to the bouncer. There was a line outside the club, but security took one look at Waverly and waved them in. Cellphone flashes were still puncturing the night behind them when they entered the club.

The pulse of the music was loud enough to feel throughout her entire body. Lights flashed lavender and yellow over them. Xavier kept her close, never breaking contact with her.

Waverly angled her head toward his ear so he could hear her over the thumping electronic dance music. "She'll be in the VIP section."

"What's under your jacket?" he asked.

"My wallet," she said casually. She didn't want to find out what his reaction would be to her carrying a loaded .38 into a club. "Come on. VIP is up there," she said pointing to the loft area above the dance floor.

He climbed the metal stairs behind her, and she could feel his gaze burning into her ass as it swayed in front of his face. But it wasn't the time to lose her focus. The section hostess put them at a small white vinyl couch overlooking the packed dance floor.

Waverly spotted Petra against the far wall of the section. She wore a hot pink halter dress and was giggling at a horse-shoe-shaped banquette filled with the young and beautiful European crowd she usually attracted in L.A.

Anatoli, the bodyguard with the leg wound, was nowhere to be seen, but his friend Yurgei was. And by her count, there were three others in plainclothes. It looked like Grigory had stepped up the security on his little girl.

"I count four," Xavier said quietly in her ear.

Waverly nodded. "I can't sneak past four. I need a diversion."

"If I start another fight in another club, I'll be banned from L.A. nightlife forever," he quipped.

"Funny. Hang on. I have an idea."

She pulled her phone out of her jacket pocket and snapped a picture of Xavier. "What are you doing?"

Waverly grinned. "Payback for breakfast at the café, Saint."

He saw phones at nearby tables light up.

"What did you do?"

"Celeb Spotting's app alerts all users to nearby celebrities," she said, pushing back from the table and standing up. "Brace yourself."

"Waverly—"

"Well, ladies," the DJ announced over the music. "It looks like your wet dreams just came true. We've got a real live hero here tonight. Let's give it up for Xavier Saint in VIP."

The women on the dance floor below, fueled by too many overpriced Cosmos, erupted as a lone spotlight centered on Xavier. It froze him in place when he would have come after her. Waverly could feel his rage following her as she slipped away into the crowd. Every table in VIP emptied as everyone tried for a better look at Xavier.

Petra's guards were doing their best to direct the flow of traffic away from their client, but with the chaos, Waverly was able to weave her way around them and come up behind the girl.

"Hey, Petra," she said, leaning over her shoulder.

Petra's face morphed from curiosity to happy surprise to wariness. "Hi, Waverly. Uh, I'm just going to catch up with my friends—"

Waverly put her hand on Petra's arm. "I really need to talk to you, Petra. It's life or death."

Petra's eyes were as wide as the lipstick stained mouths of the martini glasses scattered on the table behind her. "Sure. Just let me—"

Waverly wasn't sure if she or Petra was more surprised when Petra took off running. She dodged behind a booth and shoved through an Employees Only door.

Waverly, with two guards hot on her heels, sprinted to the door. She slipped through and slammed it behind her and thanked her lucky stars that there was a deadbolt on the door. She threw it just as the first guard gripped the handle. She was running down the short hallway after Petra by the time someone put their shoulder into the door. Hopefully the bolt would hold, she prayed. Petra dashed down a rickety set of stairs, and Waverly followed her, regretting her choice of footwear with the delicately heeled boots. Petra, on the other hand moved like a sprinter in sneakers. *The girl must have been born in stilettos.*

"Petra, wait!" Waverly called out. But Petra was turning a corner at the foot of the stairs.

Waverly followed and found herself in the club's greasy kitchen. If the staff was confused by two well-dressed women sprinting through the prep area, they didn't show it. When Petra pushed through the side door in the kitchen, Waverly poured on the speed—feet be damned—and caught her on the sidewalk off the side street that ran parallel to the length of the club's squat brick building. To the left, Waverly could see the flashing neon of the club's signage reflected in the glass of the building across the road.

"Please don't hate me!" Petra cried out as Waverly held her by the forearm. "I feel so guilty already! I wanted to call you and tell you, but my father wouldn't let me. He thinks you're trouble."

"Petra, what are you talking about?" Waverly demanded, loosening her hold and praying the woman stayed put.

"Dante. I feel terrible about Dante, and I know you're mad at me, and I'm just the worst person in the universe. I mean, you saved my life, and look what I go and do."

"What did you go and do?" Waverly asked, fear icing her belly. "He's alive, isn't he?"

Petra frowned. "You don't know?"

"Know what?" Waverly squashed her urge to take Petra by the shoulders and shake the answers out of her.

A compact car with rust around the fenders pulled up with a squeal of poorly maintained brakes. The passenger side window rolled down with a squeak.

A skinny guy with thick glasses leaned over from the driver's seat. "Uh, hi. This is my first time doing this. It really wasn't my idea. It was kind of a dare. My cousin bet me a hundred bucks that I wouldn't get laid by the time I turned twenty-two, and well, my birthday is tomorrow. So, I don't know how this works..."

Waverly blinked.

Petra frowned. "Does he think we're—"

"Prostitutes."

Petra put her hands on her hips. "Excuse me, that's just offensive. Do you think a prostitute can afford this outfit?" She gestured at her Valentino dress and Manolo Blahniks.

"Uh, maybe a good one can?" the guy ventured. "Are you a good one?" he asked.

"No wonder they call this place La La Land," Petra huffed.

The squeal of tires caught Waverly's attention. Two black SUVs careened around the corner from the front of the club. They came to an abrupt stop, and with the engines still running, doors flew open.

"Are these your guards?" Waverly asked, already knowing the answer.

Petra was shaking her head when the first man jumped out and started toward them. He made no bones about flashing the gun he had in his hand.

"Shit." Four more men dressed in head-to-toe black got out and started down the sidewalk toward them.

"Petra, get in the car," Waverly whispered.

"Okay, but I'm not having sex with him."

"Just get in the car!"

Waverly yanked the passenger door open and shoved her inside. "You are not having sex with this woman. You're taking her home. Petra, I'll talk to you soon."

The goon squad was closing in at a run. "Go! Before someone gets shot."

The little car peeled away from the sidewalk.

One of the men raced back to the first SUV and jumped in,

squealing after them. Waverly grabbed her cell and dialed Burke.

"There's a black SUV chasing a white piece-of-shit two-door down Fourth. I need you to disable the SUV!"

"On it," the driver said as coolly as if she was asking him to pick up a carton of ice cream on his way home.

Less than ten seconds later, she saw Xavier's SUV careen down the street in the direction Petra had gone.

For fuck's sake. She'd been one second away from finding out what happened to Dante, and she was interrupted by four assholes and a john, she seethed.

Someone was going to pay. She walked backward, facing the remaining men and leading them further away from the main street. The alley was ten feet behind her, and she could either run or lure them in for the ass-kicking she was more than ready to dole out.

They all had guns, but given the setting, she wasn't too worried they'd use them. The one on the left was a big dude, too big to be agile. She could work with that. The second one was a wiry guy who topped out around five-foot-eight. The way his right shoulder hunched under his tactical shirt made her think back pain or some kind of injury. She'd start with those two. She stopped at the mouth of the alley and waited.

"Looks like blondie wants to play," the one on the far right said, flashing a glint of gold tooth and a Texas accent.

"Let's get this over with boys. I've got things to do," she said, taking a wide-legged stance in the middle of the sidewalk and crossing her arms. She palmed the pepper spray from her jacket pocket.

The third guy looked vaguely familiar, but she couldn't place him.

"How about we even the odds?" Xavier's voice came from the alley behind her. He sounded dangerously angry, and she hoped he'd be willing to direct it at someone other than her temporarily. He calmly strolled out from the shadows and stepped in front of her without sparing her a glance. His attention was on the four menacing figures in front of them.

"Four on two looks fair to me," the chatty Texan said.

"Stay behind me," Xavier said quietly to Waverly.

As if.

Chatty Cathy made his move first, swinging fast and hard at Xavier's head. He dodged the blow easily and countered with a body shot and right hook. The man's head snapped back from the hit, and he stumbled back a step. The big guy lined up next and came in at full speed to grab Xavier in a bear hug while his skinny buddy moved in to take some shots.

She saw Xavier kick the skinny one in the gut but was distracted by Number Three who skirted the grappling threesome and made a grab for her. She let him grab her by the forearm and then stomped on his instep with her icepick heel.

"Nice try," she said, spinning to throw an elbow to his gut. When he doubled over, she reached into his windbreaker and pulled out his gun. She tossed it in the dumpster behind her and kneed the man in the face.

The big guy had passed Xavier off to his friend to come to Number Three's rescue. He grabbed her from behind in a bear hug, apparently his signature move, and lifted her off her feet. She whipped her head back, connecting with his nose. When he dropped her, she landed low and swept his legs out from under him. His gun was in a shoulder holster that was stretched to capacity around his bulk. She fished out the Glock and tossed it into the dumpster with his friend's.

Xavier and the skinny guy were taking turns slamming each other against the brick of the building using some kind of bastardized martial art. It was pretty entertaining to watch, at least until Chatty Cathy got back on his feet and pulled his gun on her.

"I'm done playing, Blondie," he said, spitting blood. He wracked his slide. "Where's the girl? You will take me to her, or you will die."

"Oh, for fuck's sake." Waverly popped the cap on her pepper spray and hosed him in the face.

Xavier and the skinny ninja both paused when they heard the man's wild animal shrieks. Fortunately, Xavier recovered faster and popped his opponent in the face, knocking him out cold before he even hit the ground.

"What the fuck was that?" Xavier demanded staring at the three men at her feet writhing in various forms of agony. His battlefield calm was gone now.

He crossed to her and grabbed her by the wrist. "Who the hell are you?"

She threw herself at him knocking him off balance so the shot that Chatty Cathy blindly fired hit brick instead of flesh. Waverly spun and kicked the gun out of the man's hand and then landed another blow to his face.

Xavier picked up the gun and stared at the disabled goon squad. He picked the skinny unconscious one and started going through the man's pockets. Waverly pulled out her phone and fired off a text to Burke.

Everything OK?

His response was tacit. *SUV taken care of. Waiting for new ride.*

Are you OK??

Fine. But you're telling Saint. He attached a picture of the Tahoe, which was now sporting a smashed in front end.

She winced, wondering how pissed Xavier would be when he found out she'd given the order to total one of his fleet.

Waverly stowed her phone back in her jacket and backed toward the mouth of the alley slowly at first. She needed to put as much space between them as possible. There was no time for long explanations, even if she owed them. She had to find Petra, and Xavier would only slow her down.

She'd been so close and wasn't giving up now.

As if he'd read her thoughts, Xavier glanced up. "Waverly."

13

She spun away from Xavier and took off at a flat out sprint.

He shouted her name again, but she didn't hesitate, didn't slow. She crossed the street heading south. He was after her, but she had a good head start. She dodged through a crowd outside a jazz club and took a hard right into the alley. Music poured out of the back door of another club and mingled with the scents of garlic and tomato sauce from the kitchen door of an Italian place.

She hung a left and found herself on a quieter street. There were apartment buildings here and more cars parked for the night. A bar on the corner poured neon promises of beer brands onto the sidewalk.

"Waverly!"

God, he was gaining. It was her damn shoes, but there was no time to take them off now.

Beyond the bar was a massive stone cathedral and next to it a gated courtyard. She jumped the low fence, her feet hitting the brick of the courtyard, and skirted the fountain. The walls were brick as well. Trees formed an arching canopy creating a pocket of quiet nature in the middle of the city.

He was so close, she could hear him breathing, could feel the rush of his adrenaline as if it was her own. He was closing in, and she was going to lose Petra... and her connection to Dante.

The alley access was gated off as well, but the rear fencing was much higher. She took a running leap, her fingers gripping the top iron bar. It was as far as she got.

He caught her around the waist and dragged her off the fence. When she threw an elbow that connected with his jaw, Xavier forced her up against the brick of the wall next to the gate. "Goddamn it. I said stop!"

He wasn't gentle when he braceleted her wrists together over her head and held her in place with one hand.

Her breath was coming in shallow pants. She tried to aim a kick at his shins, but he read her like a playbook and shoved his hips against her, pressing her into the wall. "You're going to get yourself killed," he growled.

"You're the one who almost got shot," she snapped back.

His free hand roamed her body and found the .38 at the small of her back hidden by her cropped leather jacket.

"That's mine!" She struggled against him and felt him already rock hard.

"You'll get it back when I decide you deserve it." She felt his hand moving again. He slid it around the waistband of her skirt and up under the fitted edge of the long line of her crop top.

She felt his fingers pause as they found the small knife in its hidden sheath beneath her breasts, yet still he lingered there, just touching the trembling curves.

His breath was hot against her ear. "Keep your hands on

the wall, and if you try to run, I swear to God I'll break both your legs."

When she didn't answer, he tugged her hair. "Do you hear me, Angel? Hands on the wall."

She took a shuddering breath and nodded. Her brain was shutting down at his touch. She should want to run. She needed to find Petra. But his hands were skimming low over her hips, down the outside of her legs. He was patting her down, looking for weapons after ruining her chances of questioning the only one who might have answers for her. She shouldn't be turned on.

But as his palms skimmed up her ankles, over the inside of her legs to her knees, she quivered in anticipation. Her heart thrummed in her head, blood pounded through her system. First the chase, and now the seduction. She was caught in his trap and had lost the will to escape.

He brought his hands higher, coasting over the inside of her thighs. Waverly felt him hesitate when she stepped her feet apart, a moment of indecision. She made the choice for him by hinging forward against the wall and pressing her hips back to grind against him.

He growled, and she felt his breath hot on her neck. He was still just barely under control. She took one hand away from the wall to grab his and guided it between her legs.

She felt lightheaded when he pressed his palm against her aching wetness. "Touch me, X."

Her words freed him from his prison. Xavier gripped the silk of her underwear and yanked, shredding the delicate material. He grinded his hips against her, and she moaned bracing both hands against the wall again.

He slid his fingers over her exposed sex, and she whimpered with pleasure.

"You get off on it, don't you?" he whispered darkly in her

ear. "Running from me, the chase." He used his fingers to part her tender flesh and gently stroke her where she ached for him.

"Xavier," she breathed out his name as he broke her with the pads of his fingers making tiny, probing circles. He was working her over with the lightest touch, the darkest words.

"I'll tell you a secret, Angel." He dipped his other hand into the front of her top to cup her breast.

She gasped when his palm grazed her nipple. "Chasing you gets me off, too."

His fingers worked that sensitive peak, and she was already coming for him as he danced over her clitoris. She moaned as it tore through her, fast and heady, and in its wake, her orgasm left a gnawing hunger for more.

She thrust her hips against him, begging with her body for what she desired most.

"Don't tease me, Angel. I've been thinking about this moment for five long years, and I don't know if I can go slow."

"I don't want you slow. I want you angry and hard. The way you chase me. Take me that way, X," she told him through clenched teeth.

She heard him growl, and then he was flipping her skirt up and running his palms down her buttocks and thighs. The sound of his zipper as he opened it was as erotic as the promises he was murmuring against her neck. His erection fell heavily into his hand, and she trembled when it brushed against the exposed skin of her ass. He was leaking with anticipation, and the moisture transferred to her cheek.

He shoved her forward, head down and kicked her feet out a little wider. Her heels evened out their height difference enough that he only needed to bend his knees a little.

Xavier guided the head of his shaft down the cleft of her

buttocks, and she shivered when he probed between her legs. "Be careful what you wish for, Waverly."

"Xavier," she gasped out his name when he paused just outside of her entrance. "Please."

"Hands on the wall, Angel." He was stroking himself against her, working the head of his cock through her slick lips. The round, smooth crown of his penis teased her still trembling bud.

God, she wanted him. If he stopped now, if he pulled away, she knew she'd die. Her heart would simply stop beating, and she would crumple to the ground, ruined with unfulfilled desire. No one made her feel like this, no one but Xavier, and she hated him for it.

"You know what this means," he groaned in her ear as he tortured them both with shallow strokes and thrusts. She shoved her ass against him, begging with her body. She was dizzy with need, with the thrill of being overpowered, and gasped when a bead of moisture, the physical combination of both their desires, trickled down the inside of her thigh. "Tell me what this means, Waverly."

She shivered against him, so close to coming again, but she wanted him in her, filling her.

"Say it," he snapped.

"I want you," she whispered.

His lips caressed her jawline where it met her neck, and he grunted softly. "And?"

"I need you."

He growled his approval, and she wanted to feel shame for falling for him again. For needing his body to make hers feel complete. For craving the release that only Xavier could give her. But all that mattered was that he was touching her, and he wasn't going to stop.

"I don't have a condom." It was a last chance for her to put a stop to it.

She could have told him that she was on the same birth control as five years ago, could have told him that she wanted him without any barriers between them. But she kept it simple. "I don't care."

He groaned in her ear, the sound the tortured make when their torment is finally over.

"Yes!" The word exploded from her as he eased into her inch by glorious inch stretching her, filling her, so painfully full.

"God. You're so tight," he gritted out.

The pleasure that rose in her was so intense, it forced her breath out of her burning lungs in sobs. There wasn't enough oxygen here to breathe, but she didn't need it. She didn't need anything with him inside her. "Xavier," she chanted his name over and over again.

He braced his hands on her hips and pulled out slowly before slamming in, this time to the hilt. A primitive groan of triumph rose from his chest as he buried himself in her.

His fingers bit into her skin hard enough to leave bruises, and the brick scraped at her palms, but Waverly didn't care. After feeling empty for years, she was finally filled. Her body remembered this fullness, this sliver of pain and tidal wave of pleasure. It was in her DNA to crave him.

He held there, sheathed in her, for a breath then two. "Relax for me, baby. You're so fucking tight." His words were harsh with the effort to hold back.

She took a shaky breath and tried to accept him all. As she relaxed around him degree by degree, he let his hands roam her stomach, her thighs, her breasts. He pulled out and drove back in with a measured plunge, then again.

"My beautiful, Angel," he murmured.

His thrusts came faster now and with more force. His balls slapped off of the backs of her thighs as he powered into her.

He grabbed her top and yanked it down, baring her breasts. When he reached up to palm one of her breasts, Waverly let out a shaky moan. She was overwhelmed by her body's submission to him. In this moment, Xavier Saint owned her. She wanted to pause and collect herself. But she felt that inward momentum build, the inevitable hurtling headfirst into a pleasure so intense she might not survive. It was where he always took her.

While he used one hand to palm her breasts, Xavier brought his other to the apex of her thighs. He zeroed his fingers in on the one spot in her body that connected to every nerve.

"Say my name, Waverly. Who's making you come?"

"Xavier!" His name, charged with so many emotions, exploded from her lips.

His thrusts picked up speed until they bordered on wild and violent. The pads of his fingers worked her ruthlessly, and she couldn't fight the orgasm that was building inside her.

"That's my Angel. Now tell me who you belong to."

She fought it. Fought the word that was clawing its way out of her throat. Fought the orgasm that was building. She shook her head against his shoulder. But Xavier wouldn't accept that for an answer.

"We both know it, Waverly. Say it." He punctuated his demand with a thrust so deep she thought she would come apart. The angle of his thick cock and the unceasing attention of his fingers rocketed her up. He felt her tighten around him and growled out his demand again.

"Who do you belong to, Angel?"

It spread like wildfire through her body, every cell

exploded with the orgasm. "You," she sobbed. "I belong to you."

Even in the throes of her own release, she felt him lose control. The words she'd given him had set him free. He slammed into her again and again in a quest for the finish. "Mine. Mine. Mine." With every thrust, he told her again and again that she belonged to him, and then he was coming. She felt the first burst of his release as he buried himself to the hilt in her. He jerked against her again and again as he emptied himself into her. He rolled her orgasm into another, and he groaned in agonized ecstasy as her muscles tightened around him forcing every drop of his release from him.

They stood there, shuddering and shaking against the wall, trying to absorb the magnitude of what had happened between them. Xavier moved first, pulling out slowly even as Waverly clenched reflexively around him. He grabbed the shredded remains of her underwear and gently cleaned her with them.

He pulled her around to face him, pressing her against the wall and his chest, holding her as if he was afraid she'd disappear.

"Don't ever doubt what we have between us," he murmured against her hair.

14

*E*ven after his soul-shattering orgasm, Xavier already craved more of Waverly. It would never be enough with her. "We need to go someplace," he said gruffly.

"We'll need a new ride home. Burke uh, ran into some traffic." She looked guilty for a moment, but he was in no shape to run an interrogation at the moment. There was only one thing on his mind.

He shook his head. "We're not going home. I'm not going to last that long. Invictus has a property nearby."

The light in those green gray eyes told him she was as frantic for him as he was for her. "Hurry," she told him breathlessly.

They burst through the front door of an upscale condo eight minutes later and were on each other. Xavier kicked the door shut behind them and was dragging his jacket off while Waverly assaulted his mouth with hers.

He threw the jacket blindly and winced at the ensuing crash. *Fuck it. He'd pay to have the whole place redone as long as he could take Waverly here and now.* He picked her up, shoving her skirt up so she could wrap those long, beautiful legs around him. He carried her through the first door, and finding it to be a bathroom, he kicked in another door thanking God when he found a bed within.

She was driving him mad with her wet lips and quick tongue. His fingers flexed into the flesh of her ass cheeks, and she moaned against him. He didn't know precisely what it was about Waverly Sinner, but he suspected that she was in his blood. From the moment he'd laid eyes on her, his body had recognized her as his mate. She was what had been missing in his life.

He'd tried to shake it off, to ignore it, and then to fight it. But Xavier knew without a shadow of a doubt she was meant to be his. His wife, his partner, his center. He would have her no matter what it took, what it cost. Waverly was his.

Xavier dropped her on the mattress and dove after her, hating to be apart for even a second. He nuzzled into her neck and tasted a trail to her jaw. Her breath was hot against his face.

He needed to slow down, needed to get control. This was his chance to show her they belonged together, to make her choose him. *She had to choose him.*

He slowed intentionally and began to savor the feel of her neck under his lips, the lean muscles in her shoulder. She gasped his name when he nipped his way over her clavicle.

"Xavier."

"My Angel."

He pressed his face to the hollow between her breasts. "It's never enough," he murmured to her. "I could have you a thousand times, and it still wouldn't be enough." His cock strained against the confines of his pants as if to confirm it. The curves of her breasts threatened to spill over the molded cups of her top. Xavier trailed his tongue along the exposed flesh, taking pleasure in the hiss of her breath.

"Too many clothes," she whispered.

"I agree." Xavier kicked off his shoes one at a time, letting them land with a thunk on the floor by the bed. He pulled back, and Waverly levered up on her elbows to watch what he was doing. On his knees between her legs, he loosened his tie. When the knot came free, he draped the tie over her and moved on to the buttons of his shirt.

She wet her lips watching him work them free one by one. When his shirt hit the floor, Waverly reared up. She grabbed him by the belt buckle, and as her mouth worked his over, her fingers undid the belt and the button and zipper beneath.

She shoved his pants down his thighs until the only thing keeping her from his throbbing dick were the black briefs. He recognized that gleam in her eyes. She was going for control. He let her have it... or the illusion of it, let her pull down the waistband of his briefs until he sprang free.

The hunger in her eyes nearly did him in. And then her sweet lips closed around his crown, and he nearly did lose it. His balls tightened instantly, and he fisted his erection at the root. Control. He needed to find it and use it to show her what they had together.

But still she worked her mouth over him, around him, drawing him in deeper. He distracted himself momentarily by dragging open the zipper at the back of her top and letting her breasts tumble out pendulously as the top fell to the mattress.

She'd been spectacular five years ago, young and lithe. But she was a goddess now.

She teased the slit of his cock and purred when she was rewarded with another drip of moisture from his tip. He let her take him deep until he felt her throat close around him.

He was hanging on by a thread, and then she took one of his hands and held it to her breast.

He drew back, pulling his erection out of her mouth with an audible pop.

"Not yet, Angel. I've got plans for you."

He shoved her on her back and yanked at her skirt. She levered her hips up to help him. Free of the binding, he almost felt sorry for having shredded her underwear because it would have been a fantasy to slip his fingers beneath them and pull them slowly from her body.

He settled for trailing wet kisses up the inside of her thigh. Her knees fell open, giving him unfettered access to what he craved most. Xavier sampled his way to her sex, dipping his tongue between her folds and teasing at just the right spot.

Waverly writhed beneath him, and he knew his touch was driving her mad.

When he slicked his tongue over her opening, dipping it ever so slightly into her slick center, she gasped. And when he ran it lower still over the tight bud between her ass cheeks, she cried out.

He was sending her a message that every inch of her belonged to him. Every orgasm, every whispered gasp—he laid claim to them all.

Again and again he stroked over her, back and forth, and all it took was the two fingers he slid into her to send her falling into the abyss. She shuddered over every single wave as they rolled swiftly, smoothly through her body.

Then he was ranging himself over her, and he closed his lips over the peak of her breast. Even sated, he could tell her body demanded more. Her nipple pebbled, in excruciating sensitivity, as his tongue teased it. He pulled on it, sucking deeply, and she reached between their bodies to grip his shaft. He growled against her breast when she touched him. But he let her stroke him as he moved his attentions to her other breast.

He felt himself go impossibly harder beneath her fingers. He let himself nuzzle her breasts, admiring the red that appeared on her skin from his beard. He wanted to mark Waverly everywhere, to send her back into the world with his marks on her so there would be no doubt who she belonged to, who she'd chosen.

"I'm going to fuck you until you forget there was ever anyone else."

"There is no one else," she groaned back.

It was the words he needed to hear. Her surrender to him, to their destiny. He loomed over her, bracing his weight on his forearms so that her nipples just brushed his chest. He was settled between her spread thighs and felt his dick notch into place.

She flexed her hips against him, those wet folds kissing the head of his shaft, welcoming him.

He held there, watching her writhe beneath him. Her angelic face tortured with the sharp edge of desire. The power snapped through his body. She was his to take, his to pleasure.

Waverly bucked against him again, pleading without words for him to fill her. But still he waited until she opened those hazy eyes. And then, only then, did he bury himself in her. Joined, they were one. One soul. One pleasure. One need.

He wanted to go slow, to savor the way her delicate muscles clenched down on him, drawing him in and holding him there. But with every stroke he felt himself losing control. He'd wanted this for so long and it was nearly impossible to stop the crushing need for taking everything she offered now. *Now.*

He reined himself in and pushed into her with slick, measured thrusts. Each one taking him closer to heaven as she gripped him in her velvety vice. His balls slapped against her rhythmically and began to tighten. It was too soon. He needed to send her over first.

With the last ounce of self-control he pulled out, feeling the pulse of blood demanding orgasm in his erection. Waverly was trembling beneath him, and he was afraid he might still come just from that. But then she was shoving him up and over onto his back and mounting him.

This time, she cuffed his hands over his head. "My turn," she said, biting at his lower lip.

"Go slow, Angel. I can't hold back—"

His words were lost as she worked herself down onto his rigid shaft until he was fully embedded. "Oh, God—" his abs tightened, and his head lifted reflexively off the pillow. It brought him to her breasts, and as she began to ride, he took a nipple into his mouth, plumped it with his tongue.

Her moan of pleasure spurred him on. She wasn't riding him slowly. She set a breakneck pace that had her breasts bouncing against his face. He sucked her nipple into his mouth and lapped at it.

She was a goddess, his to worship, as she rolled her hips over him, her blonde waves tumbling down her back in a golden curtain.

"Xavier, you're making me come," she warned him, her lips parting as she sought breath.

He wasn't sure if it was his name from those plush lips, the tender peak he worshipped with his mouth, or the way she slammed down on his cock, but he was coming. And there was no stopping it.

His hips jerked against her, abs freezing in flexion as he thrust in to her hilt. The first wrenching explosion of his orgasm triggered hers, and he felt the waves tighten her channel around him, milking jet after jet out of him as she gripped him between her thighs to ride out the storm.

She cried out, and he sucked deeply on the nipple he'd claimed, grunting softly as he emptied himself with violent thrusts.

15

*X*avier hated to wake her. He wanted this moment between them to last. Waverly was curled on her side, her back cuddled against his front, wrapped in the embrace of his arms. He was still hard as a redwood—as if he hadn't just been gutted by two violent orgasms.

But that wasn't why he needed to wake her. He needed answers.

She'd left three goons incapacitated without breaking a sweat and had anticipated the shot that could have ended his life or seriously pissed him off before he had. He'd seen the gun in the split second that she'd knocked into him, sending him off balance and out of harm's way.

That wasn't luck. That was training.

He now had a good idea what Micah's text had meant. He'd gotten it as he was frantically sprinting down the club's emergency exit staircase trying to dial Waverly.

Big news on Tomasso and Target. You're not going to like it. Call ASAP.

He'd barely escaped the crowd that had closed in on him in the VIP section after Waverly's stunt. It was a first-hand experience with how Waverly must feel on a regular basis. So many people, each wanting a piece of you. He was going to have a talk with her about using him as a distraction, about separating herself from him, and trying to handle an armed squad of someone's enforcers on her own. By the time he'd hustled through the door leading to the alley, his instincts were screaming that she was in trouble.

And it looked like it was bigger trouble than he'd anticipated.

He nuzzled into her hair and stroked his palm over her arm and taut stomach. "Angel, wake up."

"Again? I'm not going to be able to walk tomorrow," she murmured into her pillow.

He liked that picture enough that his dick twitched against her, but they needed to talk first.

"Baby, wake up. We have to talk."

"We're not getting married, X," she yawned.

"Yes, we are. But that's not what we have to talk about."

"I know," she grumbled and rolled over in his arms. Looking at her swollen lips and those full breasts that pressed against his chest, he started to change his priorities. And when she threw one leg over his hips to cuddle closer to his erection, he almost lost his resolve.

Reluctantly, Xavier pushed her across the mattress until she was an arm's length away. "Hang on. We have to get out of this bed and get some clothes on or we're both going to die of orgasm-induced dehydration."

He dragged himself out of bed and padded over to the closet door. Invictus made it a policy to stock certain basics in each safehouse, and he was relieved to find sweatpants and t-shirts that would fit them both.

Waverly had rolled to her side and watched him approach with a feline smile. "God, you're magnificent," she sighed.

"Which one of us are you talking to?" he asked, glancing down at his still hard shaft.

"Bravo to both," she said. When she stretched, the sheet slid down to reveal one perfect, supple breast.

He turned around.

"Angel, please get dressed so we can get this conversation over with."

"And then what?"

"And then I'm undressing you again and keeping you that way for at least six or seven months."

He heard her shift on the mattress and the sound of her pulling on clothes.

"Better?"

He turned around to find her pulling her hair up into a knot on the top of her head. Her nipples were visible through the soft white cotton of the t-shirt. He felt his cock move in appreciation.

"There's got to be a parka or something in here," he said, hurrying back into the closet. He found a sweatshirt, three sizes too big for her and hurled it in her direction.

She humored him and pulled it over her head. "Better?" she asked.

"Not really. Maybe it's the bed. Let's go back to the living room and sit on opposite ends of the couch."

She padded out of the room in front of him and veered into the kitchen where she riffled through drawers and cabinets until she found sandwich bags. She filled one with ice and wrapped it in a dishtowel.

"Here. For your eye."

He frowned and probed his left eye. He'd taken a good

169

shot from the ninety-pound ninja but had forgotten about it in the heat of the chase and the... after.

He took inventory of the rest of his body. Besides feeling sated, the knuckles on his left hand were split, and he felt a bruise blooming on his jaw. Everything else seemed to be intact.

Waverly grabbed two bottles of water out of the refrigerator and slid one to him across the black onyx of the counter.

He opened an app on his phone, and after some fiddling, the overhead lights dimmed on.

"Isn't that handy?" Waverly said.

"All of our properties are wired to our system," he said, drinking deeply from the bottle.

He let her fidget for a few more moments.

"You're going to have to eventually tell me," he said.

She raised her gaze to his. "I know. I just don't know where to start."

"Let's start with where you learned to beat the hell out of men twice your size, and then we'll wind our way around to what made you sic a hoard of women on me while you chased Petra into an alley."

When she began to pace in front of the sink, Xavier pulled out a barstool and sat at the island.

"I have two jobs," she began. "I've been acting my entire life, and in college while I was taking classes in psychology and international relations, I saved my summers for filming. Dante and I made another film together for Target Productions. I didn't realize it at the time, but it was a test."

Xavier stayed still, focused on her words.

"After graduation, Dante approached me with a job offer. Brad Tomasso, the CEO of Target, had identified a unique need that the government's intelligence gathering organizations all had. There were certain places that agents couldn't get into, places that celebrities had access to."

"Like the Lake Tahoe home of a Russian billionaire."

She nodded. "Exactly. Dante and I do contract work, gathering intelligence from people in situations where we wouldn't necessarily be seen as a threat."

He swiped a hand over his face. The love of his life was telling him she was a spy.

"How long have you been doing this?" he asked, keeping his tone even.

"Since I graduated. I have a good grasp of languages, so I do well with European and Russian targets."

"When you say, 'do well...'" he trailed off, not really wanting to know the answer.

She rolled her eyes. "I'm not James Bonding my way through assets if that's what you're asking. It's just the kids of weapons dealers have looser lips around drunk party girl movie stars. Or a mogul's lonely daughter needs a new BFF. Occasionally, Dante and I double-teamed targets. We've hacked phones, searched private offices, gotten information out of coked up entrepreneurs with shady business dealings."

He took a slow deep breath and fought the pounding headache that suddenly appeared.

"It was a pretty strategic move on Brad's part," she continued. "The income from the contracts padded the studio's bottom line, and Dante and I both received a cut. The organizations we worked for were happy to farm out some of their case load."

"When you say 'organizations,' who do you mean exactly?"

"NSA, FBI, DIA, occasionally the CIA and the SEC. And I see the line is back between your eyes," she noted.

Xavier closed his eyes. The idea was actually fascinating, but the fact that his Angel was taking assignments from the intelligence community destroyed any objectivity he had. A thousand scenarios raced through his head—ways things could have gone horribly wrong, had gone horribly wrong.

"So what happened in Tahoe?"

"The whole assignment to get close to Petra? It felt off. Usually there's a clearly stated objective, but this time I was just told to befriend her and stay close. There were no further instructions. And after a few weeks, the studio told me to bring Dante into it."

"Do you know why?" Xavier asked.

She shook her head. "I felt like the whole thing was off. Petra's not into anything, and she's not involved in her father's business, so I didn't think it was likely that she'd know anything. I assumed Grigory was the actual target, and Dante thought the same. So when Petra invited us to Tahoe, Dante decided to do a little digging."

"So you got her out of the house while he went snooping," Xavier filled in.

Waverly nodded. "Grigory had a locked study on the second floor. So I suggested a walk down to the lake." She paused and took a sip of water before continuing on.

"The shooting started about five minutes after we left the house. The office door was open and riddled with bullet holes when I got back to the house."

"So Dante got caught in the study?"

She shrugged. "I don't think Petra's security would have shot up the house like that or shot me for that matter. Their boss is an international mogul. He's not going to want to be answering questions about two murdered houseguests."

"So it was someone on the outside."

"I think someone sent an armed team into that house, and I think they were after Petra."

"But they got Wrede instead?"

Waverly scrubbed her hands over her face. She looked tired, frustrated. "I don't know. He wouldn't have gone easily."

"Have you considered the possibility that Wrede was in on this? That he used his time alone to report to someone that he was in place?" If Wrede had played any role in Waverly being shot, Xavier would make him pay.

Waverly was shaking her head. "Dante wouldn't do that. And if he was, he would have called them in when Petra was easily contained. In the middle of the night, probably. Not traipsing around in the woods. It wasn't him," she said firmly.

"Don't let your feelings cloud your judgment," Xavier warned her. It was a lesson every operative had to learn, and one that he still struggled with where Waverly was concerned. Objectivity with her was impossible. "He abandoned you in a firefight. That's not what partners do."

"Dante didn't abandon me," Waverly snapped. "He trusted me to do my job. I got Petra away from the house. If he didn't come for me, there was a damn good reason why. A reason I was about to find out tonight when some moron mistook Petra and I for prostitutes."

"I beg your pardon?"

She relayed what had happened on the sidewalk outside the club prior to his arrival. "Also, I owe you an SUV. Burke's fine, thank God. That guy does not half-ass his job."

Xavier stared at her and very slowly lowered his head to the cool countertop.

"Are you okay?" she asked cautiously.

"I think I need some time to process this," he announced to the granite.

"I understand," Waverly said.

He heard her pad around the island, felt her arms come around him. When she moved to release him, Xavier sat up and tugged her in to stand between his legs. He brushed a loose tendril back from her face and held her jaw gently. "Thank you for trusting me with the truth."

She glanced down before meeting his gaze again and nodding.

"I want you to know that you're not in this alone anymore. You have me, and I'll commit every resource I have to helping you find out what happened." *And protecting you,* he added silently.

Waverly dipped her head. "Thank you, X. I can't tell you what that means to me."

He rubbed the pads of his thumbs over the smooth skin of her jaw. "But, Angel, you need to be prepared for the fact that you might not like those answers."

"Dante didn't do this. You'll see," she said earnestly before kissing him on the cheek and threading her fingers through his hair.

"That's not my only concern here, Waverly. There's a good chance he might be dead."

Her fingers stilled in his hair. "I hope you're wrong," she whispered.

The unwavering faith she had in another man ate away at him. Wrede had abandoned her as Xavier had done. Only Xavier had walked out after he knew she was safe. Yet Wrede was the one she trusted, the one she believed in. The one who didn't need to beg for forgiveness.

Xavier had been inside Waverly not twenty minutes ago, and already he felt the distance between them growing. Xavier pulled her in for a tight embrace. He wanted her thinking of *him*, needing him, loving him.

"I'm going to make some calls. Why don't you get some sleep?" he suggested.

"It's after one in the morning. Who's going to answer the phone now?"

"Burke and Micah if they know what's good for them," he said lightly.

She wrapped her arms around him tighter. "You won't... I mean..."

"I won't tell anyone who doesn't need to know. You're my priority, Angel. Nothing has changed that."

He felt her sigh against him. She pulled back and studied him in that disconcerting way she had. "Will you come to bed then?"

The tightness loosened in his chest. She may believe in Dante Wrede, but it was him she wanted in her bed.

BURKE ANSWERED on the first ring and sounded almost chipper. "Hey, boss."

"I heard you had an eventful night," Xavier said dryly.

"On the bright side, the airbags worked great," Burke quipped.

"I take it the bad guys didn't get the girl?"

"I caught up with them about a mile from her house. The idiot driving her car has to be the worst driver ever. I took a shortcut around the block and t-boned the chase car. Looks like Stepanov made it through the gates okay and the other guys limped off."

"You get the plates?"

"Called 'em in to the office when I was waiting for a tow."

"What did you tell cops?"

"That some asshole ran the stop sign."

Xavier sighed. "Good work tonight, but next time Angel gives you orders, maybe double check with me first?"

"Sorry, boss. She sounded very persuasive on the phone."

Xavier thought of Waverly in the alley, three men crumpled at her feet. There was a possibility that the woman he was protecting didn't actually need his protection.

He hung up with Burke and dialed Micah and took great pleasure in waking up his friend.

"There better be fire and blood," Micah groaned into the phone.

"More like four armed assailants in the alley, one car crash, and an escaped asset."

"I take it this ties in to my text?" Micah yawned.

"I'm guessing it does. You go first."

He heard Micah murmur something. "Sorry, Suz wanted to know if anyone was dead."

"Pretty sure the guys crawled out of the alley under their own power," Xavier told him.

He heard Micah stumble through the dark and then a thud and a string of curses. "Jesus, man. Thank God you're not back on night raids," Xavier muttered.

"I'm a fucking ninja when I need to be," Micah snorted. "Just not when someone leaves Barbie's Corvette in the middle of the dark hallway."

Xavier smiled in spite of himself. "Can you hurry up and finish traversing the dangers of family life so you can fill me in on Tomasso?"

"Yeah, yeah," his friend yawned. "Okay, so I had a chat with our old pal Travers."

Agent Malachi Travers was the perpetually irritated FBI agent that had worked the Ganim case and more recently turned up squat for Xavier on Waverly's purported car wreck and the Stepanov home invasion.

"I dropped a few names—Brad Tomasso, Target Productions, Dante Wrede, Stepanov," Micah continued. "Three of them rang bells. Are you sitting down?" Now that he was awake Micah was having fun dangling the carrot.

"Tomasso turned Target into a contractor for the intelligence community."

"You're an asshole in the middle of the night, you know that, Saint?" Micah complained.

"Just trying to speed things along. What did Travers have to say about the Stepanovs?"

"Zip. He's not aware of any investigations into any of them. In fact, he made a few unofficial inquiries to pals in other agencies. No one's looking at them, or at least no one's willing to admit they're looking at him."

Xavier's brain started firing on a theory. "What about Wrede?"

"No one's aware that he's missing. Travers did know about Wrede's moonlighting though. Said he's been helpful to the Bureau in a couple of sticky cases. They like siccing him on ladies with information. If you know what I mean."

"I don't need you to draw me a picture," Xavier told him. "So Wrede went missing on an investigation that no one wants to own, and Target covers his disappearance by leaking an open-ended vacation."

"Essentially, yes."

"Well, I've got one more piece of intel for you. Waverly works for Target, too."

Micah's silence stretched on for five full seconds before he said anything. "You're shitting me."

"Nope. She told me tonight after she kicked the shit out of three of the four armed assholes outside of a club."

"You're shitting me," Micah said again.

"Still not shitting you." Xavier filled him in on Petra and the excitement at the club.

When he was done, Micah blew out a breath. "So what are we doing?"

"We're going to help her find Wrede," Xavier said.

"You realize that you're delivering your dream girl's boyfriend back to her?"

"It's what she wants," Xavier said lamely.

"Who are we bringing in on this?" Micah asked.

"Just you. For now."

"I'll be by in the morning."

"Thanks, man. Do me a favor and text me when you're on your way."

Micah was silent for a moment, processing. "I sure hope you know what you're doing, Saint."

Xavier hoped so, too.

16

When Xavier crawled into bed in what was left of the night, he'd pulled Waverly into his side. What started as a sweet goodnight kiss Waverly was all too happy to push farther. They made love again, this time leisurely as if they had all the time in the world. And it was just as shattering, if not more so. They savored each other, moving slowly, whispering softly as streetlights played across the bed.

She could have told him all of it. Confessed that Dante was her partner, not her lover. But she needed that one last layer of defense between them. Tonight was a reminder of how devastating Xavier Saint could be. As he murmured words of love against her neck, she clung to that shield. And when he said the words her heart craved, she felt her grip slipping, the shield falling.

"I love you, Angel. I love you."

"Xavier." She sighed into the blooming ecstasy as it lifted her up and carried her away, but he was there with her, holding her to him as if he was afraid she would disappear beneath him.

~

Morning began abruptly with a brisk knock on the bedroom door. Waverly and Xavier both reached for guns before realizing it was the Invictus knock.

"I'm guessing you slept through my text," Micah's voice carried through the door.

"Fuck," Xavier swore under his breath.

"I'm leaving both your bags from the truck outside the door in case you need clothes for some reason."

"You're never living this down," Waverly predicted.

"Shut up, Angel."

He softened his words with a kiss on his way to the door. She loved the way he looked in suits, so sexy and urbane. But naked Xavier prowling a room was a breathtaking sight.

He opened the door, grabbed the bags, and tossed a middle finger in the direction of the kitchen for good measure.

He returned to her bedside and dropped her bag at her feet.

"Are you ever not hard?" Waverly wondered, studying his thickly veined erection with fascination.

"Jesus, Angel. Stop looking at me like that. You're already not going to be able to walk. Do you want to be incapacitated?"

She reached for him and laughed when he danced out of her way. "Get dressed, and if you behave yourself for the next hour, I'll make it worth your while," he promised.

She watched him prowl into the bathroom. He glanced back out at her. "By the way, this wasn't a fluke or a one-night stand or a mistake. We're back together," he announced and slammed the door on any denial she tried to throw his way.

While she wasn't thinking of the night before as a one-night stand, Waverly was by no means ready to consider a reconciliation either. It was a topic she would tackle with him later.

Enjoying the delicious soreness in her body, Waverly tugged on yoga shorts and a sweatshirt she had buried in the bottom of her bag and went to visit Micah in the kitchen. The loft looked different in the daylight and without the sexual haze that had clouded her vision last night. Everything was sterile, modern, and state-of-the-art from the gleaming kitchen countertops to the arresting canvases on the exposed brick walls.

Micah took one look at her and raised his gaze to the ceiling. "I feel like I shouldn't be looking at you right now."

"We're all adults, Micah," she reminded him, snagging a mug of coffee and digging for sugar in the pantry.

"Well, as a slightly older adult, I hope you both know what you're doing. I'm not looking forward to picking up any pieces this time around."

Waverly patted his shoulder. "Micah, I think we've all grown up a bit. Trust Xavier to make his own decisions, okay?"

"If you two fuck this up again, I don't want either of you to come crying to me about it."

"Your support means a lot," Waverly said dryly.

The door to the bedroom flew open, and Xavier hustled into the room. He was wearing another custom black suit, this one without a tie. The evidence of bed and sex head had been combed out of his hair. He stopped in his tracks when he saw Waverly, and she saw the relief flood his face.

"I thought you took off again," he sighed.

Micah grumbled something that included the word "pussy" under his breath, and Waverly glared at him. "Behave," she warned him.

Xavier came into the kitchen and, ignoring the mug she held out for him, dipped his head to capture her mouth. The kiss was swift and hard, possessive. Waverly knew he was using it to remind her of last night and the fact that he'd staked his claim once again.

"I can come back later if you have better things to do than discuss espionage and missing persons," Micah grumbled.

"Jesus, Waverly. Couldn't you have put some pants on?" Xavier complained.

"Oh, my God. Both of you sit down and shut up," she ordered, pointing at the glass and iron dining table.

Xavier opened his mouth again, but she cut him off with a stern look. "Uh-uh, sit," she told him, shaking her head.

Both men grumbled their way over to the table and sat. A knock at the door had them both rising again.

"Relax. It's Kate," she called over her shoulder as she moved to the entryway.

Xavier ignored her and followed her to the door. He wouldn't let her open it. Instead, he shoved her behind his back and turned the handle.

"Hey, X-Factor. Nice digs," Kate said, brushing past him. "I brought donuts." She scented the air. "I'm willing to trade them for coffee."

Once everyone was settled around the table with sugary baked goods and caffeine, Waverly deigned it time to begin.

"So, to make sure everyone is up to speed, Xavier I assume you blabbed to Micah about my alternate line of employment."

Xavier nodded, pulling his chair closer to her. "I did."

"Kate, everyone knows about my work with Target," Waverly confirmed to her friend.

"Great." Kate bobbed her blonde head. "Uh-huh. So can we get to the part where Xavier causes a mob scene at Volt?"

"He was my distraction to get to Petra. I had her cornered

after we slipped her guards. She has information about Dante, but we were interrupted—"

"Someone thought they were prostitutes," Xavier filled in.

Waverly shot him a look. "*Anyway*, I need to get to Petra again, which is going to be more difficult now that her guards think I'm Satan."

"Did she say why she hasn't contacted you since that night in Tahoe?" Kate asked.

"She said her father wouldn't let her. I don't know if he thinks I was part of the raid, or if I'm just trouble. Either way, after last night, her guards aren't going to let me within a five-mile radius of her."

Xavier was kicked back in his chair angled toward her and watching. "So what do we do?"

"I want you to find a way into her house."

"You want the owners of Invictus Security to break into a house?" Micah clarified.

"It takes balls to play the game," Waverly said sweetly.

"I've been in her house before. It's a twelve-bedroom mausoleum that sits on five acres. There are guards aplenty. And, as Micah probably knows, an Invictus Security system."

The pained look on his face told her he was probably hoping she didn't have that information.

She leveled her gaze at him. "Micah, I know this isn't easy. But I believe that Petra is being targeted. Someone has tried to get to her on two separate occasions by sending in armed teams. I need your help to make sure they don't succeed."

"Are you sure you're not just doing this to find out where your boyfriend is?" Micah challenged.

"Micah." Xavier's voice held a measure of restrained anger.

"This is my company, too, Saint," Micah reminded him. "I still have a say."

Waverly cut in. "Ultimately, yes. I do want to find Dante.

But my first priority is to get to Petra and keep her safe. She's the one innocent party in this mess, and I'm not going to let her pay a price for it," Waverly said coolly.

"I'm on board, of course," Kate put in. "But where do we stand with the studio? Brad wasn't too happy with you for flying home early. He's going to go ape shit when he hears you were clubbing together."

"I was ordered off of the assignment. I'm supposed to be lying low," Waverly said for Micah's benefit. "So Brad's going to take last night as a personal affront. Especially if there's any coverage of what actually happened. He's going to see it as me going rogue."

"What are the consequences for going rogue?" Micah wanted to know.

She shook her head. "I honestly don't know. We don't do the heavy lifting that other agencies do. We just gather intel. For all I know, Dante doing a little extra research into the assignment could have been labeled going rogue, and they could have sidelined him somehow."

"Do you think that's a possibility?" Xavier asked, watching her closely.

"I'm working under the hypothesis that Brad decided to expand the side business by accepting contracts from the private sector. I had a friend look into Grigory Stepanov, and she couldn't find a speck of dirt on the guy."

"Travers with the FBI confirms that there's no official investigation into Stepanov on his end," Xavier added. "He also found no record of a police report regarding the incident in Lake Tahoe, which is interesting considering that no one called the cops when a heavily armed team turns a house into a shooting gallery."

"So unless it's another agency trying to keep this very quiet, I'm leaning toward a private player," Waverly told them.

When Xavier nodded, she was pleased to realize he'd come to the same conclusion.

"This has the potential to be a lot bigger than finding a missing person," Xavier said, addressing the table. "If Tomasso started picking up jobs he shouldn't be touching, we've got some serious problems."

"Another reason to not get involved," Micah tried again.

"Brad strikes me as the kind of guy who'd be willing to go pretty far to clean up a mess," Kate spoke up, through a mouthful of donut.

Including taking out one of his own agents, Waverly thought. "I agree with Kate. Dante and I both felt there was something off with the assignment from the get go. There were no objectives—just get and stay close. Brad knew we were going to Tahoe, and Dante was supposed to check in with him that evening."

"So either Tomasso sent in a backup team, or the client just needed inside surveillance so they could make their move," Xavier ventured.

Micah sighed and poked at the half-eaten donut on his napkin. "I really don't like it when you guys work together," he said morosely.

"Cheer up, pal. Weren't you just saying how things had been quiet for a while?" Xavier said.

"I was saying that so you'd take a fucking vacation, not drag me into some kind of espionage plot."

"What do you need from us?" Xavier asked Waverly with a spark in his eyes.

"A lot, and I hope you're feeling generous. Brad kept his players list under wraps. The only other agent I worked with was Dante. But if I go back through our assignments, could you have your research team take a peek and verify that they were legitimate investigations?"

Micah nodded, finally finding a task he felt comfortable with. "If you can get me the backgrounds and timelines I should be able to pull some information together for you."

"Great. Then I'm going to need a way into Petra's estate, and I need it fast. These guys aren't going to wait, and if the studio gets it in their head to sideline me—"

"That's not going to happen," Xavier cut in. "No one gets to you."

"That's why I want you going after Petra with me, X," Waverly smiled.

"What about the money trail?" Kate piped up.

"I've got a friend who'll follow that. If Brad's not just taking government contracts anymore, I need to prove it. Micah, once you pull together the data about any fishy investigations, I'll have her see if there's money to follow there as well."

"I'd like to talk to your friend," Xavier said. "Invictus can extend our resources to her."

Kate and Waverly shared a look. "I don't know if that will be possible, but I'll be sure to extend the offer," Waverly said, choosing her words carefully.

"So how do we find out what Brad's up to? And if he's going to come after you?" Kate asked, graciously changing the subject.

Waverly's phone rang, and she glanced down at the screen. "I guess I just answer the phone."

Xavier and Micah both stood up abruptly and began heatedly debating the best course of action.

Waverly sent Kate a signal and took the phone into the living area while Kate chucked a donut at the guys to get them to shut up.

"Brad, what do I owe the pleasure?"

17

"He wants you to do what?" Xavier snapped.

Micah looked like he was going to barf up his donut.

"My new assignment is to kidnap Petra Stepanov," Waverly repeated, tossing her phone down on the table.

Kate picked up another donut and shoved half of it at Waverly.

"I'm to snatch her Saturday." Four days from now.

"You said you just gather intel," Micah began.

Waverly nodded. "My recent performance has led to some doubt about my loyalties," she said, quoting Brad. "I can redeem myself by stepping up my game and collecting 'the asset.'"

"This is insane," Xavier argued. "What are you supposed to do with her?"

"I'm supposed to keep her in a secure location until I can deliver her personally to Brad."

"Sounds like a freaking trap to me," Kate said, shaking her head.

Waverly shook her head. "It makes perfect sense. He can't

get to her. I'm the only one who's been able to get close enough. So either I fulfill the assignment, and he gets what he wants, or I fail, and I'm out of the way anyway."

"You mean going down in a hail of bullets," Xavier said. He was pacing now. Gone was the calm, calculating man from moments ago. He'd been replaced by a caged animal. Waverly saw it then, the vulnerability he carried because of her. She was his weakness... and he was hers.

"This doesn't change step one," Kate reminded everyone. "We still need to talk to Petra and find out what she knows."

"It's a big jump from breaking and entering to kidnapping," Micah put in.

"Between Xavier and I, I'm sure we can convince Petra to come with us. So we're back to just breaking and entering," Waverly reassured him. Micah didn't look like he was buying it.

"Are you actually considering doing this?" Xavier demanded.

"I just want to talk to her, and I want your help in assessing how safe she is in that house. If I don't take her, Brad will just have someone else do it."

Xavier closed his eyes and took a slow breath. Waverly went to him and put her arms around his waist. "I need your help, X."

He dropped his forehead to hers. "And you'll have it. But I'm not letting you walk into a trap."

"Oh, my God! Xaverly's back!" Kate cheered from the table.

"No, we're not," Waverly warned. "I just... we're just..."

"Yes, we are," Xavier said arrogantly.

"You might want to look away," Kate warned Micah. "The smolder they put off is kind of eye-searing."

Micah grumbled and got up from the table. "One of us has to get to the office to make sure we still have a functioning company until we destroy it by getting involved with this shit," he said, buttoning his jacket. "Get me that information, Sinner, and I'll have Research start on it ASAP."

"Thanks, Micah," she called after him as he headed for the door.

Waverly turned her attention back to Xavier. "Are you going to be okay, X?"

"You'll have to forgive me. I've had a lot happen in the last twelve hours," he said with sarcasm.

"Poor baby. I'll make it up to you," she promised.

"I told you it wasn't a one-time thing," he smirked.

"Just because we're having sex doesn't mean that we're a couple. It doesn't even have to mean that we like each other."

"Oh, we like each other, Angel."

"So listen, sorry to interrupt your foreplay banter, but you're not making anything up right now," Kate said, checking the time on her phone. "We've gotta go, Wave."

Waverly frowned at Kate. "Where?"

"Spa day with Sylvia. She put it in the books with me when you got back. Limo will pick us up here in ten."

"I'll go with you," Xavier said, holding her hips closer.

Waverly smiled up at him. "You can't, X. I need you to do something else for me."

"What?"

She dragged him toward the bedroom.

"Nine minutes," Kate called after her. "Do not get naked! I have a massage booked in an hour."

Waverly stuck her tongue out at her friend and shut the bedroom door behind her. She sat on the bed while Xavier wandered restlessly. He was trying to process the astronomical amount of information he'd been dealt since last night. The woman he'd resumed a smoking hot sexual relationship with was a spy, and he was about to be party to a kidnapping. It was a lot to take in. *What he needed*, Waverly decided, *was a task to keep him busy*.

"Listen, X. I can't cancel on my mother. She's doing this as a checkup to make sure I'm taking care of myself and all that. So I need you to go to my house and get the assignment information for Micah."

"You kept files?"

She nodded. "They're on an offline hard drive in my study."

"We can just wait until after the spa and take them to him together," Xavier argued. She knew what he was doing. He didn't feel safe leaving her alone.

Waverly grabbed his hand on his next pass around the room. "Brad isn't going to try for me. Not when I'm about to get him something he wants. The sooner we can get some answers about what he's actually up to, the sooner we can get out of this mess."

"What happens then, Waverly?" Xavier knelt on the floor in front of her. "What happens when this is all over?"

She shook her head and pushed her fingers through his hair. "I don't know. But I do know that I need you."

He swore quietly. "Tell me where the hard drive is."

She gave him instructions and a key. "We're not back together, by the way," she reminded him.

"Do you mind if I have sex with other women while we're having sex?" Xavier asked casually.

She saw bloody murder red at just the thought of it. "You're not putting that anywhere near another woman," she said, pointing at his crotch.

"I don't plan to ever again, Angel. And you sure as hell aren't sleeping with anyone else because I'll kill them. Which means we are exclusively seeing each other."

"Exclusively having sex with each other."

"Exclusively having sex and living together."

"Until this is over and you go back to New York or D.C. or London or wherever the hell you live." Waverly crossed her arms over her chest.

"After this is over, I'm flying you to Barbados, and we're getting married."

"You drive me insane!"

"Get used to it, baby."

~

THE LIMO PULLED AWAY from the curb and Kate raised the privacy glass. "You'd better call Chelsea, but make it fast because I want to hear about the sex."

"You're vicariously insatiable," Waverly shot back as she dialed Chelsea's number.

"Hey, Wave! You guys were hysterical on the show last night! I've never seen my brother covered in puppies like that before."

Good God. Waverly had forgotten all about the Max Heim show. It felt like it had been a lifetime ago. "Thanks, did your parents get to see it?"

"They did. We video chatted during the broadcast. You realize there's not a soul on the planet who's going to buy that you're not together, right?"

"I'll deal with that when I have to. Right now, I've got some money quests for you."

"Yippy! I love a good money trail."

Waverly filled her in on what she was looking for.

"No problem. I can start digging here on my end and see what I can come up with."

"Also, your brother now knows about my other employment," Waverly warned her.

"I bet that went over well," Chelsea said dryly. "The woman you've been pining over for years just told you she's basically Batman."

"I don't think it's fully hit him yet. But I wanted to let you know that I'm not going to blow your cover. He asked to speak to my hacker friend so he could offer you any of his resources. I told him it wasn't possible."

Chelsea snorted. "I appreciate that. Zave would freak. He'd go apoplectic."

"I don't know. Maybe we underestimated him. He handled my news okay."

"Just wait," Chelsea warned her. "It'll catch up with him, and he'll go ballistic."

Waverly hoped Chelsea was wrong.

She hung up and flopped back against the buttery leather of the limo's seat. "Don't you go all mental hibernation on me," Kate said, throwing aside the glossy magazine she'd been looking at. "Tell me what happened last night."

XAVIER SAT BACK in his desk chair and stared at his screen. It was just another unprecedented surprise to add to the teetering pile of the last twenty-four hours. He'd followed Waverly's instructions and found her hard drive under the false bottom of a locked drawer in an unassuming credenza in her study.

The hidey hole also held a small arsenal including three handguns, six knives in varying sizes, and a jumbo pack of pepper spray all with cozy homes in the molded foam base.

The hard drive had been tucked in next to a package of tiny listening devices and GPS trackers.

He and Micah had handpicked a small team to start sifting

through the assignments detailed in her files. She'd been meticulous with what she recorded. And she'd been damn good, too, he realized as he scrolled through case after case on the offline workstation.

Waverly was a spy. The woman whose safety he'd been obsessed with purposely chose to put herself in harm's way. And for what? Information that other agencies were too lazy or busy or clumsy to collect.

He could see how it had happened. Fresh out of college, Dante Wrede tempted her with the offer of a little excitement. Finally, something she could choose. Given her unpredictable childhood and then the cage of expectations she'd found herself in as a young adult, Waverly had always found small ways to feel that rush of adrenaline. Jumping off yachts, racing motorcycles. But running around playing spy games? Operatives got killed. It could and did happen. It had likely happened to Wrede. And if the man was alive, odds were he'd led Waverly into a trap.

Things had seemed so clear last night. The magnitude of the need that each felt for the other, the moments when they were so close they stopped being two and became one. It didn't happen like that for everyone. They had *it*. And he'd finally had tangible hope that she'd find her way back to him. She had to feel it, too. There was no denying what they ignited in each other.

But when he'd looked around her study and now at her assignment notes, at the evidence of her worlds of screen and spy, he wondered how he would fit in anywhere besides her bed. Could he handle it if she chose to continue her work?

So many questions and so few answers. He roused himself from his reverie. He would find a way to make Waverly his, even if it killed him. For now, he'd settle for putting her two steps ahead in the game.

Micah was making calls to intelligence community buddies trying to unofficially confirm some of the more hush-hush investigations. Cayman, Invictus' ever-fashionable head of research, was plowing through the rest with a handpicked team. With the investigation moving forward, Xavier decided to do a deeper dig through Waverly's case notes.

He was cross-referencing a particularly hairy assignment to clone the phone of a playboy son who looked to be in line to take over his ailing father's Middle Eastern weapons business. He pulled up paparazzi footage of Waverly entering a Miami hotel in South Beach for the son's midnight club party. She looked like the picture perfect party girl. The short kimono dress in jade green covered what he could only assume was a very tiny bikini. Her blonde hair was pulled up into a knot on the top of her head, and despite the dark, she wore oversized sunglasses to protect herself from the photographers' flashes.

He spotted Kate a few paces behind her. Casual in a ball cap and jeans and a t-shirt.

Where she once would have kept her head down and scurried inside, this Waverly smiled and waved, blowing kisses as photographers and fans shouted her name. She strutted inside on ankle-breaking platform wedges. The videographer followed her shapely ass to the door and then panned away as another celebrity arrived.

Xavier did a search for videos from that same night and found one of Waverly leaving the party at two o'clock in the morning. The amateur quality left much to be desired, but the video showed Waverly teetering out of the hotel on the arm of a burly security guard. She was grinning and cracking her gum, and though the crowd outside the hotel was smaller now, she thrust an arm up in a salute. The cuff bracelet on her arm slipped a bit, and Xavier paused the image.

He zoomed in, enhancing the image on screen, and kicked back in his seat. That wasn't Waverly. That was Kate dressed as Waverly. It was a trick they'd pulled back when he met Waverly. He'd almost fallen for it, too. It made sense here. "Waverly" would be long gone before the host's phone disappeared and magically reappeared. No one would suspect a woman who wasn't even there.

Memories of the day he'd caught her leaving the house as Kate, of kissing her that first time, pushed to the surface. It was the first of many times that he'd lost his cool around her. He'd thought being older and wiser and with the distance of so many years between them that her pull on him would have lessened.

But that longing that he'd refused to name had made him just as reckless now with her. He'd taken her in the courtyard of a church. *Sinner and Saint*, he thought wryly. If that wasn't the perfect definition of their relationship, he didn't know what was.

He stared at the image of Kate dressed as Waverly onscreen and smirked. Kate was incapable of walking in heels, and he wondered if that's where the drunken party girl rumors had begun. With Kate stumbling out of clubs in shoes that didn't fit. He'd have to ask them.

For now, satisfied that he could confirm one of her assignments, he moved on to another. This was a joint assignment with Wrede handed down from the SEC. They were to get information that could confirm suspected insider trading by a young tech startup billionaire. This case Xavier recalled from the extensive press coverage. The weasely little dick had taken investors' money out of his company and used it to short sell securities. When the market price tanked, he'd purchased it all back at a huge profit.

According to Waverly's cryptic notes, after attending a

dinner party hosted by the weasel in London, not only were they able to confirm the man's participation in the short sell, but they'd also uncovered a Ponzi scheme. Xavier's eyebrows winged up. While it was impressive work, it was the paparazzi photos of Waverly and Dante leaving their hotel together that he couldn't stop studying.

They looked as though they belonged together. Wealthy, confident, decked out in designer fashions, they'd paused to pose for the cameras outside the hotel before sliding into the back of a white Range Rover. Waverly wore purple, a body-hugging dress that drew the eye and didn't let it go until it had skimmed every perfect curve. Beside her, his hand at her back, Wrede wore a couture crushed velvet dinner jacket in navy with satin lapels. Xavier didn't know if he wanted to punch Wrede more for daring to touch Waverly or wearing that douchey jacket.

Waverly was looking up at him, her expression sweetly serene. Xavier tilted his head and keyed in a command. The image of just her face filled his screen. God, she was beautiful. Flawless skin, eyes that drew a man in just to drown, that thick curtain of hair that made his fingers twitch with the need to dive in. And her lips, painted a dusky rose here.

Lips that were curved subtly. He frowned and looked again. Waverly Sinner had a bombshell smile that could reach into a man's chest and stop his heart. And then she had her "working" smile that never quite lived up to her genuine one. It didn't light up her eyes. That was the smile she was giving Wrede.

Hope bloomed in his heart, and Xavier abandoned his research to pull up every picture of Waverly and Wrede together. Over and over again, he spotted that smile. Never quite the full wattage. Was it his imagination? Or was there really hope that when all was said and done, Waverly loved him more than Dante Wrede? He wanted to call her and demand an answer.

Micah ambled in the door and took a glance at Xavier's screen. "Oh for Christ's sake. I thought you were helping out, not obsessing over Lover Boy," he accused.

Xavier shut off his monitor. "I'm researching."

"What? How to dress like an asshole?"

"What kind of a man goes out in public wearing red skinny jeans?" Xavier complained.

"Apparently your girl's boyfriend does."

"What's your take?" Xavier asked. "Dead or double cross?"

Micah shrugged his linebacker shoulders. "My take is that there's something rotten in Denmark."

"Look who's quoting Shakespeare," Xavier said, giving his friend a sarcastic golf clap.

"Suzanne's latest obsession. Family book club."

"When is she going to get into something you can get behind like home brewed beers or fantasy football?"

"Why would she do that when it's so much fun making me quote Hamlet and knit shitty potholders?"

"The joys of marriage," Xavier empathized.

"You want to talk about last night?" Micah offered.

"Nope," Xavier shook his head. As protective as he was of Waverly, he'd prefer that no one knew the heights their love-making took them to.

"I could draw a few conclusions from that cozy scene this morning."

Xavier shot him a look.

"All I'm saying is I don't want either of you to end up in the same place you were five years ago."

"Micah, she's it for me."

"Is that why you're dragging our company into your personal business?"

Xavier stared at him coolly. "I know you're not happy with where this investigation could take us."

"It's not *our* investigation. We should be passing this off to the feds."

"Micah, I'm asking you as a friend to trust me here. If we turn this over, it's going to sit for a year before they assign anyone to it. We don't have a year. She's in trouble. And this is going to go deeper than a missing actor in skinny jeans."

Micah covered his face with his hands. "I know it is. And your ass is going to owe me big time for this."

"Yeah, yeah."

"Shut that shit down," Micah sighed. "We're going to lunch."

Xavier obliged and followed Micah out the office door.

"Have you seen any of the intel from Sinner's hacker pal?" Micah asked on the way out. "She's good. We should talk to her."

18

The Palisade Spa Resort was a luxurious slice of heaven on earth. Perched on the edge of a golf course, the rambling white adobe buildings clustered around a courtyard with a huge saltwater pool and private cabanas. Inside skylights and walls of glass brought the natural light and expansive canyon views indoors.

Sylvia Sinner greeted them at the front doors. She was decked out in capris and a flowing, crisscross back tank top from her own line of yoga wear and holding a glass of cucumber lemon water.

"I'm so glad you girls could join me today," she said, her face bright with enthusiasm.

Sometimes Sylvia's evolution from a downward spiraling alcoholic to the picture of health and vitality still struck Waverly. It hadn't been that long ago that her mother had passed out in a puddle of her own sickness on a family vacation in the Mediterranean. Xavier had been there for that, Waverly remembered clearly. He'd seen her family at their worst, and he'd stuck... until he hadn't.

"Hi, Mom," Waverly gave Sylvia a kiss. "Thanks so much for organizing this."

"What better way to welcome you home? Now, you and I are starting with a yoga class in fifteen minutes, and Kate has a sixty-minute massage with Arturo."

"Arturo?" Waverly arched an eyebrow.

Kate fanned herself in anticipation.

They went their separate ways, Kate heading off to the languid promise of Arturo's heavenly hands and Waverly and Sylvia peeling off toward the yoga studio. It was a bright, glassed-in yoga studio with wide-planked oak flooring. The room was naturally heated by the spectacular southern California autumn sunshine.

Waverly chose a pink and purple tie-dye mat from the shelf and spread it out in the front row. Her mother hopped onto the elevated stage at the front of the room and smiled prettily as the rest of the mats began to fill up.

Sylvia's recovery had drawn her from the arms of addiction into the exact opposite direction. During her journey, she had become a certified yoga instructor and occasionally, when her schedule allowed it, would lead a class. Venues clamored for her, and any class she taught booked full within half an hour of its announcement.

She winked at Waverly and sent her a little finger wave before calling the class to order.

Waverly spent the next hour flowing through poses and finding soreness in every posture. The twinges in her side from the bullet wound were negligible compared to the marks her night with Xavier had left on her body—and her heart.

There was zero chance of her moving on unscathed. She'd known better yet still couldn't say no.

No one made her feel the way Xavier Saint did. Raw, stripped bare, vulnerable yet still protected, cherished. It was impossible to maintain a safe distance as they worshipped each other's bodies into the night. There wasn't an inch of her he hadn't touched, hadn't loved.

And still she wanted more. It was the pull that he had over her. The more she had him, the more he feasted on her, the more she needed.

He knew nearly all of her secrets. The last obstacle, her last layer of protection, was Dante. What would happen when Xavier found him for her? Because she knew he would. He'd stop at nothing to give her whatever he thought she wanted. But if Dante was found alive, that last secret would be told. There would be nothing left to stand between them.

Not that her "relationship" with Dante had been enough to slow Xavier's seduction.

Waverly rolled onto her back and closed her eyes and followed her mother's instructions into the final pose.

"It is in savasana, or corpse pose, that we finally let go," Sylvia's soothing voice sighed through the studio. "Here we find the spaciousness in our bodies, in our hearts. Here we let our worries, our fears, our need to control gather and die away. Here we welcome everything as it is."

Waverly let everything go on her mat, everything except Xavier. There was no letting go of him.

"How do you feel, darling?" Sylvia asked, joining Waverly on her mat after the classroom emptied out.

Waverly stretched luxuriously. "Like my body melted. You're an excellent teacher, Mom."

Her mother waved away the praise. "You were moving through sun salutation as if you'd finished a marathon yesterday. Is it safe to assume that Xavier got his way?"

Sober Sylvia was eerily perceptive.

"Mom!"

"I know you don't feel comfortable sharing everything

about your love life," Sylvia said patting her leg. "But this is Xavier."

Sylvia knew exactly how gutted Waverly had been over him. In the wake of Sylvia's stay in rehab and Waverly's near-death experience, they had bonded over therapy sessions and late night talks.

"We may have resumed a particular area of our relationship last night," Waverly said vaguely.

"I thought I recognized a satisfied woman," Sylvia said.

"Gross, Mom!"

"Darling, if you don't want people thinking about you and Xavier like that, you're going to have to tone down the sparks that fly between you two. When you came to dinner, I thought you'd start a wildfire."

"He says he loves me."

Sylvia nodded, waited.

"I don't want to love him."

"Because he hurt you before?" Sylvia prompted.

"That and... I don't know how to describe it. He's so all consuming. There's nothing safe and steady there. He makes me *feel* too much. The highs are meteoric, and the lows are devastating. It's not healthy."

Sylvia reached for her hand, squeezed it. "Waverly, did it ever occur to you that seeking the safety of numbness is what's not healthy?"

Waverly sat with that for a moment.

"You can't protect yourself from life, daughter of mine," Sylvia said with a sad smile. "I would love to keep you from feeling any of the hurt that it brings, but that wouldn't be fair. The point isn't to get through life unscathed. It's to throw yourself into it and experience every drop of it. Get scarred, get scared, soar high, love whenever possible."

"Jeez, Mom. Did you chug the yoga holy water today?"

Sylvia laughed. "Okay, darling. I'll leave it alone. I believe you'll find your way. Let's go drag Kate away from Arturo, and we'll treat ourselves to some facials."

On impulse, Waverly pulled her mom in for a hug. "Thank you for being here."

Sylvia smiled sadly. "I wish it wouldn't be so new for us. But I'll take what I can get."

"I think I love him, Mom."

"I know, sweetheart."

Kate poked her head in the studio door.

"Well, you look wrung out," Sylvia commented.

"Arturo and his magical hands. I swear to God that man must have been a baker in a previous life. He had hands like a dough kneader," Kate sighed.

Sylvia laughed. "If you girls will excuse me, I'm going to visit the ladies' room, and then I'll meet you for facials."

As soon as Sylvia breezed out of the studio, Kate's expression went serious. "I have interesting news."

"Dante?" Waverly asked.

Kate shook her head. "No, more Xavier-related."

"What is it?"

"Calla Cabot. She wants a meeting with you."

Waverly's eyes widened. Calla Cabot was the woman Xavier had dated seriously after their breakup. Waverly had spent an embarrassing number of hours poring over pictures of Calla and Xavier together and the woman's social media accounts.

"What does she want?"

Kate shrugged. "She didn't say. Just said she'd be grateful if you could set aside a few minutes for her today."

WAVERLY WALKED into the Polo Lounge at precisely three o'clock. The hunter green walls and plaid carpet gave the large room the requisite equestrian feel. It wasn't too busy yet, so it was easy to spot Calla at a small two top table in the corner.

It was odd seeing someone in the flesh after spending so much time studying them onscreen, Waverly thought. Though it was a common feeling in L.A. where you spent years worshiping actors from afar only to run into them at the next booth in your favorite restaurant.

With Calla it was different. She cut her hair, Waverly noted. Before she'd worn her blonde tresses long with a touch of waves. Now, she rocked a short, sleek pixie cut that angled across her forehead with a sexy sweep. She was tall and slim with a pert nose and a dimple in her chin. Her eyes were gray as storm clouds and currently taking in Waverly.

Waverly patted herself on the back for having the spa give her the full works for hair and makeup and wished she'd worn a more formal outfit. Her suede booties, distressed jeans, and white tunic blouse were far more casual than Calla's simple gray suit.

The woman rose as Waverly approached.

"Thanks for meeting me," Calla said, coming to her feet and extending her hand. "You're even more gorgeous than I was expecting."

"I was just thinking the same thing," Waverly said, grasping her hand in a firm shake.

"Please, sit," Calla said, gesturing at the empty chair.

Waverly sank down keeping her chair angled to the room.

"I'm sure you're curious why I reached out to you," Calla began. She tugged at one of the simple platinum hoops in her ears, and Waverly realized the woman was as nervous as she was.

"I'm guessing it has to do with Xavier," Waverly confessed.

Calla nodded briskly. "I'm sticking my nose in where it doesn't belong. But because I care about Xavier, I told myself it's warranted."

A waiter appeared and took their drink orders, hot tea for Calla and sparkling water for Waverly.

Calla waited until the waiter left before pressing on. "I saw you both on Max Heim's show last night. And I'm not going to pretend to understand the ins and outs of relationships in Hollywood. But I hope you're not playing him against your old boyfriend."

Waverly's eyebrows winged up.

"I really don't want to come across like a hard ass," Calla said, "But I can't stand the idea of Xavier getting hurt because of some publicity game or whatever it is."

"You two were serious, weren't you?" Waverly asked steering the conversation away from Dante.

"I thought we were more serious than he did," Calla said honestly. "I loved him, but he never got over you. So part of me hates your guts, part of me is thrilled that he's getting a second shot with you, and part of me wants to make it very clear that I don't want you taking his feelings lightly."

"You still care about him," Waverly said, stating the obvious fact.

"I think you do, too," Calla said with a wry smile. "I fell hard for him, but I think from the beginning I knew Xavier wasn't going to be it for me. I'd hoped with time he'd be able to move on and open up. But..." she shook her head. "He's a good man."

"He is. He's in a league of his own," Waverly agreed.

The waiter returned with their drinks and disappeared again, sensing this was not a table to hover over.

Calla sighed. "I'm just going to go ahead and put it all out there, okay?"

"Go for it."

"He never talked about you or what happened that night. But he had dreams. He'd say your name in his sleep over and over again."

Waverly grimaced. "That couldn't have felt good."

"It stung," Calla agreed. "He thinks he's not worthy of you because he didn't protect you."

"Oh for fuck's sake," Waverly muttered. "He saved my life. I wouldn't be sitting here today if it weren't for him, and he should know that."

"He's not stupid, but he's—"

"Irresponsibly mule-headed?" Waverly supplied.

Calla laughed. "You do know him well."

"I thought I did at one time," Waverly said, stirring the straw through her drink. "Things didn't end well between us."

"I gathered that. He loves you the way every woman wants to be loved by a man. And I guess, in a way, I owe you for where I am now."

"How's that?" Waverly asked, leaning in.

"Once I realized that Xavier's feelings for you were never going to go away, I realized I wanted to find that with someone. I wanted to find a man who felt that deeply for me." She held up a hand and flashed her rings. "Married a year last month, and we're seven weeks pregnant."

"Wow," was all Waverly could say.

"Yeah. It happened fast, but I recognized it when I felt it. If it hadn't been for you and Xavier, I might have missed out on this 'wow.' Not that I'm naming the baby after either one of you, of course."

It was Waverly's turn to laugh. "I understand."

"It's none of my business what your relationship with Xavier is, but I will say, I hope you give him a chance. A real chance."

Waverly bit her lip. "It's hard for me to trust people. And I've never been a second chance kind of girl."

"Don't turn your back on once-in-a-lifetime," Calla advised. "Especially not when it comes around the second time."

Waverly fingered the chain around her neck while Calla sipped her tea and studied her.

"You know he's it for you, don't you?" she asked. "And you're trying to decide if you can take another kick in the chest if it doesn't work out again or if you should just settle for something safe."

Waverly blinked, and Calla waved her hand between them. "Sorry. I'm a family therapist. Sometimes words of wisdom just spew forth from my mouth."

"Remind me to consult with you about all of my future decisions," Waverly quipped.

"Maybe just start with this one and go from there," Calla suggested. "Xavier's a good man. Anything he does? It's not to hurt. It's to protect. That's how he shows his love."

Her mind flashed to their final scene together all those years ago. The pool house, eerily quiet and empty after he left. Was Calla right? Had he left her because he didn't believe he could protect her anymore?

Waverly sat back in her chair and held her glass with both hands. "I was insanely jealous of you," she confessed.

"Back at you," Calla said raising her cup in a toast.

19

My bed tonight?

*T*he text from Waverly pulled him out from under hours of work. Xavier had tried to isolate his personal connection to her so he could be objective. But it was an impossibility, and in addition to his anxiety about her dangerous second career, he found a growing pride. She was damn good. So good that, under other circumstances, he would have head hunted her to bring her onboard at Invictus.

She had instincts and talent, and she'd committed to her training, and it paid off. Not only was she able to successfully build cases and handle assignments, but her gut had told her that something was off with Target.

And she'd been right.

Cayman and his team noticed a subtle pattern starting nine months ago. While there were still legitimate investigations that could be traced back to the intelligence community, there were also a handful of assignments that had gone unclaimed by any one organization.

Waverly had forwarded him some preliminary information on the money trail that her hacker friend had unearthed. The studio was showing some nice profits under "consulting services" with deposits lining up with several of the confirmed jobs. The mystery hacker had also unearthed an account under a shell company in Luxembourg and traced it back to Tomasso.

Interestingly enough, a deposit in that account lined up with the initial Stepanov assignment Waverly accepted. They'd find more. Xavier was sure of it.

He texted her back, feeling warmth slide through his belly as he reread her invitation.

Your bed, your table, and your tub.

Her response brought a curve to his lips.

Aren't we feeling cocky in our prowess? I'll be home in an hour.

An hour's good. I'll make sure my hands are the only ones you remember on you today.

He turned back to his screen, prepared to start wrapping up, when something caught his eye.

Brat5torm.

Waverly's hacker went by the moniker BratStorm. The anticipation he'd felt moments ago went to ice in his veins. He closed his eyes, opened them again, and refocused on the screen. The tag was still there.

It couldn't be a coincidence.

He'd called his sister Chelsea "bratstorm" since they were both kids, and she'd used every one of her waking moments to annoy him. His sister, the network security administrator. His sister who had hit it off with Waverly when he brought her home all those years ago.

"Fuck." He shoved back from his chair and shut the computer down quickly as if he was afraid the information would leak out of the system and go public. His future wife was a spy, and his sister was a freaking hacker. If he found out that his college professor mother moonlighted as a stripper, he was going to lose it.

He picked up his desk phone.

"Do you have a profile on this BratStorm?" he asked Cayman when he answered the phone.

WAVERLY WAS MORE than ready for him by the time Xavier finally walked in the front door. Not only did she have more money trail news from Chelsea, but her body was revved for him. She'd chosen her lingerie carefully. The black Agent Provocateur bodysuit was cut low at the breast and high on the hip. She topped it with an open flutter sleeve robe and left her hair down and curling past her shoulders.

When he let himself in, Waverly perched on the arm of the couch in the great room. And when he spotted her, he tossed the files he carried onto the table and didn't slow his speed. He knocked her backward over the cushions and followed to cover her body with his.

She lost her breath when he kissed her fiercely. There was anger in the kiss, a roiling, dangerous rage that she didn't understand. But she was lost to anything but his touch. He pulled back, and she could see it in his eyes. He was furious but in control. And with those tight strings of control engaged, he traced his fingers over her neck, across her clavicle, and down the plunging V of the body suit to the coin that hung on the long chain.

She shivered with anticipation when he inched under the lace edge to skim over her full curves. Her nipples pebbled against the gossamer thin material begging for his attention. But he merely circled them with a lazy finger.

He moved his hand lower to skim over the flat of her stomach to the curve of her hip. He followed the black edge down. Restlessly, she shoved her knee out to the side giving him better access. But when he moved his fingertips over the lace that covered her, it was feather light, and she needed more.

Waverly flexed against him, begging for the friction that would set her off. He ignored her body's pleas. Instead he pulled the edges of the body suit's crotch together over her center and tugged. She gasped when the material bunched and slipped between her slick folds.

He ran the top of a finger over her bared flesh. Back and forth, he stroked without making the contact she craved. Light strokes that made her beg for more.

"Please, Xavier."

"Please what, Angel?" his voice was mild, but that fire was still in his eyes.

"Please touch me."

"I am touching you. Can't you feel me?"

"I need more," she whispered.

He was stone hard against her, yet he made no move to free his straining shaft from the confines of his pants. He made no attempt to grind into her with a promise of pleasures to come.

His finger looped beneath the crotch of her bodysuit and tugged it away from her.

"God, yes," she gasped, anticipating what would come

next. But nothing did. When he pulled the material to one side, he didn't plunge his fingers into her. He ignored the slick flesh that pleaded for his touch. Instead, he brought his face to her neck and pressed a soft kiss to her pulse there.

"You know what I love about you, Waverly?"

She shook her head. She didn't want to talk. She wanted to feel.

"I love that you trust me." The bite of his teeth against her throat excited her. But she felt anxiety at his words. He was up to something and was using seduction to get there. Unfortunately, her body didn't seem to care. It shuddered when the crisp heat of his shirt brushed over her hardened nipples.

"You do trust me, don't you?" he murmured. He used his index finger to hook under the lace strap and dragged it from her shoulder. She could see the pulse in his neck as he stared down at her breast. She knew he wanted to dive into her, but something held him back.

With his palm, Xavier made lazy circles around her breast, again too light to do anything but make her demand more. She arched under him, but he was careful to pull his hips up, denying her the contact her body needed. When he lowered his head to her breast, Waverly rejoiced.

Until he pressed a chaste kiss to the upper curve. He circled her nipple with soft kisses, never getting close enough to the straining peak.

"You trust me enough to tell me if you or anyone else I love is in trouble."

Uh-oh. She shivered as his lips skimmed closer. "Of course," she whispered.

"Or if they were doing something they shouldn't be, something illegal."

She had trouble concentrating on his words. Her breast and sex were bared to him, waiting, craving. The throb between her legs continued to grow more powerful. But she knew what he was asking. Chelsea. He'd figured it out somehow, and he was mad enough to kill them both.

She shot her hand down to cup him through his pants and felt a small spot of dampness. He wanted her, damn it. He wanted her so badly he was leaking, but he was happy to torture them both instead.

"What are you talking about?" she asked, playing dumb.

He shoved her hand away and worked his fly open. He freed his cock and fisted the engorged length in his hand. "Is this what you want, Angel? Is this what you're begging for?"

"Yes," she nodded, squeezing her eyes closed so she wouldn't have to see him withholding himself. "What do you want?" She'd give it to him. She knew she would if he pushed her.

He slowly, carefully, nudged the blunt head through her folds stopping between the begging bundle of nerves and her empty entrance.

When she tried to buck against him, he held her hips in a vice-like grip. "Not until you tell me what I need to know," he growled.

She gritted her teeth.

"Do you want me inside you? Do you want me to push into you and fill you?"

"God, yes!"

He did on one violent thrust. Pushing off of the arm of the sofa with his foot, Xavier powered into her.

She screamed out his name. She hadn't been prepared. He hadn't worked to soften her up to accept him, but it didn't matter because they were finally one.

"I'm inside you Waverly, and I won't tolerate you lying to me." He didn't pull out, just stayed sheathed to the hilt inside her taut channel. She flexed her hips, trying to find a millimeter of space inside. But he'd claimed it all, and he wasn't moving.

"It's not my secret to tell," she gasped.

They were both sweating, him with the effort to hold back and Waverly with the fight to chase down her release.

"Look at me," he ordered her on a ragged breath. She opened her eyes and took him in. He was struggling, fighting the primitive urge to mate. But behind that was hurt, and she couldn't stand to see that. The man who made it his life's work to protect those he loved couldn't understand when the women in his life turned their back on that protection. She brought a hand to his face.

"Tell me my sister isn't a hacker, and you didn't willingly drag her into this clusterfuck," Xavier gritted out.

"I'm sorry, X. I'm sorry," Waverly panted. "She didn't want you to worry."

He swore ripely, but her confession was enough to have him giving in.

"Hang on to me, and don't let go." The words snapped out in a command.

The second her hands gripped his shoulders, he let his control snap. He pulled out of her and slammed back in, riding her hard and without finesse. It didn't matter. Waverly was already coming. It was a fast, brutal orgasm that slammed into her and detonated throughout her entire body. He groaned as she came, clutching and bucking against him. She sobbed as he finally gave her what she needed.

Xavier's shout of triumph echoed in her ear as he poured himself into her. His thrusts continued wildly until he was empty, and she was full with everything he had to give.

They lay there, joined, crushed, decimated for long minutes. Heartbeat to heartbeat.

"What was that?" Waverly asked, her voice muffled against Xavier's shoulder.

"Angry sex," he said, lips moving against her tangle of hair.

"Think we'll ever get to make-up sex?" she wondered.

"Maybe in a couple of years."

As she washed out her teacup, Waverly could hear him on the phone and took his low voice as a good sign. The shouting had only taken a few minutes, and knowing Chelsea, she'd given as good as she'd gotten.

They'd showered after he'd tortured her with his body into confessing. And then he'd excused himself to her study to call his sister. Waverly was relieved the secret was out and had confidence that Chelsea would talk him down. But Xavier was still hurt, and that hurt her.

Calla's words from that afternoon echoed in her head.

Xavier showed his love by protecting, defending, and when that was rejected, he felt like it was his love that was being spurned. Waverly felt guilty. It's what she'd been doing since the beginning of their relationship.

As angry as she had been with Xavier, she didn't mean to hurt him like that. He had to have felt rattled, first learning her news last night and then discovering his sister's secret today. There was only so much a man could take before he broke.

Maybe she could at least help ease his stress. After all, she was the cause of most of it.

She poked through the fridge and pantry and fired off a quick text to Marisol and Louie thanking them for taking charge of restocking everything. There was no time to whip up Xavier's favorite pot roast, but a nice pasta dish with fresh garlic bread? That she could handle.

She started the creamy sauce and set the water to boil. With the French bread buttered and dotted with garlic and a light layer of mozzarella, she slid it into the oven.

They'd forgo the dining table and instead keep it cozy and relaxed in front of the fireplace, Waverly decided.

She added a handful of spinach to the sauce for the illusion of health and sliced a dozen cherry tomatoes in half and froze. Was this how she showed her love? By caretaking? By anticipating needs? Had she and Xavier been showing how much they loved each other the entire time?

By the time Xavier wandered out of her office and into the great room, she was plating up pasta and bread into shallow bowls. She pointed at the beer she'd opened for him on the island.

Marisol certainly had faith in Xavier's ability to get into my bed, Waverly thought when she'd spotted the six-pack in the fridge.

After their shower, he'd changed into jeans and a worn t-shirt. His feet were bare, and his hair had dried with a little curl to it. He looked gorgeous and a little sad.

Waverly went to him and wrapped her arms around his waist. He hesitated for just a moment, and it told her he was still at least a little mad.

"Chelsea's flying in in the morning," he told her.

Waverly pulled back and looked up at him. "Is everything okay with you two?"

"No," he sighed. "But it will be."

Waverly handed him his plate and his beer and led the way to the couch by the fireplace.

"What's this?" he asked.

"Thought you could use some dinner," she told him. They settled against the overstuffed cushions and ate in silence for a few minutes.

"What is it with the women I love being hell bent on seeking out danger?" he asked finally.

"Maybe it's because we know you'll always have our backs," Waverly said, twirling her fork into the pasta.

She felt the weight of his gaze on her but focused on her plate. He said nothing, but he did run his hand down from her neck to her back in a light stroke. She could feel it in the air— a shift between them—and wondered if he felt it, too.

That night, long after the dinner dishes were cleared and lights turned off, Waverly showed Xavier what it was like to have someone look out for him for a change. When she knelt between his legs on the wide expanse of her bed, when his hands fisted in the sheets, when he bowed up from the mattress, abs rippling, her name a shout from his throat, only then did he lose the hurt.

20

$\mathcal{W}$averly tagged along with Xavier to meet Chelsea's flight to keep the family bloodshed to a minimum. Xavier had sent the jet for her, and given the sensitive nature of her visit, they were picking her up at Van Nuys Airport, a small airport half an hour northeast of Waverly's Calabasas home.

Burke drove a sleek, new Cadillac Escalade that Waverly assumed had replaced the totaled Tahoe. She sat next to Xavier in the backseat, his arm anchoring her to his side, and she didn't even pretend to fight it. They'd made love again before dawn broke in the hours before they would be consumed with what lay ahead.

And for a time, their world was just the two of them. Waverly found herself reluctant to give that up, yet. They rode in silence, his hand stroking her arm. And when she rested her palm on his thigh, he leaned in to nuzzle her face.

"You might want to be careful," he warned her with a whisper of lips against her ear.

She looked down at his lap at the growing evidence of his interest.

"You're insatiable," she whispered back.

He pulled her hand off his leg and cupped it to his erection. "As if you're not soaking wet right now, Angel."

Her fingers tightened around his shaft through his navy trousers, and he gave a soft grunt of approval. He let her play for a moment before pulling away. When she pouted, he flicked her lower lip.

"We'll be there in a minute. I can't meet my sister with a raging hard-on, now can I?"

"Let's find out," Waverly suggested.

He playfully pushed her across the leather to the far side of the bench seat. "Stay," he ordered.

Minutes later, Burke brought the Escalade to a stop on the tarmac near a sleek private jet. Chelsea Saint emerged from the plane onto the stairs, her thick dark hair blowing in the breeze. Xavier pushed the SUV's rear door open and beckoned for her.

Paparazzi were less aggressive at Van Nuys, but there were still a few photographers hanging around the fence hoping for a glimpse of fame.

Burke loaded her bags in the back while Chelsea propelled herself into the backseat wrapping Xavier and Waverly in a double hug.

She gave Xavier a smacking kiss on the cheek, "I hope you're not super mad at me because I'm so excited that I can show off my mad skills for you now."

Before he could respond, she was giving Waverly a loud kiss. "And I am so glad we get to hang out even though it's work-related."

Waverly and Chelsea chatted the whole way home while Xavier watched them in that brooding way of his.

"What's the matter, Zave?" Chelsea asked.

"Just realizing what a long week this is going to be," he commented dryly. They both smacked him.

~

THEY WERE GOING to have to take Petra early. Waverly couldn't see a way around it.

They'd gathered in one of Invictus' conference rooms in the back away from the bustle of the office. The privacy glass was frosted to keep any unwanted eyes from prying. She looked around the table. Xavier, impeccable and urbane in a navy suit with subtle pinstripes, sat on her left at the head of the table. They talked business, but every once in a while, his gleaming oxford nudged her calf. Micah, in shirt sleeves and a frown, sat opposite him.

Kate sat next to Waverly in yoga pants and a Zoolander sweatshirt. Across from them was Chelsea in full-on work mode with her hair pinned up and wearing sexy, nerdy glasses.

As Xavier walked those gathered through what his team had discovered so far, Waverly realized this went a lot deeper than just Petra and Dante. Three of her last four assignments appeared to have no legitimate government oversight. Which meant that Brad had gone fishing in the private sector. Xavier's research team had been able to pull enough intel together to speculate that the CEO's phone she'd cloned in Miami had given a brokerage firm in D.C. a head's up on a top secret merger. The early stock acquisition had earned the firm—and Brad—a huge profit.

Then there was the twenty-year-old playboy that Waverly had teased on the dance floor of a club in L.A. His whispered brags about his congressman father's ties to the New York mafia had corresponded to the congressman suddenly announcing he wouldn't seek re-election for a fifth time and was throwing his support behind a young and hungry female candidate. A very generous deposit had been made into Brad's Luxembourg account from said hungry female candidate.

Chelsea—in sterling trousers, a white ruffled blouse, and red Jimmy Choos—walked them through the finer details of the money trail.

"This is just what I've been able to glean from the Luxembourg account," she concluded. "There will be more, most likely in other tax havens. But I think there's more than enough here to turn this over to the authorities and have them start to comb through this mess."

Xavier and Micah shared a glance. Micah cleared his throat before responding. "And therein lies the problem. We're considering the possibility that Tomasso has someone or multiple someones inside the government clearing the way for him to pick up odd jobs."

Waverly frowned at Kate. This was news to both of them.

Xavier's foot touched her again under the table. "Our research team occasionally gets sucked down the rabbit hole of information," he began. "Cayman uncovered a connection between Tomasso and a member of the Special Collection Service."

"Quick question," Kate said, raising her pen like a reporter at a press conference. "What the hell's the Special Collection Service?"

Xavier winked at her. "The SCS is a joint program between the CIA and the NSA. Their job is to eavesdrop in places that are complicated to eavesdrop in."

Micah took a spin at the wheel. "It turns out that our pal Brad went to college with one of the suits at the SCS. On a basic review of Tomasso's social media accounts, Research turned up several photos of the two of them but nothing recent. We haven't connected the financial dots, but it's an area of concern."

"So what you're saying is, we can't dump this information on just anyone because we don't know who else is in bed with him," Waverly filled in.

"Yep." Micah looked even unhappier than he had when she'd told him she was kidnapping Petra.

"What leads you to believe that someone else is involved?" Kate piped up again.

"After every deposit into his Luxembourg account, he transfers thirty percent of that fee out of the account," Chelsea answered. "I haven't been able to track where that percentage is going. Yet."

Waverly took a peek at Xavier to see how he was handling his sister in full-on hacker mode. His face was impassive, but she caught a glimmer in his eye. Familial pride. She knew he was still hurt that Chelsea hadn't trusted him with her secret, but they would get past it. And judging by how intently he was listening, he'd poach her for Invictus within the year. Waverly rubbed her toes up his shin, and those brown eyes warmed when his gaze moved to her face.

Crap. She was sunk. She was staring at the man who was putting every resource he had at her disposal to get her out of a disaster. A man who loved her enough that he was trying to track down the man he thought was her boyfriend. A man who, hurt by his sister's deception, was still big enough that he could be proud of her skill.

She loved him. She'd never stopped loving him. And wasn't that hard to swallow? She'd deal with it later, she decided. Just because she loved him didn't mean she could trust him. He'd run before. He'd stuck through the hard times and then walked out of her life, leaving her to pick up the pieces of her shattered heart and hopes. And it could happen again.

"So this buddy who's collecting on these jobs could be Frat Boy, or it could be someone else," Kate clarified. Her comment brought Waverly back to the present and the problem at hand.

"Exactly," Micah nodded. "And if we take this information to the wrong person at the wrong organization, we could be looking at a lot of trouble."

"There's one more problem to consider," Waverly spoke up. All eyes turned to her. "I'm supposed to take Petra on Saturday. Brad said most of the staff have the day off, and she's planning to be home until going to a restaurant opening that night. Which means he's got someone on the inside feeding him information."

She saw Xavier's wheels turning.

"So we've got a source on the inside to worry about, and I think the deadline is important."

Micah blew out a breath and eyed Xavier.

"Either they're planning on taking her from you as soon as you get her out, or we're walking into a trap," Xavier said.

"I'm the squeaky wheel at Target right now. They need me to get Petra, but once I'm no longer useful, they're going to want to shut me up and sooner rather than later. We need to take her early."

"DON'T LOOK at it as kidnapping," Xavier advised Micah. "Look at it as us illegally saving someone's life." The girls had cleared out of the conference room to begin reviewing security footage from the Stepanov estate, leaving Xavier the unenviable job of convincing Micah that this was the only play that would work.

"We don't know that she's in danger!" Micah's voice was on the low side of yelling. He paced in pissed off laps around the oval conference table, pausing every once in a while to kick one of the wheeled chairs out of his way.

"Someone wants her kidnapped—that's textbook danger. She's a client. We owe it to her to—"

"To what? Be the ones to kidnap her? Saint, this isn't what we do. And if we break this rule now, what's to stop us from doing it again?"

"I understand where you're coming from, Micah, but I don't see a choice. Either we do it this way, or you're sending Waverly and me in there without support. Those guards aren't just hired muscle, and they don't trust Waverly. They're not going to detain her if they see her jumping a wall. They're going to shoot first and ask questions later."

"Listen, Saint, next time I bust on you about settling down and starting a family, make sure you do it with some PTA-attending cookie baker who has a regular job."

"So noted."

"I wouldn't put this company on the line for anyone else but you," Micah sighed, sinking down onto one of the leather seats."

"I appreciate that, and if this goes south, I'll take full responsibility for it. I'll sign everything over to you and walk away with the heat."

"Let's make fucking sure it doesn't come to that," Micah said, swiping a hand over his forehead.

If it meant that Waverly would be safe, he'd walk away from everything he'd spent the last seven years building. And he wouldn't regret a damn thing.

Xavier picked up the pen Waverly had left behind and tapped it on the table. He'd won the battle, but there was a war to fight yet.

WHILE XAVIER WORKED on convincing Micah that snagging Petra was the best course of action, Waverly commandeered Xavier's office. She focused on reviewing the security footage Micah had pulled from previous Thursdays. Kate poked her head out to talk to Xavier's scary efficient assistant, Roz, about what to order for lunch. Chelsea worked furiously on her laptop doing God knows what.

When Waverly spotted the pattern at the front gate, she backed up and reviewed eight weeks of footage. Same time every Thursday like clockwork. And it would be better than scrambling over a ten-foot wall and ending up with a gun in her face.

"Sandwiches are on their way," Kate announced when she came back in. Her eyes narrowed. "You have the 'got something' look on your face."

"Oh, boy, do I."

21

*L*averne's Organic Produce was an exclusive delivery service that brought the bounty of a farmer's market to the door of those who would prefer to purchase non-genetically modified broccoli and chemical-free avocados in their own kitchen.

Every Thursday at nine a.m., Laverne's biodiesel-powered van stopped at the gate of the Stepanov estate before being ushered up the drive. And every Thursday between 9:25 and 9:30, the van exited the gate.

Laverne herself had driven a hard bargain. Waverly spun the tale of researching a role about an organic farmer. The cost of a ride along in her produce van was the promise of a special appearance by "Xaverly" at her new juice bar when it opened the following month.

It would be worth it, Waverly thought from her hiding spot under a crate of yellow wax beans and behind a stack of Bok Choy boxes.

Xavier, who would be less recognizable to Petra's guards, was sitting up front with Laverne's driver. He was a quiet man by the name of Tony who asked no questions and wore a thin mustache under his nose. Waverly couldn't help but wonder if the man bought their expanded role research story—she was now doing a movie about an organic farmer spy who needed to break into a house—or he just didn't care. Tony's instructions were clear. Get them inside the gates, and if they returned in time, get them back out again. Either way, there was a hefty bonus in his future.

"Doing okay back there?" Xavier asked from the supremely comfortable passenger seat.

She was hunched over in a literal vegetable prison. She glanced at the basket of fruit on her right. "Just peachy."

"Ha."

"You're five minutes out," Micah's voice rumbled in her ear through the earpiece she'd been fitted with.

"Copy that," Waverly whispered into her shoulder mic.

"Try not to fuck this up, guys," Micah warned.

"Yeah, yeah, yeah," Waverly grumbled.

She closed her eyes and steadied her breathing. This had to work. Right now, Petra was the only key they had. She brought up the interior of Petra's house in her mind's eye. She'd been there a handful of times, and Invictus had stored the blueprints from their security system installation.

From the kitchen, it would be a fast jog down the back hallway to get to the rear stairs. With the all clear from Micah, who was monitoring the system's camera footage, they'd take the stairs to the second floor, fourth door on the left to Petra's suite. Petra was not a morning person. In fact, she considered anything before 11 a.m. to be an inhuman torture so Waverly was confident they'd find her sleeping. They'd have a few minutes to talk her into leaving with them, packing whatever she needed, and then smuggling her back downstairs to the waiting van. If all went according to plan.

She felt the van slow and then come to a stop. She heard

Tony roll down his window to greet the guard.

"Hey, Tony, how is it going?" the guard asked with a thick Russian accent.

"Can't complain," Tony replied. "I got a whole bushel of them Brussels sprouts Ms. Stepanov loves."

The guard laughed. "Then I guess I won't be seeing you again, my friend."

"Maybe I'll leave them in the back of the van then."

"That would be wise. I see you have company today."

Waverly's heart tripped. Her fingers brushed the reassuring metal of the .38 she wore at her back.

"This is Gus. I'm training him," Tony lied blithely.

There was a silence that stretched on for what felt like hours, and Waverly was sure they were going to have to shoot their way out.

"Don't let Tony take the Brussels sprouts inside, Gus," the guard warned. And then they were moving.

Waverly let out the breath she'd been holding.

"Coming up to the top of the drive. Looks like we've got a guard in the backyard doing a patrol," Xavier said quietly from the front.

"I see him," Micah announced in Waverly's ear. "If you can park angled toward the back door, you can cut off his view."

"Park angled toward the door," Xavier relayed to Tony, and the van came to another stop.

"Show time," Waverly muttered into her mic.

"Break a leg. But make sure it's not one of yours," Xavier said lightly. "Prepare to cut the feed on my mark," he told Micah.

Waverly heard the driver's side door open and close as Tony got out.

"Cut the feed," Xavier announced.

"Cutting," Micah responded.

"Angel, we're giving Tony twenty seconds to get the chef occupied, and then we're moving," Xavier said quietly.

"Ready when you are."

She felt the familiar adrenaline of an operation build in her as she counted down from twenty. She was already crawling out of her hiding spot when Xavier gave the okay. He slid smoothly out of the van and opened the sliding door. He settled his hands on her waist and lifted her down.

She teased the line between his eyes with a finger. "Don't worry. This is going to work."

"It better because otherwise we're going to get shot or arrested in pajamas," he said looking down at the black sweatpants he wore.

"Trust me, it's all part of the plan," she said, hefting a box of raspberries at him. She took the crate labeled "Stepanov" from the floor behind the front seat. "Let's roll."

The kitchen was a modern monstrosity of chrome and black. It was as if the architect had wanted to smother the soul of the room. And he'd accomplished just that.

They ditched their produce on the stainless steel counter next to the industrial side-by-side fridge and freezer, and while Tony had the chef cornered in the walk-in-pantry, Waverly silently led the way down the back hallway.

"I've got you in the hallway." Micah's voice was calm. "You've got company coming down the stairs. Big guy, black suit. You'll want to duck into that door on your left."

Xavier was already opening the door and dragging her inside.

"A fucking walk-in linen closet?" Xavier hissed.

Waverly elbowed him as the door clicked shut and the light automatically turned off. "Shh!"

She turned in the dark to shove her hands through Xavier's thick hair. It would take security a bit longer to process two sleepy-eyed guests yawning through the halls as a threat than it would if they showed up with guns. They'd both worn clothes that could pass for pajamas, just in case.

They went silent and still as heavy footsteps approached. Waverly felt his hand cup her breast and squeeze when the footsteps moved past the door. In the dark, she reached out and cupped him through his sweat pants.

"You two are breathing funny, everything okay?" Micah asked.

She felt Xavier shake with silent laughter.

"Clear?" she whispered.

"Clear."

They moved soundlessly as a unit down the hallway to the foot of the back stairs. Xavier let her lead but was never more than a foot behind her. She felt his presence like a bulletproof vest. The stairway was narrow and dark. It was designed to spare the homeowners from experiencing the unsightly spectacle of staff coming and going on the home's main staircase.

"You're clear to the second floor," Micah said.

They climbed the carpeted stairs quietly. Even with Micah monitoring the live feed of the security cameras, her senses felt sharp, ready to identify and respond to any threats. She felt rather than heard Xavier moving behind her. They reached the top of the stairs and squeezed close to the wall so they wouldn't be seen from below.

"You're almost there," Micah said. "Fourth door on your left."

They were closing in fast. She could hear her heartbeat as it ticked up just a notch. The doors to the suite were a glossy white with gold scroll levers for handles. Waverly was just reaching for the left one when Micah blasted in her ear.

"Ah, shit. Company downstairs."

She opened the door swiftly and shoved Xavier inside. She

could feel eyes on her and purposely gave a lazy stretch. "Good morning," she yawned as she wandered through the door closing it behind her.

"Nice acting, Sinner," Micah said. "Guard is still looking at the door thinking."

It wouldn't buy them much, if any, time, but she was hoping that Petra's security team suffered the same breakdowns in communication every other organization did.

It was then that Waverly noticed that Xavier had his gun drawn and pointed at the bed.

Petra was sitting up looking terrified, a sparkly eye mask shoved up on top of her head. Beside her stood a very familiar and very naked figure clutching a sheet to his waist.

"Dante?" Waverly hissed. She crossed the room at lightning speed and locked him into a hug. "You asshole, I thought you were dead!"

Dante returned the fierce hug. "Where the fuck have you been?" he whispered back, his British accent lending a delightful weight to the words.

"Me? You're the one who went missing!" she said, shoving him back a step. And then it hit her. Xavier had his gun on Dante, and she knew why.

She took a step back and then another and pulled her own weapon. She made sure she stopped directly between Xavier and Dante. If someone was shooting her partner, it was going to be her. "Someone is trying to kidnap Petra, and they're being fed information from inside the house. You wouldn't know anything about that, would you Dante?"

"Oh for Christ's sake, do I look like a mole?" he demanded, raising his arms.

"Do us all a favor and keep the sheet on," Xavier said mildly.

"So you two really are back together?" Dante said, looking

over Waverly's shoulder at Xavier. "Are you sure that's wise?"

"Shut the fuck up, Dante" she and Xavier said together.

Petra whimpered, and Waverly realized how this must look to her. "At the club, you were worried that I knew you and Dante were... together, weren't you?"

Petra gave a nod, tears shimmering in her blue eyes. "I feel so guilty. I knew you two were together, but then it just kind of happened and—"

"Let's get back to the kidnapping, shall we?" Xavier suggested with murder in his tone.

"What the hell's going on in there? Grab the girl and move," Micah ordered through the earpiece.

Waverly nudged her gun in Dante's direction. "Swear to me that you had nothing to do with the shootout at Tahoe. And nothing to do with Brad trying to kidnap Petra."

"Jesus, I swear!" He held one hand in the air and one at the sheet around his waist. "Well, I mean I returned fire. But I didn't start it."

"Good enough for now," Waverly said. "Both of you go put some clothes on. You're leaving with us."

"Oh, so you're the kidnapper? Did Brad give you a raise?" Dante teased.

Xavier had advanced into the room and was at Waverly's back. "Put on some goddamn pants, or you'll regret it." He lowered the gun to line up with a particularly beloved part of Dante's anatomy.

"I'm going. I'm going. Come on, Petra love. It's going to be all right." He put an arm around the shivering girl. Waverly rolled her eyes and gestured toward the dressing room.

"Incoming," Micah said quietly.

Xavier moved back to the door and flipped the lock.

"I don't know if we should go with them, Dante," Petra said in a wavering voice.

Dante tenderly cupped her face in his hands. "This is going to be an adventure that we'll tell our children about someday. Trust me, darling. Okay?"

A short sharp rap at the door had them all freezing.

"Ms. Stepanov, is everything all right?"

Xavier moved to the side of the door, gun leveled and ready.

"Just tell him everything's fine," Dante whispered in Petra's ear.

She hesitated, and Waverly thought she was going to have to answer for her.

"Everything's fine. Anatoli, can you check on breakfast for me?" Petra said unconvincingly.

There was a pause on the other side of the door this time. "Of course, Ms. Stepanov."

"He's moving," Micah reported.

"Good girl," Dante purred to Petra.

Waverly breathed a sigh of relief. "Back to the putting on clothes thing," she ushered them into the closet.

When they disappeared, Waverly could feel Xavier's gaze boring into her.

"You and I are going to have a long talk," he said, in that calm, cool voice. She winced at the threat behind it.

"Did you guys really find Dante?" Micah asked.

A minute later, Dante and Petra reappeared fully clothed. Petra's idea of a kidnapping appropriate outfit was leggings with leather patches, knee-high boots that looked like she'd slaughtered Chewbacca, and creamy mock neck sweater with the shoulders cut out. Dante was wearing skinny jeans and a checkered button down under a thick knit cardigan. He was carrying a pink Louis Vuitton overnight bag. Something in the bag barked.

"Why are you guys wearing pajamas?" Dante asked.

22

They had four minutes left in their timetable to get everyone downstairs and out the door if they were catching a ride with Tony. With one more body than expected, it was going to be damned crowded in the back of the produce van.

This time, Xavier claimed the lead and signaled Waverly to bring up the rear. He hated to let her get that far from him, but right now, she was the only one out of their motley group that he even remotely trusted. And after what he'd witnessed upstairs, he wasn't feeling too generous with that trust. Xavier was thankful that his training allowed him to compartmentalize. Because seeing Waverly completely unfazed by finding her "lover" in bed with another woman meant she'd been lying to him the entire time. Again.

He wasn't going to think about that now. No, he was going to save that for when they were alone... and then possibly shoot her.

But first they had to get out of the house. With the all clear from Micah, he led the way down the back stairs.

"I'm missing one," Micah muttered in his ear. "I'm only

counting six. There should be seven guys lurking around the house and grounds."

Shit.

Xavier's hand flexed restlessly around his gun. They made it to the first floor without incident. But with the way Petra clomped down the stairs like a prized Clydesdale, he'd be amazed if they made it out of the house. The girl had no stealth. She kept whispering questions to Wrede, who only half-heartedly tried to shut her up.

"Shush, darling."

Xavier hoped he'd get the chance to shoot him in his British ass.

"Stop!" a thickly accented voice rang out.

"Oh, fuck. Found him," Micah muttered.

Xavier spun around, pulling Dante and Petra behind him. A short, beefy guard in a black-on-black suit had his gun trained on Waverly.

He didn't know what surprised him more: when Waverly held her hands up toward the ceiling or when she began speaking in rapid-fire Russian. The Russian meatball nodded and frowned.

Xavier caught the name Anatoli and the word leg. And that was it.

Waverly looked at him. "Linen closet," she said. "Dante and Petra first, then you."

He wanted to argue, but there was no time. He wrenched open the closet door and gestured Dante and Petra in. He followed, keeping them at his back, his gun trained on the guard.

Waverly backed in in front of him and then the guard entered. When he shut the door, the man flicked the switch on the wall and the light stayed on this time.

She began spouting off again in fluent Russian. It seemed like a question and answer session to Xavier.

Then Anatoli was asking Petra something and she was nodding her head violently through tears as she gripped Dante's arm. Wrede, for his part, kept Petra at his back against the wall.

"A minute and half. Where are you guys?" Micah demanded.

Waverly was speaking again, drawing Anatoli's attention.

He swallowed hard, his Adam's apple working in that tree trunk neck.

"What's happening, Angel?" Xavier asked.

"Dah." Anatoli said with a brisk nod.

Waverly tucked her gun back into her waistband and patted the guard on the shoulder. "Anatoli's coming with us to help ensure Petra's safety."

"We're not all fitting in the fucking van."

"You have to leave in the van. If the guard at the gate catches on that you didn't leave with Tony, we're in trouble. The rest of us are leaving with Anatoli in one of Petra's cars."

"No." He wasn't leaving her alone on this. Not with an agent he didn't trust and a private security guy who would probably shoot her in the driveway.

"X," she cupped a hand to his face. "Please trust me. We'll meet up down the road and switch cars."

"I've got her back, Saint," Dante promised.

"I do as well," Anatoli agreed in English.

"Uh, me, too," Petra piped up. Her pink bag gave a tiny yip.

Only Waverly Sinner could garner the support of the woman she was kidnapping and the man paid to protect her.

"If anything happens to her, I'll hunt down each and every one of you," Xavier swore. "Micah, we're going to need a ride.

"On it."

Xavier had the impossible job of sneaking back out to the driveway without getting caught by security or the chef. Meanwhile the F-Team got to swagger out the front door with Anatoli leading the way to the garage.

He listened as Micah detailed the position of the chef and then moved like a shadow through the kitchen when the man wandered out to the butler's pantry for a nip at the cooking sherry.

"Go!" Micah hissed in his ear. Xavier hustled through the kitchen at full speed and didn't stop until he was sliding onto the seat of Tony's van.

"Let's get the hell out of here, Tony," Xavier said. He couldn't relax. His entire body was tuned. He was just waiting for the sounds of gunfire to come from the front of the house.

If anything happened to Waverly, God… what had he been thinking? How could he have let her talk him into this?

Tony cruised down to the foot of the driveway where the chatty guard waved. "You two have a good day," the man said with a friendly nod.

"You do the same," Tony offered through the window and cruised on through the opening gate.

"Pull over up here," Xavier ordered, pointing up the block. "Waverly? Do you copy?"

"Ouch, get off my boob!" Her voice crackled in his ear.

"What the fuck is going on?"

"Hang on," she whispered.

Several seconds of silence passed.

"The suspense is killing me," Micah said.

Xavier saw a dark blue Range Rover pull out of the Stepanov estate and then Waverly's voice was like a miracle in his ear. "Sorry, Dante and I are laying in the back. It's—" He heard muttering and then something like a slap and an "ouch." "Cramped."

"Tell Wrede if he lays a finger or anything else on you, I'm going to break it."

"Believe me, I will," Waverly laughed.

Xavier forced his fingers to relax on his knee. She was in the SUV behind him. She was safe and laughing. He felt better just having that confirmation.

"I got new wheels for you with a driver in the lot at the Beverly Center," Micah told them.

"See you in ten," Xavier said. "Nice work, Angel."

"Back at you, X."

THEY REGROUPED in the shopping center's lot and piled into an Invictus SUV. Xavier slid into the back with Waverly and kept her anchored to his side. She smiled up at him, but he wasn't ready for that yet. She was safe, and he was mad. Warring feelings had him glaring at her while he tucked her head under his chin.

"You're the only operative I know who goes after a girl and comes back with the girl, a movie star, and a Russian bodyguard," Micah said as he watched them all file out of the elevator into the offices.

Waverly grinned at him and hurried ahead to bump shoulders with Dante. Xavier didn't like the camaraderie. There was no reason to trust the guy. He'd been lounging around in Petra's bed since the shoot-out and hadn't once bothered to reach out to Waverly. *He was going to get some answers, and if he didn't like them, Wrede would pay.*

Xavier saw the questioning looks from staff. No one would dare ask any questions. But the sight of Xavier strolling through the office in sweatpants and a t-shirt with Waverly Sinner and the man she allegedly loved in tow was bound to raise a few eyebrows.

He veered off and swung by his admin's desk. Roz was the guardian of his time and office, and even though he'd worked mainly from the New York and D.C. offices in recent years, they still spoke every day.

She eyed him from under her silvery sweep of hair. "Is this a new casual Thursday look?" she asked in her smoky voice.

"Hilarious, Roz. I need you to sit on a Russian heiress and her burly bodyguard in Micah's office. Maybe order up brunch for everyone because this is going to be a long day. Reschedule any meetings Micah and I had until next week. And see if you can find me some work appropriate attire somewhere around here."

"Is that all?"

"One more thing. I'm going to need a place big enough to hold this disaster of a team. Somewhere secluded and secure with no ties to any of us. We need it stocked." That was Invictus code for necessities include food, clothing, and weapons.

"Consider it done," Roz said without batting an eye.

"You're a treasure, Roz."

"You just be sure to remember that when it's time for my lovely holiday bonus," she suggested.

They put Petra and Anatoli in Micah's office with Roz as the guard. She'd watch them like a hawk as she ordered up a brunch fit for a Russian heiress. Once the guests were settled, Xavier led the rest of them to the conference room and activated the privacy glass. He pulled a chair out for Waverly and claimed the spot next to her.

"Wrede, we're starting with you," he announced. "What

the hell happened in Tahoe, and why haven't you been in touch?"

If Dante was pissed off by Xavier's attitude, the affable bastard didn't show it. "Right. So, Waves and I both thought the assignment was a bit wonky," he said, launching into his explanation as if he'd been dying to tell it. "She was going to get Petra out of the house so I could do a little snooping around. At this point, our orders were to stay close to Petra. So when Waves and Pet headed outside, I reported in to Brad and let him know that we were in."

He must have caught the narrowing of Xavier's eyes because he quickly explained. "Some of Brad's assignments had strange caveats. I took the request to report in as one such caveat."

Waverly leaned forward and poured a round of waters into the glasses that waited at the center of the table.

"I let myself in to Grigory's study," Dante continued.

"It was open?" Micah interrupted with the question.

Dante flashed him a grin. "I'm a bit of a locked door enthusiast."

"So you broke into the study," Xavier pressed, his annoyance palpable, but Dante was unfazed.

"Yes, well I wasn't even in there for five minutes when a particularly canny security guy found me. He called two friends—by the way, Waves, that Wild West butler was not a butler—and they had me pinned down. I was right in the middle of convincing them I'd taken a wrong turn when the front door was breached."

Xavier's gaze slid to Waverly's face. She was listening raptly, taking in the answers she'd been so desperate for.

"How many?" she asked.

"Five with semi-autos all wearing ski masks, which at the time, I thought was ironic given that we were in Tahoe. They were on a mission. Two of them pinned me and Stepanov's security down in the loft from the foyer." Two more started a sweep, and the other disappeared through the back of the house.

"That's probably the one who shot you," Xavier said mildly to Waverly.

Dante came out of his chair. "You were shot?"

"Your girlfriend there took a gut shot while hustling the bodyguards and Petra to safety. And then she climbed up the mountain looking for your ass, but you'd already abandoned her," Xavier snapped, rising also.

"Abandoned her?"

That's when the yelling and insult hurling started. It felt good to shout at Wrede, like a release valve had just been opened, at least until Waverly slapped the table with a palm of her hand.

"Enough! Micah, please keep Dante company while I talk to Xavier." She latched onto his arm and dragged him from the room. She didn't say a word until she'd pulled him into his office and slammed the door behind them.

She stood with her back to the door, her arms crossed in front of her. The fine line of her jaw was clenched tight. "I need you to chill the hell out in there, X," she told him.

"Excuse me? Why should I give you anything that you need?" he demanded, still looking for that fight. "You've done nothing but lie to me this entire time."

"And I had my reasons for that, which I will get to later with you. For now, you are personally standing in the way of me getting the answers I need."

"Yeah, well right back at you, baby."

That shut her up for a second. "Dante and I are not together. Let's leave it at that for now," she said.

"This is my life we're talking about right now. We are not

leaving it at that!" Xavier railed. "You've strung me along, lied to me, used me. I put my company, my reputation, on the line for you. For what? Why the fuck am I doing any of this?" He shoved his hands through his hair.

She crossed to him, got into his space, and just her physical presence reminded him of why he was doing it. He loved her so fiercely he was willing to sacrifice it all. What a joke it was, to have worked his whole life to build something he could be proud of only to ante it up for Waverly in a game of Jenga. If she slid the wrong piece loose, the whole thing would crumble and he wasn't sure she'd care.

"You're letting your personal feelings get in the way of the job, Xavier. I need you to pull it back and help me with this."

"This *is* personal. Everything with you is personal, and there's no way to draw that line. It was personal five years ago, and it's still fucking personal. Don't jerk me around, Waverly. You don't get to use me anymore."

He didn't know how it happened, whether she'd jumped or he'd grabbed, but she was in his arms. Her arms were wrapping around his waist and hanging on for dear life and he was crushing her to his chest.

"You make me feel so angry and so possessive I can't see straight," he murmured into her tangle of hair.

"You make me so everything, X."

It hit him then. They'd found Dante, yet Waverly was in his arms. The fear he'd had since the beginning felt looser, less strangling. She wasn't holding Dante, breathing him in and hanging on. Maybe she and Dante weren't together. He'd figured that out the second she didn't shoot him in Petra's bed. But he'd still had that worry, that jealousy over their history, over her forgiveness of Dante's abandonment.

He needed one more reassurance before he was willing to let her go, before he'd walk back into the conference room and not punch Dante in his smug, British face. He fisted his hand in her hair, pulling her head back. Those gorgeous gray-green eyes weren't looking for answers now. They were looking at him, only him.

His mouth was hard when it lowered to hers, unforgiving and controlling. But she knew that's what she was getting with him. With a hand on her jaw, he forced her mouth to open for him even though he knew she'd give it to him willingly. He was reminding her who she belonged with, who she belonged to. No matter what her history was, Xavier was her present, her future.

He thrust his tongue into her mouth, demanding her response. She sighed into the kiss, their first kiss with no one else between them. There was no nebulous threat of Dante coming back. He was back and she was still here returning heat for heat, need for need. Xavier backed her up until they hit the wall. Her teeth sank into his lower lip, and he felt the growl rumble in his chest.

No matter what, they had this, they had each other.

"Hey, Zave, do you want me to—Ah! My eyes!" Chelsea covered her face with her hands.

Xavier and Waverly sprang apart.

"Get out!" he ordered, turning his back on them both to spare his sister the sight of his hard-on through sweatpants.

"I'm going to go disinfect my eyes," Chelsea said, practically sprinting from the room. She shut the door behind her.

"Uhh..."

"Don't say anything or do anything or even breathe too loudly," Xavier said, his back to Waverly. "Otherwise I'm going to bend you over that couch and the entire office is going to hear it when I make you come."

He heard her exhalation come out in a whoosh. He took

several deep breaths himself. "Do you see what you do to me, Angel? Do you see how crazy you make me?"

"Why do you want me, Xavier?"

"Why?" He turned to face her.

"People have wanted me before. They wanted to tagalong into fame, to take advantage of my connections, to get a front row seat for whatever surrounds me. Tell me why you want me."

He risked his blood flow and put his hands on her again. He gripped her upper arms. "You don't get it, Angel. I don't just want you. I love you. You're under my skin and you're in my veins. I've been looking for you my entire life. I don't give a shit about the fame and the drama. It's you. You're the girl who talks me into motorcycle rides up the coast and beach picnics. You're the girl who leads me on a chase and then completely surrenders to me. You're the girl who takes me inside her and makes me feel like I am finally the man I was meant to be."

Tears glistened in her eyes. "Damn it, X!"

He cupped her jaw. "I'm in love with you, Waverly, and I'm not going to let you fuck this up for us."

She threw herself into him, held on tight. "Promise me you won't let me."

"I swear to you, Angel."

She took a shuddery breath. "Okay. We'll talk later."

"You're damn right we will. And no distracting me with sex."

"Maybe we should have it out on the phone, then," she joked.

"Funny." When she moved for the door, he held her by the wrist. "Waverly, I haven't heard anything yet that means Wrede wasn't involved."

She looked at him, her eyes still damp. "I haven't either."

23

They returned to the conference room where Micah and Dante were discussing the Lakers' chance at the playoffs.

"Where were we?" Xavier asked, holding Waverly's chair for her.

"You were accusing me of abandoning my partner in a firefight."

"As good a place as any to start," Xavier snapped.

"Okay, how about I ask some questions?" Waverly suggested. "The five guns who showed up, did you get a nationality on them? Could they have been back-up for Stepanov's men in the house?"

Dante shook his head. "They were American. Except for one Eurotrashy accent. They didn't say a whole lot and took a great deal of pleasure shooting the place up."

"Amateurs?" Waverly asked.

"More like overzealous new recruits."

"So they fired on you from below. What happened next?"

"I had my piece on me, and I returned fire."

"That must have been terrifying for everyone," Waverly

said dryly. "Dante here is a terrible shot," she explained to Xavier and Micah.

"Let's just say it's not where my expertise lies," Dante shot back. "Anyway, once the Russian goon squad realized I wasn't part of the raid, they stopped worrying about me and started shooting, too."

"Someone got hit upstairs," Waverly said. "There was blood by the door and on the doorframe.

"One of the guards got clipped in the arm. We were taking fire from two sides and had to get out. They took my gun, dragged me out, and threw me in a van."

"Not very trusting, those Russians," Micah commented.

"My phone was upstairs in the office, I didn't have a gun, and I had these three angry men shouting questions at me in Russian. It turns out they didn't know who the welcoming party was either."

"So you've been where since that night?"

"We rendezvoused with Petra and her guard Yurgei on the other side of the lake. Security called Grigory to report what happened. He certainly didn't trust me, but when I told him I thought Petra was the target, he was less inclined to turn me over to the cops and more inclined to listen. He grudgingly believes I didn't have anything to do with turning his Tahoe place into the O.K. Corral, but without knowing who exactly we were dealing with and what they wanted, we both thought it would be better if I stayed off the grid with Petra. I've been basically a prisoner, though a well-kept one since. I knew someone would try for her again, especially after Stepanov told me about a business deal gone south."

"The drug manufacture licenses?" she asked.

"Very good, Waves," he said with pride. "Those guys never learned that no means no. They're prepared to go to war to get the licenses."

"But the drugs sell for less than a dollar a pill. Why the strong-arming for a product that isn't going to pay off?" she asked.

"Ah, that's the reason Stepanov squashed the deal. Axion Pharmaceuticals was going to put the drugs in question into closed distribution and jack up the prices. With limited distribution channels and no generics available? They'd make billions on everyone who needs to manage their blood pressure or survive malaria."

"Dicks," Micah muttered.

"Agreed. Stepanov saw me as an asset that he might be able to trade for his and Petra's safety, or I could be sent back to Target and work from the inside for Stepanov, but it was clear that Brad was done with me. So he kept me and Petra on lockdown and tried to come up with a different plan. I think he was hoping to make himself a target, staying away from Petra and doing all these public functions."

Waverly drummed her fingers on the glossy surface of the table and Xavier could see her wheels turning.

"It was the studio, wasn't it?" she asked. "Axion hired Target to make Stepanov sell and Brad sent those guys in to grab Petra."

"That's my thought, yes," Dante agreed. "They showed up almost immediately after I called into Brad. That's too much of a coincidence."

"Did you happen to notice if one of them had a gold tooth?" Xavier asked.

Dante frowned. "I do believe there was one who had a very shiny maniacal grin. You know him?"

"Waverly and I had the pleasure of meeting them in an alley this week."

"When Petra was at the club," Dante said, understanding dawning.

"Stepanov has you on lockdown and he's aware of the threat against his daughter. So why send her out clubbing?" Xavier asked.

"That was a desperate move on my part. Waverly had finally resurfaced, and I had no way to get in touch with her. I knew she had to be wondering where I was, but I couldn't reach out in any of the usual ways for fear of Brad realizing I hadn't been shot and dumped in the woods as I assume were his orders. I didn't know if Waverly knew she could be a target, too. So I asked Petra to make an appearance without giving her the details on why. We've become... close, and she was happy to help."

"You knew I'd track her down," Waverly filled in.

"I know you," Dante said, grinning at her. "You're tenacious. You wouldn't let that opportunity to grill Petra on what happened pass by."

"Only we were interrupted," Waverly sighed.

"Imagine my surprise when she returned home with a virgin trying to solicit prostitutes instead of you," he quipped.

"And here we are." Waverly interlaced her fingers and sat back in her chair to process.

"I'm still not buying that you had no way to send a text or an email or make a phone call," Xavier said.

"I wasn't kidding about being locked down. Petra is Stepanov's diamond, his princess. He cut the phone and Internet to the house, confiscated her phone, and threatened us both with my death if we tried anything. We took him seriously. In fact, he's still royally pissed at me for talking her into going to the club that night. Plus, I couldn't be sure that Brad hadn't tapped your phone or hacked your accounts. I imagine he's got some high up friends who enjoy the benefits of his side work."

"What makes you say that?" Micah asked.

"I've been suspicious for a while," Dante said. The assignments started changing, and I started asking questions. He told me he was taking on some new assignments. I guess I asked too many questions because I think first priority in Tahoe was to get Petra, and the second priority was to eliminate me."

"Brad doesn't know where you are or if you're alive," Waverly frowned. "He wasn't lying about that when I met with him. But if he has someone on the inside at Petra's, how did he not know you were there?"

"No one but security and the chef have been allowed onsite since Tahoe. And a cleaning crew once a week, but I hide in the closet while they're there. Security is tight, and they seem pretty loyal to Petra and Grigory. Maybe Anatoli will have an idea? I think he has a crush on you," he winked at Waverly.

"We'll be sure to ask him," Xavier said dryly. "How much time do we have before everyone knows you and Petra are missing?"

"Anatoli texted the house and let them know he'd taken Petra shopping. But I imagine by this afternoon they'll be putting things together. We should call Grigory before that happens. He'll be more receptive to hearing you out if he doesn't know you kidnapped his daughter from his house."

Grigory Stepanov was still not very receptive to their news. He steamed and turned a furious red on the video screen in the conference room.

It had been very wise to include Petra and Anatoli on the call, Waverly thought as she watched his daughter, clutching the tiny Pixie to her chest, try to calm her father.

"You were to stay in the house, Petra," he said, his accent thickening as he desperately tried to control his temper.

Anatoli stepped in to defend the situation and soon an animated discussion was taking place in Russian. They were losing ground and Grigory was refusing to listen.

"Mr. Stepanov," Waverly stepped in, addressing him in his native language. "This is not an ideal situation for any of us, but your daughter is safe. And that's what matters right now. However, if Petra is out of the way, I fear you may be the next target. Which I think you have considered and have taken measures to encourage that."

She glanced around the table. Xavier was grinning at her with pride. Micah's jaw was on the table.

"And just who in the hell are you?" Grigory snapped.

"Mr. Stepanov, this is the woman who saved Petra, myself, and Yurgei from the gunmen. She is a friend. I promise you that," Anatoli said fervently.

"Sir, I think we need to speak in person," Waverly suggested.

The Russian grunted and mopped at his brow. "I feel as if I am walking into a trap. But I would walk anywhere for my little girl."

"Papa, please come. I miss you, and I would like you to spend more time with Dante as we will be married."

"Married?" Grigory shrieked.

"Married?" It was Waverly's turn to be shocked. To Dante, marriage held all the appeal of a firing squad. She wondered if he was aware of Petra's plans.

"Someone please tell me what the hell is going on," Xavier asked. "All I caught was gunmen and married."

Petra and her father were yelling again and when Dante put an arm around Petra's shoulders to comfort her, Grigory howled in rage.

"Dante, if you value your life, please stop touching Petra right now," Waverly hissed in English.

"I will meet you," Grigory said also in English, finally regaining a modicum of calm. "If only to kill this man!"

And the calm was gone.

"I'm starting to like this Stepanov guy," Xavier whispered to Waverly.

~

THE HOUSE ROZ procured for them was a rambling eight-bedroom Spanish villa in Malibu. It sat on two manicured acres behind thick brick walls and an iron gate. The neighborhood itself was gated as well. The interior was all rustic beams, graceful arched doorways, and timber ceilings. Bedrooms were divvied up, and everyone dispersed to claim their space.

Roz had done an impressive job stocking it with all the necessities from toothbrushes to frozen pizza.

Grigory arrived alone that evening, adding to the fleet of luxury SUVs already in the drive and garage. He was a short, stern little man whose eyes shone like diamonds when they looked at his daughter. Xavier noted that they showed something like malice when they looked in Dante's direction.

Through stilted discussions, Xavier and Micah were able to assure Grigory that they were here to help. And after a long chat with Anatoli, during which Xavier was convinced that the man did have a significant crush on Waverly that sprung from her saving his life, they were able to identify the possible inside source.

Target Productions had been in preliminary talks with Petra over a reality show starring foreign heiresses as they navigated the L.A. scene. To sweeten the deal, the studio had hooked her up with a part-time assistant who managed her calendar. Xavier had to admit he was impressed with Target's creativity. When Petra had been identified as an asset to the negotiations, they most likely made contact with her under the guise of a show business deal. What better way to keep tabs on a target?

To Xavier, it made sense that Target's moonlighting wasn't limited to just acting talent. Having a stable of behind-the-scenes spies could come in handy for assignments or run-of-the-mill blackmail, he mused. From the outside, it looked as though Brad Tomasso was building his own intelligence network.

However, since Petra's untimely lockdown, the assistant had communicated with her through Stepanov's security and had what Anatoli referred to as "a cow" when they hadn't told her in advance about Petra's spontaneous outing to the club.

Xavier and Micah agreed that it was enough that it warranted another call to Travers. The ever rumpled, ever grumpy Travers arrived after dark and took one look at the assembled crew and shook his head. "I'm out," he announced.

Kate surreptitiously locked the front door behind him, blocking his escape.

"You haven't even heard what's going on yet," Micah said, putting a hand on Malachi's shoulder and helpfully shoving him toward the house's library. "Come on in, take a load off, and *then* tell us to fuck off."

Waverly plied him with coffee and a plate of the apple crumble Anatoli, the man of many talents, had made as his contribution to dinner.

Settled in around the library's walnut table, Xavier laid it all out—minus what could have been misconstrued as a kidnapping, as well as the stickiness of Grigory sort of holding Dante prisoner.

Travers had the reaction Xavier had expected.

"Why is it everything with you guys is a freaking mess? Can't you just stick to protecting celebrities?"

"Malachi, don't tell me you don't want in on this," Waverly said, turning those big eyes his way. Xavier felt pity for the man who didn't yet realize that he had no chance against her persuasion.

"Look, from what you've told me, this has to go higher than someone in the Special Collection Service. This has to be someone with oversight. Maybe even Joint Intelligence Community Council. There's no way that Tomasso is operating out of bounds without someone serious in his corner. You sure you want to stir up this hornets' nest?"

"Yes," Xavier, Waverly, Micah, Chelsea, and Grigory chorused.

"First off, we can't start digging based on the detective work of a hacker," Travers cautioned. "No offense," he tossed out to Chelsea.

"None taken," she said, with a feline smile. Xavier narrowed his eyes at her. He was just getting used to seeing his sister as a hacker. He wasn't ready to see her as a woman yet.

"We need *legal* reasonable cause before I can take this anywhere," Malachi continued. "Even the SEC is going to want something actionable before they go after the biotech firm or the studio."

"So how do we get something legally actionable?" Waverly asked.

"California is two-party consent, so without a warrant, I can't just send you in there with a wire and get Tomasso to spill his guts to you."

"We wouldn't be putting Waverly in that position in the first place, would we?" Xavier said coldly. He knew how the FBI would want to play it. Waverly holding all the cards was the best bait they could have in luring Brad out into the open and making an actionable threat. And that was *not* happening.

No one was putting her in harm's way. Not this time and not ever again.

Waverly, of course, had other ideas. "What if an agent personally overhears a conversation that concerns him? He'd be ethically required to pass it on up the chain, wouldn't he?" she asked.

Xavier's fingers tightened reflexively on the arms of his chair. Their talk tonight was also going to involve her reckless willingness to become a target.

Travers reluctantly agreed. "That would warrant some phone calls, but these are Russian nationals," he pointed out. "I don't have jurisdiction."

"But it's an American company that's playing espionage games with private entities, including one U.S. Senator who was blackmailed into retiring and supporting his successor," Waverly argued. She pushed a file at him.

"Where'd you get this?" he asked, eyes skimming the text.

"This would be a very nice success on your bureau record. Are you in or out?" Xavier asked him.

Travers looked down at the file again. "Fuck it. I'm in."

"We'll get another room ready," Xavier nodded.

24

It was well past midnight by the time Xavier and Waverly closed the door to their bedroom. It was actually a private apartment on the third floor secluded away from the rest of the house. A queen-sized wicker bed dressed in white sat under the room's white washed rafters and faced glass doors that led to a tiny balcony where a bright sliver of moon was visible in the sky. In the corner, a small fireplace was ready to push off the autumn chill. The bathroom was charming with a Spanish tile floor, a small but serviceable walk-in shower, and a copper soaking tub.

It was a beautiful room in a beautiful house, but Waverly couldn't help but feel like she was walking onto a battlefield. She'd had all day to think about what she'd say to Xavier and still felt unprepared.

He didn't bother with the overhead lights or the bed. Xavier prowled across the room to the overstuffed couch along the wall. He slid his jacket off his shoulders and sat down, switching on a lonely lamp.

"Don't you want to take your shoes off?" Waverly asked, toeing off her sneakers and stretching.

"Not until I'm sure you won't run tonight."

She looked down at her bare feet and back up at him.

"Never stopped you before."

He was right, of course. She'd once jumped off of a yacht and swam to shore to get away from things she couldn't control. He'd jumped after her and chased her down. The memory of that night slid over her skin like a warm caress.

Xavier had been there catching her when she fell, chasing her when she ran, and holding her when she stopped. And then one day he hadn't been. It had taken her a long time to come to terms with that. It had taken even longer before she understood that she was responsible for herself. She couldn't blame anyone else for holding her back. Couldn't point the finger at someone who shoved her forward when she wasn't ready. Couldn't depend on someone else to clean up her messes. In the end, she was responsible for herself, and somewhere along the line, she'd come to like it.

But none of that took into account the feelings she had tangled up in Xavier Saint. Love to her was complicated and messy. She didn't know if she was ready to make room for complicated and messy.

She sat down on the coffee table in front of him. "I don't know where to start," she said.

"You and Wrede," Xavier stated, his voice low and quiet. But she heard the thick emotion there. He'd held it in all day giving orders, making arrangements, coordinating his small, rag-tag army, all to keep her safe once again. And now she owed him answers.

"We were never together," she admitted in a rush. "It's not good to mix personal feelings with a working relationship. We worked well together, but it never went beyond friendship. I trusted him to have my back, but our romantic relationship was a fiction created by agents and movie studios and exploited by Brad."

He stared at her, dazed and hurt, and then closed his eyes.

"You made me think I was delivering the love of your life to you. I thought that you'd choose him over me! Why the hell would you do that to me? I've been gutted over this, Waverly!"

Her heart twisted painfully in her chest. "You knew it wasn't like that with Dante. You told me how you deduced that our relationship wasn't as serious as it was made out to be."

"You know I don't think straight with you. Everything gets tied up and inside out because all I see is you. All I feel is how much I want you and how nothing else is ever enough for me. Evidence was pointing me in that direction, but I still felt like there was a man between us, that you loved someone who wasn't me. That's a cold thing to do, Waverly."

"That's how I operate now, X. You know how hard it was for me to trust anyone before you came along. So you can imagine how it went after you walked out."

He swore quietly. He moved restlessly on the couch, his elbows on his knees and then pushing back to lean against the cushion. "You told me you loved Dante." His fingers dug into his thighs.

She nodded. "That wasn't a lie. I love him like a friend, a brother. Not like..." she trailed off, not willing to say the words. "Not like I led you to believe."

"Why would you do that to me? You knew why I came back. You knew I loved you. You knew I wanted to marry you."

"That's exactly why," she said in exasperation. "X, I have no way to protect myself when I'm around you. You broke my heart, and I still want to be near you. I can't stop myself. If you're in the room, I'm gravitating to you. And when you touch me?" She shook her head. "Nothing else in the world exists in that moment."

He took a shaky breath and reached for her hand. "Do you think that happens with just anyone? Because it doesn't."

She shook her head again. "I know it doesn't, Xavier. But I can't go back to what we were. It can't be you protecting me from life. I need a partnership. I need someone who trusts me and believes in me, who doesn't think I'm weak and vulnerable."

He studied her, emotions strong behind his eyes.

She changed tactics. "Do you know why I pursued this work?"

He shrugged. "You wanted to call your own shots. You wanted control and excitement."

"I wanted to be closer to you. And I didn't figure that out until you came back." That motivating factor hadn't hit her until she'd seen him there on the beach in Belize with that cocky grin and eyes that followed her everywhere. "We didn't fit into each other's worlds before. The only way we worked together was in bed. In every other situation, you were in charge. You were a guardian. That's not a sustainable relationship. I wanted to be your equal, not your dependent."

"I *worship* you, Angel. Don't tell me that's not enough," his voice was jagged with pain.

"I want even more than that from you, Xavier. I *need* more than that."

"Tell me what you need, Waverly. You know I'll move mountains to give you what you want."

She held his chin in her free hand. His beard prickled against the skin of her palm. "I want you to see me as an equal and treat me that way. I want you to believe in my abilities and trust me. I'm good at what I do. I'm not that impulsive kid jumping off yachts or running away from home. I'm solid, and I need you to see that. It tore me up when you lost it at Petra's house about me leaving with Dante."

"I didn't trust them, Waverly. What if they'd turned on you? What if it was you against all of them?" She could hear the panic in his voice.

"X, your instincts were telling you they were okay. But you got it all tangled up and I get that. I do. You haven't worked with me. You don't know what I'm capable of. But what I'm asking is for a chance to prove myself. Let me prove to you that I can be trusted. And in return, I'll give you the chance to show me you can be trusted."

"How?"

"I know you're already looking for ways to cut me out of this operation." He tried to look away, but she pulled him back. "I understand, Xavier. I really do. You show people you love them by keeping them safe, and me asking you to do this feels like I'm just throwing that back in your face. But I swear I'm not, X. I want to earn my place with you and I want you to earn yours with me. Let me work with you. Let me help take Target down."

"And how do I earn my place?"

"By treating me like an equal, not a goddess up on a pedestal and not a child who needs her hand held. A partner."

"You want this? You want us?" He squeezed her hand in a death grip.

"I'd be crazy not to, X." The smile split her face as the words finally set her free.

Xavier wasn't as ready to celebrate. "Say it, Waverly."

He was so bossy, and that would probably never change. But there were a thousand things that she'd never change either. They could learn to work together, learn to trust each other. "I want us."

He was yanking her to him, pulling her off the table and settling her in his lap. "Thank fucking God," he said raggedly.

"We're going to have to be patient with each other," she cautioned him.

"Yeah, because that's our strong suit," he said dryly, pressing a kiss to her throat.

"We can't just have sex all the time. We're going to have to talk every once in a while. But that's the only way we can make sure nothing else stands between us."

He pulled back and stared up at her as if he was deciding something. And then he yanked her down for a sweet, soft kiss. When she moved for more, he tucked her head against his chest and took a deep breath.

"There's still something in the way," he said. She heard his voice like a rumble in his chest. "Something we haven't talked about."

"What?"

"I was angry with you," he began. "Probably more mad at myself because I felt so helpless. We were flying back to L.A., and I felt like I was delivering you to everyone who could hurt you again. Your parents, the studio, Ganim." Xavier swiped a hand over his face. "So I picked a fight with you on the plane. I wanted to blame you for putting my team in danger, but really it was everyone in your life who was willingly shoving you in harm's way."

Waverly's heartbeat picked up. He was talking about the night Ganim had taken her, the night everything changed for them. It was the night they never spoke of.

"I saw you weren't feeling well at the club, thought it would be an out, a reason to take you home. But I didn't stay with you. I wanted to get your drink and bring it back to you and then convince you to leave. But when I followed the waitress to the bar, I saw the bartender pull out this vial..." He shook his head, took a steadying breath.

She pressed her hand against his heart, felt it thunder beneath her palm.

"I lost it, Waverly. Someone was trying to hurt you right in front of me, on my watch. I grabbed him, pulled him over the bar. I don't even remember how many times I hit him. By the time they got me off of him, let me back up off the floor, you were gone."

She saw the flash in her own memory, felt the residual roll of terror. There were screams over the music and then Ganim's face swam before her, but she was too weak to scream or fight.

"I lost it. I completely lost it," he shoved his hand through his hair. "You were my world and not just because you were a job. You know that, right?"

She nodded but said nothing.

"Micah was there, Travers and Hansen, too. And everyone was just standing around talking on phones, looking at security footage. I needed to move. I needed to find you. We were going to take Travers' SUV," he remembered. "And then I realized you were wearing your tracker. It took me ten minutes to remember. Ten fucking minutes, Waverly. That's how gone I was. If I'd remembered five minutes earlier, you wouldn't have had a scratch on you."

She shook her head. "He had a gun," Waverly reminded him. "He would have just shot me in the car. It could have gone even worse."

He took another breath. "Micah was driving because I... I couldn't. I was tracking you, and I knew where he was taking you. I knew he was going to kill you. And then Kate calls and she's hysterical."

"And Kate is never hysterical," Waverly said with a sad smile.

"She's just sobbing in my ear that I have to save you, that it's streaming live. And then we were there, and I saw you. I saw him. I don't even remember pulling my gun. Micah knew exactly what to do. He just floored it up over the curb onto the sidewalk, and I threw the door open.

"He knew we were coming for him, that I wasn't going to let him live. I saw the knife coming down and I fired. Three times. Center body mass. The truck was still moving, and I dove for him. As soon as I touched him, I knew he was gone. He just kind of crumpled under me like a doll. And then I was with you. And there was so much blood. So much blood," he repeated, his voice choking.

She rested her head on his shoulder, stroked his chest tenderly with her hand.

"I've never loved anyone that much, and almost losing you broke me." His voice broke with emotion.

"Do you remember what I said to you?" she asked quietly.

He nodded, but didn't answer.

"I told you I knew you'd come for me. And I meant it. I had no doubt that you'd move heaven and earth to find me. And when I opened my eyes and saw your face I knew that everything was going to be okay."

"I almost wasn't fast enough." He swiped at a tear that had escaped the corner of his eye. "I almost cost you everything."

She cupped his face in her hands. "You were fast enough. You saved my life, Xavier. I'm here today because you were there. You didn't hesitate. Your instincts, your skills, your control stopped a killer."

He wiped his face again, trying to absorb her words yet still fighting them against the truth he believed.

"I have to tell you something, X. Something I never told anyone about that night."

"What?"

"I could have faded away. I *was* fading. Everything was going black, and I knew I could just let go and nothing would hurt anymore and no one could hurt me ever again." She felt the goose bumps rise on her arms at the memory of the cold concrete under her and the warm spread of her blood as it left her body.

"Jesus, Waverly." His arms banded around her tighter.

"But I held on because you did. You held my hand, and you talked to me. I heard every beautiful word you said, and I hung on to them, to your voice. I knew you were with me, and I didn't want to leave you. You didn't just save me from Ganim. You kept me here."

She was crying now, and he crushed her against his chest, cradling her in his arms.

"My Angel," he whispered.

"So don't you ever tell me that you made mistakes that night. If it weren't for you, Ganim would have gotten me long before then, and there wouldn't have been anyone to save me. There wouldn't have been anyone to hang on for."

He kissed the top of her head. "And then I walked out on you like a scared, selfish asshole. I'm so fucking sorry, Waverly. I just loved you so much, and thinking that I almost got you killed... it destroyed me. If I couldn't protect you, couldn't keep you safe. I wasn't good enough for you."

She wrapped her arms around his waist. "It's about time you apologize for the right thing."

He gave a broken laugh. "I love you, Waverly Sinner. And nothing is going to stand in my way this time. I'm going to marry you, and we're going to spend forever driving each other insane."

She pulled back, but he wasn't having it and yanked her against him. "Don't argue with me. I'll wear you down eventually. Even if it takes another five years. You will be my wife."

"X—" But his mouth found hers and silenced her protest.

She broke the kiss breathlessly. "How about we just work on dating for a little while? We've never tried that before."

He laughed against her hair. "You are the most infuriating, exhausting—"

She glared at him.

"Beautiful, sexy, smart, sweet, surprising woman I have ever met in my entire life," he amended.

Waverly winced. "Crap. In the interest of honesty and stuff, I should tell you I met Calla for drinks."

"Calla?"

"Jesus, X. Get some blood flow back to your head." His penis was rigid against her. "Calla, your ex-girlfriend."

He froze. "Why the hell were you having drinks with her?"

"She called and asked. And I was very curious about the woman after me, so I went."

"What did you talk about?" he asked gruffly.

"Oh, you know, what's hot in hair care for fall and whether or not we think global warming—" He pinched her. Hard. "Ouch!"

"Smartass," he complained.

"You, you ass. We talked about you."

"I assumed as much," he said, exasperated now. "What specifically?"

"She wanted to let me know that you're a great guy and I better not jerk you around."

"She threatened you?" He didn't sound mad. He sounded incredulous.

Waverly smiled, enjoying herself. "Not in so many words, but I'm willing to be extra nice to you just in case."

He squeezed her.

"She's good, X. Happy. Married and pregnant, and she wants to see you happy, too. She thinks that might involve me."

His hands skimmed up to cup her breast. "Let's stop talking and work on making me happy."

"Okay."

Her immediate acquiescence must have thrown him because it took him another five seconds before he rose, carrying her from the sofa to the bed. Xavier lay her in the middle of the mattress and stared at her with an unreadable expression as he loosened his tie.

Waverly felt like she was watching something erotically artistic as he unbuttoned his shirt. The powerful chest that gave way to a rippled expanse of abs, the V of muscle that drew her eye down and down. He shed the shirt carelessly on the floor, and when his hands moved to his belt, Waverly licked her lips. She rose up on her knees and stripped the sweatshirt over her head revealing the purple lace of her bra. She saw his throat work as his pupils zeroed in on her breasts.

Xavier's fingers deftly opened his belt and moved to the button on his trousers. She could see the bulge beneath the fabric, felt the liquid pull of desire between her own legs. He shoved his pants down and stepped out of them. The flushed crown of his cock peeked out of the waistband of his gray briefs. Waverly eagerly peeled off her yoga pants one leg at a time. And when Xavier shoved his hand into his briefs to fist the root of his erection, she crawled across the mattress to him.

He must have liked what he saw because as he stroked his big hand up the shaft, the tip glistened with a pearl of moisture, and he grunted softly. It made her bolder. He offered himself to her, and she held Xavier's gaze as her tongue darted out between her lips to taste him. His intake of air was a hiss, and when her lips flowed over the broad head, it became a groan. She took him into her mouth, tonguing and tasting his hard flesh. His hand fisted in her hair hard enough to draw a moan from her lips.

He pumped himself into her mouth, and she eagerly accepted the assault. Pushing him over the edge gave her a dark pleasure. "You're my fantasy come to life," Xavier gritted out.

She closed her eyes on his words of praise and worshipped him back. With a ragged rumble deep in his chest, he pulled her off of his cock. He met her on the mattress and easily pinned her beneath him. Waverly bucked against him, craving the friction of his cock grinding against her sex.

"Be patient, Angel." He teased her lips with his, biting and licking his way to her surrender.

Waverly ran her hands over his muscled back and lower, squeezing his tight ass and yanking him against her. He obliged and rubbed his dick over the purple lace of her thong. "You could make me come just like that," she gasped.

"I have a better idea," he said, sliding down her body. He paused at her breasts, tonguing under the lace to tease each nipple before licking his way down her stomach.

He pushed her thighs wide and slipped his palms under her ass.

"Show me," he ordered, his voice harsh with desire.

Desperate, Waverly grabbed her thong and yanked the material to one side.

He groaned, low and guttural. "Hold it there. Stay open for me." His tongue blazed a trail through her sex, sliding through the wet folds to tease her greedy bud. Waverly's thighs trembled when he skimmed lower. He tasted the very center of her, and she purred out her praise. When the tip of his tongue probed even lower, she felt her breath catch.

"Every inch of you belongs to me, Waverly," he murmured.

Teasing that secret spot. *It shouldn't feel so good*, she told herself. She shouldn't want this, but she did.

Xavier made everything feel so good, so right. He gave her the things she didn't know she needed. And when he pressed the pad of his thumb to where his tongue had just been, sliding it inside past that tight ring of muscle she didn't fight him. She took slow, steadying breaths getting used to this new invasion.

"Good girl." His breath fluttered against her bared flesh. With his other hand, he probed her sex gently before sliding his fingers home. Waverly was so close to coming that she clamped down on his fingers, holding them inside her.

He was breathing heavily, and she could feel him grinding his hips into the mattress, as desperate for the friction, the touch, as she was.

"Not yet, baby. Not yet." Xavier lowered his mouth to her, and when his tongue danced over her clitoris, he began to move his fingers. She gasped for breath, her hands fisted in the sheets as she rode his mouth and hands. She couldn't hold back if she wanted to. The orgasm had her in its ironclad grip.

Full. So beautifully full, his tongue and his hands triggered her release, and she saw constellations erupt behind her closed eyes. She closed around him, squeezing those fingers in shattering waves. He moaned against her. Her pleasure was his. Still quaking from her release, she gripped him by the hair and pulled him up her body.

"I want to make you feel what I feel." She straddled his hips pulling her thong off to the side again as he guided his thick erection to her center.

"Oh, God!" The words were wrenched from his throat as Waverly lowered herself onto him. His stomach muscles were rigid, holding his head and shoulders off the bed.

"Don't move," he begged, his eyes pinched closed.

She waited until he opened his eyes. Blurry and unfocused, they zeroed in when she slid the straps of her bra down her arms. Without the support, the curves of her breasts threatened to spill over the top of the lace that contained them.

"Fuck it," he whispered.

He reared up and shoved her bra down. The second her breasts were free, he latched his mouth onto one of the nipples, and Waverly began to ride. She was too close to the edge again. She wanted to be the one to drive him over, but those deep needy pulls on her nipple were driving her insane.

He palmed her ignored breast, squeezing and kneading it to the rhythm his mouth set. She followed suit, riding him with long slow strokes. His mouth released her with a pop. Her nipple was pink and swollen. Xavier growled and took the other peak between his lips.

She felt him swell inside her, knew he was close. His hips were bucking off the mattress, begging for more. More speed, more friction. She gave it all to him, wrapping her fingers around the headboard and riding his cock as if her life depended on it.

She heard him grunting softly as he sucked. Then he was thickening, swelling, and just that was enough to send her over the edge. She exploded, and instantly he was jerking inside her, coming in thick, hot spurts as she pulsed around him. His name, she chanted it over and over again as their orgasms joined. Only when it was over did he release her breast.

Waverly collapsed on him, and the change in angle had his cock twitching in her. "You're still hard after that?"

He rolled, still inside her, and pinned her to the mattress. "Angel, I'm always hard for you."

He pulled out and stroked back in. There was no way she

could go again, Waverly told herself. But her body sent a delicious shiver through her when the crown of his cock angled over the perfect spot.

Her sigh of pleasure had him lowering onto her. "One more time for me, Angel."

With slow, smooth strokes, he was rock hard again, and she was floating into the bliss. He smoothed his hand over her forehead, brushing her hair back. Her gaze met his and held. Xavier rolled his hips, and staring into the depths of each other, they sighed together.

She hiked her knees up higher on his hips and held on. Every deep, masterful stroke took her higher. Her nails dug perfect crescents into his shoulders as if she hoped to anchor him to her forever.

He moved in her endlessly, languidly. Taking his time, he carried her toward the light with measured strokes. Every thrust perfect, every sigh magical.

She felt it then, that slow, glorious build like the dawn breaking. He felt it too and paced himself. "I've got you, baby," he promised her.

It swept through her like gravity, like the magnetic pull of the moon on the tide. Infinitely powerful. "Xavier," she sighed out his name as she tumbled with it, rolling and falling, floating and flying.

She watched him as he came, her name from his lips. He was unblinking, staring into her as if he could see inside to where he filled her with his seed. They possessed each other in the most beautifully carnal of ways.

Waverly wasn't sure if it was minutes or hours before they moved. Maybe it was days. But when Xavier finally pulled out of her, she missed the connection immediately. He pulled her into him, positioning her head on his chest. She could see the self-satisfied smile on his face as she toyed with his chest hair. It was probably a reflection of the one on her own face.

"Xavier?"

"Hmm?"

"Don't go to sleep yet."

"Angel, I'm going to need at least another twenty minutes and a gallon of water if you want to go again."

"No! It's not that. It's work related. And don't get all huffy," she told him when he opened one eye disapprovingly. "I have an idea, and if I get you onboard tonight, it'll be that much easier to convince everyone else in the morning."

"I already hate this," he complained.

"I already made it worth your while," she told him, nibbling at his neck.

25

*I*t was a good plan. He'd give her that, Xavier thought as he lay in bed staring at the ceiling. Waverly was curled up against him, her head resting on his chest. She had certainly made it worth his while. He could barely walk, let alone escape her while she talked work. But he'd have liked the plan a hell of a lot better if it were someone other than Waverly running point. He hated even the thought of her facing danger. It didn't matter how strong, smart, or capable she was. She was Waverly, *his* Waverly. He wanted her somewhere safe and happy.

Like right now. Right now was pretty damn perfect. The girl he loved sleeping on him, a quiet house on a crisp fall night. If it could stay just like this, life would be perfect.

Perfect ended four seconds later with an ear-splitting scream. Waverly woke with a start, blindly reaching for the gun she'd stowed in her nightstand. Xavier was already pulling on pants and grabbing his piece. He tossed his discarded t-shirt at her, and together, they silently made their way down to the second floor.

There was shouting now. Some English, some Russian,

some the Queen's English. The hallway off the media room was full of people waving weapons and yelling. Micah, wearing rubber ducky boxer shorts, held a Ruger at his side. Anatoli had muscled in next to him in a white tank top, black silk boxers, and a rifle. Chelsea, his lovely sister, wielded a bat. She was wearing a boxer tank top outfit, and Xavier did not like how Travers with his Glock and flannel pajama pants was eyeing her up.

Kate sat on the hallway stable bench with a box of cereal and watched the show.

It was only then that Xavier realized what the fuss was all about. Grigory Stepanov was shouting at Dante who was holding only a bed pillow over his crotch. Petra, in a purple silk negligee alternated between sobbing and yelling.

"I thought someone broke in here and was murdering people," Chelsea said, shouldering the bat.

"If we stick around long enough, we might see a murder," Kate told her, helping herself to another handful of cereal. "Looks like they weren't the only ones getting some." She wiggled her eyebrows at Waverly's attire and sex hair.

"Don't make me shoot you, Kate," Waverly joked, tucking her gun behind her back.

"Okay, everyone. Let's calm down," Xavier said, wading into the fray. "Wrede, go back to your own room."

Dante decided escape was in his best interest and scurried his bare ass down the hallway. Everyone watched him go.

"His ass is a lot smaller than I thought it would be," Kate murmured.

"It really is," Chelsea agreed.

Xavier shook his head. "Grigory, I know this is hard, but try to pretend this was just a horrible, horrible nightmare. Let's all go back to bed, get some sleep, and never speak of this again."

He herded them all off toward their rooms, weapons in hand.

Waverly waited for him at the foot of the stairs to the third floor.

"You're going to be a great dad someday."

"If I were Grigory, I would have shot the bastard."

AFTER BREAKFAST, Kate took Petra-sitting duty and dragged the girl away from Dante to use the basement gym... or the basement wine cellar. Xavier wasn't clear on which.

The rest of them convened in the upstairs media room, the only room large enough to hold everyone. Xavier and Waverly sat on a leather chaise while Chelsea and Malachi claimed the barstools against the mahogany bar. Grigory, Anatoli, and Micah all chose positions on the large leather sectional. Dante lounged on the floor by the cedar plank coffee table looking every bit the casual playboy.

Xavier leaned forward resting his elbows on his knees and began. "As you're all aware, we're in an awkward position of being aware of having evidence of certain crimes committed while not being able to turn said evidence over to the proper authorities. And instead of marching each and every one of us down to the FBI's office to tell our stories and hoping for the best, we're looking for a way to speed the investigation along."

He glanced at Waverly and nodded, giving her the floor. *See? He could do this partner thing.*

She rolled her eyes at him as if she'd read his mind before addressing the group. "While we don't have much in the way of legally collected evidence, what we *do* have is all of the players that Brad wants. We'd like to use Brad's inside source to inform him that Petra has already gone missing. It will motivate him to contact me."

"Travers, you'll also be on the line, and if Tomasso throws any threats around or demands that Waverly turns Petra over to him, it should be enough for the FBI to start digging," Xavier said, taking over again.

Malachi was frowning thoughtfully across the room.

"I'll tell Brad that I want a cut of the Axion action in exchange for turning Petra over to him," Waverly said, smoothly picking up the thread. "Which, of course, won't happen, Mr. Stepanov."

Petra's father had been looking a little green at the direction the conversation was going. He nodded.

"We'll arrange the swap for Saturday, which should give the FBI enough time to call in the SEC and start their investigations."

"And you want us to stake out the exchange," Travers predicted.

Xavier nodded. "Invictus will be there as backup, of course. But you'll be there to slap on the cuffs."

Micah cleared his throat. "It's a good plan. We can start by identifying a location for the swap. Somewhere public that feds would have no trouble blending in. Waverly, since you're the cardholder, you'll want to lay it all out for Brad. You pick the place and the time."

"And my Petra? She will be safe?" Grigory asked.

"Brad won't get anywhere near her during the exchange," Xavier promised.

"What can I do?" Dante asked. "I'm tired of being a home-bound prisoner."

Waverly cleared her throat. "I was thinking if Dante comes back from the dead, it might be a good distraction during the exchange. Brad would have his hands full trying to deal with me making demands and a shiny, British loose end suddenly reappearing."

Xavier thought about it. "It might be dangerous," he said with a grin.

"And we know how devastated you would be if something happened to my gorgeous face," Dante said, heavy on the sarcasm.

"You should do it," Grigory said, getting a laugh out of everyone.

"Grigory, don't tell me you're trying to get rid of your soon-to-be favorite son-in-law," Dante quipped. Xavier had to hand it to the man. He was unflappable.

Grigory was back to looking green. "This we will discuss much later. Perhaps after you have mysteriously disappeared again."

WAVERLY RELISHED the speed with which Xavier moved. There was no debating over countless lesser options or overthinking. He was decisive and intensely focused, and God she found that attractive. Never in this lifetime would Waverly have expected to find bossiness sexy. But with Xavier Saint, that's exactly what it was.

He issued orders and ran herd like a general commanding his troops while Waverly watched his every move with female appreciation.

With everyone on board, Xavier gave Anatoli the go ahead and listened as the man gave an Emmy-worthy performance when he hysterically called the assistant to ask if she'd seen Petra. The assistant leaned on Anatoli and suggested that telling Grigory right now would only cause the man needless worry. She advised that he give it a few more hours. Petra would probably show up.

It took just seventeen minutes for Waverly's phone to ring.

She held up the screen for everyone to see.

"Let it go to voicemail first," Chelsea suggested. "Keep him worked up and off-balance."

"Yes!" Waverly pointed at her with enthusiasm. "You're a smart woman."

Chelsea grinned. "It works on men like a charm."

Xavier glared at her. "I'm packing you up and sending you to a convent after this."

She tossed a throw pillow at him.

"Children," Dante said, pointing at Waverly's phone that had begun to ring again. "Showtime, Waves."

She took a breath and answered with just the right edge of annoyance in her voice. "Brad, you're interrupting an amazing massage."

Brad's voice rang out of the speaker loud and clear. "Where is Petra Stepanov?" he demanded.

"What are you talking about?" she asked airily.

"You were supposed to take her Saturday."

"Well, you know I'm an overachiever. I wanted to have a little extra time with my friend. Have a little chat with her about her father's business and a couple of drug manufacturing licenses."

The only sound coming from Brad's end was heavy breathing.

"What do you want?" he asked finally.

"This deal is worth billions from what I hear. I want a cut."

"And then you'll give me the girl?"

"You give me twenty-five million and leave me the fuck alone permanently, and you can have the girl."

He tried to bluff his way out, which she hoped he would.

"How am I going to get that kind of cash together?"

"Nice try, Brad. I have a feeling this isn't your first freelance job. I'm sure you've got cash reserves handy for situations like this. Tomorrow, 9 a.m. I'll call you with the place once you've wired the money into the account I send you."

"Don't play games with me, Waverly. I had Dante Wrede taken out, and I won't hesitate to do the same to you," Brad snarled.

"Honey, you're going to have to get a better goon squad than a bunch of washed up stunt men if you want to take me anywhere," she said, her tone icy. She felt the weight of the gazes in the room settle on her questioningly and ignored them.

"You could have been a huge asset for Target," he said snidely.

"I've seen how you handle your assets, asshole. I can do better than working for you. Now you can pay me to keep my mouth shut about your little side business, and I turn Petra over to you, or I can start calling gossip sites now with the biggest story of the year."

His laugh was cold. "You're a cold-blooded—"

"Take it up with someone who cares. And keep your phone on you." Waverly said snidely. "Oh, and Brad?"

"What?" he snapped.

"Watch out for our little Russian princess. She's not too happy about being our guest." She disconnected the call.

"What the fuck was that?" Xavier demanded.

"What? I improvised a little," she shrugged. "He's always underestimated me, and we wanted him off-balance."

"You're practically begging him to take a shot at you!" Dante scolded.

"I hate to agree with this terrible man," Grigory said,

pointing in Dante's direction. "But you seem to have poked a bear who has already proved willing to attack."

Micah and Malachi weighed in with equally damning opinions, but Anatoli and Chelsea stood firmly in her corner.

"If I had a penis, would you all still be up in arms about this?" Waverly demanded, crossing her arms.

She could tell by Xavier's expression that she'd at least scored a small point with that. But the victory felt hollow. It was their first test in trusting each other, and they'd both bombed it.

"Let's all pretend that Waverly does indeed have a penis and realize that she just got this guy to confess to taking Dante out." Chelsea argued.

"Speaking of taking me out," Dante began. "What was that bit about washed up stunt men?"

Waverly shot a furtive glance at Xavier. "The one guy seemed oddly familiar to me. I kept seeing him behind the wheel of a speeding car, and it hit me this morning. He was a stunt driver on a movie I did when I was a kid."

"So Tomasso poaches acting talent for espionage and stunt men for muscle," Micah mused out loud.

"Can we get back to the part about Waverly going off script?" Xavier muttered.

Chelsea cleared her throat. "Bottom line is, not only can Agent Travers go back to the feds with an attempted kidnapping, but we've also got Tomasso on conspiracy to commit murder."

"On that note, I've got some serious convincing to do," Malachi announced, standing. "Let me know where your team wants this to go down, and we'll make it happen... somehow," he said to Xavier. "And you," he pointed at Waverly. "Don't poke any more bears."

"I'll walk you out," Chelsea volunteered.

One by one, they all filtered out until Xavier and Waverly were left alone.

"I feel like we both dropped the ball already," Xavier sighed.

Waverly rested her head on his shoulder. "I should have told you I was going to push Brad."

"I shouldn't have jumped on you, especially not in front of the rest of the team."

"We're new at this. We'll get better... right?" she asked. She hoped they would.

"God, I hope so." Xavier put his arm around her and pulled her back into his side. "When this is over, when the studio's operations are shut down, what are you going to do?" he asked her. "Is acting enough for you?"

She felt herself freeze up. "You think I should give it up?" This had been the one thing in her life that she'd felt she'd chosen. And now Xavier, a force she never saw as a choice, wanted her to give that up.

"Think about it, Waverly. How else would you continue? Your value as an operative comes from you being a celebrity. You can't just go work for the FBI or the CIA. They don't work that way," he said.

She hadn't really considered the future beyond finding Dante and now nailing Brad to the wall for his sins. Brad had made her a pawn as so many others had in the past, and it wasn't something she'd stand for anymore. And then there was Xavier. She was part of an "us" now, and that would mean making decisions together, moving forward together. Could acting be enough for her now that he was back in her life? It hadn't been before, she remembered.

"What do *you* want to do after this is over?" she asked, turning the question back on him. Her fingers traced a heart pattern on his thigh through his pants.

Invictus allowed Xavier to call his own shots, play by his own rules. But from what she'd gleaned from Chelsea and Micah, it consumed his life.

"Maybe we could try normal?" he suggested.

"Oh, something new and different for us."

She felt him smile against her hair.

"Do either of us even know what normal is?" he wondered.

"Maybe we could learn. We could take some time off after all this. I hear there's this really nice lake town in Colorado where normal people live."

"My parents would love to have you back," he said, brushing a kiss across her mouth.

"We'll find our own normal," she predicted. "Whatever it may be." At least she hoped they would.

26

Waverly decided to give Xavier some space to play general and was helping Anatoli assemble two-dozen sandwiches for lunch when Dante slunk into the kitchen.

"Aren't you supposed to be a spy?" Anatoli asked him innocently.

Dante preened and reached for a chicken salad on wheat. "I've been known to run an operation or two."

"But how does a spy get caught in his girlfriend's bedroom by her father?" Anatoli wanted to know, his Russian face perfectly deadpan. "James Bond would never be caught by a father."

Waverly let out a peal of laughter. "Excellent burn, Anatoli," she commended, offering him a fist bump.

"Very funny. Hilarious," Dante said, taking a bite.

Waverly stowed her sandwich knife and wiped her hands on a paper towel. "You got a minute?" she asked Dante.

He gave an elegant shrug. "Lead the way, my love." He gestured toward the back door.

"Don't start that, or Xavier won't be so quick to holster his gun next time," Waverly warned him. They stepped out into the balmy California fall. The backyard stretched on before them, a hidden paradise of avocado trees and emerald green lawn. The freeform pool curled around the outdoor kitchen and thatched roof cabana.

Waverly stuck her hands in the back pockets of her jeans as they wandered toward the back wall of the estate. "So we haven't really had a chance to talk."

"No, we haven't. It's been a special brand of chaos, these past two days," Dante agreed, rolling up the sleeves of his blue and red checked shirt, another special find by Roz, Xavier's right-hand wardrobe magician.

"I have so many questions," Waverly sighed.

"Like why did I leave you with a bullet hole in your side?" He kicked at an avocado on the ground with a glossy loafer.

"No," Waverly said firmly. "You had no idea I was shot."

"I'd have come for you." He looked at her, his blue eyes earnest.

"I know you would have. Jesus, Dante, I thought you were dead... or thought that you could be dead." She shaded her eyes against the sun. "I got back in that house, and there was blood outside the office door."

"I can't believe you went back in the house," he shook his head. "Petra's cowboy-slash-butler-slash-security-guard got winged in the shoulder. Stepanov's security hustled me out pretty fast under fire, and then they shoved me in a van and took my gun, and we went after Petra. Two of the able-bodied men went back for Anatoli after he called in. By the time they got back in the house the next morning, it had been cleaned, and the security videos had been corrupted."

She let out a breath, walking through the scene in her mind again. "I'm glad you're not dead."

"Me, too," he said, giving her that boyish grin that had

charmed women from screens for the last decade. "So exactly how did you end up letting Saint back in your bed?"

Waverly gave him a playful shove. "You of all people should understand the power of the irresistible male."

"Waves, the way he looks at you? It's not just a hot fuck he's after."

It was her turn to kick at the ground. "I know," she said. "We're going to give this couple thing a real try."

"Is that wise?"

One night, long ago while shooting on location, Waverly had confessed to Dante just how badly her heart had been smashed to bits over Xavier. Dante had patted her head, promised her she'd find someone more worthy of her in the future, and then dragged her out to a karaoke bar. Despite his outward appearance, Dante was a good, solid friend.

"I have no idea if it's wise or not, but I can't seem to help myself."

"He loves you, you know. You can see it in the way he devours you with his eyes every time you enter a room. It's like a light turns on, and then he's glaring at me for looking in your general direction."

"Which you probably do just to piss him off," Waverly predicted.

"Guilty as charged. Just be careful there, Waves. You've got a lot tied up in this guy, and he's putting his entire life on the line for you. If you aren't careful, you could get hurt again, or you could wreck him."

"Whose side are you on anyway?" Waverly asked.

Dante threw an arm around her shoulder and ruffled her hair. "Always yours, my love. But I do have a newfound kinship with your Saint since I met Petra."

"You're dead serious right now, aren't you?"

"I kid you not, my dear Sinner. She's beautiful, kind, sweet, and she thinks I'm the most incredible man on the face of the earth. What's not to be in love with?"

Waverly grinned up at him. "I'm happy for you, Dante. Shocked, but happy."

"She's not like us," he sighed. "Not jaded and afraid to be vulnerable. She makes my world bigger."

"Wow. That's the most beautiful thing I've ever heard you say about a woman."

Dante laughed. "I know. I can't wait until this bit of nastiness is over. I'm going to marry that girl and find out what all the fuss is about normal."

"Will it be enough for you?" Waverly asked. *What she wanted to ask was if it would be enough for her.*

"What does it matter how big my next movie is? Or if I do another twenty missions for some government agency? I'm still going home to my empty house afterwards. I want someone to be there at the end of the day. Someone who cares about me, someone I can't wait to talk to. That's the part that matters. It's the sharing that counts, not the life in between."

"Holy crap, Dante. Did Petra feed you some kind of love potion? I've never heard you talk this way."

"Love makes everything clearer," he said, turning his face up to the sun.

In Waverly's experience, love only muddied things and made them infinitely more complicated.

"So how are you going to get Grigory to give his blessing?" she teased.

"I'll just sweep him off his feet like I do everyone," Dante said, picking her up and throwing her over his shoulder.

He spun around in the golden sunshine, and Waverly giggled like a girl without a care in the world.

❧

Xavier watched them through the window. His Angel and the man he'd thought she loved. There was an easiness between them, something that had never been present in his own relationship with Waverly. Nothing had ever been easy for them. Every step forward was a hard-fought battle.

He envied the history she shared with Dante. A history during which he'd never let her down. Xavier, on the other hand, had abandoned her. Where Dante was playful and charming, Xavier was broody and intense. He'd been told so by every woman in his life beginning with his mother and ending with Calla.

His stomach clutched as he watched Dante pick her up and toss her over his shoulder. He could hear her laughter, light and easy, through the window.

Waverly might not have been *in* love with Dante, but she did love him. She trusted him. And Xavier wanted that with her... and so much more. He wanted to be the one to give her everything, to make her laugh, to make her smile, to make her come. He wanted to be her everything.

Things moved quickly on their end. The Invictus Advance team had ranked their choice of public locations for a sting operation, and while Xavier and Micah weighed the options, Waverly poured over the profiles of employees who would be involved in the operation.

Chelsea set her sights on tracking down Brad's partner and spent hours staring and swearing at her laptop.

Anatoli worked with the hand-selected security staff from Invictus to keep the house locked down and took on the bulk of the cooking. Dante and Petra were caught making out in a variety of nooks and crannies around the estate.

Kate coordinated with Roz for the rest of the supplies they needed, and Grigory handled his business from the house trying to make sure his presence was still felt publicly.

Xavier found Waverly in their room staring off into space, the laptop open in front of her. She looked so serious and focused the way she bit her lip as she stared at the screen. He loved this side of her, too, he realized, the competent operative. She had always taken her work seriously, and it had clearly transferred to her moonlighting.

"Angel?" he said softly, sliding onto the bed next to her.

When she looked at him, it wasn't with the brooding frown. Her face lit up, and he felt the knots in his gut that had been there since he saw her with Dante smooth out. "Micah and I are going to scout out the two potential sites for the sting."

"I promise to stay here," she teased.

"You're damn right you will," he said, leaning over to look at the screen and brush his lips over her hair.

"What do you think of her?" Waverly asked, showing him the picture. She was a pretty brunette with bright blue eyes.

Xavier studied the picture. "She's good. Still new to the field, but she's got good instincts."

Waverly closed the laptop and reeled him in with his tie. "You look concerned," she said, pressing a kiss to his lips.

"There are a lot of ways this can go wrong," he reminded her. "We're making assumptions here that we can't be one hundred percent sure about."

"We'll make it work," she promised. "We stay flexible and vigilant, and when we close this deal, Brad will be behind bars."

"And you and I will be lying on a sandy beach in Barbados," Xavier predicted with a heavy sigh.

She laughed. "You and Barbados."

"I love you, Angel," he breathed.

She bit her lip. "I might be getting used to hearing you say it."

"There's a lot more you're going to have to get used to," he said wolfishly.

"Go do your recon and come back to me," she said. "Bring pizza."

He kissed her good-bye and reluctantly broke away from her before she could tangle her fingers in his hair and convince him to stick around a while longer.

She looked up at him, her lips swollen and pink, her eyes wide and trusting. Was it any wonder he was willing to go this far for her? "Behave," he reminded her, before giving her a final squeeze and walking out.

He and Micah hadn't been gone for ten minutes when Waverly called Xavier's phone. "There's been a new development," she warned him.

"Don't tell me Grigory murdered Dante," Xavier quipped.

"Cute. Grigory just got a call from building security for the condo he keeps in the city. Someone broke in between two and three a.m. this morning."

"Petra's gone, so Tomasso went after Grigory," Xavier guessed.

"Thank God you talked him into staying here," Waverly said.

"This means he's getting desperate, Angel," he warned.

"I know. Watch your back for me."

XAVIER AND MICAH returned that afternoon with the logistics mostly worked out and enough pizza to feed their small army. With the location set for the sting, he gave Waverly the go ahead to text Brad with instructions and the account number that Chelsea set up for her. When she received a terse "okay" in response, there was nothing more for her to do but wait. And eat pizza.

As much as he wanted to be alone with Waverly, Xavier knew he couldn't afford the distraction. He would make it up to her once this was over and she was safe. There were details to see to and plans to put into motion. So he chose to work in the media room turned war room. Everyone had a job to do, and had the situation not been so tense, Xavier would have been amused by the ways in which they all worked.

Waverly sprawled on the floor at his feet in the media room pouring over street and aerial views of downtown L.A. while he juggled team assignments and worked out positions for his undercover operatives. Micah spent a good two hours in the garage running through the inventory of gear Roz had delivered to them at the house.

Kate and Petra dug through the Roz-supplied wardrobe for just the right outfits for the exchange.

They were running with eight onsite players. Xavier had another five in reserve who would be a mobile Plan B in case it all went to hell. Micah would be heading that team. Between making out with Petra and verbally sparring with Grigory, Dante got in touch with his agent and publicist to let them know he was back in town, but that the news was to stay hush-hush for now.

They had yet to hear back from Travers, and it was starting to make Xavier itchy. Something was up.

Dante strolled into the room wearing black skinny jeans and a loose gray V-neck worn under a faded blue blazer.

"How do I look?" he asked, doing a slow twirl in front of Waverly.

She looked up at him from the floor and held her hand out

to him. Dante pulled her to her feet. "Very sexy," Waverly grinned. "And very alive. Brad is going to crap his pants when he gets a load of you tomorrow."

Xavier studied their interaction. He could see how the world had fallen for their relationship. Waverly was a phenomenal actress, of course, but the easy affection she and Wrede had for each other was real. And even knowing that their love affair had been just another part to play, it didn't make the reality of their friendship any less disconcerting.

It wasn't that he didn't trust Waverly. *Okay, to be fair, there were a handful of situations in which he didn't. Namely if there was danger, she'd run to it with open arms.* But in this particular instance, it was Wrede he didn't trust.

Waverly glanced back at Xavier, those eyes bright and warm, her silky tresses tossed over her shoulder. She stood between the two alleged loves of her life and she was looking at him. Xavier felt the warmth that always flooded his chest when she looked at him like that. She *had to* love him, even if she wasn't willing to say the words yet. But until he heard those words from her, he'd still feel the urge to pound Wrede into the ground. And he'd still worry that she wasn't one hundred percent his.

Xavier's mental torture was interrupted by Micah climbing the stairs.

"That was Travers," he said, stuffing his cellphone into a pocket. "We've got a problem."

"I bet it's the same problem I've got," Chelsea said, storming into the room from the hallway, laptop in hand.

"Ladies first," Micah insisted.

"Tomasso moved twenty-five million into the account all right. He did it from the shell corporation in Luxembourg."

"Which is what we asked him to do," Waverly clarified.

"Yeah, but he also moved fifteen million into a brand

spanking new account in the Cayman Islands and another nine million to a new account in Switzerland. Both are in your name."

"What?" Waverly asked, her eyes wide.

"That dovetails with my news," Micah said grimly. "Travers caught wind of a new investigation that just got handed down in the L.A. office. The FBI is looking into one Waverly Sinner on the suspicion of running unsanctioned ops in the country, including the possible abduction of Petra Stepanov."

Xavier shoved out of his chair so hard it flipped over. Waverly seemed frozen in place, her face pale and her jaw set. He pulled her into him as if he could protect her from the words. She looked up at him, shocked, but at his touch, something fiercer than shock bloomed behind her eyes.

It pleased him more than he could say to see that Waverly was ready to kick someone in the balls instead of wilt under the new threat.

"I don't get it," Kate piped up. "Petra, do you feel kidnapped?"

"No, of course not," she said, cuddling into Dante's side. "I feel very safe."

"Give you three guesses who tipped them off," Micah said, swiping a hand through his thick, dark hair.

"That sneaky wanker," Dante muttered, stroking a hand through Petra's hair.

"Travers is on his way over, but we already know we can't count on the feds' help tomorrow," Micah said, flopping down on the sectional and loosening his tie.

Waverly gave Xavier's arm a squeeze and slipped out of his grasp. She walked over to one of the shelving units that framed the TV and stared without seeing at the books and designer knickknacks before her. She crossed her arms, drumming her fingertips on her biceps.

"Waverly Sinner's gone off the deep end," she murmured to herself. "She kidnapped a celebrity we were in negotiations with for a reality show. Maybe she wanted the show and got jealous? She just had that stay in rehab. We know she's not stable." She frowned thoughtfully. "So where would the money have come from?"

Xavier watched in fascination as Waverly worked her way through the problem.

Her eyes lit up. "He's going to pin all the backdoor deals on me. He obviously can't disavow the legitimate operations we've done for other agencies. But no one else knows about his side ops."

"Besides his partner," Xavier reminded her.

Waverly moved away from the shelves and stood in front of a cheerful window seat to stare out into the fall night.

"This would throw any suspicion off of them, if they can hang it all on me. 'She did a few jobs for us and must have gotten cocky or greedy. She thought she could moonlight—'" She froze where she was and then turned slowly to face Xavier.

And Xavier knew exactly what she was thinking. "Dante," he said.

She nodded at him.

"What?" Dante asked.

Waverly held her breath and waited for Xavier to say it.

"They think you're dead," Xavier answered. "So why not pin that on Waverly, too?"

27

Malachi arrived with the setting sun to a tense crowd gathered upstairs. He'd lost his jacket somewhere during the course of the day. His tie was askew, sleeves rolled up, and his narrow shoulders hunched. Waverly kept herself between Xavier and Malachi, just in case Xavier was feeling ready to fight.

"Agent Travers," Petra rose so quickly the fashion magazine she'd been reading tumbled to the floor. "How can the FBI think that Waverly kidnapped me? She saved my life! I will tell them this."

Grigory nodded gruffly coming to his daughter's side. "Of course we will tell them, my daughter." He patted her hand.

"I'm sure that will be a big help, Mr. Stepanov," Travers said unconvincingly.

"How exactly does Brad think he's going to get away with pinning a fake kidnapping on you?" Dante asked Waverly.

Her gaze skimmed to Petra and Grigory and back to him. Xavier saw realization dawn on Dante's face. The man swiped a hand through his perfectly styled curls.

"What? What are you not saying, darling?" Petra frowned.

Dante went to her and reached for her other hand. "I'm not going to let anything happen to you or your father, okay?"

"What is he saying?" Grigory demanded, his usually flushed face pale and covered with a light sheen of sweat.

"What he's saying," Xavier began. "Is that Tomasso is counting on there not being any witnesses left. If he is trying to cover his tracks, once he has possession of your daughter and you sign over the drug licenses, he has no more use for either of you."

Petra gasped and clasped Dante and her father's hands to her chest. "No!" Pixie, the tiny ball of fluff, yipped from her pink satin cushion as if responding to her mother's distress.

"We aren't going to let that happen," Dante promised.

Malachi joined Waverly and Xavier. "Travers, what the fuck is going on in your office?" Xavier demanded.

Malachi shook his head. "All I know is it came from somewhere on high. They've got ten agents assigned."

"Isn't that practically your entire office?" Micah asked, approaching with a diet soda in his hand.

"Do you think Brad's partner leaned on someone?" Waverly asked Malachi.

The man shrugged. "I think it's likely. We're the FBI. We don't move that fast without extreme motivation."

"How does this work without the FBI?" Waverly asked. "The whole point of the plan is to catch Brad in the act. We can't just walk up to him and yell 'citizen's arrest.'"

Xavier shook his head. "It's too late to move the exchange. If we put it off, it puts you at risk in case the feds are tailing one of their own," he looked pointedly at Malachi.

Malachi held up his hands. "I ran a surveillance detection route on the way here. No one's any the wiser as to your whereabouts," he assured Waverly.

"Look on the bright side. At least no one knows where you, Dante, and Petra are," Micah said.

"Okay, Pollyanna." Xavier crossed his arms. "How do we make this work?"

"Travers here isn't my only buddy in law enforcement," Micah said, taking a sip of his soda. "Let me make some calls."

"Dial fast," Xavier warned him. "We're almost out of time.

Roz had a four-course Italian dinner sent over to the house that evening, and they all gathered around the massive dining table. Ten of them around the table laughing and talking as if lives didn't hang in the balance. They told stories of childhoods and movies and missions and life over bottles of wine and plates of lasagna.

They felt like a team to Waverly, almost like family. All these people coming together for her. She'd spent almost her entire life feeling alone, facing obstacles by herself. And to have all these men and women who were willing to go head-to-head with an enemy for her? It hit her in the heart. The lives and livelihoods of so many people were riding on her getting this right. The responsibility weighed heavily on her. She owed them all so much more than she'd ever be able to repay. But she vowed she'd find a way.

Kate winked at her across the table, reading Waverly's mind as she'd always been able to. The woman always had her back, and Waverly decided that as soon as this mess was done, she was sending her on an all-expenses paid vacation to wherever Kate wanted to go.

After dinner, Malachi decided not to spend the night so he could stay close to anything that went down in the field office.

When she watched him leave, Waverly closed her eyes for a moment.

She tried to zone out with Kate, Petra, and Dante while they watched reruns of *Gilmore Girls*, but her mind kept running through the plan.

When Xavier came up behind her and nuzzled her ear, it was a very welcome distraction. "Come with me," he whispered. "We're going to go have some fun."

"Now?" She followed him upstairs to their bedroom. When he only studied her outfit rather than stripping her out of it, she looked down, too. She wore jeans and a fitted black sweater in the softest cashmere.

"What?"

"Just making sure you can move. Go find some shoes that you can walk in."

"I take it your version of 'fun' doesn't involve sex?" she asked, slipping on a pair of sneakers.

"Consider the first part of our date foreplay. Bring your gun," he told her.

Well this was going to be interesting foreplay, she decided.

They took the Escalade, and before they'd left the driveway, Xavier was reaching for her hand. She looked down at their linked hands. How quickly things had changed between them. It had taken Xavier a matter of days to reawaken feelings she thought were long dead. Waverly knew the truth now. She'd loved him then and had never stopped. For better or horrible, her heart belonged to Xavier Saint.

"So what's with the sudden craving for fun?" she finally asked. "Shouldn't we be hunkered down with the rest of the team preparing for tomorrow? This isn't exactly your style."

"I can be fun!" Xavier said with a fierce frown.

"Can you?" She was mostly teasing. Though Xavier was many things—invincible, brave, gorgeous, powerful, dark—

fun just wasn't what came to mind first. It wasn't even in the top ten. "Don't be mad, X. You can't possibly be everything, can you?"

"I'll let you be the judge of that," he said, still looking vaguely annoyed.

Twenty-five minutes later, she was still turning it over in her head when Xavier pulled the Escalade into the parking lot of a long, squat building the same color as the desert that surrounded it on all sides.

"Harry's Guns and Shooting Range?" Waverly asked, reading the sign. "You're taking me shooting?"

"Gotta make sure you can handle your piece," he winked.

"I handle your piece just fine," she said dryly.

"Angel, there's nothing 'just fine' about the way you handle my piece." He slid out of the driver's seat, and Waverly followed him to the back of the SUV. When he lifted the hatch, she just stared.

"Did you bring an entire arsenal?" she asked, taking in the dozen neatly stacked cases packed in the back.

"Angel, you haven't seen anything yet," he said with a steamy look.

She felt the warm glow spread from her belly. Would she ever get used to the way he looked at her? She hoped not.

Together they carried the cases to the darkened storefront. Xavier, his hands full, kicked lightly at the door. Almost instantly, a light turned on in the back. Waverly could just make out a shadowy figure shuffling toward the door. The shadow jingled keys in the lock and pushed the door open.

"Evening, Xavier."

"Good to see you, Harry." Xavier motioned Waverly inside. "Harry, this is Waverly."

"I'm not blind, son. I know a beautiful movie star when I see one." In the dim light, Waverly could see snowy white hair and broad shoulders on a short frame. The man wore bifocals and a red and black flannel shirt.

"Hi, Harry," Waverly offered the greeting as she slid her load of cases onto the glass counter that housed the usual gun shop treasures.

"Well, this must be a special occasion. As long as Xavier's been coming here, he's never brought company before, let alone company as pretty as you. Hope to see more of you," Harry said, in a lopsided cadence.

"I hope you will, too," Xavier said, laying a hand on the man's shoulder while looking at Waverly.

"Well, I'll leave you to it. You know how to lock up," Harry said, stuffing his hands into the pockets of his Dockers.

"Thanks again for opening up," Xavier said.

Harry shuffled out the front door and locked it from the outside. He threw a little half wave, half salute and Waverly waved back.

"You do this often?" she asked, picking up her cases again.

"When I'm in town and need to blow off some steam," Xavier said, leading the way through the retail and repair section into a narrow hallway of whitewashed concrete block. One wall had a large glass window overlooking the six-lane indoor firing range.

He opened the door to the range and slid his cases onto a long shelf that ran the length of the window. While he organized the weaponry, Waverly pushed the recall button on the first lane, calling the target clip home. Xavier reached over her and clipped the full body target in place and sent it back out to ten yards.

He settled ear protection over her ears and gestured toward the safety glasses. "Ladies first."

She slid the eye protection on and plucked her Glock out of the molded foam compartment.

Waverly ejected the magazine, checked it, and slapped it home. Racking the slide, she adopted a wide-legged stance and sized up the target with a smooth inhale. On her exhale, she emptied the magazine into the target.

She placed the gun on the shelf and smirked as Xavier hit the recall button. She was a damn good shot and knew it. Dante had taught her tradecraft, but he was a terrible shot, so she'd hired a private coach for training. She had shown talent from day one, and with a few lessons and a lot of practice, she was solid.

Xavier let out a low whistle. Six shots were neatly clustered in the center of the chest. Any of them would have been fatal.

"Not bad," Xavier said. "Now, what if the guy is wearing a vest?" He sent the target back out.

Waverly loaded in a fresh magazine and repeated the process. This time, when Xavier pulled the target back there was a grouping of four shots to the head and two in the groin.

"Remind me not to piss you off," Xavier said with amusement.

"As if you need that reminder." She handed him her gun. "Let's see what you can do, Mr. Saint."

He reloaded and with a cheerful smirk, fired off six shots. Xavier ejected the spent magazine, reloaded, and emptied that one, too.

Xavier was the essence of a man: raw, masculine, powerful, and cocky. He'd shed his suit jacket and fired the handgun in shirt sleeves and a tie. Waverly could feel her mouth spread in a slow smile of female appreciation for the fine picture before her.

"Damn," she sighed.

His target was toast. Six shots to the head in a tight little grouping. Six more opened up one big gaping hole in the chest.

"I like what you do with a gun, X."

He laughed. A real laugh like the kind he reserved for family and close friends. "I like what you do with *my* gun."

"Aren't you playful tonight?" Waverly commented, slyly arching an eyebrow.

"I can be fun. Why does everyone think I'm so serious?"

"They also think you're dark and intense and maybe a little scary."

He meant to tease her with a quick kiss, but Waverly shifted those intentions with her response. There was so much going on behind those deep brown eyes of his. She wished she could tease it out of him. She settled instead for teasing his lazy tongue and nipping at his lower lip until Xavier was pressing her against the divider wall of their booth.

Playful or not it was a marvel what he was able to do to her body. With just a kiss, he set her afire. His hands cruised up her side, sneaking under the softness of cashmere. But he stopped short, resting his rough palms against her waist.

He pulled away from her mouth with a sound akin to a growl. "That's not why I brought you here."

"I won't complain," Waverly said, trying to catch her breath. No matter who instigated the kiss, they both always ended up affected. She leaned into him, resting her face against his chest. He was always so warm, so solid. His body meant comfort and security to her. Strength, power, and heat were the hallmarks of what she felt under her hands when she let her palms wander his skin.

He was protector, predator, hero.

Now it was her turn to take a step back. Xavier overwhelmed her. Her feelings for him threatened to drown her. And tonight, she needed air and space. "Maybe we should shoot some more before we get naked?" she suggested.

THEY BROKE OUT EIGHT HANDGUNS, firing them and stripping them down one at a time. Xavier had to admit Waverly was good. Not only was she an excellent shot, but she also handled the weapons with competency and a healthy respect. He was confident she could physically hit a human target. But he wasn't sure she'd be mentally prepared to do so. Taking a life, no matter how necessary, wasn't easy. It could weigh heavily, and he prayed his Angel would never be in that position where it became necessary.

He would always put himself between her and any danger. *But not tomorrow,* he reminded himself. Tomorrow she'd face her threats head-on while he stood in the wings. He shoved the thought aside. There was no room for worry. But he could test her skills *and* prove to her that he too could be fun.

Xavier grabbed her around the waist and pulled her in again. "You ready for some real fun?" he asked her, his voice husky and full of dark promises.

She smiled coyly, her fingers curling into the neck of his t-shirt. "I'm always ready for some fun."

He liked that she pouted when he broke away from her. He took her hand and led her back into the narrow hallway. "This is a top secret Invictus project," Xavier warned her, sliding the key into the lock of the last door. "I have to swear you to secrecy before I allow you to enter."

Waverly held up three fingers. "Scouts honor," she promised.

The knob turned in his hand, and Xavier let Waverly enter first.

"I don't know what I was expecting, but it was definitely something more exciting," she confessed, eyeing the room.

A large screen hung from the ceiling to cover most of the sidewall. On the opposite wall was a serviceable metal locker.

"You'll be impressed in a minute. Be patient." He closed the door behind her and crossed to the cabinet. Brandishing yet another key, he unlocked it and beckoned her over.

"Tell me you don't have a severed head in there," she said, approaching cautiously.

"Don't be ridiculous. Everyone knows you keep those in the freezer. Here." He handed her a headset with goggles and took one for himself.

She studied the set in her hands. "Is this VR?"

"First person shooter virtual reality in beta testing for law enforcement and private security capacities," he explained, handing her a weighted plastic pistol.

"No way!"

"Yes way," he smiled. "Testing is underway at the farm for CIA recruits and four police departments across the country."

"How did you come up with this?" Waverly asked, ejecting the gun's magazine.

Xavier shrugged. "There've been other basic VR programs out there but none with the programmable and randomized scenarios we've built. Cops can train on domestic disturbance, shots fired, and hostage calls. The CIA wanted drop scenarios with evasions and counterterrorism situations."

"You must have been developing this for years," she guessed.

"After you. After Ganim, I stopped working in the field and instead focused on revamping our training program. Micah and I, our backgrounds are military. We know what it feels like to be in a firefight, to have that adrenaline pumping through you when your life is on the line. But without that experience..."

"You can't anticipate how someone's going to react in a situation when it's life or death," Waverly filled in.

Xavier nodded, pleased that she got it. "Exactly. You can have all the training in the world and still freeze up when someone pulls a gun on you. Or in the case of some law enforcement, you can error on the trigger-happy side. We're building a program now for traffic stops to help troopers determine real versus perceived threats."

"X, that's amazing," Waverly said, impressed.

He shrugged lightly and pulled a vest from the locker.

"I need Kevlar for virtual reality?"

"Dual function," he explained, sliding the vest over her head. "It gets you used to the weight of a vest, and this one lets you know when you've been hit in the training." He tightened the side straps, sizing the vest down for her.

"Awesome!" She danced in place. "You take the girls on the best dates!"

He gave her a grin, feeling like a different kind of hero. "I tell you what. If you can make it through the scenario without getting tagged, I'll stop for tacos on the way back."

"You are so on!"

"It's not easy," he warned.

"Have a little faith," she told him. "There's nothing I won't do for tacos."

"I'll have faith, and you have fun," he suggested.

Xavier suited up and turned on the program. "The scenario is a report of shots fired in a shopping center," he explained. "You ready?"

"Bring it!"

An hour later, on their fourth run-through, Waverly held up her arms in victory. "Yesss! Suck it, bad guys!"

"Said the girl who took two rounds to the head," he teased.

"That was the first time through. I learn from my mistakes."

Xavier curled his fingers into the neck of her vest and pulled her to him. The energy of battle still pumped through him, made him hungry for an outlet. "Not all of them," he reminded her. "And I'm grateful for that."

She met his mouth eagerly enough that he was cursing himself for pulling back. "It's late," he whispered, his lips moving over hers gently.

"And you owe me tacos."

They made it a mile down the road from Harry's before Waverly's wandering hands had him pulling over. "I'm so amped," she murmured into his mouth when she climbed into his lap.

"It's the rush," he explained on a groan. "There's only one way to get rid of it."

28

*T*hey woke edgy and ready before dawn and found
Kate had beaten everyone to the kitchen where the
scents of fresh coffee and slightly burnt eggs hung in the air.

"You're up early," Waverly said, throwing her arm around
Kate's shoulders. Kate sagged into the embrace.

"I'm really nervous," she confessed.

"You'll do great." Waverly gave her friend a reassuring
squeeze.

"It's not me I'm worried about. My part's easy. Brad wants
what you have. He's not going to just roll over on this without
a fight."

Xavier stepped in and shifted Waverly out of the way. He
put both hands on Kate's tense shoulders. "Kate."

She nodded, wide-eyed.

"Everyone is going to do their jobs to the best of their abilities today, including me. Do you know what that means?"

Kate shook her head, still staring up at him like a deer in
headlights.

"It means no one gets to Waverly. I swear to you, I won't let
her get hurt."

Kate threw herself into Xavier's arms and hugged him hard. Xavier eyed Waverly over Kate's blonde head, unsure of what to do.

Waverly grinned at him from where she leaned against the counter.

"Wow, you even smell good," Kate murmured against his chest.

"Okay," Waverly said, stepping in. "Stop mauling Xavier." Waverly tugged Kate out of his arms but not before hugging her herself. "Everything's going to work. I promise."

Kate nodded. "I just wish that I could do more to help."

"Kate," Xavier said smoothly. "You're an integral part of what's happening today. And timing is essential. So don't fuck it up."

It got a snort out of her, and Waverly smacked him on the shoulder.

"I know, and I'll make sure everything is perfect. I just... worry."

"Don't worry. Be ready, be good. And we'll all be celebrating with a big dinner tonight," he promised.

"Okay," Kate nodded.

"It's going to work," Waverly reassured her. "Now how about some of those well-done eggs?"

They congregated in the kitchen, everyone too nervous to sleep. Xavier surveyed his small army. Micah, his right hand, the man who always had his back even knowing it could cost him the company they'd both worked so hard for. Kate, the steadfast and loyal friend who wanted to help in any way possible. Petra, the heiress with the big eyes and a sweet heart. Her father, Grigory, a man who had done the right thing and was now facing the danger of paying the price for saying no to those without souls. Anatoli, the loyal guard charged with protecting Grigory's prize. He'd extended that protection, that loyalty, to include the rest of them.

Then there was Chelsea, his sister still in her pajamas looking as if she hadn't slept, her fingers furiously working the keyboard of her laptop. Chelsea was the only one who wouldn't be directly involved in the operation today. But her job was as important if not more so than Xavier's. She was hunting. Brad's partner was out there, and even if Brad was behind bars by the end of the day, his partner still posed a threat.

Dante ambled in, already dressed and looking as if he hadn't a care in the world. But Xavier could see a sharpness, an edge in the man's eyes. His devil may care attitude aside, Dante knew what was at stake today. And, as with Kate, his timing had to be perfect.

Malachi Travers wasn't in the room, crowded around the breakfast table and island with the rest of them. But Xavier still counted him as a member of the team. With the FBI looking hard at Waverly, having Malachi on the inside would prove valuable... as long as they could count on him. Xavier still wasn't sure if they had his loyalty if it came down to choosing between saving Waverly or saving his job.

They had one shot at turning this around today. One chance at making the feds change their minds about the target of their investigation.

And that rode squarely on Waverly's shoulders. He watched her as she sipped her coffee and bantered with Micah and Petra over something that had them all laughing. She was smart and capable, handled a weapon like a pro, and thought on her feet better than nearly anyone he knew. Yet she was the team member he was worried about the most.

She could handle herself, Xavier told himself. If they stuck with the plan, if everyone did their job, she would be fine. But if things fell apart, there was no telling what the outcome would be or if they would all come home alive tonight.

And it was eating at him. He trusted her. Knew she would do whatever it took to make the mission a success. It was the sign of a good operative. But it was also what terrified him to his bones. If something happened and the plan went to hell, Waverly would be facing Brad alone. And Xavier would have failed her again.

The thought of that possibility was killing him.

His phone signaled an incoming call, and he answered it tersely.

"Saint."

"Good morning to you, too," his mother chirped in his ear.

"What's wrong?" Xavier demanded.

"Nothing's wrong! Can't a mother call her son?"

"Mom, it's six in the morning," he said, cursing himself for not checking his caller id. Chelsea looked up from the table and mimed laughing at him. Xavier threw a napkin at her.

"You've been avoiding all my normal hours calls," Carol Saint reminded him.

It was true. He'd been avoiding his mother. He knew she'd be curious about Waverly and what their time together meant. And he hadn't been prepared to answer questions. He'd resorted to calling his parents when he knew they were at their monthly book club and leaving a voicemail so they wouldn't realize he was avoiding them.

It obviously hadn't worked.

Xavier sighed. "I've been busy," he said, pushing away from the breakfast table. Chelsea, in her infinite maturity, hissed "neener neener neener," at him as he headed into the great room.

"I gathered that from the news and the Max Heim show," she said dryly.

"You saw that, did you?"

"No thanks to you. Your sister told us to tune in."

The Katy Perry ringtone on Waverly's phone suddenly made more sense to Xavier.

"I've been spending time with Waverly," he said, making the unnecessary confession.

"No shit," Carol said succinctly. "Is it personal or professional?"

"Both," Xavier admitted. "I can hear you happy dancing," he said dryly.

"I don't know what you're talking about," his mother responded, proving his point by being slightly out of breath. "When are you bringing her home again?"

"As soon as humanly possible, and don't use that as an excuse to renovate the entire house," he warned.

"What was that? I couldn't hear you. I was looking up the contractor's number."

"Mom!"

Chelsea put her thumbs in her ears and wiggled her fingers at him from the kitchen. Xavier flipped her the bird.

"I'm just kidding. Relax!" Her voice softened. "I'm really happy for you, Xavier."

His mother had guessed all those years ago how deep his feelings for Waverly ran. And she, and the rest of the Saints, had been there to help him pick up the pieces when it had all gone to hell.

He sighed. "Thanks, Mom. I don't want to jinx anything. There's still a chance she could come to her senses."

His mother laughed. "Then you just do your best to make sure she doesn't have enough time or space to change her mind."

"Good advice, Mom."

"That's how your father wooed me."

Xavier smiled despite himself. His parents' relationship, that committed team effort, was what he wanted in life. They challenged each other, supported each other, enjoyed each other. And he could have that with Waverly.

If he could keep her safe today.

"I'll have to take a page out of Dad's book," Xavier promised.

"I'd put him on for you, but I have a bit more motherly interrogation to do."

"What now?"

"Have you heard from your sister? Chelsea hasn't been answering my calls either, and I'm worried."

"Chelsea?" Xavier grinned at his sister, who went from flipping him off to shaking her head so violently he thought it might snap off her neck. "She didn't tell you?" he asked, taking great joy in selling out his sister.

"Tell me what?" Carol demanded.

"She's here. She's helping me with a project. I can't believe she didn't tell you."

"She's what?" His mother was almost shouting.

"Here. You can talk to her," Xavier held his phone at arm's length to Chelsea. "Mom wants to talk to you, Chels," he said loud enough that their mother could hear him.

Chelsea stomped on his foot for good measure before taking the phone from him.

"Hey, Mom."

Xavier smirked as Chelsea left the great room dodging their mother's questions.

"That wasn't very nice," Waverly said, entering the room with her arms crossed.

"But necessary. My mother wants to know when you're coming to visit."

"What did you tell her?" Waverly asked, slipping her arms around his waist and looking up at him.

"Only enough for her to start hoping for grandchildren in the next six months," Xavier teased, running his hands down her back.

"Are you ready for this?" Waverly asked.

"What? Kids? I think we'll catch on eventually."

"Xavier! I meant today. Are you ready for today?"

He looked past her at their breakfast eating compatriots. He'd prefer to go into this knowing that the feds were in their pocket, knowing that his team held all the cards. But it wasn't to be. "Maybe we could postpone this? Come at it from a different angle," he suggested. The sudden desperation for a Plan B ate at him.

"Xavier," Waverly sighed out his name. "It's going to be fine. We've got this. I believe in you, and I need you to believe in me."

He shook his head. "We're rushing this. There has to be another way." *There had to be.* Maybe the timeline could be finessed enough to keep the FBI at bay until they found an in with the SEC? Maybe if Chelsea could find the partner, they could sway the FBI?

Waverly tugged out of his grasp and latched onto his arm. She dragged him out of the great room and into a very small, very purple powder room. The quarters were cramped with a long single sink vanity occupying most of one wall. But it would have to do for privacy.

"Talk to me, X," she ordered, flicking the lock.

He moved restlessly in the confined space.

"I'm having a hard time with this," he confessed, pacing the three steps to the sink and back again.

She got in his path and put her hands on his chest. "I know. Tell me what's going on in that sexy brain of yours."

He grasped her hands and kissed her fingers. "I hate using you as bait."

Tension crackled off of him, filling the air around them.

She cupped his face in her palms. "I can do this. I need you to have faith in me."

He nodded, but his eyes told a different story. There was anxiety there and something edgier. She'd been there before, the line between fear and panic. He slipped out of her grasp and roamed past her. Waverly slid up on the vanity to give him room. She let him pace it out for another minute before catching his arm and caging him in between her legs.

"X, I've been trained. I've done this before."

"Something could go wrong. What if—"

She put a finger to his mouth and then replaced it with her lips. She pulled back when she felt his rigid length stiffen against her. "This is going to work, and it's all going to be over soon," she promised, stroking her hands through his thick hair.

"Promise me."

"I promise you, X. This is important to me. I need you to trust me. I need you to believe in me."

"I do, but..."

She silenced his protest. "My poor Xavier," she sighed. "I know why this is so hard for you. You're the protector, the fixer. It's what you do. You stand between everyone you love and the danger they face. But I can face this myself, and I will with you backing me up. I need this, X. *We* need this. You can't always stand for me. I need to stand for me."

He kissed her hard, leaning into her, over her, as if he could change her mind with just his mouth. She felt it all from him: the fear, the determination, the pure power of him. Everything that he was, he poured into her. When he took the kiss deeper, Waverly let him and gave him everything she had in return. Separately, they were impressive. Together, they were unstoppable.

She broke the kiss and dropped her forehead to his chest. "I love you, Xavier."

His fingers gripped her upper arms so hard she knew she'd have fingerprints on her skin. He squeezed his eyes closed tight. "Say it again," he whispered, his voice rough as gravel.

She kissed him first, lightly, sweetly. "I love you, Xavier Saint. Even more now. And even more every damn day. You're my protector, my partner, my heart."

His breath came out on a ragged sigh, and his eyes flew open. He cupped her face. "We're getting married."

"You're insane," she laughed.

"Say it. Say you'll marry me."

"When this is all over, if you still want to, yes. I'll marry you." She felt tears prickle behind her eyes. But of all the tears she'd cried over him, these were joyful.

He took a half step back and shoved his hand in the pocket of his jeans.

"I imagined doing this in much different circumstances, but this feels right. This feels like us."

"You're not going to shoot me or something, are you?" Waverly asked.

"Maybe later, Angel." His long fingers slid out of the pocket holding a diamond ring between them.

"Oh, my God."

"We're making this official, Waverly. You're not backing out of this, and I'm not waiting any more. I bought this the day before I flew to Belize." He slid it onto her finger and kissed it and then her. She was crying now, and he took his time kissing each tear on her cheeks.

"You are my heart and my center. Nothing means what it

should without you. I want to build a life with you. I want to wake up holding you every damn day of my forever. I want to give you everything you've ever wanted. Normal, kids, maybe a couple of sloppy dogs. I want to spend the rest of my life making love to you every chance I get because I will never have enough of you."

She couldn't answer him through the tears that clogged her throat.

He squeezed her again. "Angel, baby, I need you to say it. I need to hear the words."

She nodded again, sucked in a breath. "I must be insane, but yes. Hell yes, I'll marry you."

Xavier crushed her to him. "It's about damn time," he said before his mouth met hers.

29

"You have the worst possible timing," Waverly laughed breathlessly against him as she held up her hand to admire the ring.

The laugh died on her lips when Xavier hitched her legs higher over his hips and she felt how rigid his shaft was. The light in his warm brown eyes turned to fire as she rolled her hips to grind against him.

"Now who has bad timing," he asked, nipping her lower lip. He stroked a rough palm up her thigh, his fingers slipping under the hem of the shorts she wore. She watched those brown eyes go molten when he realized she wasn't wearing underwear. He used the pads of his fingers to stroke over her delicate folds once then twice before gripping the waistband from the inside and tugging the shorts down.

He was gorgeous, she thought, lifting her hips so he could ease the shorts all the way off. That straight nose, high, patrician cheekbones, his solid jaw hidden under the days of scruff he'd stopped trying to tame. But his appeal went deeper than those beautifully carved features and those impossibly deep eyes. There was power that radiated from him. It was in the way he moved, the way he spoke, the way he zeroed in on her and looked inside her.

That connection they'd had years ago, the one she sensed from their first handshake, had only deepened.

A handshake hadn't been nearly enough then and Waverly felt a desperation for something much more rise up in her now. She reached for his jeans, freeing the button, but he caught her fingers when she touched his zipper.

He scooted her to the very edge of the vanity so she had to lean back. Xavier curled her fingers over the lip of the counter.

"I want you wearing nothing but my ring," he said, his voice a ragged whisper. "I'm going to take you now, and every move you make today, you're going to be thinking about me inside you until we're back together."

His busy hands changed their course, running back up her shins, her thighs, over her hips, and sliding under her sweater. She wanted to say yes, to promise him that she already thought of him perpetually, constantly. Xavier had once told her he was obsessed with her. He'd compared himself to Ganim, the man who had stalked her, hurt her, tried to destroy her.

But this? This heaven that she found in his arms? It was nothing like that darkness. This was beautiful, consuming, soul shaking. It had always been love between them, and now that the words had been spoken, promises made, it would grow even stronger.

He worked her sweater up, and she saw his breath catch when he bared her breasts. Only after he'd tugged it over her head and let it fall to the floor did he release his zipper. He was already rigidly hard, that thick column of flesh fought against the thin cotton of his briefs, straining toward her.

Waverly couldn't wait any longer. She used her toes to dig into the waistband of the last barrier between them, shoving his black briefs and jeans down to free his erection. He was beyond ready for her, she noted, wetting her lips as she studied the slickness at the head with fascination.

The ache that built at her core, simultaneously everywhere and nowhere, intensified.

"You're so fucking beautiful," Xavier breathed the words with reverence as he fisted the root of his cock. "And you're mine."

"I've always been yours," she said, finally forming the words she needed him to hear. "Even when we were stupid and stubborn and scared."

"I'm still all of those things when it comes to you," he confessed, watching her as he lowered his mouth to sample the pink nipple that budded under his warm breath. A low moan of pleasure escaped her throat when his tongue lashed over the peak.

"Oh, Angel," he sighed, stroking the bud again, this time with the flat of his tongue. "I need hours with you now, years." His cock flexed with need. "A lifetime."

"Right now we have minutes," she breathed. "Make them count, X."

He relinquished her breast and planted her feet on the counter just inside her hands.

Waverly's head fell back against the mirror. She was splayed open for him. She should have felt vulnerable, but instead, she was awash in power. She was craved by Xavier Saint.

He notched the head of his penis at her entrance and groaned at the slickness he found there. "I love how wet you get for me."

Waverly moaned as he used his hand to slide that flared head over her, parting her flesh until it nudged the spot that ached with desire. Her sigh sounded more like a sob to her.

"Hold on tight," he warned, guiding his cock back to her entrance.

"Hurry. Hurry. Please," she begged.

And then he was working his way into her, one thick inch at a time. "Relax, Angel," he said bringing his forehead to hers. "Relax."

Waverly breathed into the fullness that was edged with silver slivers of delicious pain. She felt those tiny muscles slowly loosen their grip on Xavier's shaft just enough.

"Ah, yes," he hissed out as he finally slid home. He hitched her legs around his waist. "Hang on, baby."

And with that warning all savoring, all gentleness was gone. Xavier withdrew and sank back into her with a primal groan. Waverly stifled the desperate noises clawing their way out of her throat by pressing her face into his chest. She felt so raw, being completely naked while Xavier was still fully clothed.

He was driving into her now, pushing them both toward the top.

"I'm going to make you come," he told her in a voice strained with effort. "And everyone out there is going to hear you. They're going to know that you belong to me."

Waverly felt herself flutter around his shaft at his words. A movement on her periphery caught her eye. She turned her head and watched their reflection in the mirror in wanton fascination. Xavier, so strong and virile, powering himself into her. She saw herself, flushed and heavy lidded. Her lips full and swollen, her breasts swaying with every plunge into her body. The ring glittered on her finger.

Ever attentive, Xavier followed her gaze. He growled low, a rumble in his chest. "I feel you working my cock, Angel. When you go off, you're going to set me off, too. Tell me what you need."

Waverly was lost to the building sensation, that tightening, that pull inward. "More," she whispered to Xavier. She wanted more of everything he had to offer.

His jaw was clenched tight and sweat dotted his forehead. The thrust of his hips increased in both power and speed. Every stroke carried her forward to the edge.

"Xavier!" His name was a gasp.

"I'm with you, Angel."

And then the light inside her exploded, blinding her behind closed lids, and he was pumping his seed into her in hot jets. She closed around him in tremulous, delirious waves that wracked her entire body.

"I love you," he groaned, his forehead resting on hers while they came together.

"I love you, X."

~

THEY SNUCK UPSTAIRS USING the front staircase to avoid a walk of shame through the kitchen where surely everyone heard their wanton display.

Xavier dressed quickly in his standard black suit and white button down before leaving her in their room to dress with a stern warning that they were rolling out in an hour. She looked at her outfit and decided it might take her that long to dress. Going into an operation was never as simple as pulling on a pair of shorts and a t-shirt. Everything had a purpose and in this case, everything had a dual purpose.

She finished dressing and then stretched and flexed in the mirror, making sure nothing bulged visibly under her long sleeve button down, and then double-checked that her lucky coin was snug between her breasts.

Satisfied, a ghost of a smile danced over her lips, and she

dug through her go bag until her fingers brushed the object she sought. The anklet was another sentimental charm from Xavier. The tiny diamond heart cleverly hid a GPS tracker. Xavier had it designed for her when he began guarding her years ago. That little heart had saved her life when Ganim abducted her. Xavier had been able to track her location and get to her just in time. She'd never worn it since but always carried it with her like a talisman warding off evil.

It seemed fitting that she wear it today. Waverly fastened it to her ankle and gave her reflection another check. Everything was where it should be, she decided. Now it was time for Hollywood armor.

She hurried into the bathroom and assembled her makeup supplies, pausing often to admire the sparkle on her left hand. It was a breathtaking ring, a breathtaking promise that they'd made to each other. Yet she didn't feel fear about their decision. It felt... right. There was no one else in this world she would ever feel this for. Love didn't even seem like a strong enough descriptor for the all-consuming fire he sparked in her. It was so much deeper than anything she'd ever hoped for.

Her parents were going to be thrilled, Waverly thought with a smile. She'd tell them tonight, after everything with Tomasso was settled.

She reached for her lipstick, the ringing of her phone caught her attention.

Brad Tomasso. Waverly's adrenaline spiked instantly.

"Brad."

"I decided I didn't like your terms. So I'm changing them," Brad announced without preamble. "You're going to drag that little Russian bitch to me, or you're going to pay a price."

"You're the one paying a price, Brad." She kept her tone

mild, but tuned into the gut feeling that she was walking into trouble.

"I've got something you're going to want even more than the money."

"What could I possibly want more than money?"

He ignored her question with a humorless laugh. "The exchange was getting a little too crowded for me. So we're going to do a little business just the two of us."

"I like the deal we have on the table," she insisted.

"Let me tell you what you're going to do today, Waverly. You're going to bring Petra to the exchange, and then you're going to wait until you hear from me with the new plan. You're going to follow my instructions to the letter, and you're not going to tell a soul. Especially not your friend Saint."

"Oh, really?" she forced a laugh of her own. "And why am I going to do all that?"

"Check your texts," he said cryptically and disconnected the call.

She had a bad feeling, one that settled like ice in her belly. Brad was too cocky not to have an ace in the hole. And when she opened the text from him, she saw exactly what that ace was.

Sylvia Sinner, sat unconscious bound to a chair. Her blonde curls fell over her forehead, her neck lolling to the side. A broad swatch of tape covered her mouth.

I invited your mother to breakfast. She must have had too much to drink.

She couldn't tell if her mother was injured or drugged or where the photo was taken. The background was dark as if her mother sat alone in a spotlight. There were no hints, no way to circumvent Brad to get to her mother.

How had she not seen this move coming? Waverly cursed herself.

She felt herself shift into autopilot, the shock crowding everything else out of her mind. Brad had taken her mother as an insurance policy. And he wouldn't hesitate to kill her if Waverly disobeyed him. Her mother's life depended on her following Brad's instructions to the letter.

"Fuck," she muttered to herself.

The diamond glinted on her finger, a flash of the promises of future and of trust, of a partnership that could last. Could Xavier ever forgive her for turning her back?

Five minutes later, a shaky but dressed Waverly made her way downstairs praying that she wasn't making a huge mistake. She was terrified that Xavier was going to take one look at her and know. So it was an odd mix of relief and annoyance that Waverly felt when Petra nervously beckoned her into the library.

The girl had Pixie cuddled to her chest.

"I wish I was brave like you," Petra announced, leaning against the massive walnut table and rubbing her cheek against Pixie's tiny head.

"Petra, you're very brave," Waverly said, dropping into a leather chair under a window. "First, for falling in love with Dante, and second, for trusting Xavier and me when we essentially broke into your house."

Petra shook her lovely dark hair back from her face. "I wish to do more. You have done so much for me. All of you, of course, but you especially."

Waverly shook her head. "Your part is so important today," she promised.

"But I wish to stand up to the man who is threatening my family! My father, he has done nothing wrong. He is a good man," Petra insisted.

"He's a wonderful man," Waverly agreed. Feeling her stomach pitch at the thought of her own parent who was now facing danger from Brad. "And we're not going to let him or anyone else pay the price for Brad's greed. I know you think your role is small today. But believe me, it's essential."

Petra sighed, and Pixie let out a tiny squeak. She put the dog down on the table, and Waverly watched as little Pixie immediately trotted toward the edge.

Waverly levered out of her chair and snatched the pup up, saving her from a steep fall or the miniature suicide she'd planned. Petra didn't seem to notice. She was too busy staring at Waverly's left hand.

"This ring?" She grabbed Waverly's hand and held it up to her face. "Four carats, cushion cut, with the slightest hint of blush," she assessed. "Does this mean what I think?"

Waverly glanced down at the beautiful stone that winked up at her. "Good eye. Yes, but we're keeping it under wraps until tonight... when all of this is behind us." *God, she hoped it would be behind them.* There was so much more at stake now.

Petra wrapped her in a tight hug, squashing the tiny dog between them. "This absolves me of my guilt!"

Waverly gave a half-hearted laugh. "There has never been anything more than friendship between Dante and me," she promised. "You have nothing to feel guilty about."

Petra waved her declaration away. "Dante often tries to protect my feelings," she confessed with a knowing smile. "But he loves me, and we will be a family soon. And now I can be happy because you are also happy with your Xavier."

"My Xavier," Waverly repeated softly. Her Xavier who

would move heaven and earth to keep her safe and give her anything she wanted.

Petra nodded. "You two are a team. It is nice to see two people who love and trust each other. Just like Dante and me!"

Waverly handed the squirming ball of suicidal fur back to Petra.

"You are sure that there is nothing more that I can do today to help?"

Waverly shook her head. "Just get dressed in that perfect Petra outfit you and Kate picked out, remember to smile and wave, and this whole thing will all be over soon." *God, she hoped she wasn't lying.*

30

*T*he Grand Central Market was an eclectic mash of cuisine and culture. Housed in a six-story reinforced concrete building, the market sprawled over the entire first floor throwing up the scents of a hundred different foods. People of all ages and ethnicities wandered the stands choosing prime cuts of meat from delicatessens and lining up for Bento boxes and fresh donuts. The noise, the smells, the entire environment was making Waverly's stomach churn.

She'd been on missions before but never with stakes this high.

She'd dressed to blend in a baseball hat, plaid shirt, and denim shorts. Her partner in crime, on the other hand, wore a pair of jeans so distressed they could unravel at any second and a voluminous knit poncho in alternating stripes of gray and pink. She too wore a hat, a floppy brimmed sunhat in chocolate brown, and oversized sunglasses.

They sat in a café just inside the market entrance at a table barely big enough for the two cups of coffee Waverly had ordered. She didn't touch hers, having had more than enough caffeine, a surprise proposal, and then a blazing orgasm already that morning. She didn't need to get any sharper, or she might shatter into pieces.

On this particular Saturday morning, the market was over-flowing with foot traffic. Xavier had chosen the venue well. Crowded and chaotic, the friendly flow of shoppers provided perfect cover for a handful of private security agents, a movie star spy, and the feds that were watching her.

"I hope you're ready for this, Petra," Waverly said without moving her lips at the woman across from her.

"You're looking a little green, Sinner," Xavier's voice rang reassuringly in her ear. "You two are going to do great."

Waverly had to stop herself from asking him to promise her they'd all come out of this unscathed. The stakes were so much higher than they had been just a few hours ago. She picked out a handful of friendly faces in the crowd. Xavier's team certainly blended better than the six men and women she'd identified as feds. They should have been here to have her back, to arrest Brad for the games he'd been playing with national security. But instead they were here for her.

In the car on the way over, a story had broken about Dante Wrede going missing and Waverly Sinner being the last person to see him alive. The article alluded that police were interested in discussing Dante's disappearance with her.

Brad was covering his tracks and planning to dump the bulk of his sins in her lap. But she wasn't going down without a fight.

She glanced around them, pretending to fiddle with her coffee. There was a woman who'd been studying the deli's sausage links with great enthusiasm for almost ten full minutes. FBI, Waverly assumed. She wondered briefly if this was Brad's plan, having her arrested here and pinning his crimes on her. She certainly looked guilty enough hanging on to a pouting kidnap victim. Even if the truth came out, she'd never see her mother again.

But he was in show business and having her picked up now lacked the drama of a showdown. Besides, she could hold her own in a battle of he said, she said. No, Brad wanted all the players here so no one law enforcement related would witness their showdown. Someplace private. Someplace he would have control of.

"You're doing great, Angel. Just hang in there," Xavier said soothingly in her ear.

"Thanks, X," she said quietly into her shoulder mic. She shoved her nerves back. There was no room to think clearly if she was panicking on the inside. This would work. She would make it work. And she'd kick Brad square in the balls before the end of the day. The thought comforted her.

Her phone buzzed in her hand. It was him.

"Hello?" Waverly answered.

"Good morning again, sunshine," Brad's voice rang out with the cheerfulness of a man who was about to get everything he wanted. "Follow my instructions, and you'll see your mother alive again. Fuck with me, and you won't."

"I'm not fucking with you. I brought Petra," she said, tightening her grip on the girl's arm.

"Take your radio out of your ear and get rid of the mic."

Waverly hesitated and glanced around her. She felt the gazes of a dozen people weighing on her. She tapped her foot nervously under the table. One long tap followed by two short ones.

"Don't sit there waiting to be rescued. Do it now!" he shouted through the phone. *Shit. He definitely had a visual on her.* It could be anyone with a cell phone out or a well-placed hidden camera.

She plucked the radio out of her ear and whispered a hasty "I love you" into her shoulder mic as she removed it, too.

"Radio's out," she confirmed quietly into the phone.

"On the count of ten, I want you to walk your friend out that exit behind the butcher. Throw your radio in the trashcan on your way out," Brad told her. Waverly gauged the distance from their table to the side door. It was about thirty feet, and a lot could happen in thirty feet.

The federal agents were reacting to her change in behavior, not even bothering to avoid eye contact. She could tell that everyone felt the change in the air.

"Go. Walk out the fucking door now," Brad ordered.

Waverly grabbed the edge of Petra's poncho and started hauling ass toward the cooler case of meat. She dumped the radio in the trashcan and felt like she had just stepped out of a plane without a parachute. A huge group of Japanese tourists chose that moment to wander down the aisle, creating mayhem everywhere.

Waverly shoved the exterior door open and kept a strong grip on the poncho.

"We're out," she told him. The sidewalk was crowded with people watching a street performer act like a statue.

"Good. Now get on the bus."

"You've got to be kidding me." A fire engine red double decker Hollywood tour bus waited at the curb.

"Do I sound like I'm kidding?" Brad yelled into the phone. Waverly heard a crash and then a scream. Her mother's scream.

"Jesus! Don't you fucking hurt her. We're getting on the bus."

She pushed the woman on ahead of her and paid in cash for the tickets. The doors closed after her, and the bus pulled away from the curb. Away from Xavier. Away from help.

"Go up onto the second level and sit in the two front seats," Brad ordered through the phone.

Waverly gestured up and followed Petra's holey jeans up the skinny staircase.

"We're up," she said. There were a dozen people on the second level, but the two front seats were open. Her phone signaled another incoming call, but she ignored it. "Where are we going?"

The tour guide's voice droned over the loudspeaker directing guests to look right and left at the highlights of downtown.

"You don't get to ask the questions. Now sit down and don't move your phone away from your ear. You're not alone up there, and if I see you trying to signal anyone or get help, Mommy's getting a bullet in her head." She heard the ominous sound of a gun slide racking.

Waverly wet her lips. "I won't try to signal anyone. Can I talk to her?"

"When you get here and hand over the girl, you'll have all the time in the world to talk."

"What are you going to do to us?" Waverly asked. She didn't have to force the tremor in her voice.

"Well, Waverly, since you've been such a headache to me, I'm going to kill you. But if you hold up your end of the bargain and bring me Petra. Then I'll let your mother go free."

There was an ice cube's chance in a hell-hosted barbecue that he'd let anyone walk away. But right now, Waverly was her mother's only chance.

"Brad, there's no way you're walking away from this. You can't just get rid of all the loose ends."

He laughed harshly in her ear. "Don't try to talk your way out of this. This isn't some contract negotiation. Your usefulness ends the second you deliver Petra, yet you're still following orders. Who's the idiot in this situation?"

"The bus is stopping," she told him evenly. They had entered a movie studio lot. Not just any studio's lot. It was Target Studios' gated lot with its fifteen huge warehouses and soundstages. The tour guide's disembodied voice was asking everyone to disembark and choose a tram car.

"Stay where you are," he instructed.

They waited until the upper deck was mostly clear. "You're going to stand up and take off your gun."

Waverly glanced at her seatmate, her eyes unreadable behind Petra's huge sunglasses.

"Just how am I going to keep her from running if I don't have a gun?" she gritted out the words.

"Be creative. Now do it."

They both stood, and Waverly reached under her shirt to pull out her .38. There were three men left on the bus, all staring at her.

"There's a good little starlet. Now put your gun on the seat and walk off the bus."

Waverly glowered at the men as she carefully set the handgun on the vinyl cushion. Keeping her hands in plain sight, she gestured toward the staircase, and together they climbed down. The brass railing was sticky under her hand. The lower level was completely empty, and Waverly chose the rear exit of the bus over the front. They skirted the crowd of tourists waiting to be assigned a seat on the tram car, and Waverly led the way, jogging down the side of one of the huge steel buildings.

She wanted to get them out of sight of the henchmen so she didn't have to worry about a bullet in her back. Thankfully, it was clear that Brad wanted one last villain speech with her before ending her life because they rounded the back of the sound stage with no interference.

"Let's get this over with, Brad. Where are you?"

"I made it easy for you," he said. Open the door on your left.

Waverly glanced over her shoulder and spotted the thick metal door. The handle moved under her grip.

She looked into Petra's gigantic sunglasses and mouthed, "Show time."

The brunette nodded, and Waverly opened the door. Sound stages all smelled the same. It was a musky scent of old props, fresh paint, and bad ventilation. The glow in the dark tape on the floor directed them forward, and Waverly could make out light ahead. They pushed through heavy black curtains and stepped into a literal scene out of a movie.

"Isn't this a little melodramatic?" Waverly asked, glancing around the dimly lit set. It was the graveyard set for the sequel to a popular zombie comedy.

"The world loves the perception of drama, even when there is none," Brad said smugly, holding a pistol loosely in his left hand.

Waverly's gaze flew to her mother. Sylvia was tied to the same chair as the picture, but she was awake now. Her blue eyes widened as she tried to process the scene before her.

"Is that why you're doing all this? The backdoor deals, blackmail, murder? For the drama?" Waverly demanded.

"Do you know how sick I am of dealing with your right-eous, spoiled, delicate egos?" Brad snapped. "I don't give a flying fuck about your set trailers or who gets top billing. You make me more money by playing spy than you ever could onscreen. But when lover boy started making noise about his assignments, I had to cut him loose before he screwed me out of billions. Do you get that? *Billions.*"

Brad was pacing over fake graveyard grass, ranting now. "I make things happen for the right people, and I'm rewarded. It could have been the same for you, but you couldn't just do your job and keep your mouth shut."

"We were working for the government, and then you decided to start dipping into other streams of income. It's not what I signed up for."

"You think every government operation was so pure and good? Wake up, Waverly. Wake up from the delusion. You actors think you're so much better than everyone else because you play dress up and you read words that other people wrote. You think you're important and special." He threw up lopsided air quotes with the pistol still in his hand. Gone was the smooth and genial man who'd promised to make Target Productions the biggest studio in Hollywood history. In his place was a raving maniac, sweaty and righteous in his fury.

"You think you have power because you get attention. How much power do you have right now, standing in front of me with no weapons, no help, no bargaining chips?" he gestured wildly with the gun.

"You were never going to let me walk out of here alive," Waverly shot back.

"And yet you still brought me what I wanted," Brad said, finally acknowledging the key to his billions. "Hello, Petra."

Waverly felt the woman tense next to her and gave the nod.

She pulled a nine-millimeter from her back and yanked off her hat, wig, and glasses.

"Who the fuck are you?" Brad screeched.

He made a move toward her, but the woman leveled the Beretta at him and bared her teeth.

31

"Oh, I'm sorry. I'm being rude. Did you think this was Petra?" Waverly laughed. "This is Carolina. She works for Xavier. She's done quite a bit of fieldwork in investigation and executive security. She also looks a whole lot like our friend Petra, don't you think? Did I mention she's an amazing shot? I wouldn't try anything funny with her."

Brad's California tan face was turning an unhealthy shade of red, and he raised his gun. "Where is Petra?" he screamed.

Waverly reached under Carolina's poncho and pulled out a Glock. Two against one. "You must feel incredibly stupid right now," she said, her voice oozing with sympathy.

"You are going to regret this," he hissed, his gun pointing in her direction.

"Yeah, yeah. That's what they all say," Waverly said, hurrying to Sylvia's side. She yanked the tape off her mouth while Carolina ordered Brad to put the gun down and put his hands on his head. Waverly worked the bindings around Sylvia's wrists free. "Are you okay?" she asked softly.

"Does getting drugged and kidnapped count as a blip in my sobriety?" Sylvia asked with a shaky smile.

Waverly grinned and worked her feet free. "I think you're in the clear. But I'll have a talk with your sponsor if you want."

"I think you're going to have to have a talk with your father and I first," Sylvia said looking pointedly at the gun in Waverly's hand.

"Yeah. Long talk later. Right now, I need you to get out of here. Are you okay to walk?"

Sylvia answered by standing and then swaying. Waverly caught her around the waist. "You got this Carolina?"

"Oh, yeah," the woman said with a deadly smile.

Brad cocked the hammer on his pistol and trained it on Sylvia. "Wait!" Brad cried out desperately. "I can still get you the cash. Just tell me where you have the girl."

Waverly glared at him. "You took my mother, drugged her, tied her up, told me you were going to kill me no matter what, and you think I still want to deal with you?"

"I can get you more than twenty-five million."

"Not interested," Waverly said as she guided Sylvia off the set.

Brad's laughter, a creepy echoing snicker, made her pause. And then she saw what he found so amusing. A half dozen shadows stepped into the light. Waverly recognized four of them as her stuntmen assailants from the alley. They all held guns. Waverly trained hers on the ninja whose ass Xavier had kicked. *Seven against two,* she calculated.

Carolina kept her gun trained on Brad and ignored the new arrivals. They stood back-to-back with Sylvia sandwiched between them. It wasn't the best odds, but Waverly still had a few cards to play.

"Don't tell me you can't do your own dirty work," Waverly taunted Brad. "You just keep calling in others to do it for you. You surround yourself with minions and then sacrifice them like pawns. Like you did Dante."

Brad lifted his hands. "When you have money and power, you don't have to get your own hands dirty. Dante was a liability just like you turned out to be."

"Sooner or later you run out of pawns," she warned him.

"I've got an army loyal to me," he bragged.

"So you have the FBI investigate me for running the espionage ops you sanctioned, and you throw my name out there in connection with Dante's disappearance?"

"It's your word against mine," Brad smirked. "And I've got enough evidence pointing at you that no one is going to believe a word you say. Not that you'll be around to defend yourself."

"It's illegal! What you're doing includes blackmail, kidnapping, murder, and probably treason. You had Dante killed!"

"So what? I'm not stopping now. I spent so many years kissing the ass of people like you. People whose power only comes from the way they look at a fucking camera. Do you know how good it feels to finally have real power?"

"Oh, I do." Waverly's laugh had no humor in it.

"You have nothing," Brad spat out.

Time to play a card. "Why don't you check Celeb Spotting and then decide what I do or don't have," she suggested.

For a second she thought he wasn't going to do it. But curiosity won out in the end.

"What is this?" he hissed.

"It's a prepared statement from Dante's publicist refuting the erroneous story about his disappearance."

"Nobody believes publicists anymore," Brad spat out.

"Oh, but what about the pictures?" Waverly said, never taking her eyes off of the man pointing the gun at her. "That's going to be a lot harder for you to spin."

"How did you get this?"

"Hmm, the one of me and Petra and Grigory Stepanov

right now, cruising down Hollywood Boulevard in a convertible? Because that's not actually me, but it *is* actually Petra. A pretty convincing alibi, don't you think?"

Brad was staring at the phone as if it were a live snake. "You have Grigory?"

"I have everyone," she said coolly. "Did you see the other photo? I imagine that one's blowing up right now. Xavier, Dante, and Petra and I all had a cozy breakfast together this morning. I believe the caption says something like 'Looks like these exes are still friendly. Dante Wrede has returned from his extended vacation with rumored girlfriend Petra Stepanov, daughter of Russian mogul, Grigory Stepanov,'" Waverly recited.

"Dante Wrede is dead!"

"I'd check your sources on that," Dante suggested, sauntering in from stage right, his gun leveled at Brad.

Thank fucking God, Waverly allowed herself a small sigh of relief. *Seven against three.* Her message had been received. Waverly could see Brad's hired guns buzz with confusion, and she hoped to God Dante didn't need to take a shot at anyone. They'd all be ducking for cover then.

"You said he was dead!" Brad waved his gun menacingly at his men.

"Looks like it's getting harder and harder to find good minions these days," Dante quipped. "None of them managed to put a bullet in me."

Brad took a step forward, and Carolina tensed, ordering him to stay put. His henchmen were getting antsy, and Waverly swung her gun from man to man, daring them to step forward. Everyone was yelling, and Waverly knew it was only a matter of time before someone's trigger finger got itchy. She pressed herself hard against her mother.

"Brad Tomasso, you're under arrest for conspiracy to

commit murder and kidnapping," Detective Dan Hansen of the LAPD stepped into the light. He was flanked by the wall of Xavier, Micah, and Malachi, all with guns drawn.

"It's about damn time," Waverly grinned at Xavier.

He winked at her before going back to frowning fiercely at Brad.

"This is not happening!" Brad shrieked.

She'd seen people lose it before, knew that their reactions were unpredictable after the point of no return. Still, she saw it in her mind's eye before it happened.

Detective Hansen made a move toward Brad. Brad raised his gun and fired. As Hansen fell, Waverly shoved her mother to the ground and spun low. A second, third, and fourth shot rang out, and the studio went pitch black.

A burst of light off to her left caught her eye. Brad was escaping through a side door on the set. "Take my mom," Waverly told Carolina. She took off at a jog, lifting her feet high to avoid any cables on the floor. She stumbled twice over God knows what before she found the wall. It took her precious seconds before her fingers found the door in the dark.

She yanked it open and wedged a folding chair in it to keep it open for the others. It was a temporary hallway as wide as a spaghetti noodle that ran between stages. She spotted Brad turning the corner fifty feet down the hallway and took off after him, the cement blurring under her feet. Brad Tomasso was not getting away.

She rounded the corner into an even longer straightaway and barely dodged the shot he squeezed off. She raised her gun and fired a shot in return. He must have decided the odds were in his favor in a foot race because he took off again, yanking open a door on the right and running inside. Waverly heard footsteps pounding down the other hallway and knew exactly whom they belonged to. "Xavier! First door on the right!" she yelled.

She went in low and blind, and the impact of the bullet nearly took her breath away. It fucking hurt like hell. That was going to cost him.

She decided against returning fire and hit the deck as the door closed leaving them in darkness. She added a moan for good measure. The fingers of her left hand closed around the one thing that sat inside the studio door of every sound stage at Target Productions.

She could hear Brad's breathing, the sharp ragged gasps of the damned. He was close and easing closer. He should have just run. There was a chance he could've gotten out of the building, off the lot. But he was beyond thinking about escape. He wanted revenge for his ruined plans. Waverly counted down, holding her breath. *Three, two, one...*

The door behind her flew open again, this time with enough force to have it slamming into the wall. Waverly turned on the flashlight and fired once. She caught Brad in the face with the beam and the midsection with the bullet as Xavier dove through the door. Brad had already raised his gun blindly and squeezed off a shot just as Waverly swung like a homerun hero connecting the flashlight to skull. "That's for kidnapping my mother!"

He went down to his knees, dropping the gun to the cement, and she kicked him in the balls. "That's for shooting at my fiancé!" She backhanded him with the light, and he went down to the floor hard. "And that's for shooting me!"

She didn't know if she would have hit him again or not, but Xavier was grabbing her arm and dragging her back.

"Are you hurt? Angel? Are you hurt?"

"I'm fine. I swear, X. Hit me in the vest."

Xavier, not taking her word, patted her down to make sure

she was, in fact, still wearing the bulletproof vest he'd outfitted her with.

Finally satisfied that she wasn't bleeding out, he let them sink down to the floor in each other's arms. Brad groaned pitifully next to them. The flashlight lay on the floor illuminating his crumpled form in its beam.

"I really wanted to shoot him," Xavier lamented, his breathing still heavy.

"Sorry, X," Waverly said. "What took you so long, by the way?"

"The tail I had on Tomasso got waylaid by security and lost him when he drove onto the lot, so we didn't have an exact location on him. Do you know how big these fucking buildings are? We went in on the far side and had to hike through some kind of Willy Wonka meets John Wayne disaster."

"I take it you got my message at the market then."

"What? The Invictus knock with the foot attached to the ankle wearing your tracker?"

Waverly smiled in the dark. "You're so damn smart. I knew you'd get it."

"We used it to track you to the stage. How is it still working by the way? I gave that to you five years ago."

Waverly shrugged under the weight of her bulletproof vest. "I had Micah replace the battery in it for me last week. I thought it might come in handy."

"God, you're sexy when you're an evil genius," Xavier chuckled.

"Please tell me we got what we needed."

"We made it just in time for Hansen to get the earful we needed."

"Thank God. I was getting a little nervous there. I was worried Carolina and I were going to have to shoot our way out. I'd already played the breakfast picture card with Kate tooling around in the convertible with Petra and Grigory. Anatoli's pictures were perfect, by the way."

Xavier pressed a kiss to her temple. "It was a good plan," he admitted.

"I changed my mind," she said leaning back against him. She felt him tense.

"About getting married?" he asked carefully.

"No. About your timing. It's excellent. Is Hansen, okay? That was a pretty direct shot."

"Yeah, took one in the vest. He's mad as hell from what I heard before I left to chase you. I hope he takes it out on the feds for fucking all this up."

"Is my mom okay?"

"Once the shock of seeing her daughter go all spy girl on her wears off, she'll be fine. She was kicking one of Brad's muscle in the balls when I came after you."

"Like mother like daughter," Waverly grinned. "Are you mad at me for going after him?"

"Oh, hell yeah. But I'm going to wait to yell at you until later."

"I appreciate you using your discretion. We should get back," Waverly sighed. "Help them clean up this mess."

Xavier nuzzled her ear. "Definitely."

She made a purring sound at the back of her throat. But when she shifted to find his mouth, she felt something warm and wet against her side.

"Xavier, either you just had the most inopportune orgasm or you've been shot."

32

He'd been shot. A flesh wound on his arm, but Waverly had carried on like it was life and death. It could have been if she hadn't blinded Brad when she did. His Angel had saved his life in a kind of perfect, poetic circle.

Brad Tomasso had been carted off to the hospital by a sore and pissed off Detective Dan Hansen and a handful of uniformed officers. Hansen had played a role in the Ganim investigation and had once again proven useful. Xavier imagined the man was enjoying the pissing match he'd started with the FBI. For tonight at least, Invictus' role in the mess was over.

They celebrated in high style in a large private room at the Beverly Hills Hotel in an event worthy of a red carpet. Micah brought his wife and daughters, whom he hadn't seen in days.

Chelsea showed up with Travers, and Xavier hated the way they were looking at each other. The two of them did pull Xavier and Micah aside. First, Travers announced that Waverly was officially no longer a suspect in Dante's non-murder and the non-kidnapping of Petra. Rather than being pissed at

Travers for going rogue, his superiors were grateful that he'd saved the FBI untold embarrassment by avoiding the very public arrest of Waverly Sinner. However, they were anxious to talk to her. It could wait a day, Xavier told him firmly.

Chelsea delivered even better news. She'd followed the money and gotten a break when she narrowed her search to members of the Joint Intelligence Community Council. Nancy O'Mara had been a three-term senator with much higher political aspirations. Now, as Secretary of the Treasury, O'Mara was privy to information about investigations and missions within the intelligence community. With first-hand information of what did and didn't happen within the bounds of the law, it would have been easy to push potential operations toward Target Productions and Brad Tomasso. The FBI was quietly beginning a classified investigation of O'Mara.

Waverly's parents joined the party in full on Hollywood glamour in a slinky ivory gown and a crisp tuxedo. While Xavier was dealing with the cleanup of a successful mission, Waverly had a long conversation with the still-recovering Sylvia and Robert that afternoon. She'd come clean from the looks of it.

Xavier greeted Sylvia with a kiss on each cheek and shook Robert's hand.

"You pulled it off again," Robert congratulated him. "Keeping my daughter safe is still a full-time job for you."

"She kept herself safe and ended up saving me this time around," Xavier corrected him. "I'm sure I don't need to tell you, but your daughter is an amazing woman."

"I gathered that you felt that way from the ring she keeps staring at," Robert said, glancing over to where his daughter greeted Grigory and Anatoli who arrived in celebratory tuxedos.

"She said yes this morning," Xavier said, feeling the grin stretch across his face. "We just haven't had a chance to make an announcement, yet." Or talk about it. That too would be remedied soon.

"Well, we're thrilled for you both," Sylvia announced from under Robert's protective arm.

"Sylvia, I owe you a huge apology," Xavier began. "I never considered the possibility that Tomasso would involve you. Let alone drug and kidnap you and use you as a bargaining chip. It was an unforgiveable miscalculation."

"I know this is going to sound strange, but having the opportunity to see you and my daughter in action like that made the whole ordeal worth it. Consider yourself forgiven, and try not to take so much responsibility for everything, Xavier," Sylvia said with a smile.

"I'll do my best," he grinned.

Petra and Dante arrived arm in arm. Petra glowed in a soft pink gown, but Xavier had a feeling most of the glow was due to Dante. To Petra, he was the hero of the day. They made a beeline for Grigory, and Xavier laughed when he saw the man's enthusiastic greeting for Petra ice over once he turned his attention to Dante. Dante was unfazed and gave the man a smacking kiss on both cheeks.

Kate surprised them all when she showed up arm in arm with Simon Shipley, the popular entertainment TV host and long-time Kate crush.

"We've kind of been dating for about six months now," Kate confessed when Xavier pressed glasses of champagne into their hands.

"You're better at keeping secrets than we are," Xavier said, giving her a kiss on her cheek.

"And don't worry, I've sworn Simon to secrecy, so if you

don't want any sparkly diamond news to get out, it won't," she winked.

"I appreciate that, and on that note, I think I'll go find my fiancée," Xavier announced and went in search of Waverly.

He found her near the bar talking to Micah's wife, Suzanne, and doling out sodas to Micah's girls. She wore fire engine red, a victorious color and sexy too in the short skirt and the low back. Her hair was down in loose waves, and while she now sported a spectacular bruise on her ribs from the shot Tomasso took at her, the shadows in her eyes were gone. The shadows under her eyes? Well, he'd take care of those. Sleep, rest, and maybe a real vacation were in order, he decided.

He slipped an arm around her waist and pressed a kiss to the crown of her head. "I see you've met Micah's women," Xavier said to Waverly, drawing smiles from Micah's three daughters.

"You've got yourself a lovely woman here," Suzanne said. "Try not to screw it up this time." She gave him a wink and hustled the girls off to where servers were hauling out trays of appetizers.

Waverly turned in his embrace and wrapped her arms around his neck, and for a second, Xavier's heart stopped. Everything he'd wanted had come true in one day. It was almost too much to handle.

She smiled up at him, and his heart started again. "I don't know where to start," he confessed.

Waverly cocked her head to the side, the ends of her hair brushing his hands. "What do you mean?"

"I mean there's so many things I want to say to you. I just don't know where to start."

"Pick one," she laughed.

"You were incredible today. You look beautiful right now. I'm the luckiest man in the world."

"That's a pretty good start."

"My heart is full, and my dick is hard."

Waverly laughed and slapped a hand over his mouth.

"Xavier, my parents are here!" But her words were undercut when she cuddled her hips against his. He heard the low purr in her throat when she rubbed against him.

He held her tight against him.

"We need to tell your parents!" she gasped.

"I think my parents know that you make me hard, and I'm sure none of us really need or want to have that conversation."

She rolled her eyes, her fingers brushing the back of his neck. "We need to tell your parents we're engaged. I don't want them to hear it from anyone else, and judging by Dante and Petra's entrance, there's going to be a herd of paparazzi outside."

Xavier shifted her into one arm and reached into his jacket pocket. He fished out his phone and opened the camera. "Smile pretty and hold up your hand," he ordered.

She did as she was told, and he snapped the picture. "There," he said, typing a quick text. "My parents have been alerted."

"We should go see them soon," Waverly decided. "I haven't seen Madelyn in ages."

"As soon as this mess is cleaned up, we'll fly out," Xavier promised.

"You're awfully accommodating tonight," she laughed.

"It's hard not to feel generous when I have everything I ever wanted."

Her face turned suddenly serious. "I love you, Xavier."

"I'm never going to get tired of hearing those words from

your perfect mouth," he said, rubbing his thumb over her lips. "Please don't make me wait to make this official."

"You don't want a long engagement?" Waverly teased.

"What are you doing tomorrow?"

"I think I'm going to need longer than twelve hours' notice."

"What kind of wedding do you want?" he asked, curious.

She shook her head. "I have no idea. One that doesn't resemble a circus," she decided.

"I can make that happen," he promised her.

"You really love me, don't you?" Waverly said, skimming her fingertips down his cheek, following the line of his jaw. "How did I get to be so lucky?"

"Angel, I'm going to ask myself that every day for the rest of my life."

33

*I*f the lead up to the sting had been stressful, the cleanup was a thousand times worse. Between the pissing contests of local law enforcement and the feds, the endless secret debriefings with just about every intelligence agency in the country, and turning over every shred of evidence they had collected against Tomasso, Target Productions, and Nancy O'Mara, Xavier was exhausted.

Throw in two trips to London to divide the new Invictus office oversight with Micah, and Xavier was ready to sleep for a week. And then drag Waverly to Vegas to get married.

He'd barely seen her since the night they'd celebrated their victory over Tomasso. Xavier had made it his mission to keep Waverly's name out of everything surrounding Tomasso's arrest, and that had involved weeks of cleanup.

Once again, their drama had played out in spectacular fashion. But this time, it hadn't also been broadcast on cell phone screens across America. This time, Xavier did everything he could to keep her name out of the fallout.

Thankfully, the FBI and the rest of the intelligence community agreed that disclosing the details of Target's role—

and by extension Waverly and Dante's roles—in operations would be detrimental to say the least.

For the foreseeable future, the entire case was classified.

He slid into the buttery leather seat of the private jet and fastened his seatbelt. The Invictus jet had become more of a home to him in the past few weeks than any building. Flights to D.C., London, and back to Los Angeles had wreaked havoc with his sleep. But he was working with a purpose.

He'd dealt with a small team made up of trustworthy, tight-lipped FBI and SEC agents who had quietly conducted an investigation into Nancy O'Mara and Axion Pharmaceuticals without the knowledge of the Joint Intelligence Community Council. Tomasso had clammed up after his arrest and hadn't spoken to anyone but his attorney since. If he was waiting for his partner to bail him out, he was shit out of luck. Guards had caught a sanctioned hit just as it began in the cafeteria. Tomasso was alive—barely—but it was clear O'Mara was tying up loose ends.

With the patient digging of the investigative team and the inmates who connected an O'Mara aide to the attempted hit, they had enough for an arrest. Travers had extended a courtesy invitation to Xavier to play a role in the takedown. He could have passed on it. But he wanted to see this through. O'Mara and then Axion were the last two dominoes that needed to fall into place before he could finally begin his life with Waverly.

The arrest had gone down quietly at O'Mara's tri-level Georgetown brownstone that morning. She was a statuesque woman in a four thousand-dollar pantsuit with what many who had faced her in committee meetings called a really shitty attitude toward the intelligence community.

And that shitty attitude had reared its ugly head when she realized the connection had been made between her and

Tomasso. It had gotten ugly enough that once she spit in the face of an SEC investigator and slapped the female FBI agent who dared try to cuff her, Xavier took great pleasure in sweeping her legs out from under her and slapping on the cuffs a little harder than necessary.

"That's for Waverly," he'd whispered in her ear as she shrieked about her constitutional rights and demanded her lawyer.

He'd turned O'Mara over to Travers and considered his job finally done. He was flying home tonight, crawling between the sheets, and sleeping next to Waverly for a week. Then he was going to make love to her for another week. And then he was going to talk her into eloping somewhere. Anywhere.

He was ready for their new beginning.

~

THEIR NEW BEGINNING was off to a rough start.

Waverly wasn't home, and her luggage was missing. He swore, looking in her closet and rifling through drawers. She was supposed to tell him when she was traveling. Technically, he should have called to tell her he was coming home tonight. But he'd wanted to surprise her.

He dialed her number and bit off a curse when it went straight to voicemail. He tried Kate's phone and got the same result. *Where the hell would she be?*

He spotted it on the dining table downstairs. A heart shaped sticky note.

> X,
>> *Taking a little vacation.*
>> *Love,*
>> *W*

Swearing, he dumped the dirty clothes out of his bag and stomped back upstairs into Waverly's closet. He'd moved more clothes in on his too-short stopovers between D.C. and London and hastily repacked his bag.

If she thought she could sneak away from him, Waverly Sinner had another thing coming.

IT TOOK NEARLY eighteen hours for him to find her, make travel arrangements, and get there himself. Xavier gave into exhaustion and slept on the nearly nine-hour flight and woke to tropical sunshine and a new country. In deference to the humidity, Xavier changed into shorts before going through customs.

He was still tired and still ready for a fight by the time he made it out onto the sidewalk and into Bridgetown, Barbados.

The cab smelled like fried food, and the driver swerved around potholes like an Indy car driver, honking his horn at locals and shouting greetings out his open window. It would have been entertaining had Xavier not had murder on his mind.

She should have waited for him. Everything he'd done in the weeks since the sting had been for her, and she couldn't wait one day for him to come home? With a honk and a wave, the cab pulled into a white stucco resort draped in pink, vining flowers. *The Palm Court*, read the gold script on the weathered sign. Beyond the hotel, he could just catch a glimpse of the kind of blue waters that made men dream of beautiful women in bikinis and trays of umbrella drinks.

The woman with a thousand curls and a pearl white smile behind the front desk directed him to Ms. Sinner on the beach. She told him she would see that his bag was taken to his room and handed him a rum punch.

"Welcome to Barbados, Mr. Saint," she smiled.

Xavier wondered if he was so tired that he was hallucinating. He hadn't introduced himself, yet she knew his name and insisted that he had a room booked. He decided it was best not to argue and took his rum punch to wander through the lobby to an open-air bar. The bartender in a smart navy vest waved a greeting. "Glad you made it, Mr. Saint."

Xavier lifted a hand in greeting and confusion. What game was Waverly playing? He plucked his sunglasses out of his shirt pocket and put them on to face the sun glinting off the crystal waters of an infinity edge pool that seemed to merge with the ocean.

The beach was dotted with palms and umbrellaed flamboyant trees offering pockets of shade on the powder fine sand. Planters spilling over with the same pink flowers as out front dotted boardwalks that looped their way through the property.

Guests in various shades of tans and sunburns crowded around the outdoor bar for the first of three daily happy hours. He didn't spare them a glance, but the bartender here, a lovely young girl with a sleek cap of black hair, called out a greeting.

"First lounger on the right, Mr. Saint!"

Puzzled, Xavier offered a wave and followed her directions. He was mid-sip of his rum punch when he spotted her, sprawled on a blue lounge chair wearing a white bikini, sipping her own tropical concoction.

Her eyes were hidden behind an enormous pair of sunglasses, but there was no hiding the smile that spread across her face when she spotted him.

"Nice of you to join me, Xavier."

He opened his mouth and closed it again. Finally he gave

up and sat down on the lounger next to her. "What the hell are you doing, Waverly?"

"I'm getting you to Barbados." She sat up and spun around so her legs dangled off the side of the chaise.

He swiped a hand through his hair. "Angel, I've flown seven-thousand miles in the last twenty-four hours. Nancy O'Mara is in custody. Axion is under investigation, and their CEO has been arrested. You're officially cleared of any and all charges, and your involvement in the case has been classified. I fly home to be with you, *finally*, and you don't even tell me you've left the country?"

She cupped his face in her hands. "My poor X. How else am I supposed to surprise you with a wedding?"

The crystal blue of the waters seemed to etch themselves in his mind. The clouds hung motionless in the sky as everything froze.

"Whose wedding? If it's Travers and Chelsea, I'm going to drown them both in the pool."

Waverly laughed. "The Sinner Saint wedding."

"We're getting married?"

Waverly turned his wrist to look at his watch. "In about six hours. So you have time to get some lunch, have a drink, take a nap, and shower and then meet me back down here for a nice little ceremony."

"We're getting married?" he repeated. He knew he sounded stupid, but he still couldn't quite grasp what was happening. Every dream he'd ever had was about to come true, and he was afraid that if he believed it for a second, it would all disappear.

Waverly nodded. "We're getting married. As long as you're okay with it."

He moved so fast his rum punch tumbled to the sand. But

it didn't matter because he was picking her up and swinging her around.

Waverly laughed and wrapped her arms around him. "Is that a yes?"

"What about rings? What am I supposed to wear? What about our families?"

"Everything is taken care of," she promised.

"I need more information than that," he insisted.

"Well, first you're going to kiss me, and then you're going to go up to the pool bar and get a fresh drink. Then I'm going to go upstairs and start getting ready. I think my dress will look familiar since you bought it for me in Greece all those years ago."

He hugged her to him, all vestiges of exhaustion gone. He heard the cheering then and, without releasing Waverly for fear that she'd disappear yet again, turned to see several familiar faces beaming at them from the pool deck. His parents and sisters, Waverly's parents, Kate, Micah and Suzanne, Dante and Petra. All grinned down at them.

"Grigory and Anatoli will be here soon. They're touring the Mount Gay Rum's bottling facility. Malachi wanted to be here, but he couldn't get away, so Chelsea is going to set up a video chat so he can watch the ceremony. And Roz is in the spa."

Xavier's mother blew him a kiss.

"We're getting married!" he shouted up to the gathered crowd.

And as they cheered, Xavier tilted Waverly's chin up. "Are you ready for our next adventure, Angel?"

"I can't wait."

AUTHOR'S NOTE TO THE READER

Dear Reader,

Thank you for bearing with me through two entire novels separated by a tricky cliffhanger! When I started Xavier and Waverly's story, I thought I could stuff it all into one book, but boy was I super wrong.

There was so much more to "Xaverly" and their story than I had anticipated and I wanted to do them justice. Waverly really needed a chance to establish herself without anyone else calling the shots and Xavier needed time to realize what an epic, lovesick idiot he'd been five years ago when he walked out.

So thank you for your patience, your understanding, and your overall awesomeness. I hope you loved the Sinner & Saint story and that you tell all your friends about the books. Unless you hated them. Then definitely don't mention the books... or me. Just forget we ever met on these pages. :)

If you'd like to keep up on the latest Lucy happenings, please follow me on Facebook or Instagram, and sign up for my newsletter on my website!

Yours Authorially,
  Lucy Score

ABOUT THE AUTHOR

Lucy Score is a *Wall Street Journal* and #1 Amazon bestselling author. She grew up in a literary family who insisted that the dinner table was for reading and earned a degree in journalism. She writes full-time from the Pennsylvania home she and Mr. Lucy share with their obnoxious cat, Cleo. When not spending hours crafting heartbreaker heroes and kick-ass heroines, Lucy can be found on the couch, in the kitchen, or at the gym. She hopes to someday write from a sailboat, or oceanfront condo, or tropical island with reliable Wi-Fi.

Sign up for her newsletter and stay up on all the latest Lucy book news.
And follow her on:
Website: Lucyscore.com
Facebook at: lucyscorewrites
Instagram at: scorelucy
Blog at: lucyscore.com/blog
Readers Group at: Lucy Score's Binge Readers Anonymous

LUCY'S TITLES

Standalone Titles

Undercover Love

Pretend You're Mine

Finally Mine

Protecting What's Mine

Mr. Fixer Upper

The Christmas Fix

Heart of Hope

The Worst Best Man

Rock Bottom Girl

The Price of Scandal

By a Thread

Forever Never

Things We Never Got Over

Riley Thorn

Riley Thorn and the Dead Guy Next Door

Riley Thorn and the Corpse in the Closet

Riley Thorn and the Blast from the Past

The Blue Moon Small Town Romance Series

No More Secrets

Fall into Temptation

The Last Second Chance

Not Part of the Plan

Holding on to Chaos

The Fine Art of Faking It

Where It All Began

The Mistletoe Kisser

Bootleg Springs Series

Whiskey Chaser

Sidecar Crush

Moonshine Kiss

Bourbon Bliss

Gin Fling

Highball Rush

Sinner and Saint

Crossing the Line

Breaking the Rules

Made in United States
North Haven, CT
11 February 2024

48649914R00221